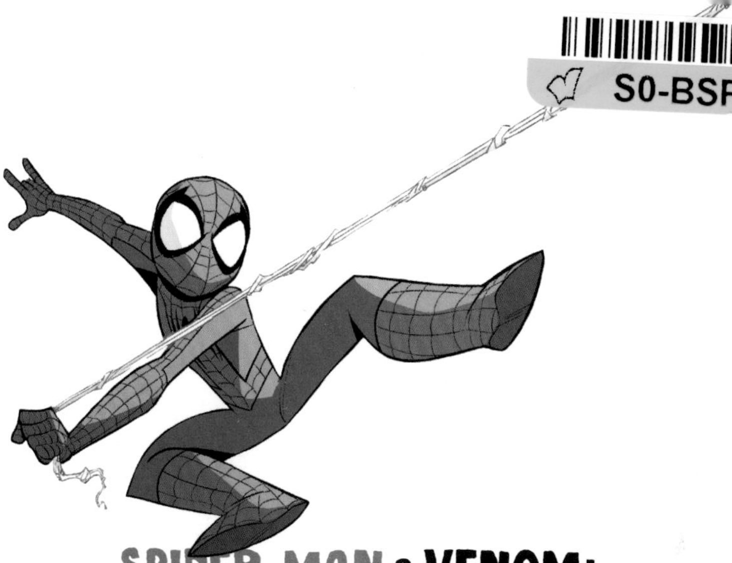

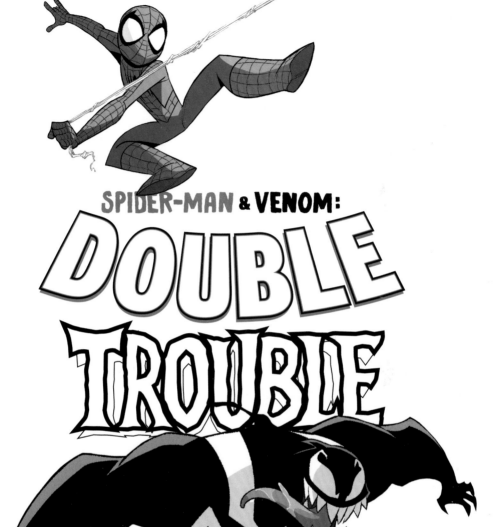

SPIDER-MAN & VENOM: DOUBLE TROUBLE

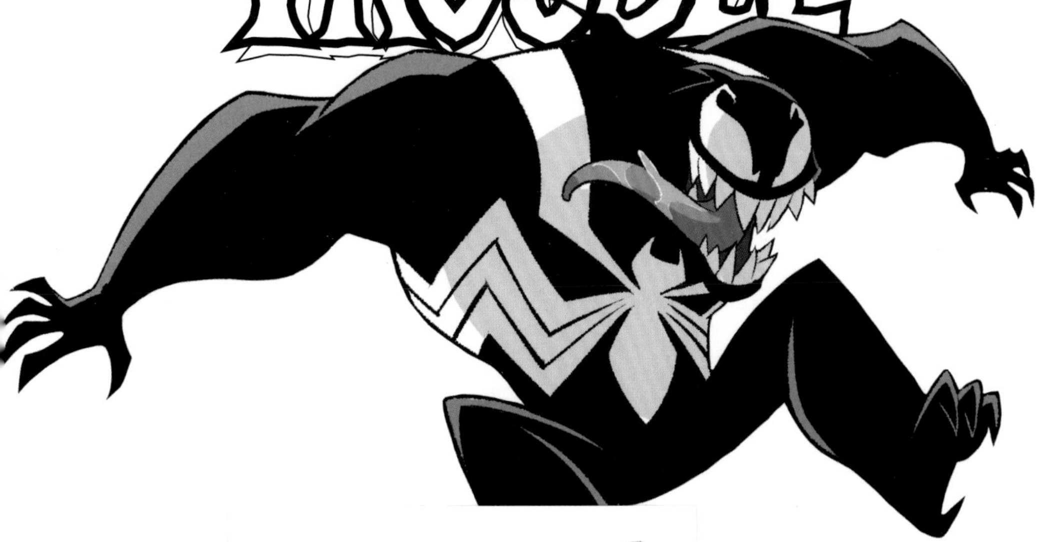

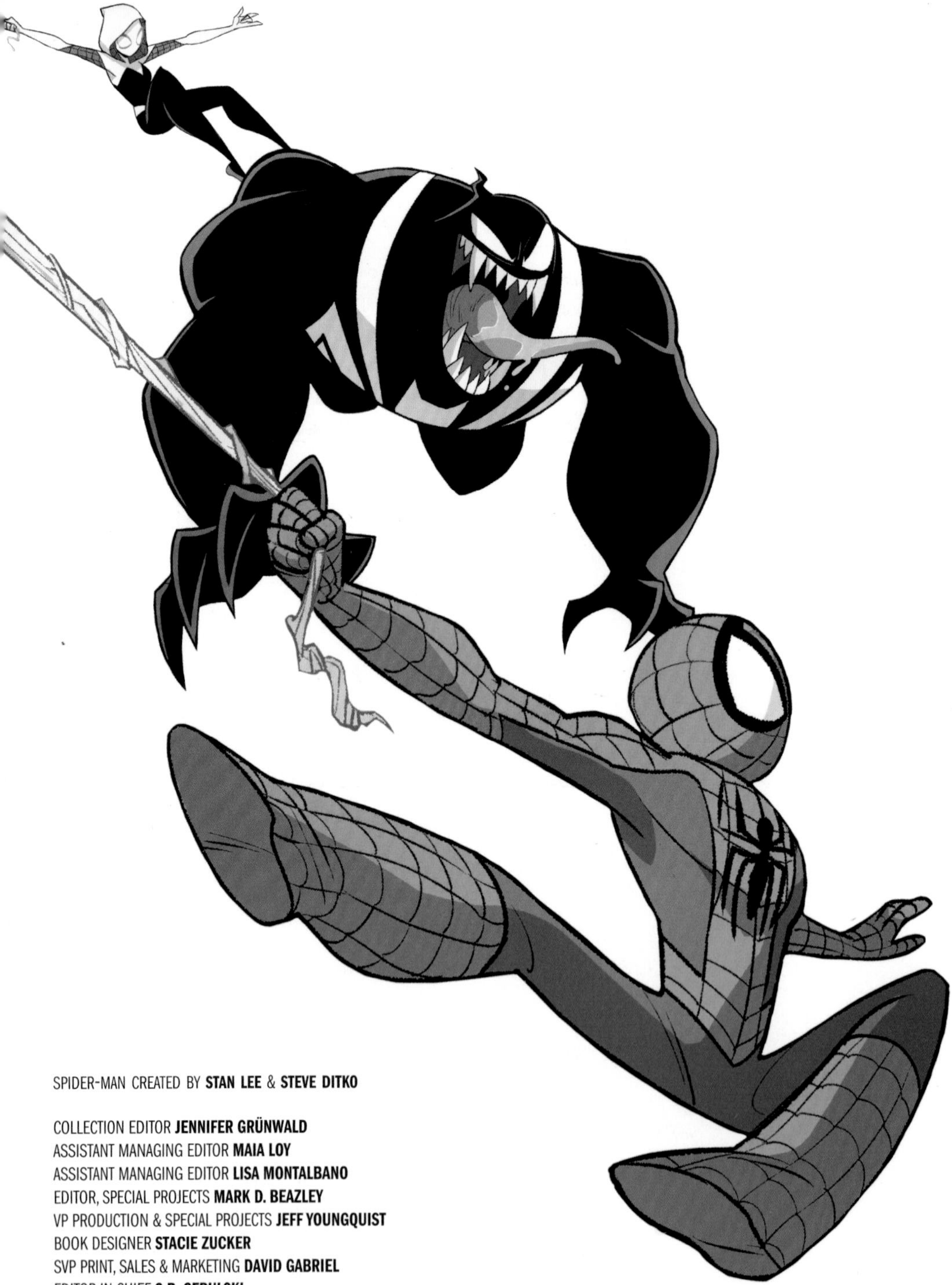

SPIDER-MAN CREATED BY **STAN LEE** & **STEVE DITKO**

COLLECTION EDITOR **JENNIFER GRÜNWALD**
ASSISTANT MANAGING EDITOR **MAIA LOY**
ASSISTANT MANAGING EDITOR **LISA MONTALBANO**
EDITOR, SPECIAL PROJECTS **MARK D. BEAZLEY**
VP PRODUCTION & SPECIAL PROJECTS **JEFF YOUNGQUIST**
BOOK DESIGNER **STACIE ZUCKER**
SVP PRINT, SALES & MARKETING **DAVID GABRIEL**
EDITOR IN CHIEF **C.B. CEBULSKI**

SPIDER-MAN & VENOM: DOUBLE TROUBLE. Contains material originally published in magazine form as SPIDER-MAN & VENOM: DOUBLE TROUBLE (2019) #1-4 and MARVEL SUPER HERO ADVENTURES: SPIDER-MAN — WEB OF INTRIGUE #1. First printing 2020. ISBN 978-1-302-92039-5. Published by MARVEL WORLDWIDE, INC., a subsidiary of MARVEL ENTERTAINMENT, LLC. OFFICE OF PUBLICATION: 1290 Avenue of the Americas, New York, NY 10104. **Printed in Canada.** KEVIN FEIGE, Chief Creative Officer; DAN BUCKLEY, President, Marvel Entertainment; JOHN NEE, Publisher; JOE QUESADA, EVP & Creative Director; TOM BREVOORT, SVP of Publishing; DAVID BOGART, Associate Publisher & SVP of Talent Affairs; Publishing & Partnership; DAVID GABRIEL, VP of Print & Digital Publishing; JEFF YOUNGQUIST, VP of Production & Special Projects; DAN CARR, Executive Director of Publishing Technology; ALEX MORALES, Director of Publishing Operations; DAN EDINGTON, Managing Editor; SUSAN CRESPI, Production Manager; STAN LEE, Chairman Emeritus. For information regarding advertising in Marvel Comics or on Marvel.com, please contact Vit DeBellis, Custom Solutions & Integrated Advertising Manager, at vdebellis@marvel.com. For Marvel subscription inquiries, please call 888-511-5480. **Manufactured between 1/31/2020 and 3/3/2020 by SOLISCO PRINTERS, SCOTT, QC, CANADA.**

10 9 8 7 6 5 4 3 2 1

SPIDER-MAN & VENOM: DOUBLE TROUBLE

MARIKO TAMAKI
WRITER

GURIHIRU
ARTIST

VC'S TRAVIS LANHAM
LETTERER

GURIHIRU
COVER ART

ADAM DEL RE
LOGO

DANNY KHAZEM
ASSISTANT EDITOR

DEVIN LEWIS
EDITOR

NICK LOWE
EXECUTIVE EDITOR

MARVEL SUPER HERO ADVENTURES: SPIDER-MAN – WEB OF INTRIGUE

"SPIDERS EVERYWHERE!"

SHOLLY FISCH
WRITER

MARIO DEL PENNINO & ARIANNA FLOREAN
ARTIST

JIM CAMPBELL
COLORIST

"THE MORE THE MERRIER"

JEFF LOVENESS
WRITER

MARIO DEL PENNINO
ARTIST

JIM CAMPBELL
COLORIST

VC's JOE CARAMAGNA
LETTERER

JACOB CHABOT
COVER ART

LAUREN AMARO
ASSISTANT EDITOR

DEVIN LEWIS
EDITOR

SANA AMANAT
CONSULTING EDITOR

NICK LOWE
EXECUTIVE EDITOR

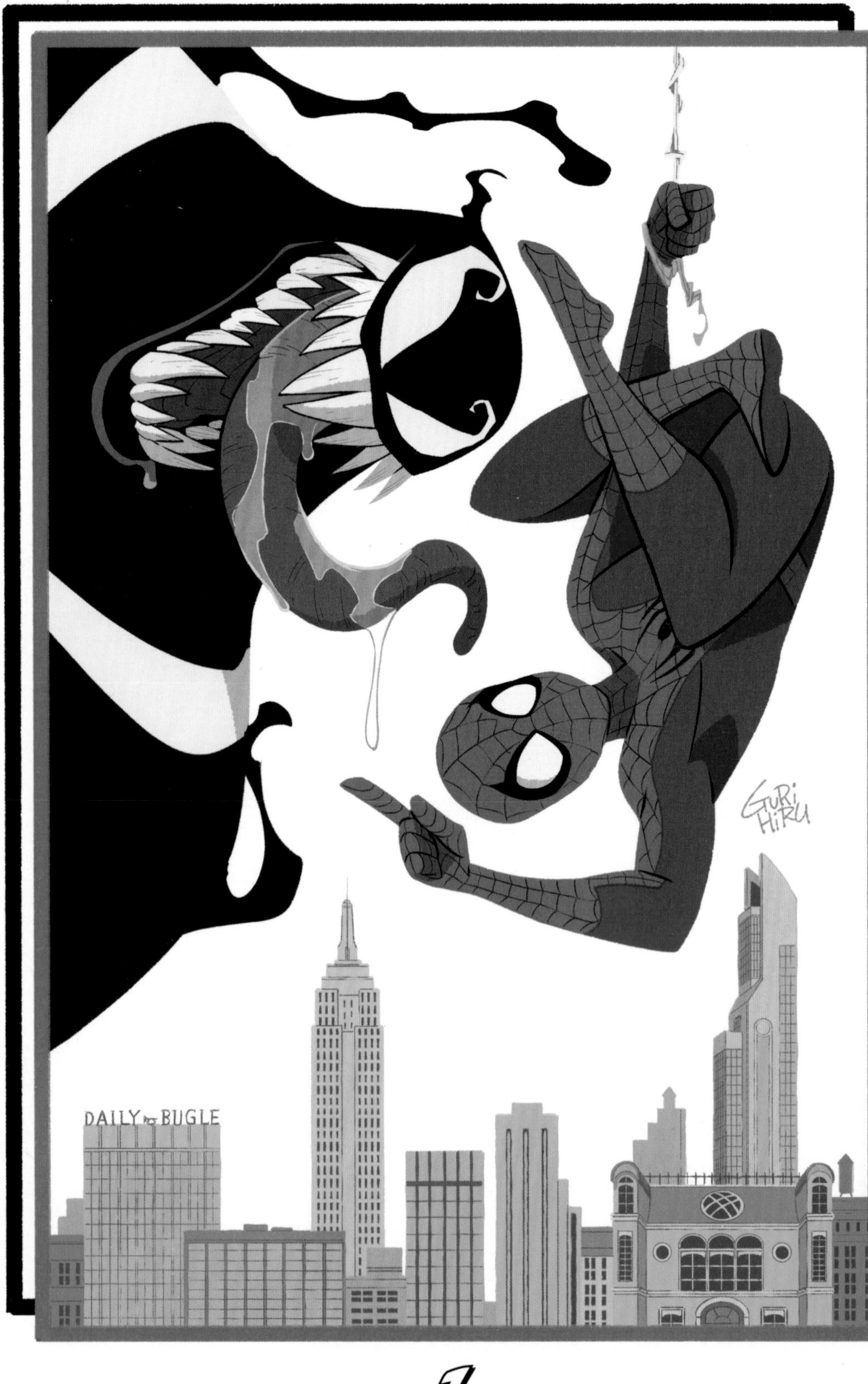

GURIHIRU
DAILY BUGLE

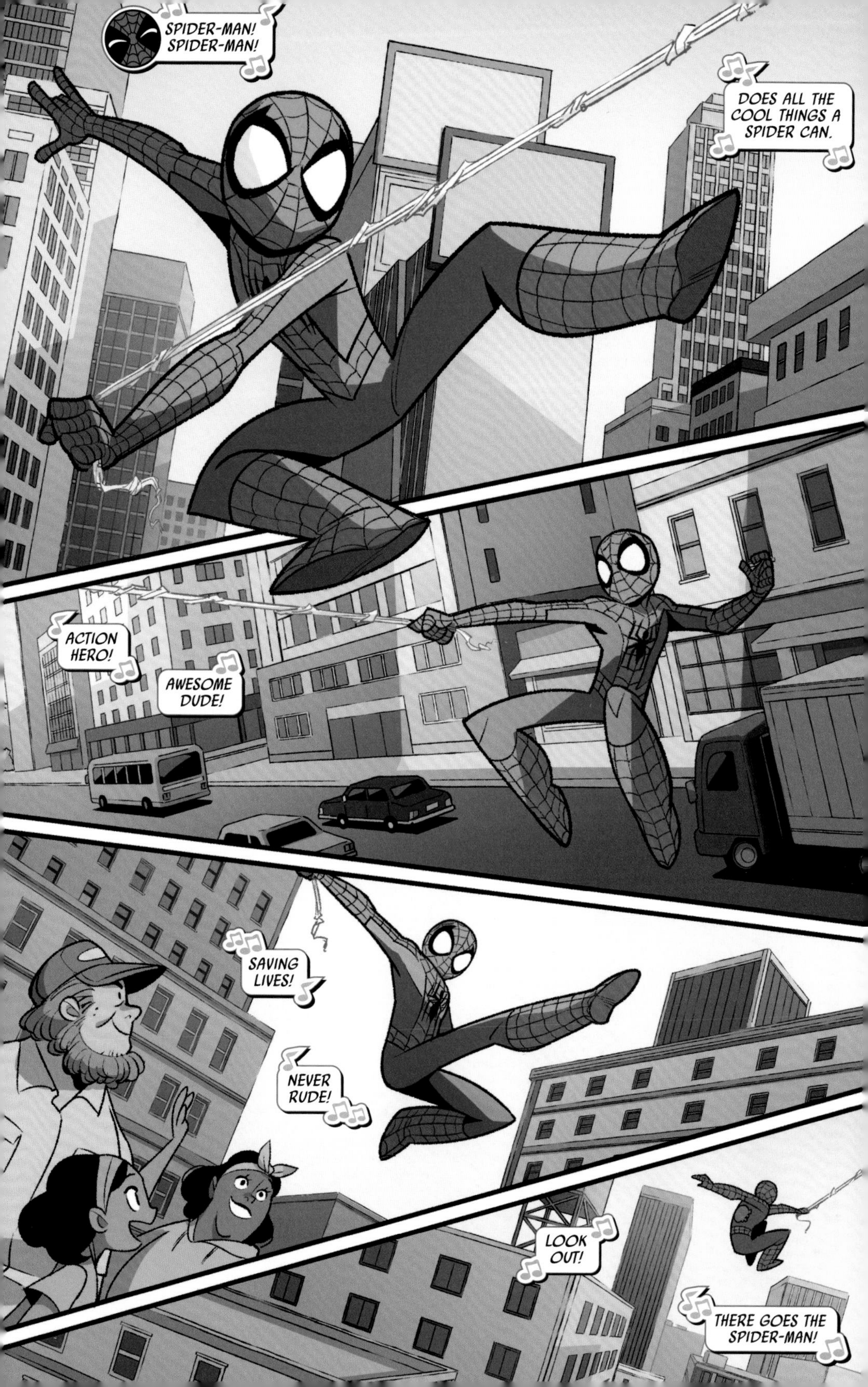
SPIDER-MAN!
SPIDER-MAN!
DOES ALL THE COOL THINGS A SPIDER CAN.
ACTION HERO!
AWESOME DUDE!
SAVING LIVES!
NEVER RUDE!
LOOK OUT!
THERE GOES THE SPIDER-MAN!

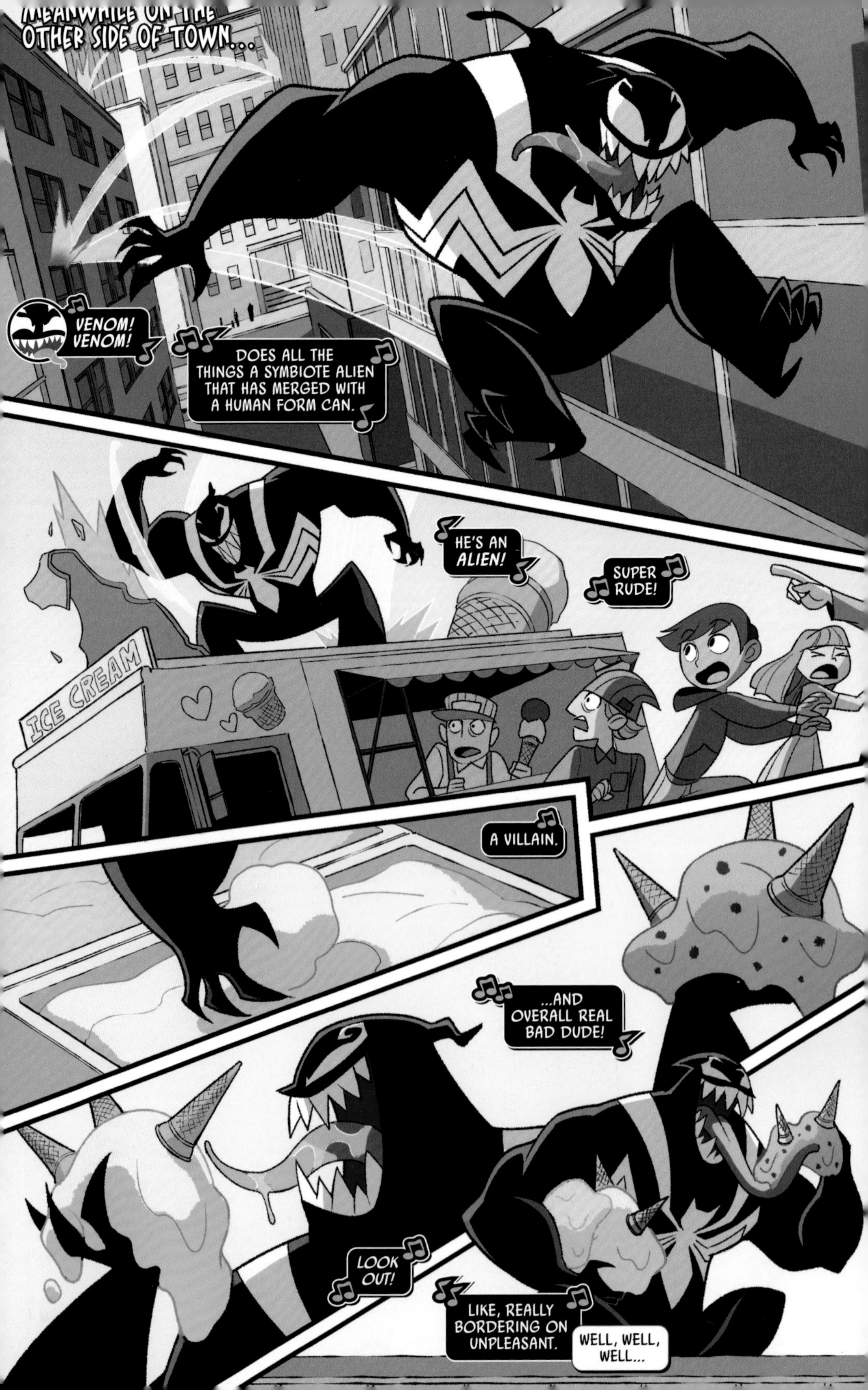
MEANWHILE ON THE OTHER SIDE OF TOWN...
VENOM! VENOM!
DOES ALL THE THINGS A SYMBIOTE ALIEN THAT HAS MERGED WITH A HUMAN FORM CAN.
HE'S AN ALIEN!
SUPER RUDE!
ICE CREAM
A VILLAIN.
...AND OVERALL REAL BAD DUDE!
LOOK OUT!
LIKE, REALLY BORDERING ON UNPLEASANT.
WELL, WELL, WELL...

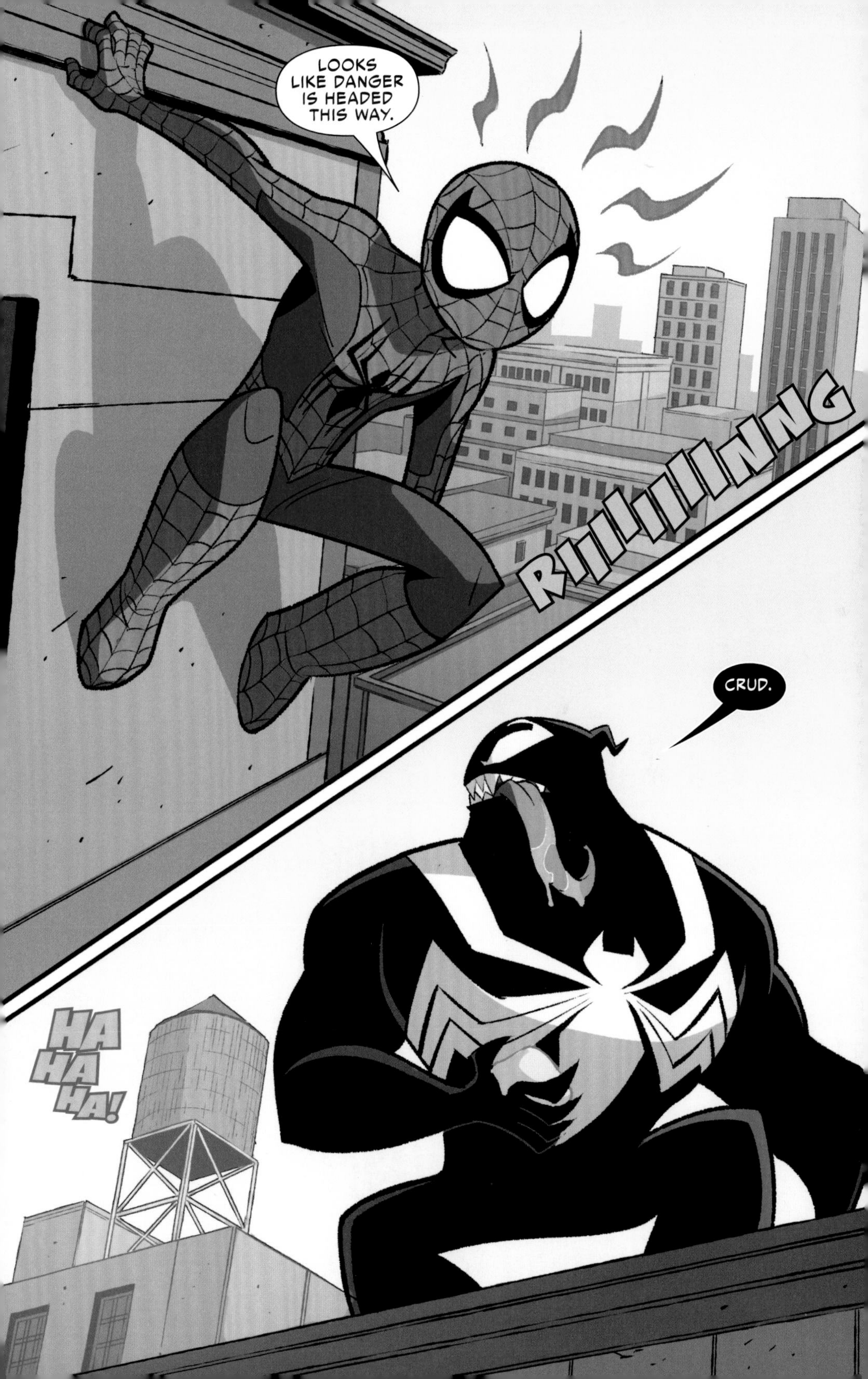
LOOKS LIKE DANGER IS HEADED THIS WAY.
RIIIIIIIINNG
CRUD.
HA HA HA!

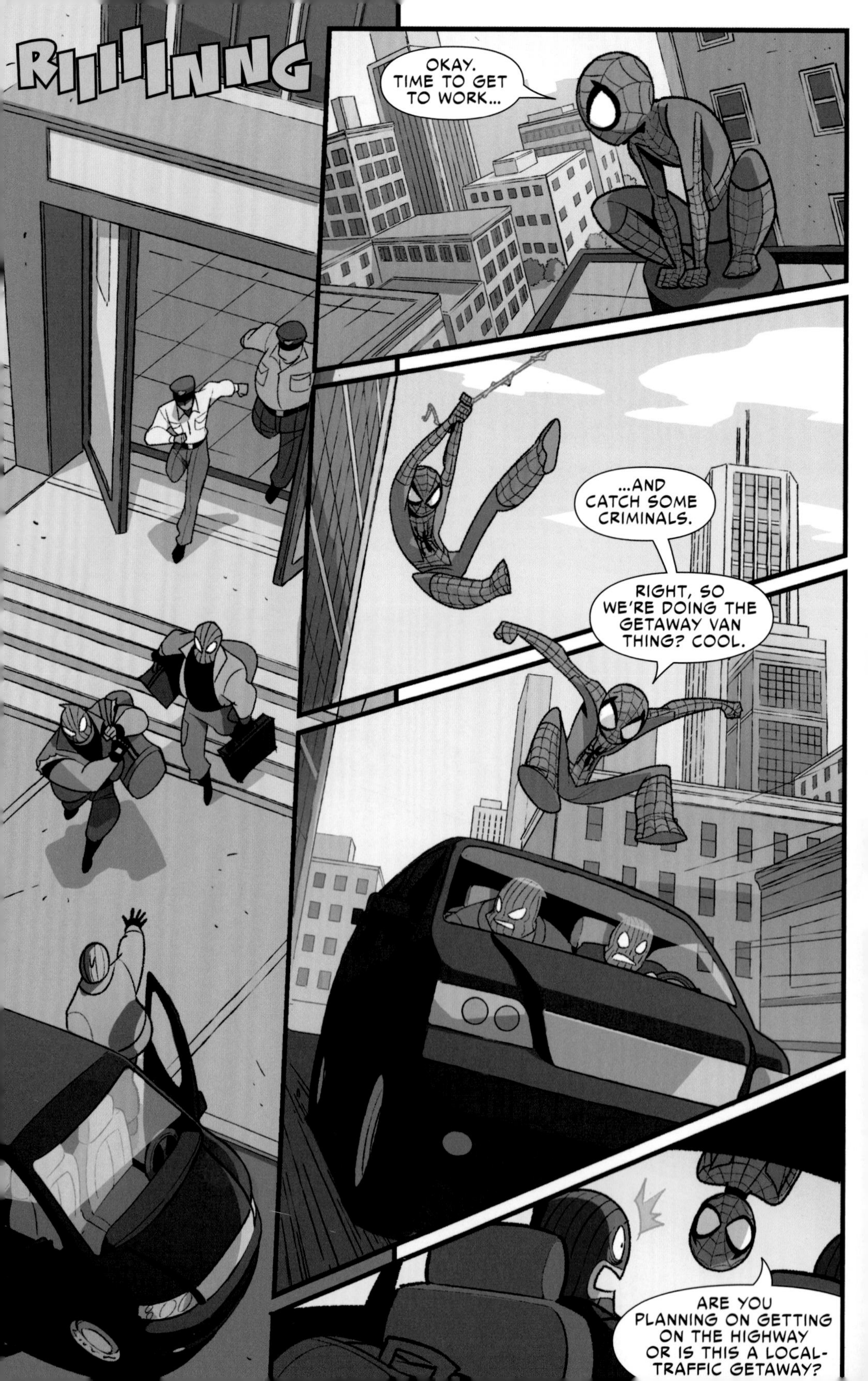
RIIIIINNG
OKAY. TIME TO GET TO WORK...
...AND CATCH SOME CRIMINALS.
RIGHT, SO WE'RE DOING THE GETAWAY VAN THING? COOL.
ARE YOU PLANNING ON GETTING ON THE HIGHWAY OR IS THIS A LOCAL-TRAFFIC GETAWAY?

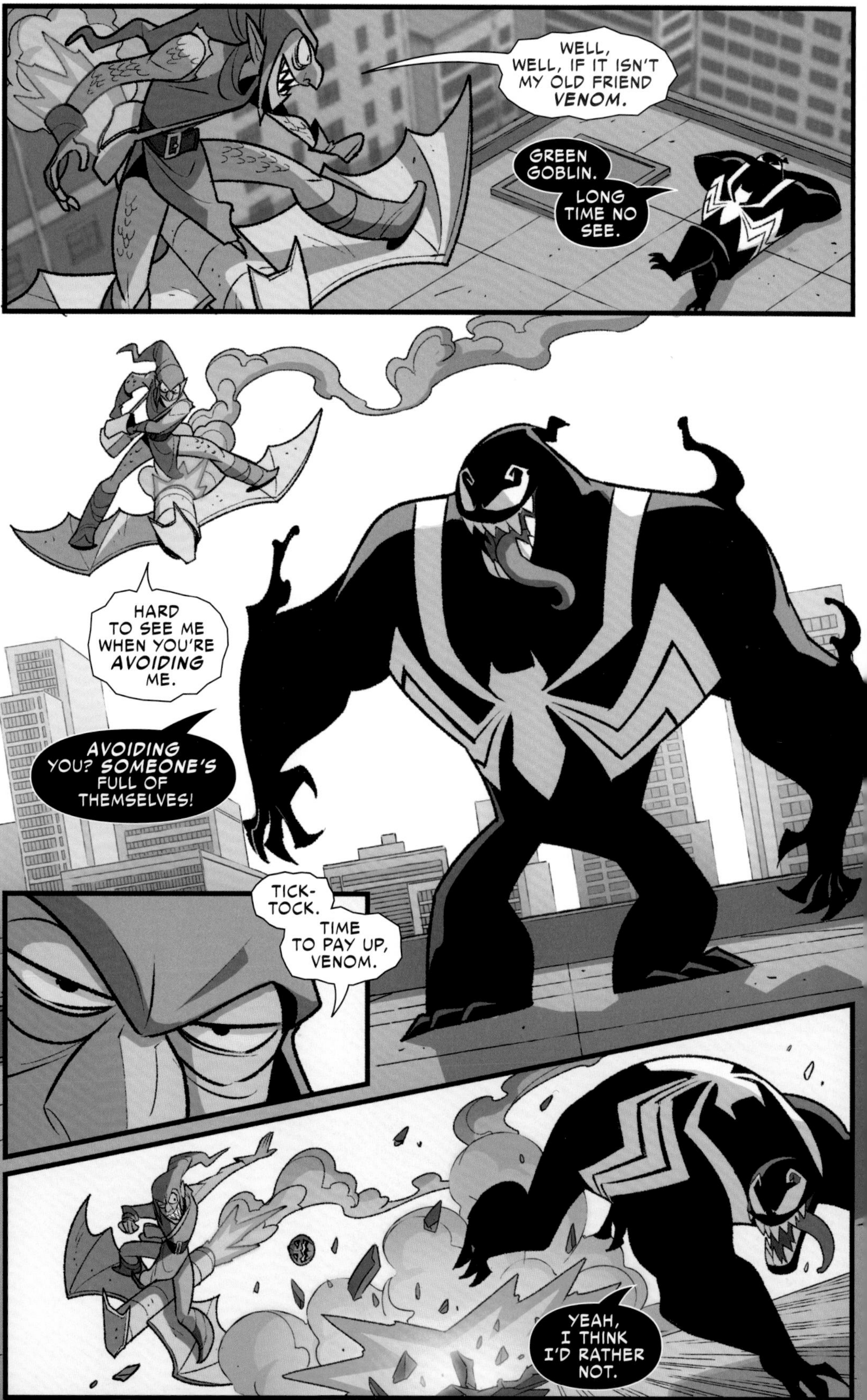
WELL, WELL, IF IT ISN'T MY OLD FRIEND VENOM.
GREEN GOBLIN.
LONG TIME NO SEE.
HARD TO SEE ME WHEN YOU'RE AVOIDING ME.
AVOIDING YOU? SOMEONE'S FULL OF THEMSELVES!
TICK-TOCK.
TIME TO PAY UP, VENOM.
YEAH, I THINK I'D RATHER NOT.

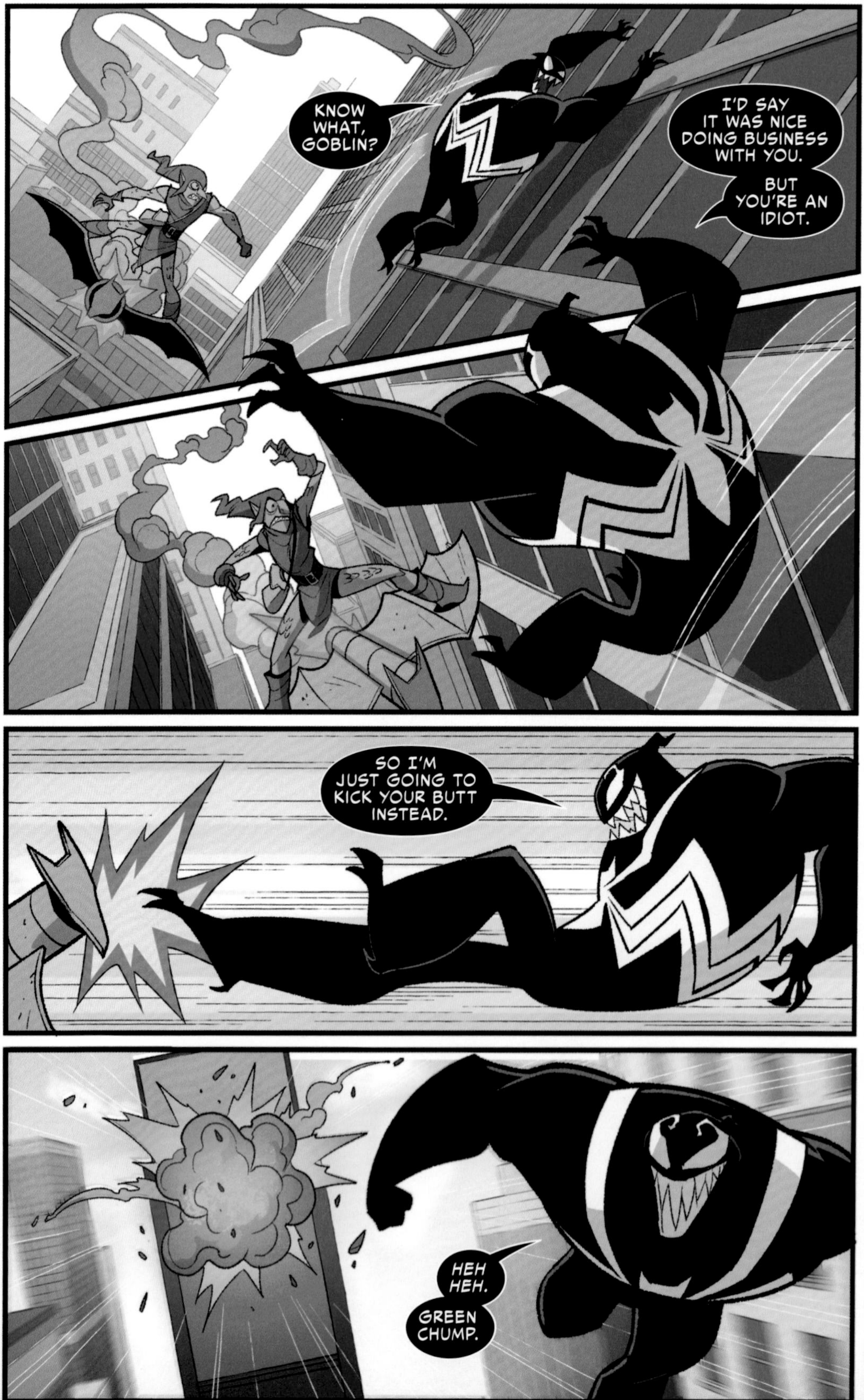
KNOW WHAT, GOBLIN?
I'D SAY IT WAS NICE DOING BUSINESS WITH YOU.
BUT YOU'RE AN IDIOT.
SO I'M JUST GOING TO KICK YOUR BUTT INSTEAD.
HEH HEH.
GREEN CHUMP.

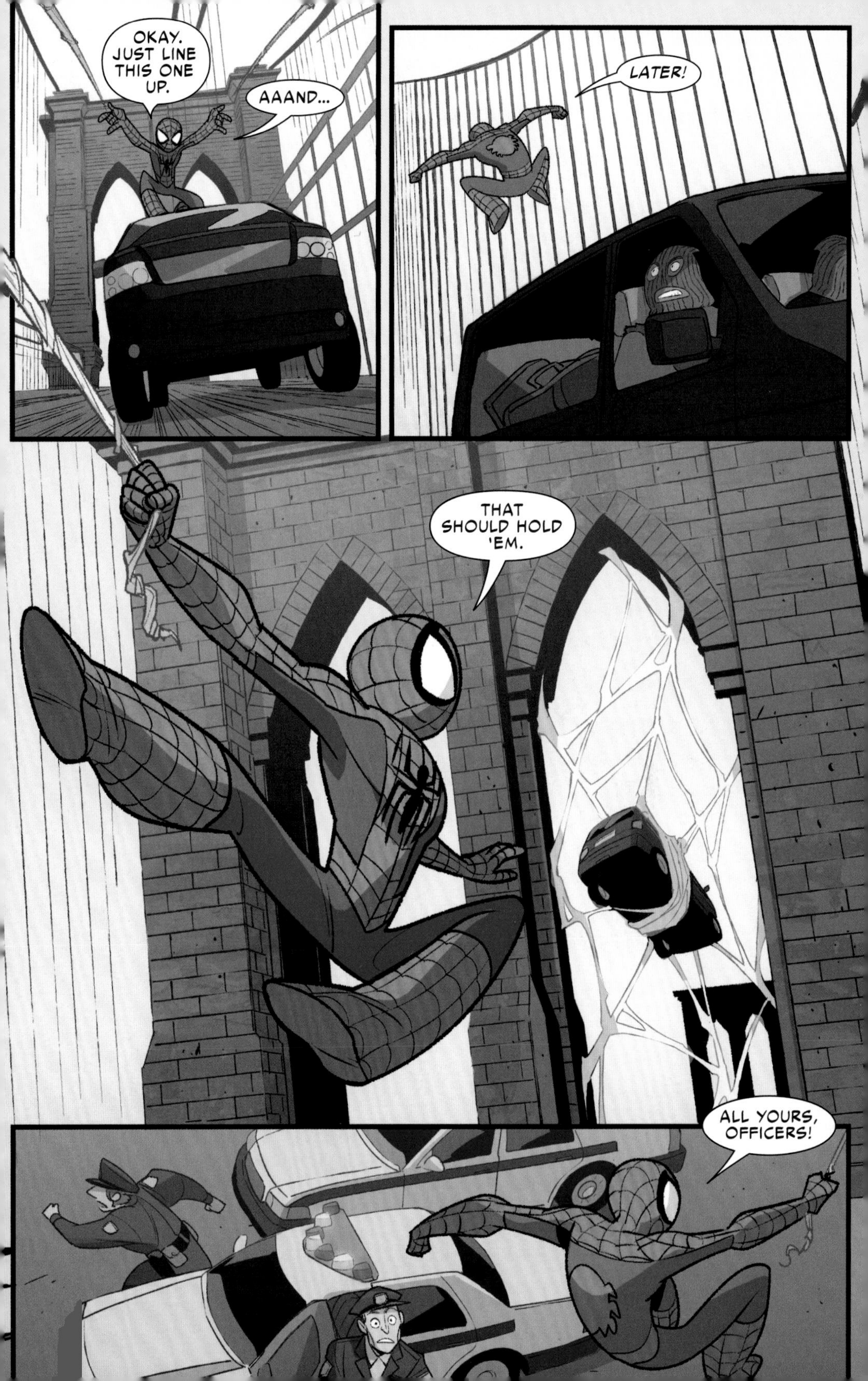
OKAY. JUST LINE THIS ONE UP.
AAAND...
LATER!
THAT SHOULD HOLD 'EM.
ALL YOURS, OFFICERS!

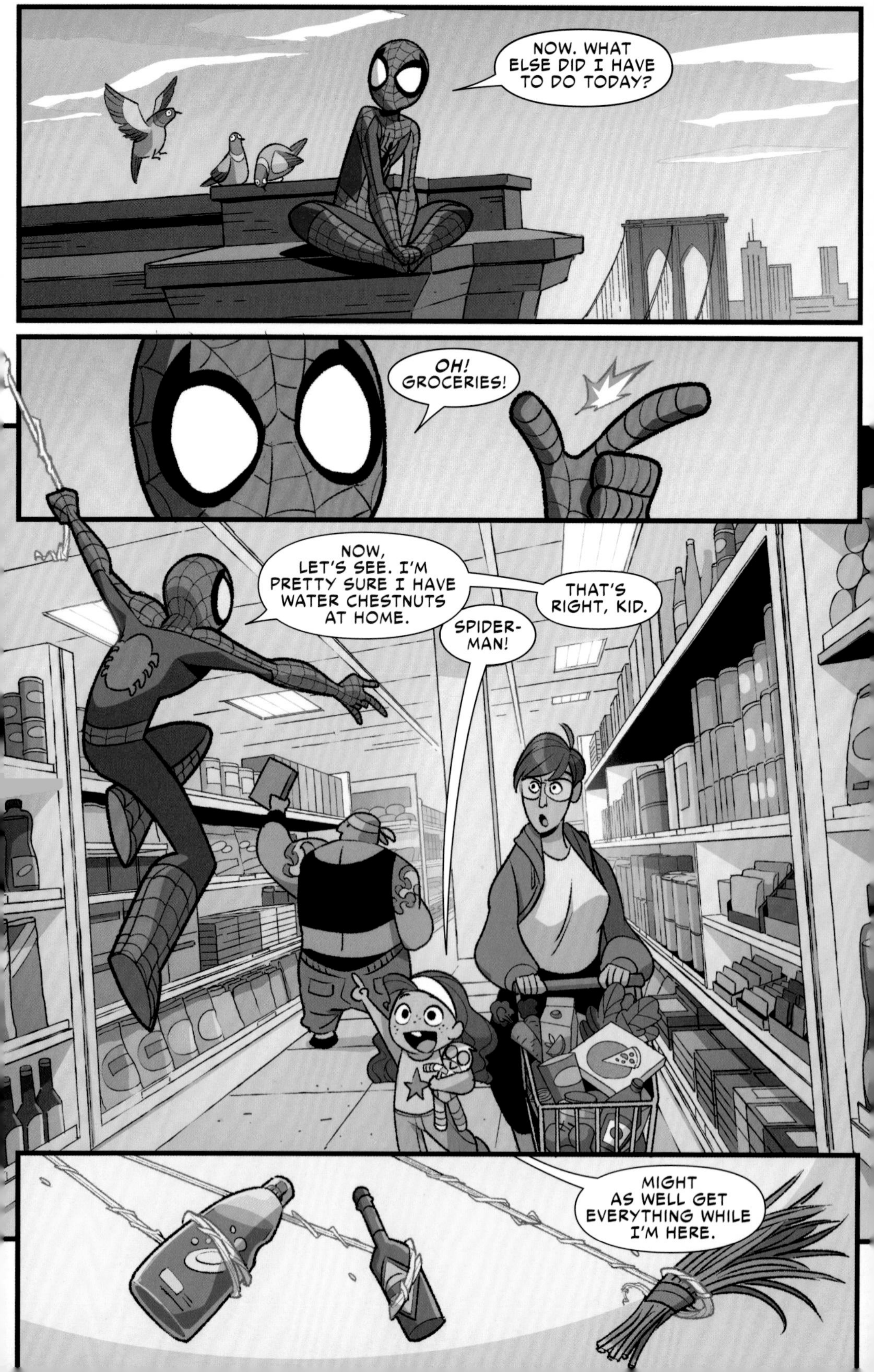
NOW. WHAT ELSE DID I HAVE TO DO TODAY?
OH! GROCERIES!
NOW, LET'S SEE. I'M PRETTY SURE I HAVE WATER CHESTNUTS AT HOME.
THAT'S RIGHT, KID.
SPIDER-MAN!
MIGHT AS WELL GET EVERYTHING WHILE I'M HERE.

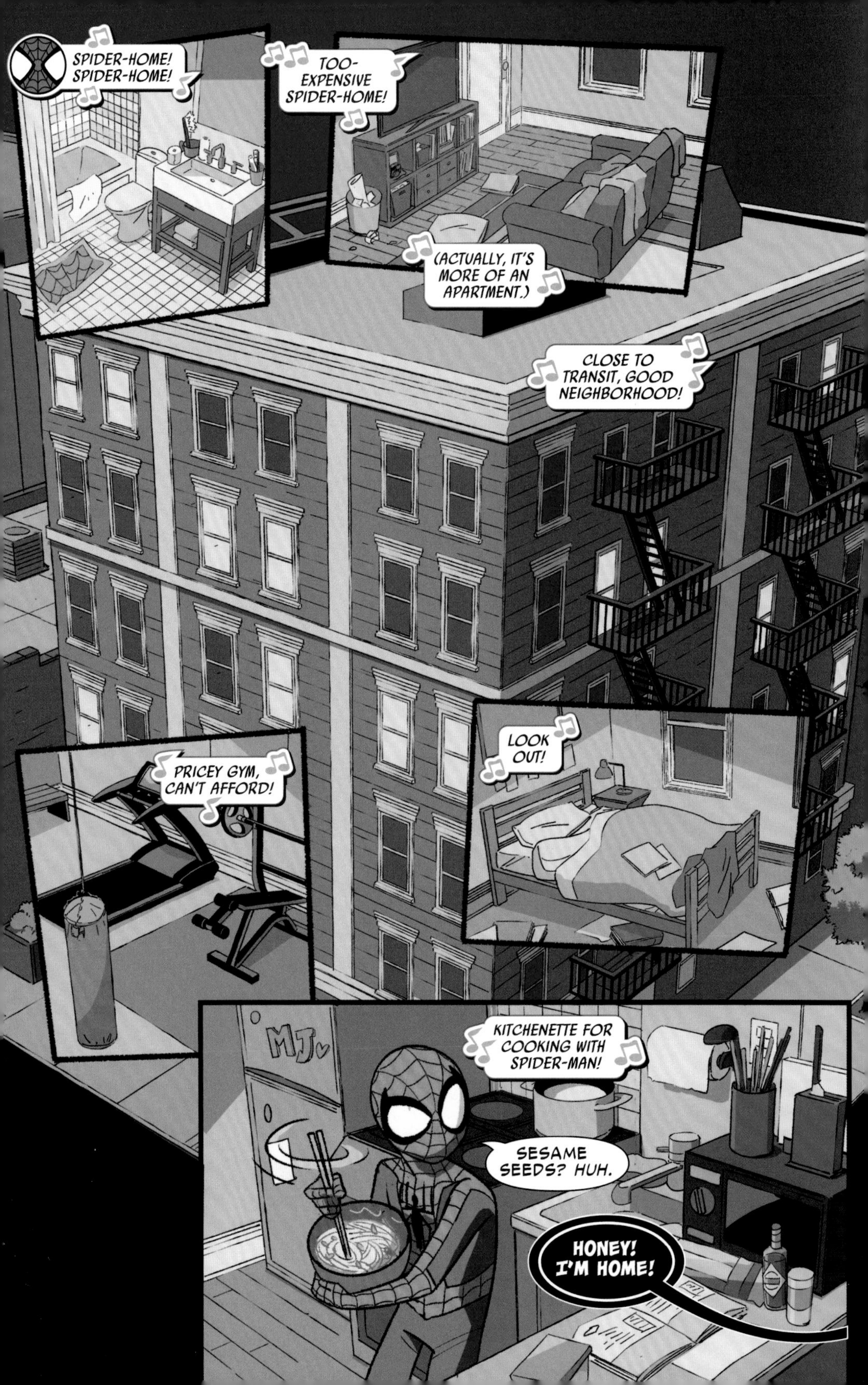
SPIDER-HOME! SPIDER-HOME!
TOO-EXPENSIVE SPIDER-HOME!
(ACTUALLY, IT'S MORE OF AN APARTMENT.)
CLOSE TO TRANSIT, GOOD NEIGHBORHOOD!
PRICEY GYM, CAN'T AFFORD!
LOOK OUT!
KITCHENETTE FOR COOKING WITH SPIDER-MAN!
MJ
SESAME SEEDS? HUH.
HONEY! I'M HOME!

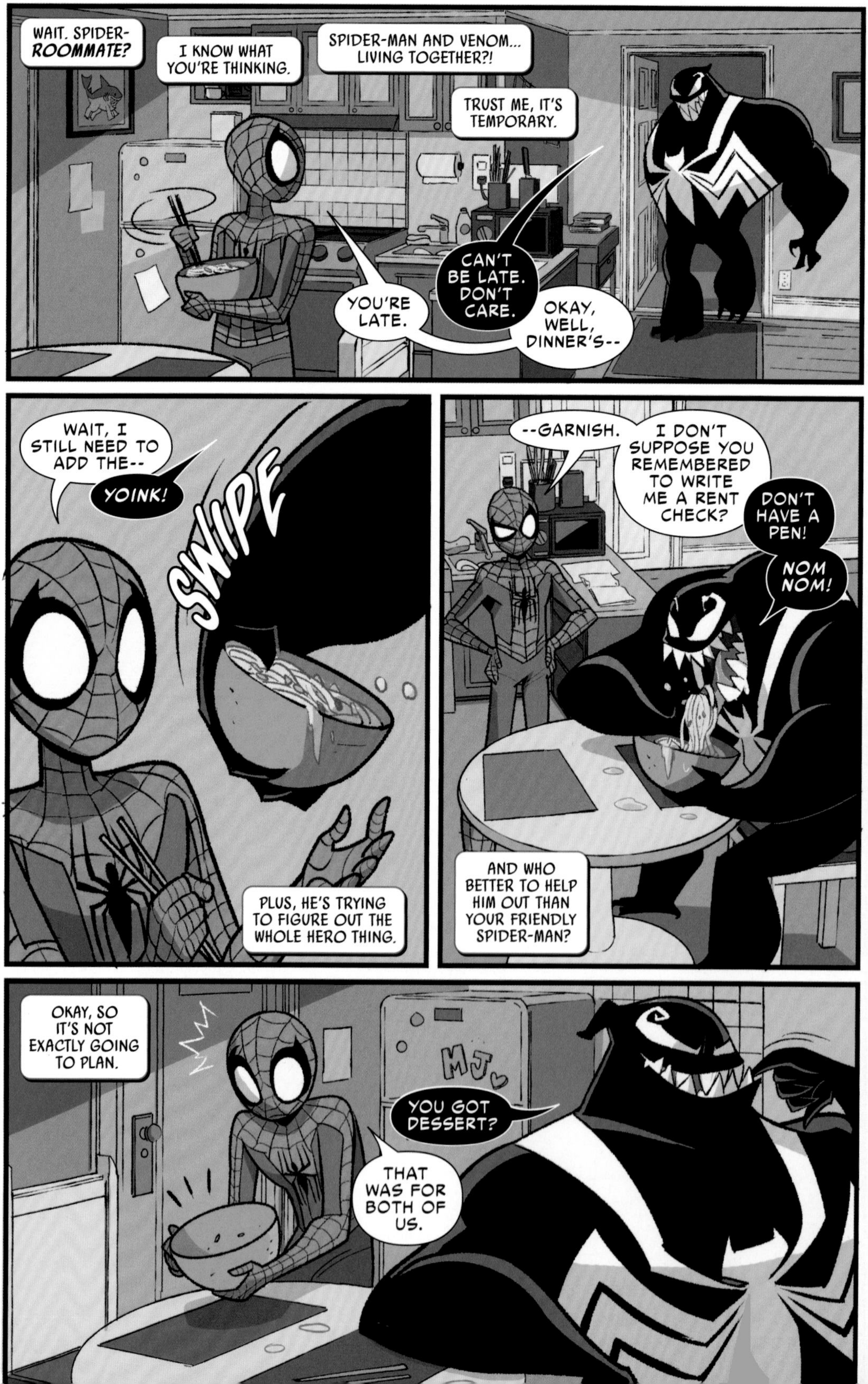

WAIT. SPIDER-ROOMMATE?
I KNOW WHAT YOU'RE THINKING.
SPIDER-MAN AND VENOM... LIVING TOGETHER?!
TRUST ME, IT'S TEMPORARY.
YOU'RE LATE.
CAN'T BE LATE. DON'T CARE.
OKAY, WELL, DINNER'S--
WAIT, I STILL NEED TO ADD THE--
YOINK!
SWIPE
PLUS, HE'S TRYING TO FIGURE OUT THE WHOLE HERO THING.
--GARNISH.
I DON'T SUPPOSE YOU REMEMBERED TO WRITE ME A RENT CHECK?
DON'T HAVE A PEN!
NOM NOM!
AND WHO BETTER TO HELP HIM OUT THAN YOUR FRIENDLY SPIDER-MAN?
OKAY, SO IT'S NOT EXACTLY GOING TO PLAN.
MJ
YOU GOT DESSERT?
THAT WAS FOR BOTH OF US.

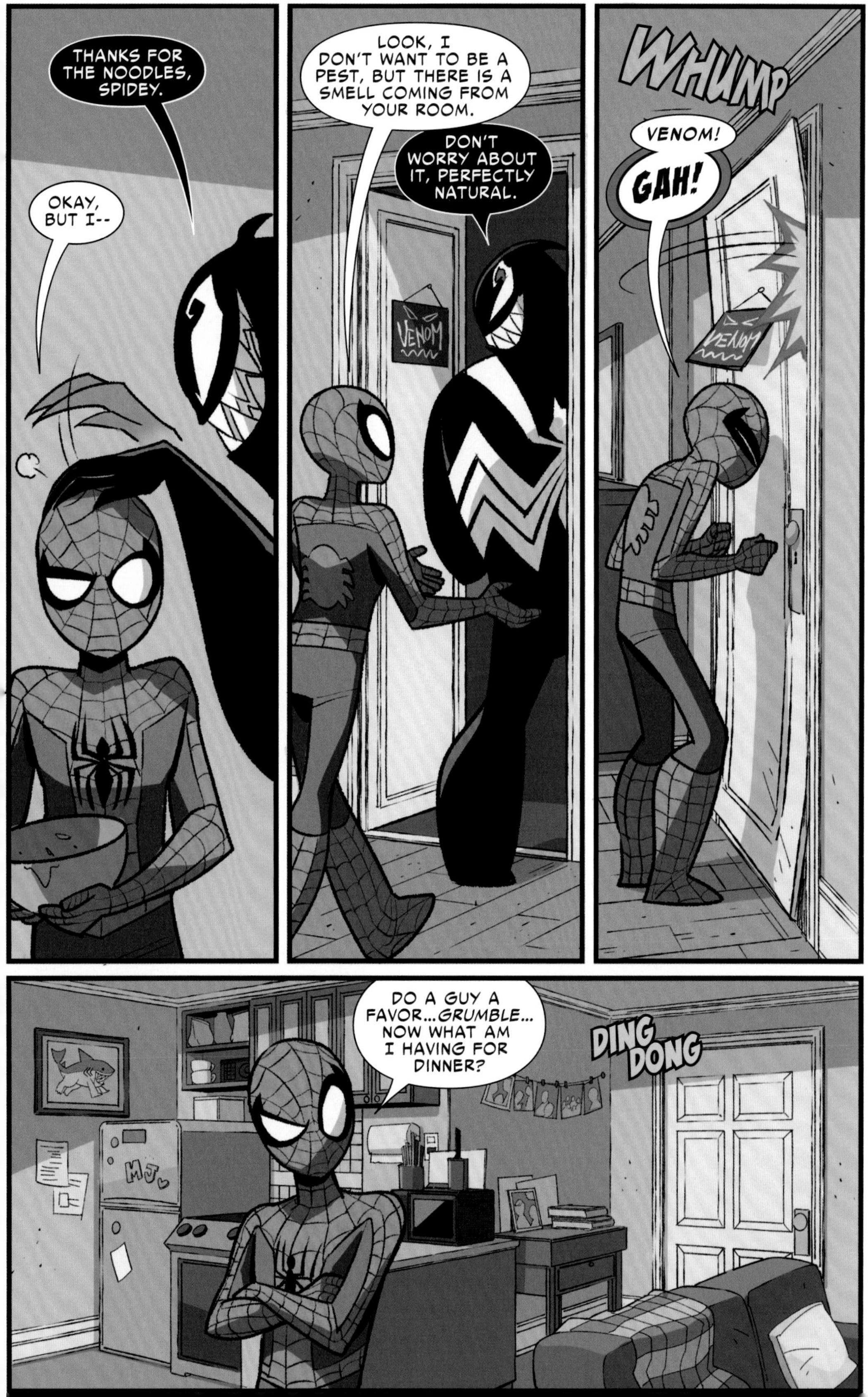
THANKS FOR THE NOODLES, SPIDEY.
OKAY, BUT I--
LOOK, I DON'T WANT TO BE A PEST, BUT THERE IS A SMELL COMING FROM YOUR ROOM.
DON'T WORRY ABOUT IT, PERFECTLY NATURAL.
VENOM
WHUMP
VENOM!
GAH!
VENOM
DO A GUY A FAVOR...GRUMBLE... NOW WHAT AM I HAVING FOR DINNER?
DING DONG
MJ

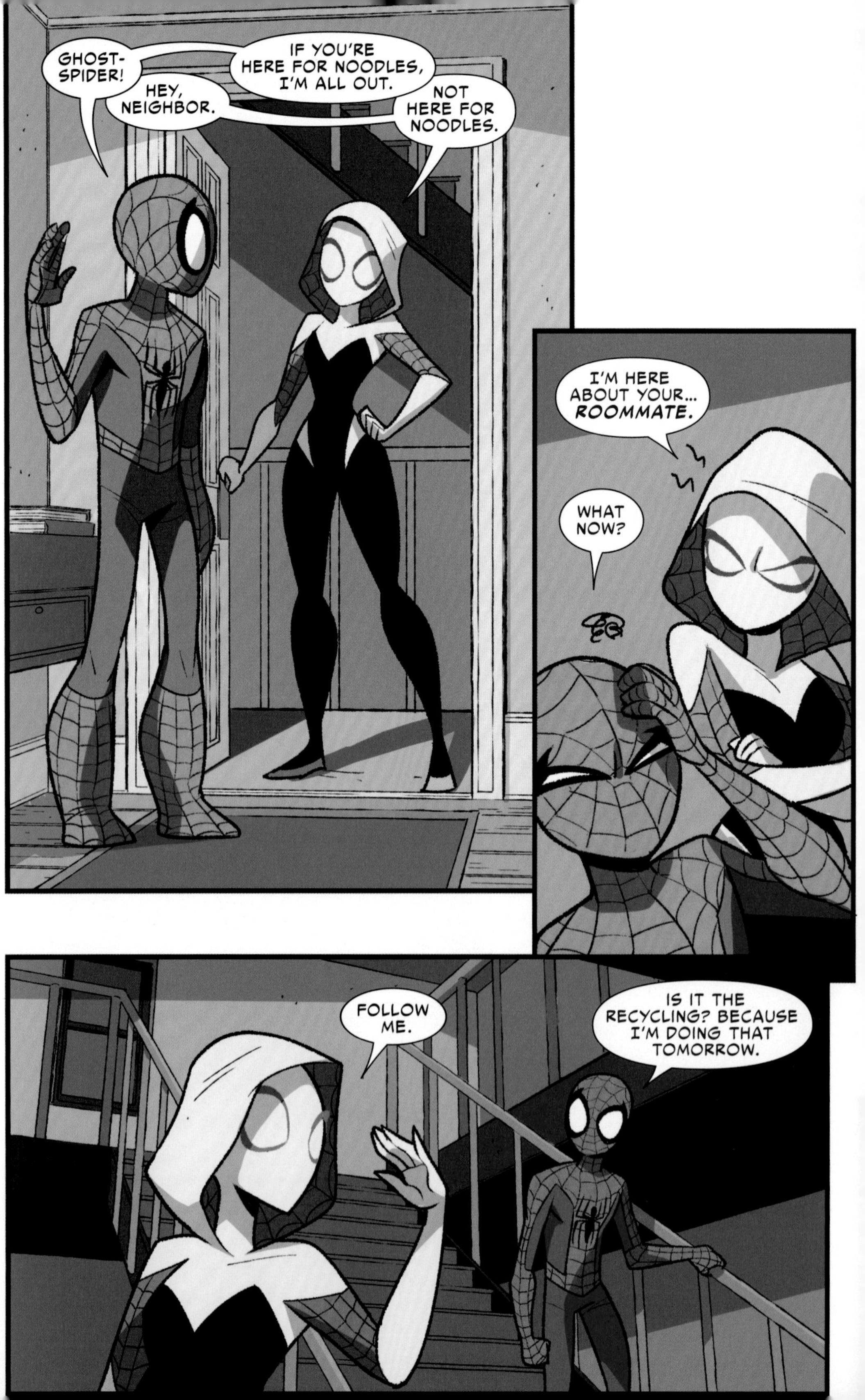
GHOST-SPIDER!
IF YOU'RE HERE FOR NOODLES, I'M ALL OUT.
HEY, NEIGHBOR.
NOT HERE FOR NOODLES.
I'M HERE ABOUT YOUR... ROOMMATE.
WHAT NOW?
FOLLOW ME.
IS IT THE RECYCLING? BECAUSE I'M DOING THAT TOMORROW.

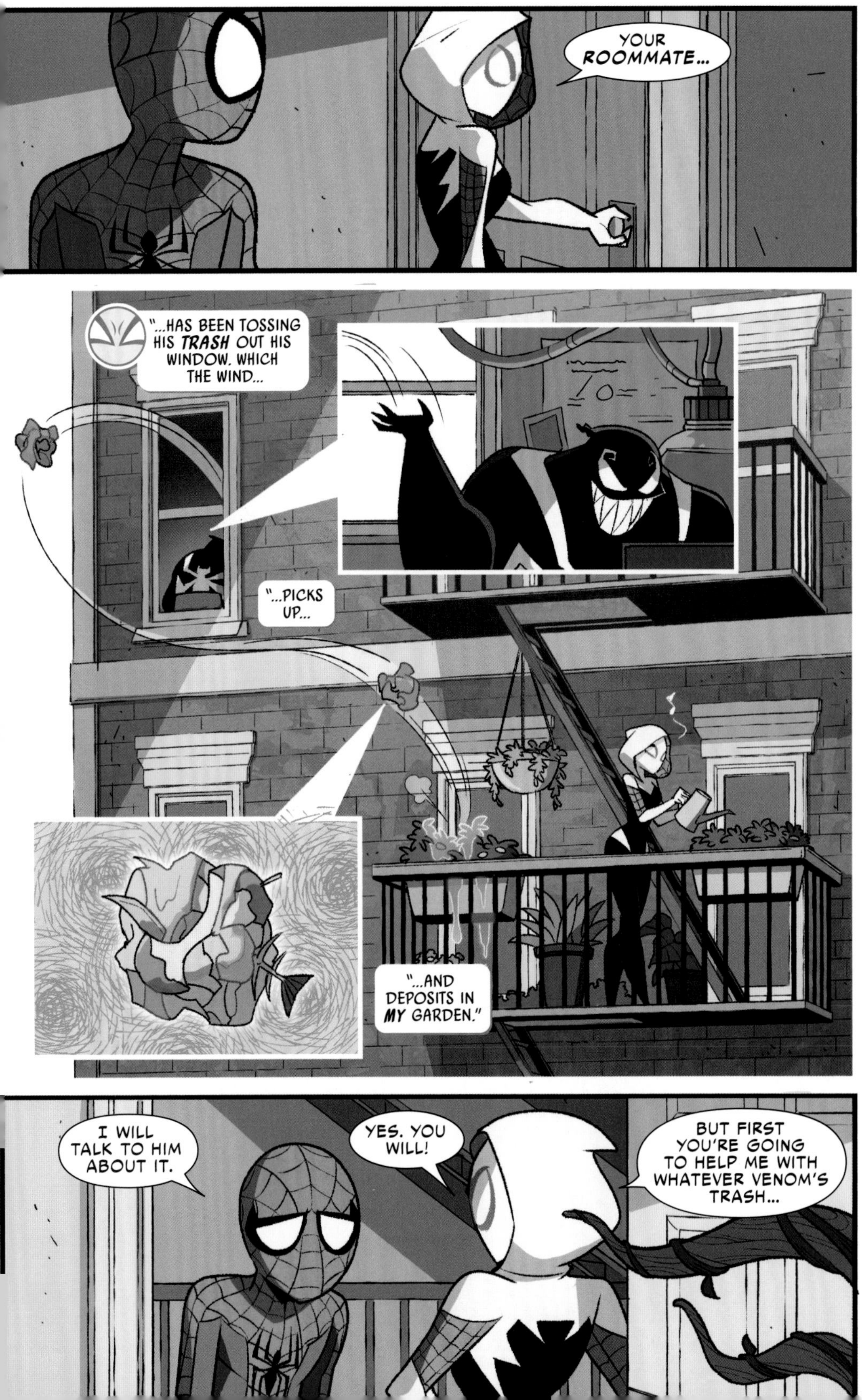
YOUR ROOMMATE...
"...HAS BEEN TOSSING HIS TRASH OUT HIS WINDOW. WHICH THE WIND...
"...PICKS UP...
"...AND DEPOSITS IN MY GARDEN."
I WILL TALK TO HIM ABOUT IT.
YES. YOU WILL!
BUT FIRST YOU'RE GOING TO HELP ME WITH WHATEVER VENOM'S TRASH...

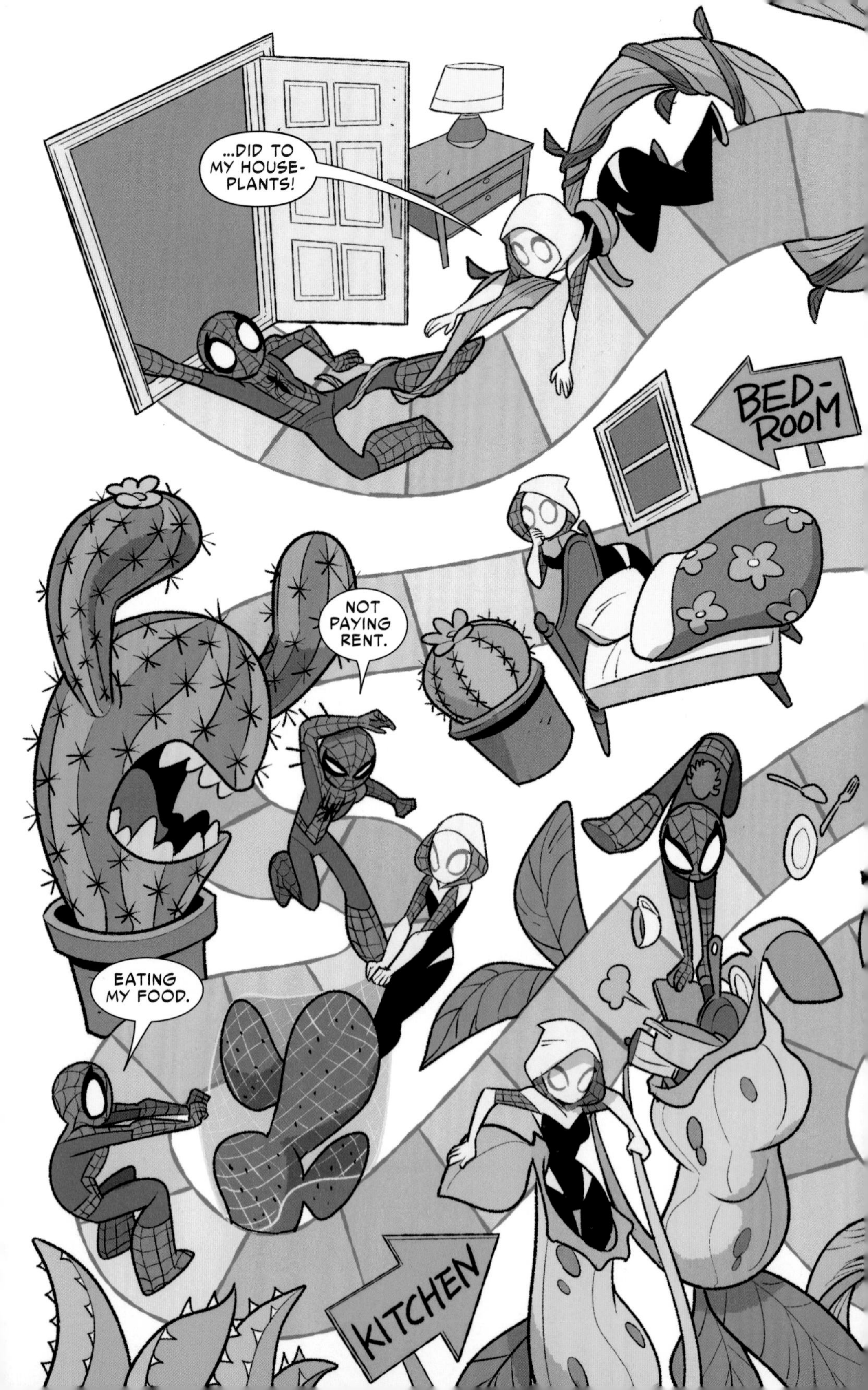
...DID TO MY HOUSE-PLANTS!
BED-ROOM
NOT PAYING RENT.
EATING MY FOOD.
KITCHEN

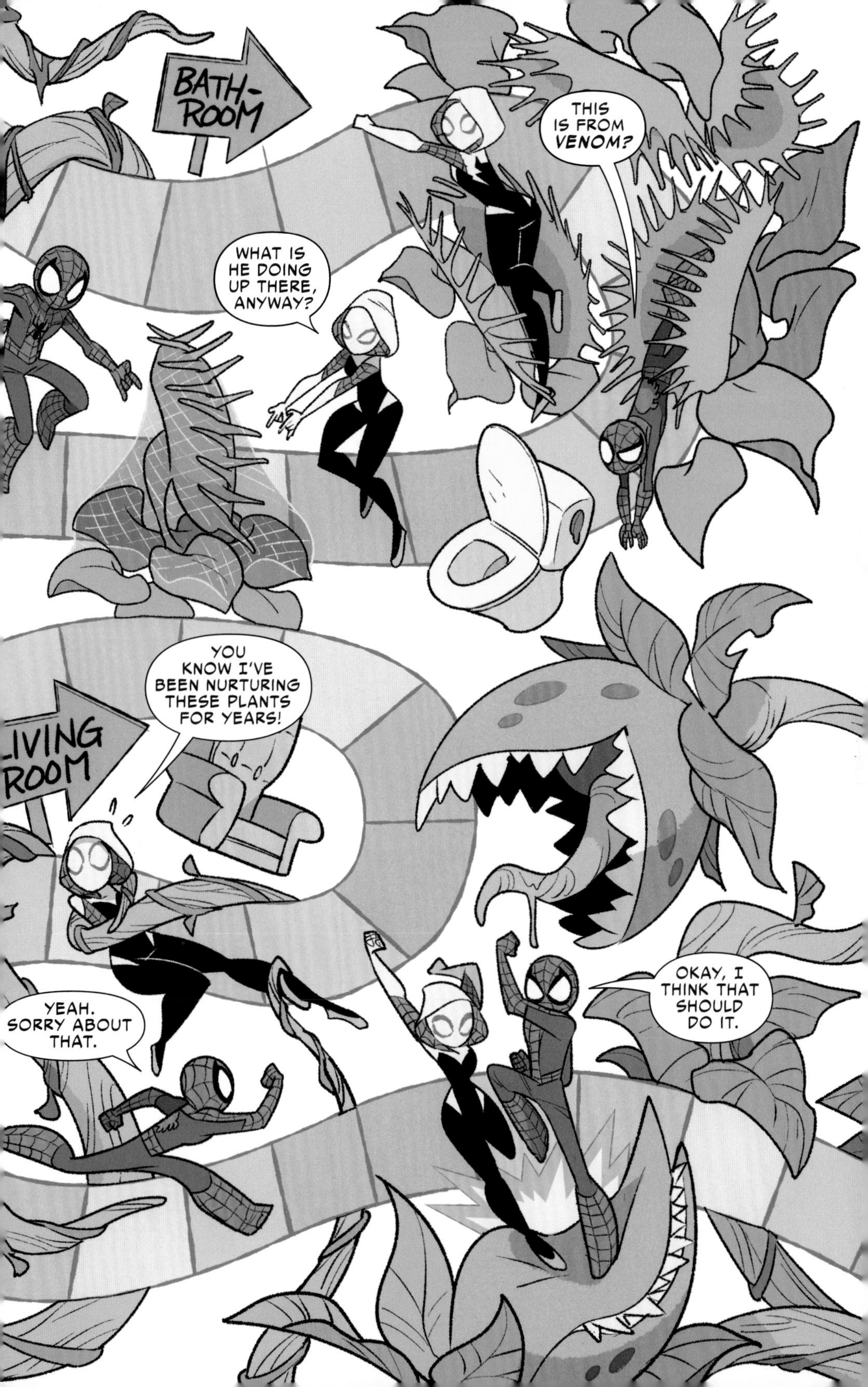
BATH-ROOM
THIS IS FROM VENOM?
WHAT IS HE DOING UP THERE, ANYWAY?
LIVING ROOM
YOU KNOW I'VE BEEN NURTURING THESE PLANTS FOR YEARS!
YEAH. SORRY ABOUT THAT.
OKAY, I THINK THAT SHOULD DO IT.

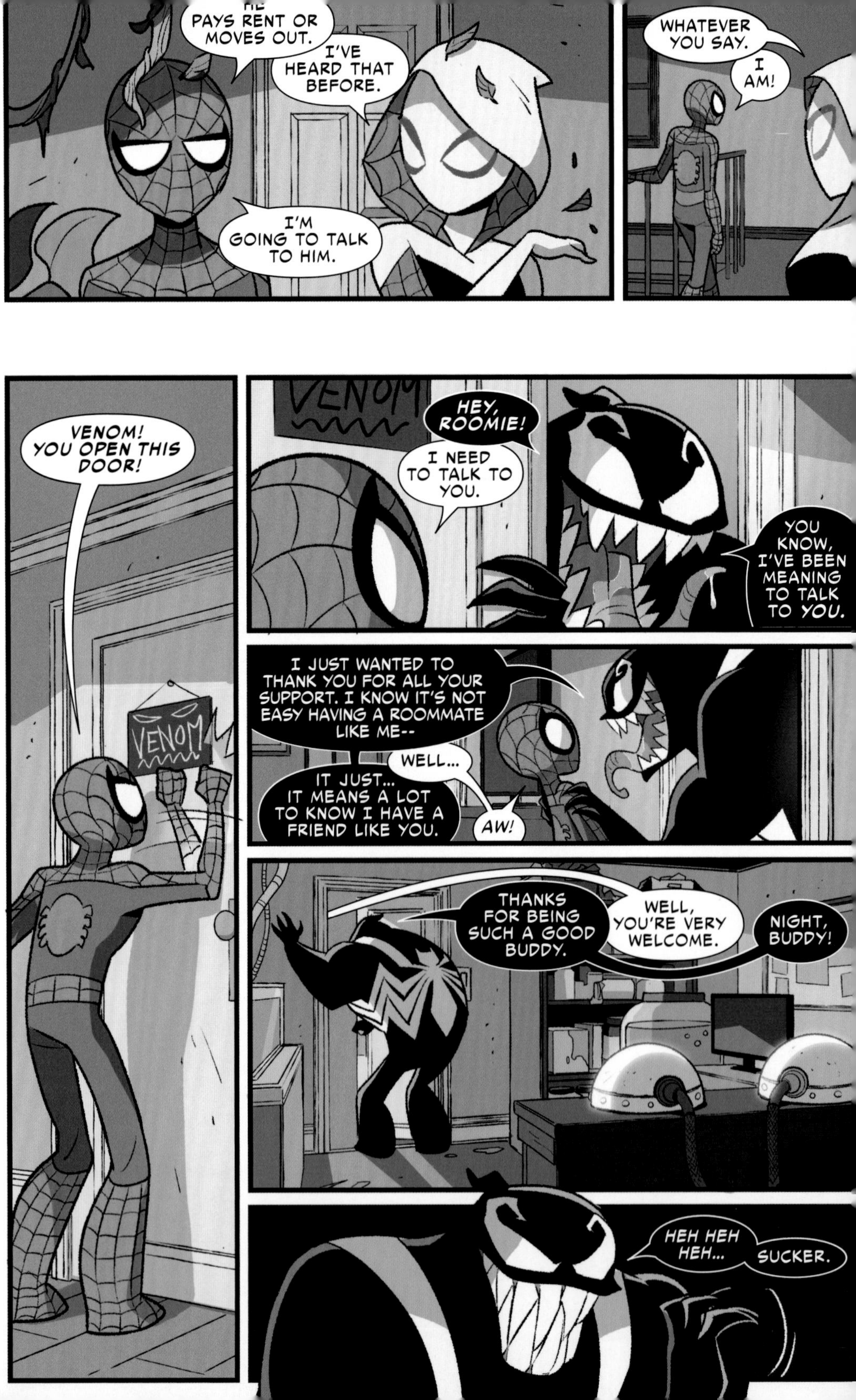

HE PAYS RENT OR MOVES OUT.
I'VE HEARD THAT BEFORE.
I'M GOING TO TALK TO HIM.
WHATEVER YOU SAY.
I AM!
VENOM! YOU OPEN THIS DOOR!
VENOM
HEY, ROOMIE!
I NEED TO TALK TO YOU.
YOU KNOW, I'VE BEEN MEANING TO TALK TO YOU.
I JUST WANTED TO THANK YOU FOR ALL YOUR SUPPORT. I KNOW IT'S NOT EASY HAVING A ROOMMATE LIKE ME--
WELL...
IT JUST... IT MEANS A LOT TO KNOW I HAVE A FRIEND LIKE YOU.
AW!
THANKS FOR BEING SUCH A GOOD BUDDY.
WELL, YOU'RE VERY WELCOME.
NIGHT, BUDDY!
HEH HEH HEH...
SUCKER.

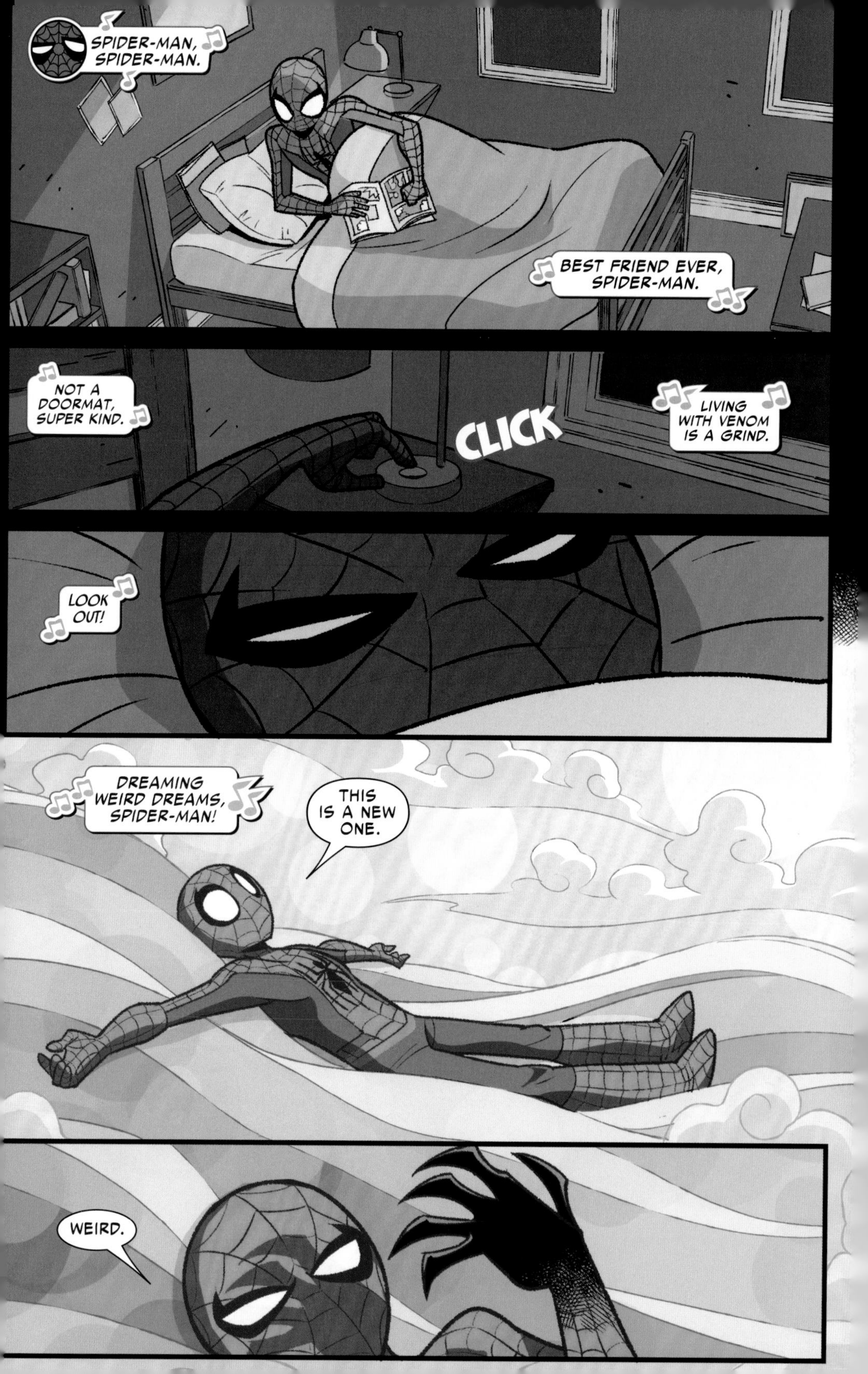
SPIDER-MAN, SPIDER-MAN.
BEST FRIEND EVER, SPIDER-MAN.
NOT A DOORMAT, SUPER KIND.
CLICK
LIVING WITH VENOM IS A GRIND.
LOOK OUT!
DREAMING WEIRD DREAMS, SPIDER-MAN!
THIS IS A NEW ONE.
WEIRD.

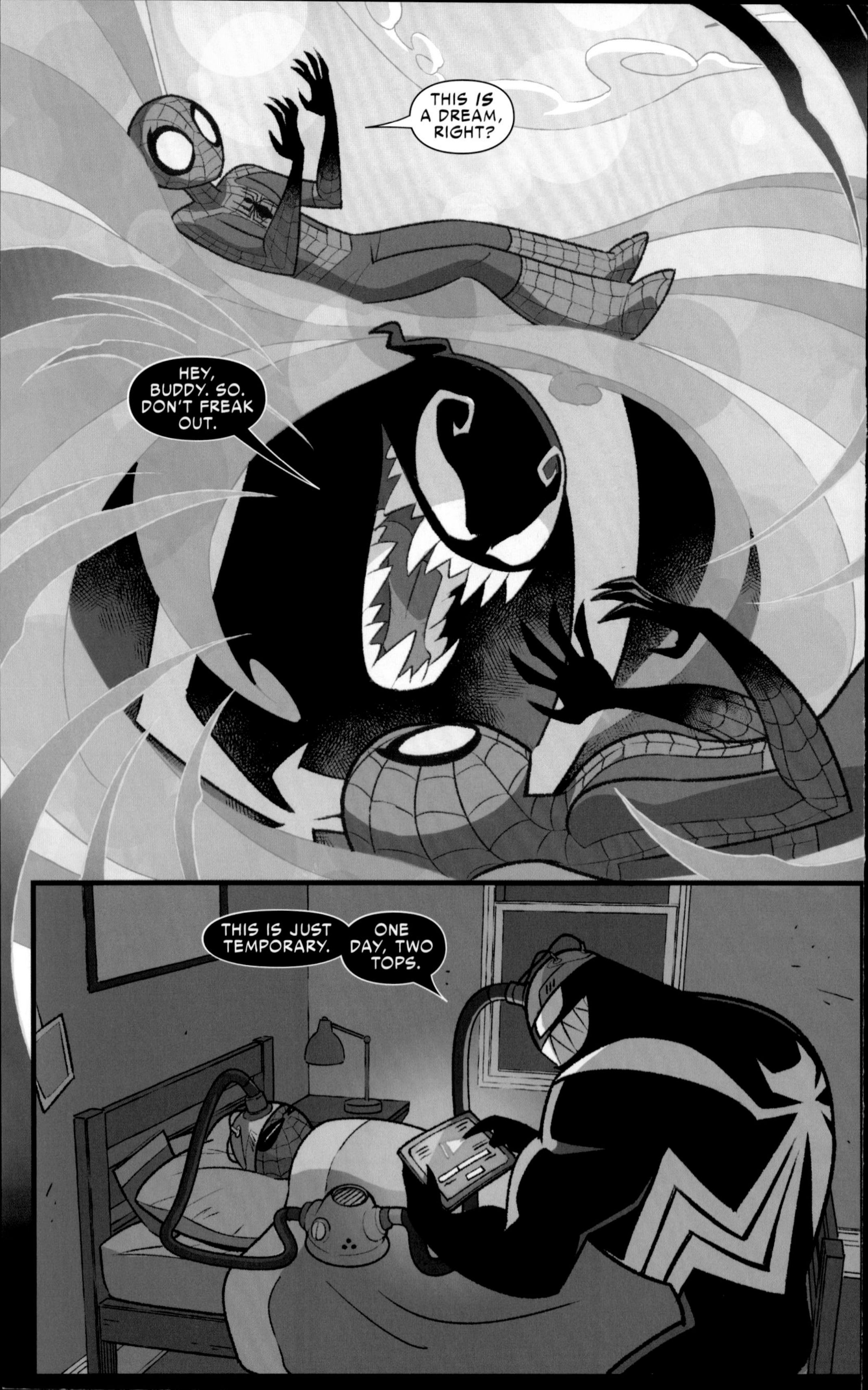
THIS IS A DREAM, RIGHT?
HEY, BUDDY. SO. DON'T FREAK OUT.
THIS IS JUST TEMPORARY.
ONE DAY, TWO TOPS.

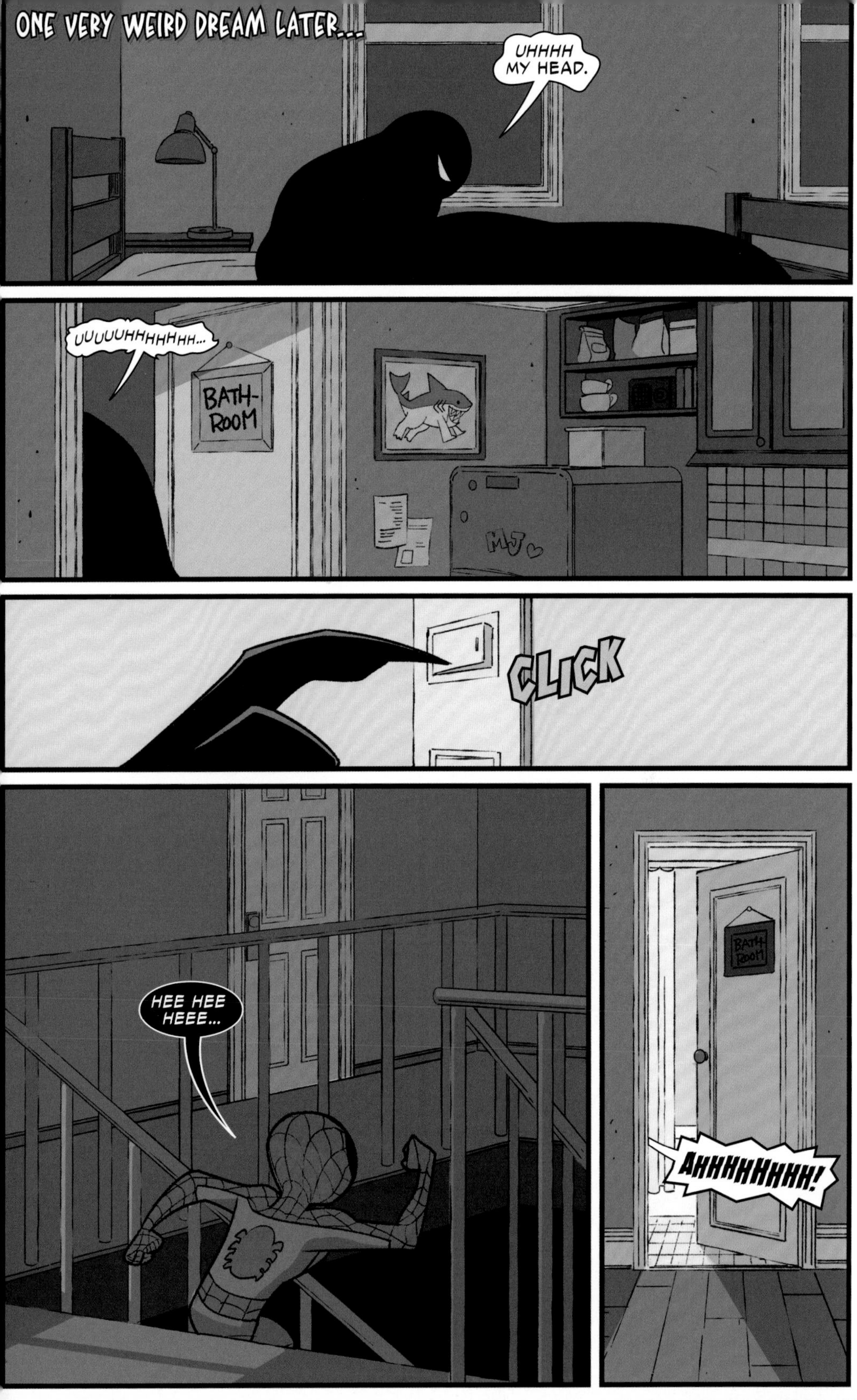
ONE VERY WEIRD DREAM LATER...
UHHHH MY HEAD.
UUUUUHHHHHH...
BATH-ROOM
MJ
CLICK
HEE HEE HEEE...
BATH-ROOM
AHHHHHHHH!

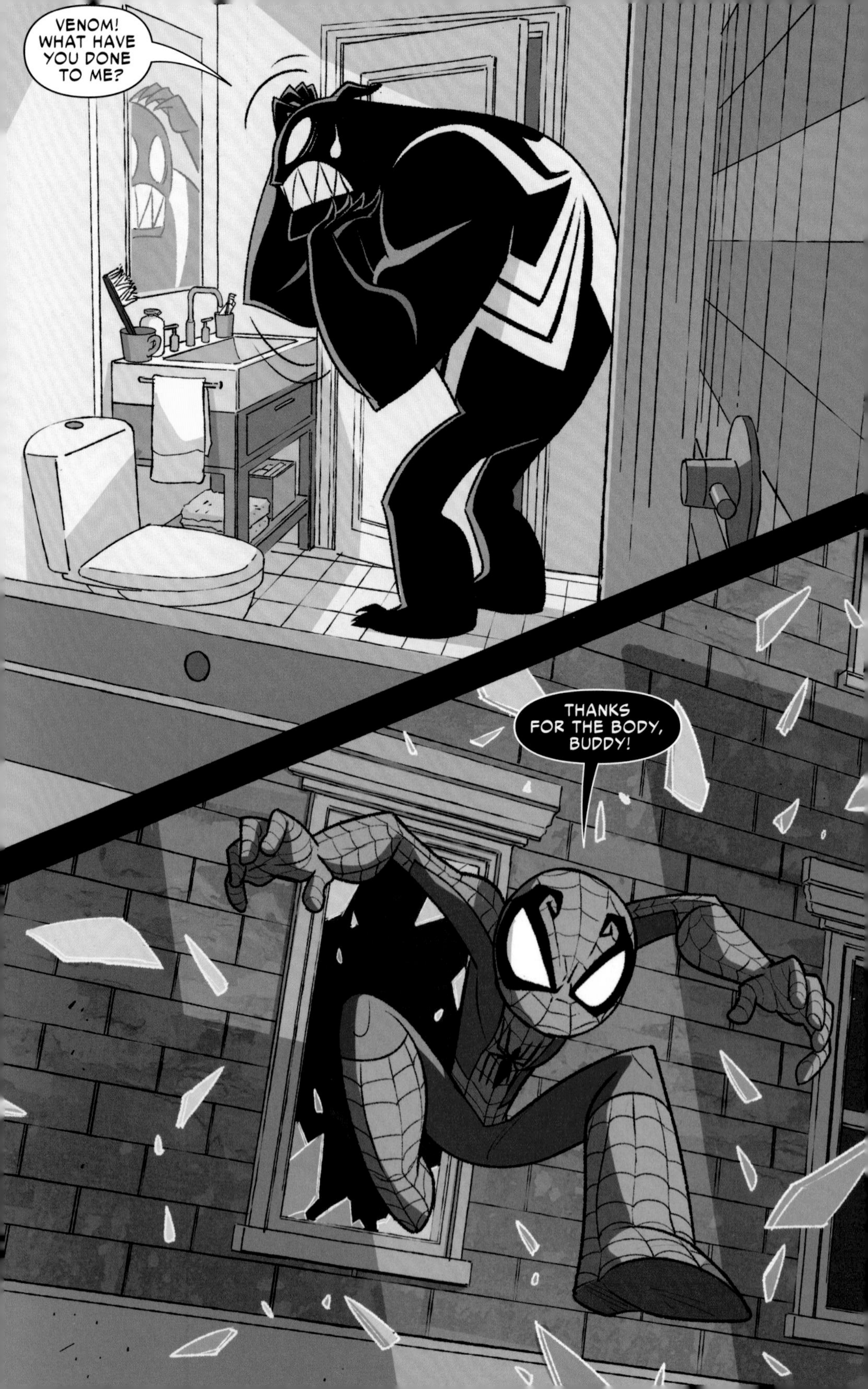
VENOM! WHAT HAVE YOU DONE TO ME?
THANKS FOR THE BODY, BUDDY!

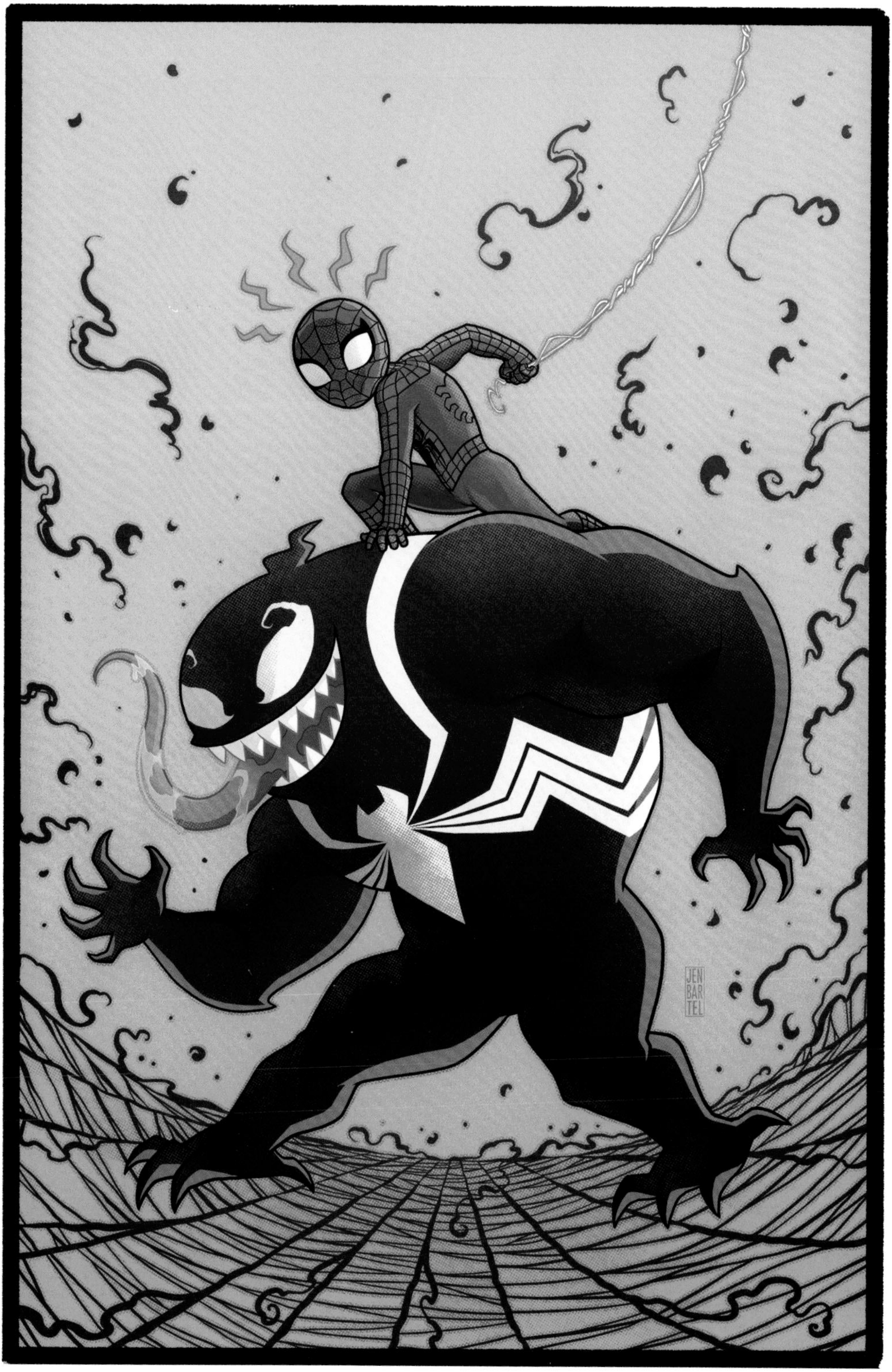
JEN BAR TEL

#1 VARIANT BY **JEN BARTEL**

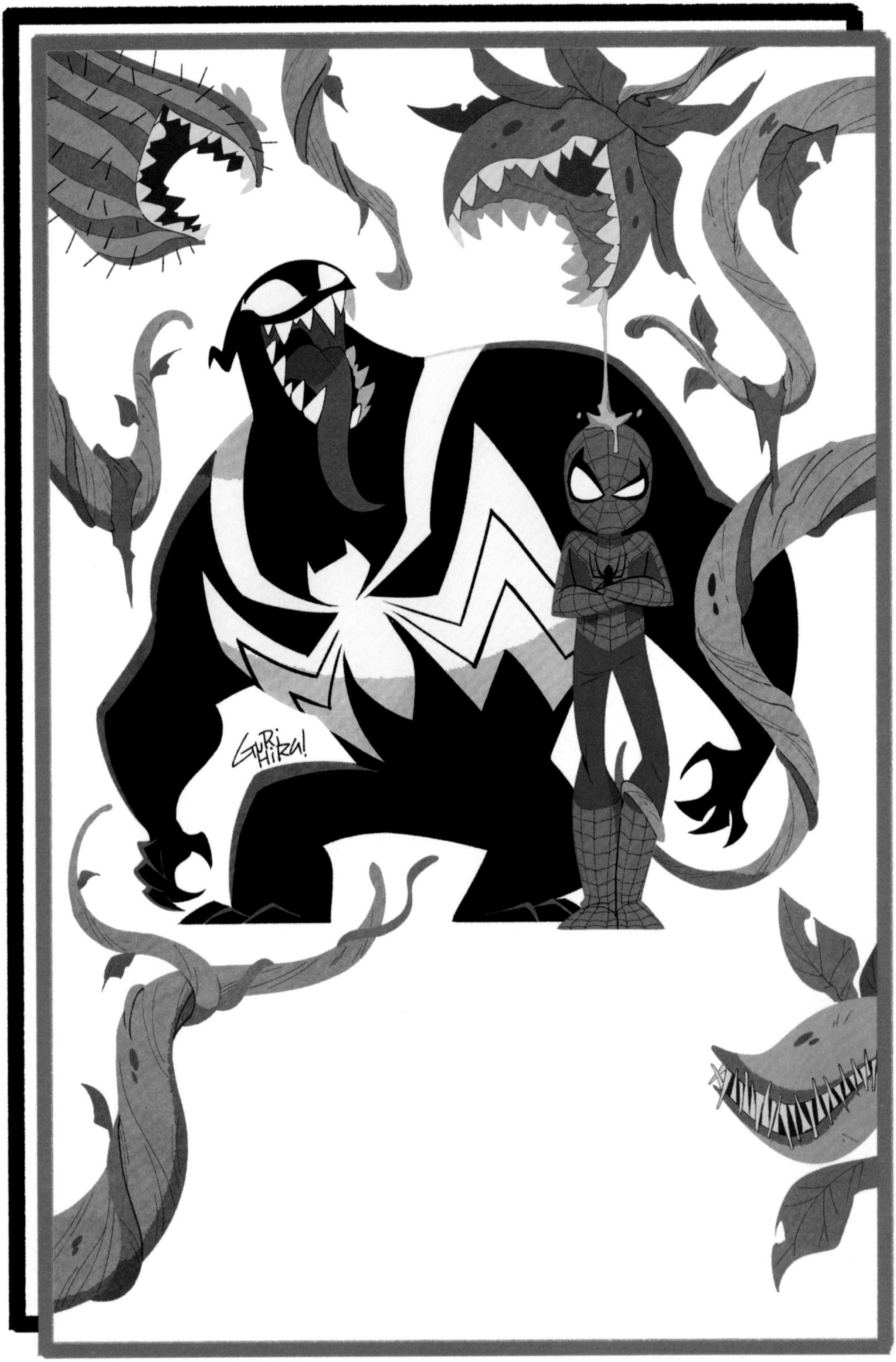
GURIHIRU!

2

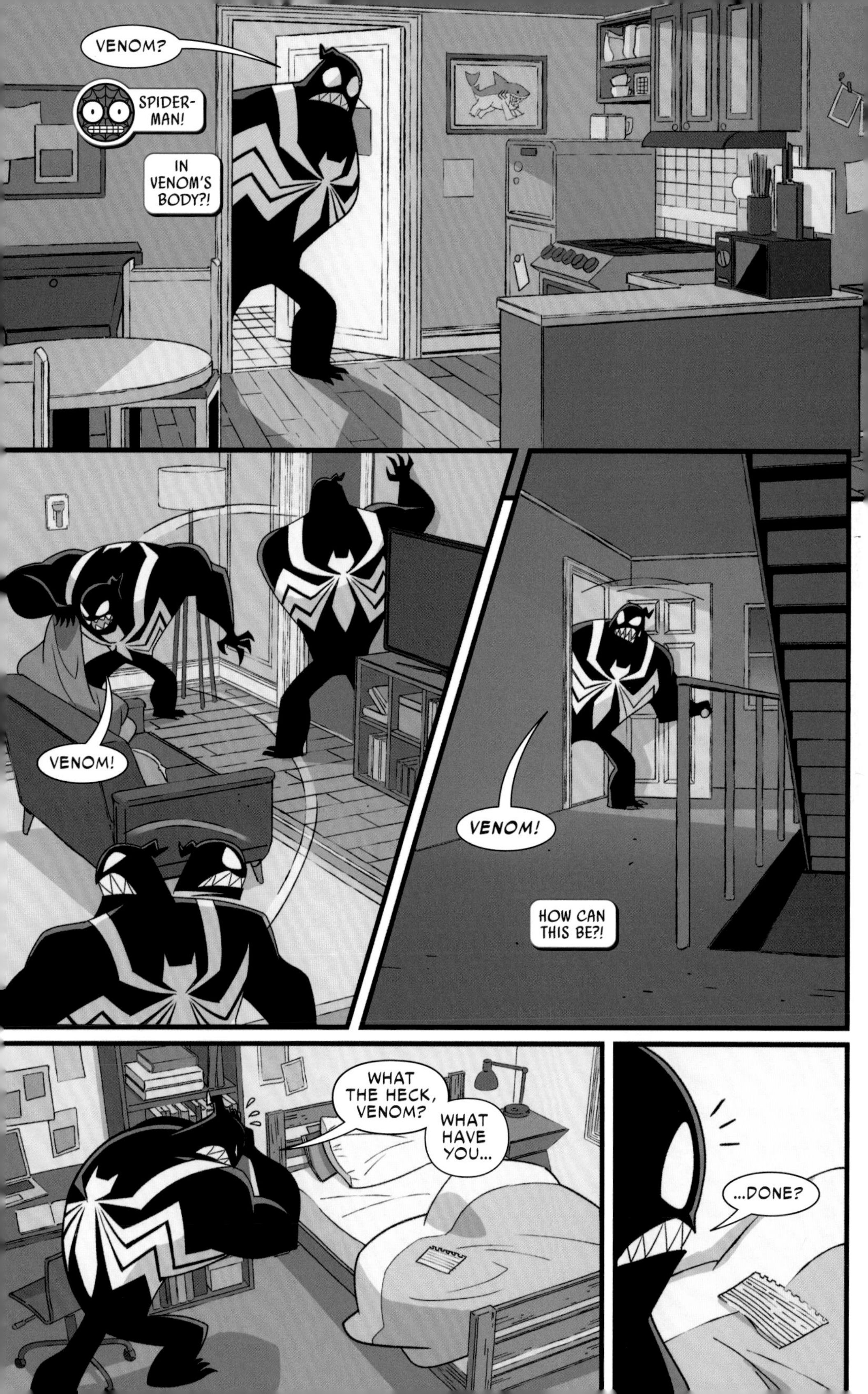
VENOM?
SPIDER-MAN!
IN VENOM'S BODY?!
VENOM!
VENOM!
HOW CAN THIS BE?!
WHAT THE HECK, VENOM?
WHAT HAVE YOU...
...DONE?

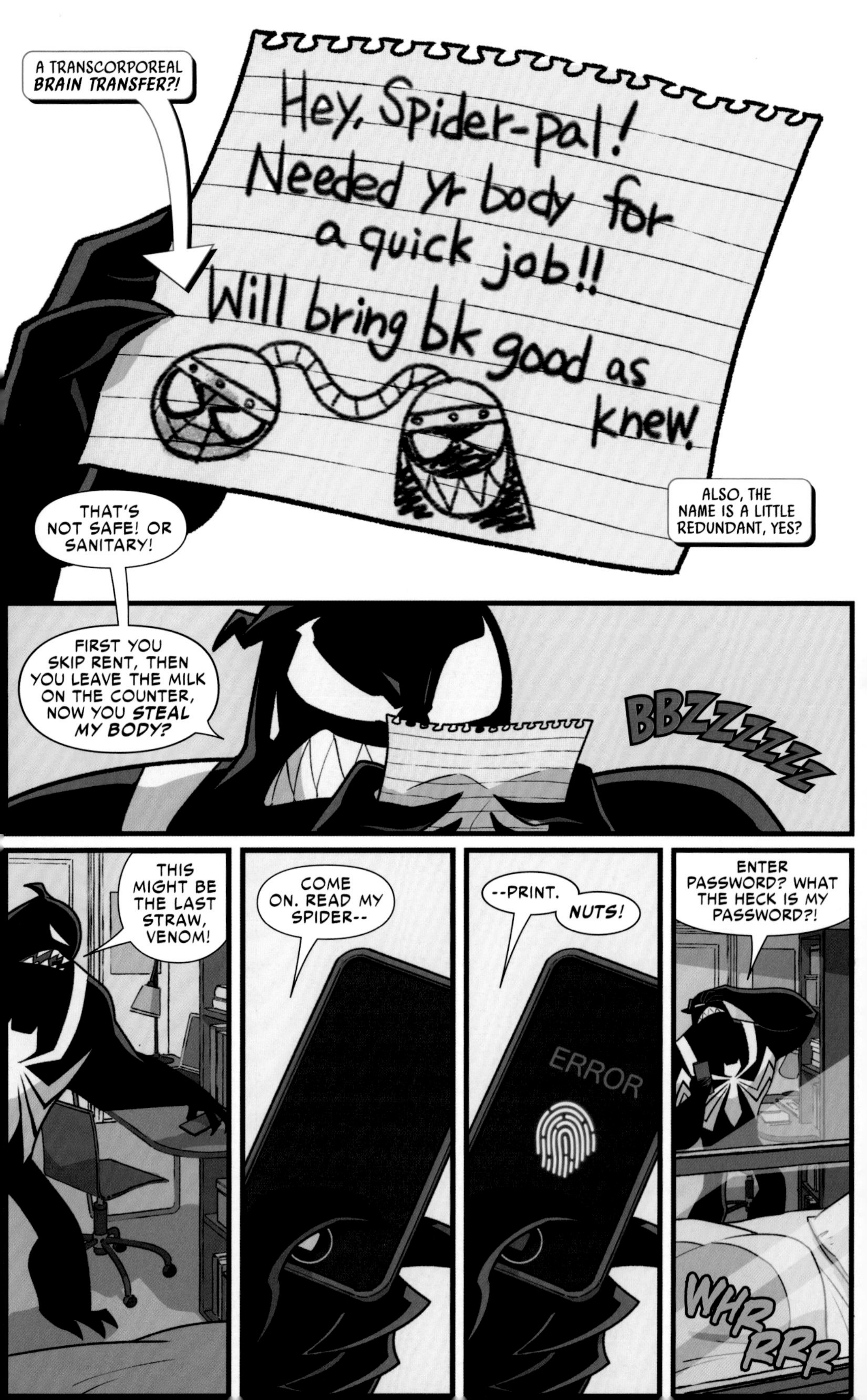
A TRANSCORPOREAL BRAIN TRANSFER?!
Hey, Spider-pal! Needed yr body for a quick job!! Will bring bk good as knew.
THAT'S NOT SAFE! OR SANITARY!
ALSO, THE NAME IS A LITTLE REDUNDANT, YES?
FIRST YOU SKIP RENT, THEN YOU LEAVE THE MILK ON THE COUNTER, NOW YOU STEAL MY BODY?
BBZZZZZZ
THIS MIGHT BE THE LAST STRAW, VENOM!
COME ON. READ MY SPIDER--
--PRINT.
NUTS!
ERROR
ENTER PASSWORD? WHAT THE HECK IS MY PASSWORD?!
WHRRRR

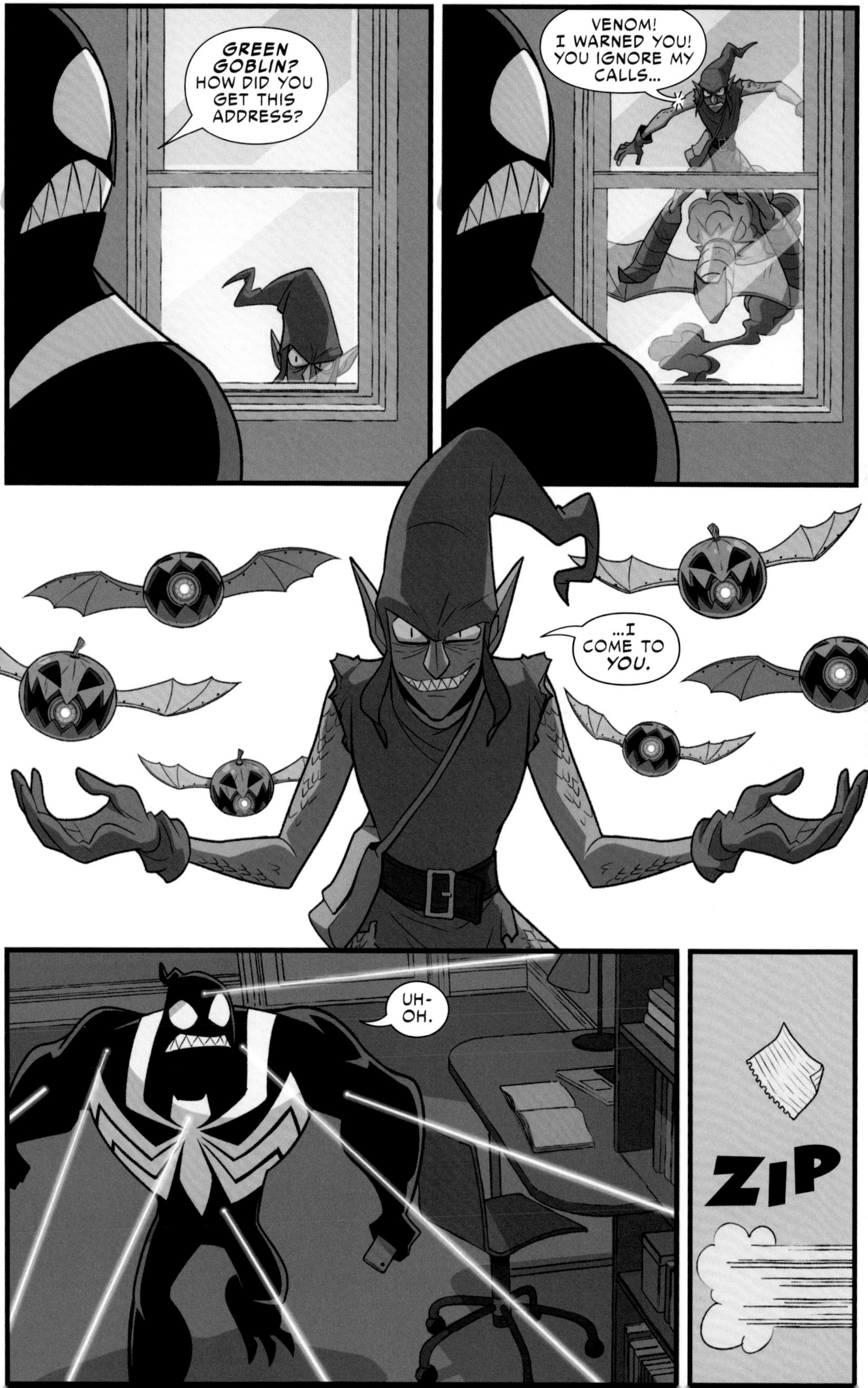

GREEN GOBLIN? HOW DID YOU GET THIS ADDRESS?
VENOM! I WARNED YOU! YOU IGNORE MY CALLS...
...I COME TO YOU.
UH-OH.
ZIP

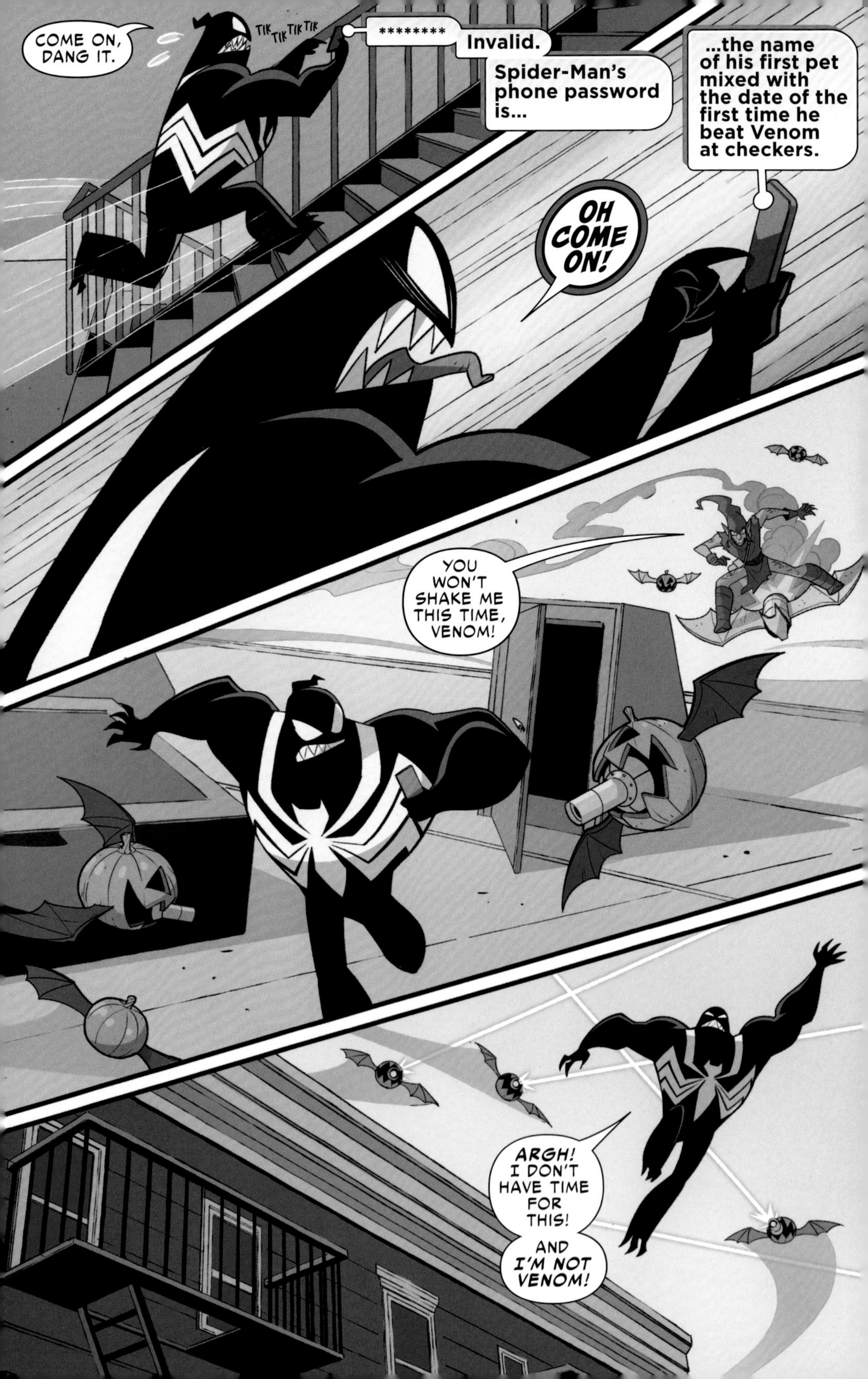
COME ON, DANG IT.
TIK TIK TIK TIK
****
Invalid.
Spider-Man's phone password is...
...the name of his first pet mixed with the date of the first time he beat Venom at checkers.
OH COME ON!
YOU WON'T SHAKE ME THIS TIME, VENOM!
ARGH! I DON'T HAVE TIME FOR THIS!
AND I'M NOT VENOM!

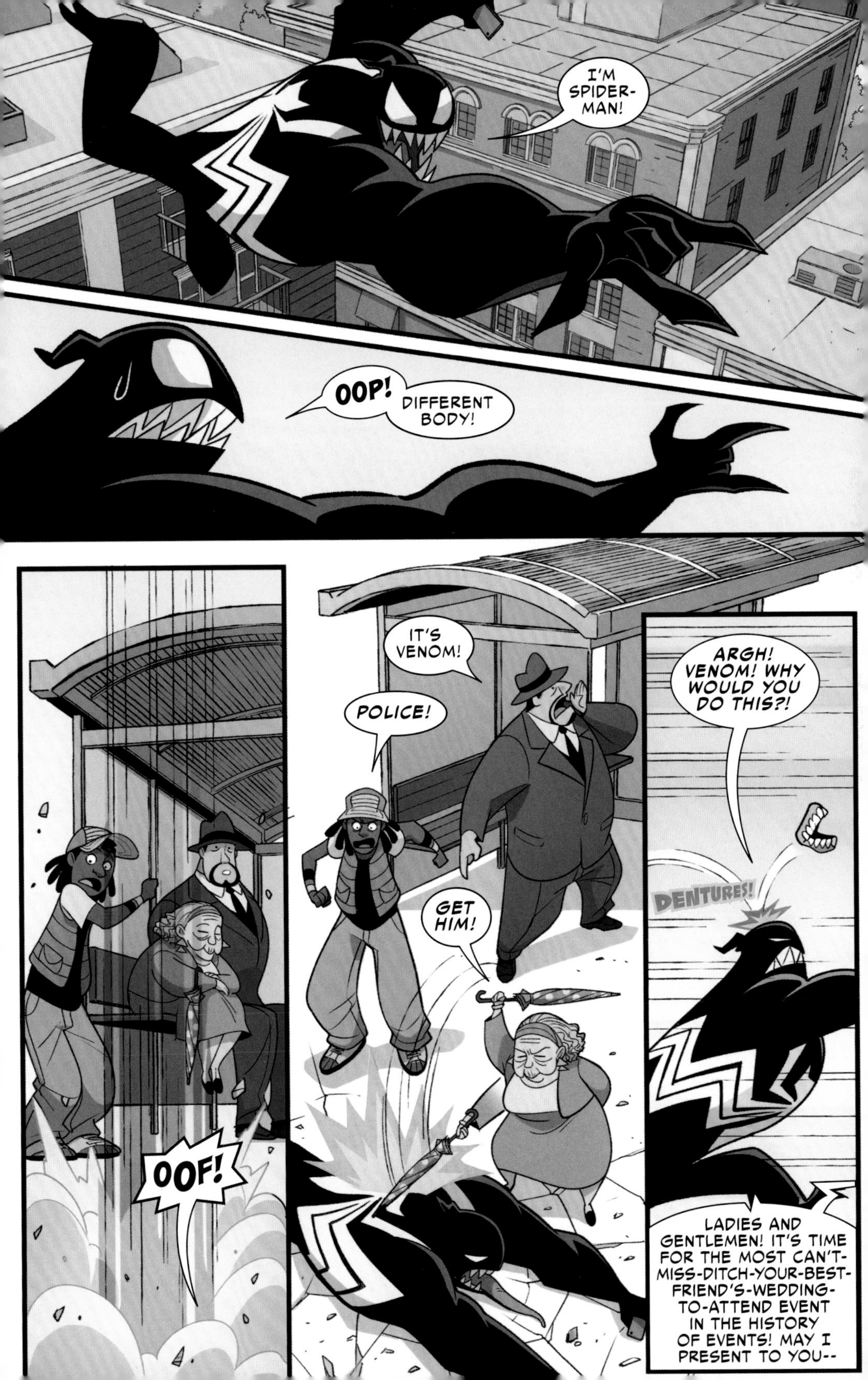

I'M SPIDER-MAN!
OOP!
DIFFERENT BODY!
OOF!
IT'S VENOM!
POLICE!
GET HIM!
ARGH! VENOM! WHY WOULD YOU DO THIS?!
DENTURES!
LADIES AND GENTLEMEN! IT'S TIME FOR THE MOST CAN'T-MISS-DITCH-YOUR-BEST-FRIEND'S-WEDDING-TO-ATTEND EVENT IN THE HISTORY OF EVENTS! MAY I PRESENT TO YOU--

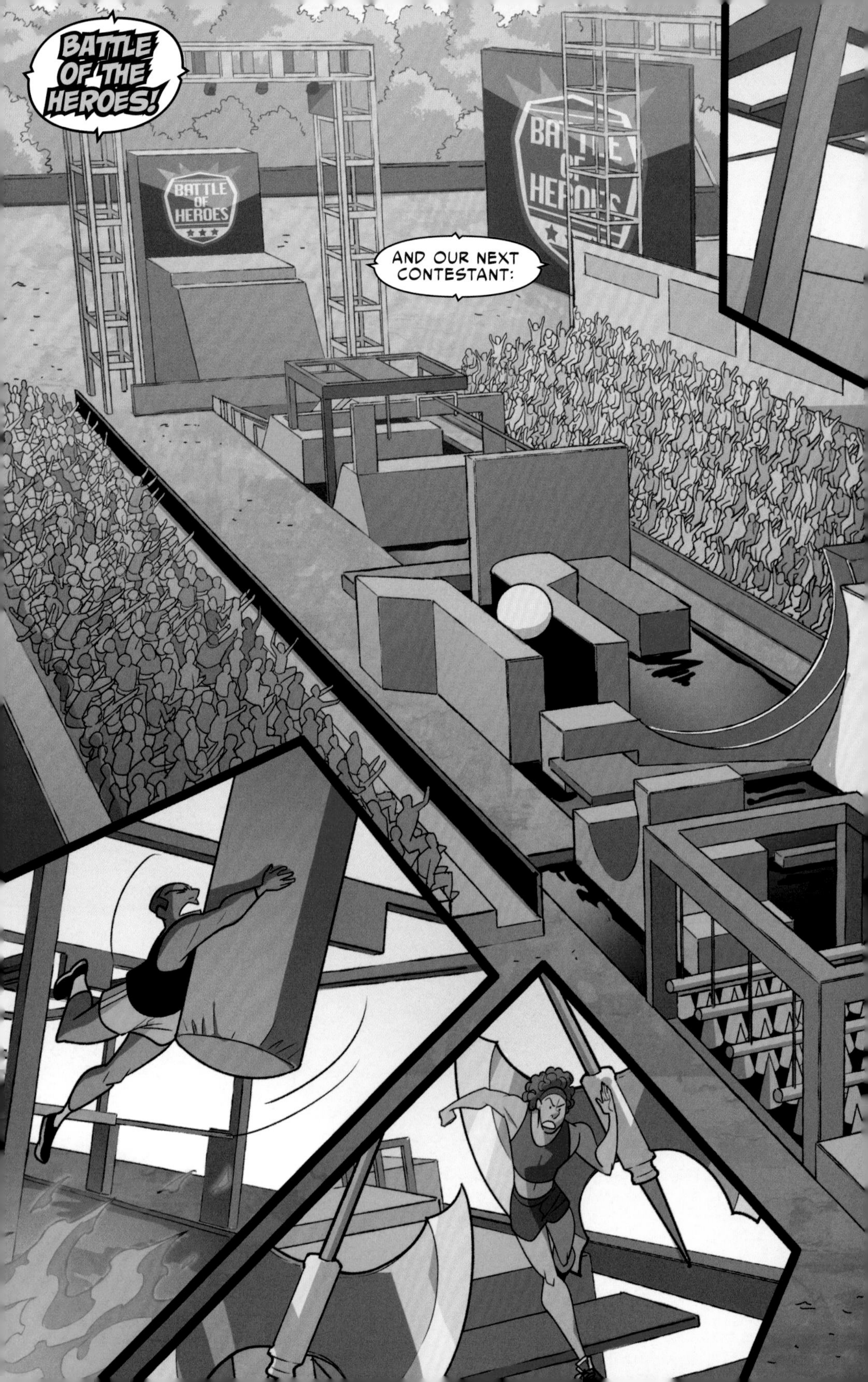
BATTLE OF THE HEROES!
BATTLE OF HEROES
AND OUR NEXT CONTESTANT:

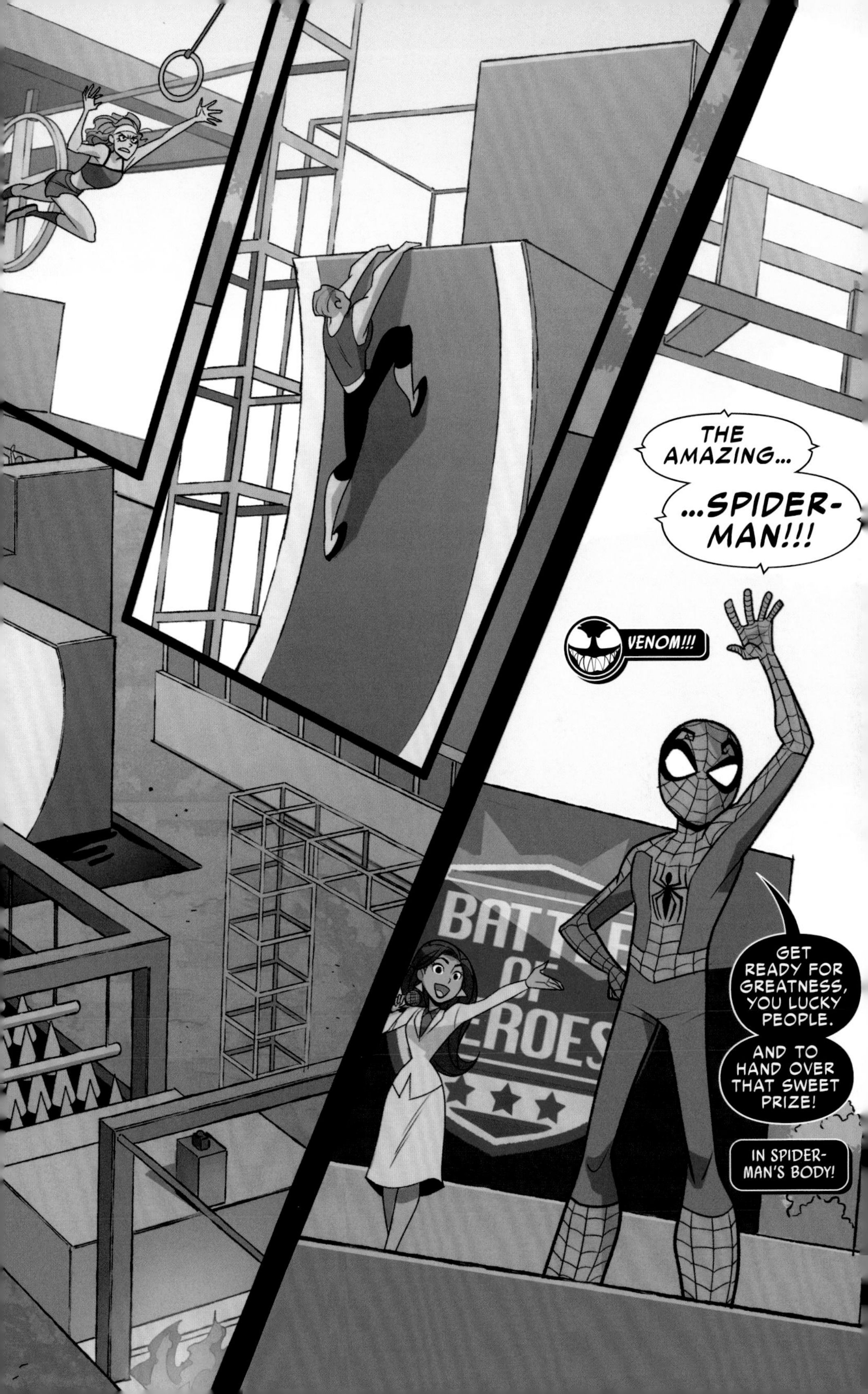
THE AMAZING...
...SPIDER-MAN!!!
VENOM!!!
BATTLE OF HEROES
GET READY FOR GREATNESS, YOU LUCKY PEOPLE.
AND TO HAND OVER THAT SWEET PRIZE!
IN SPIDER-MAN'S BODY!

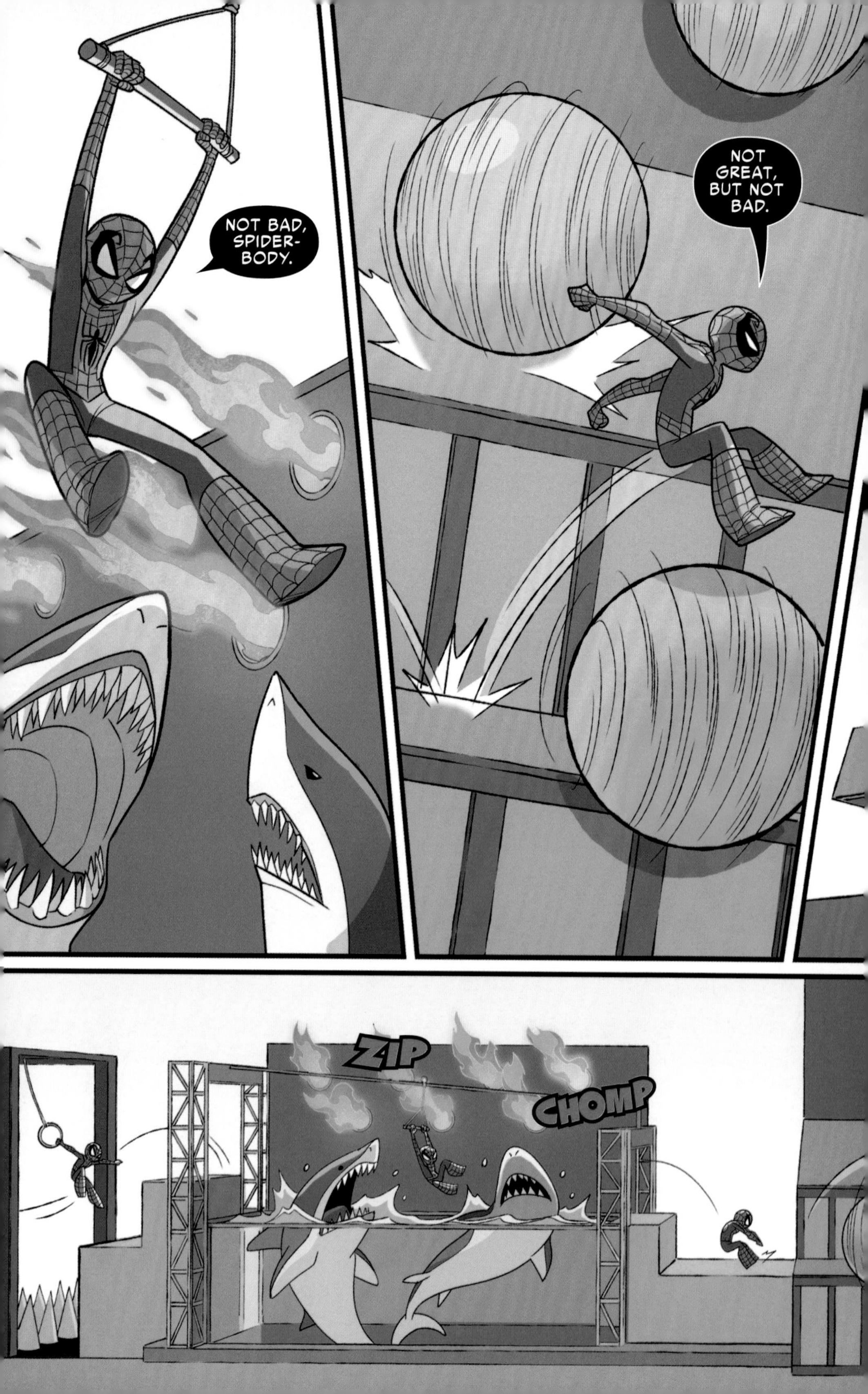
NOT BAD, SPIDER-BODY.
NOT GREAT, BUT NOT BAD.
ZIP
CHOMP

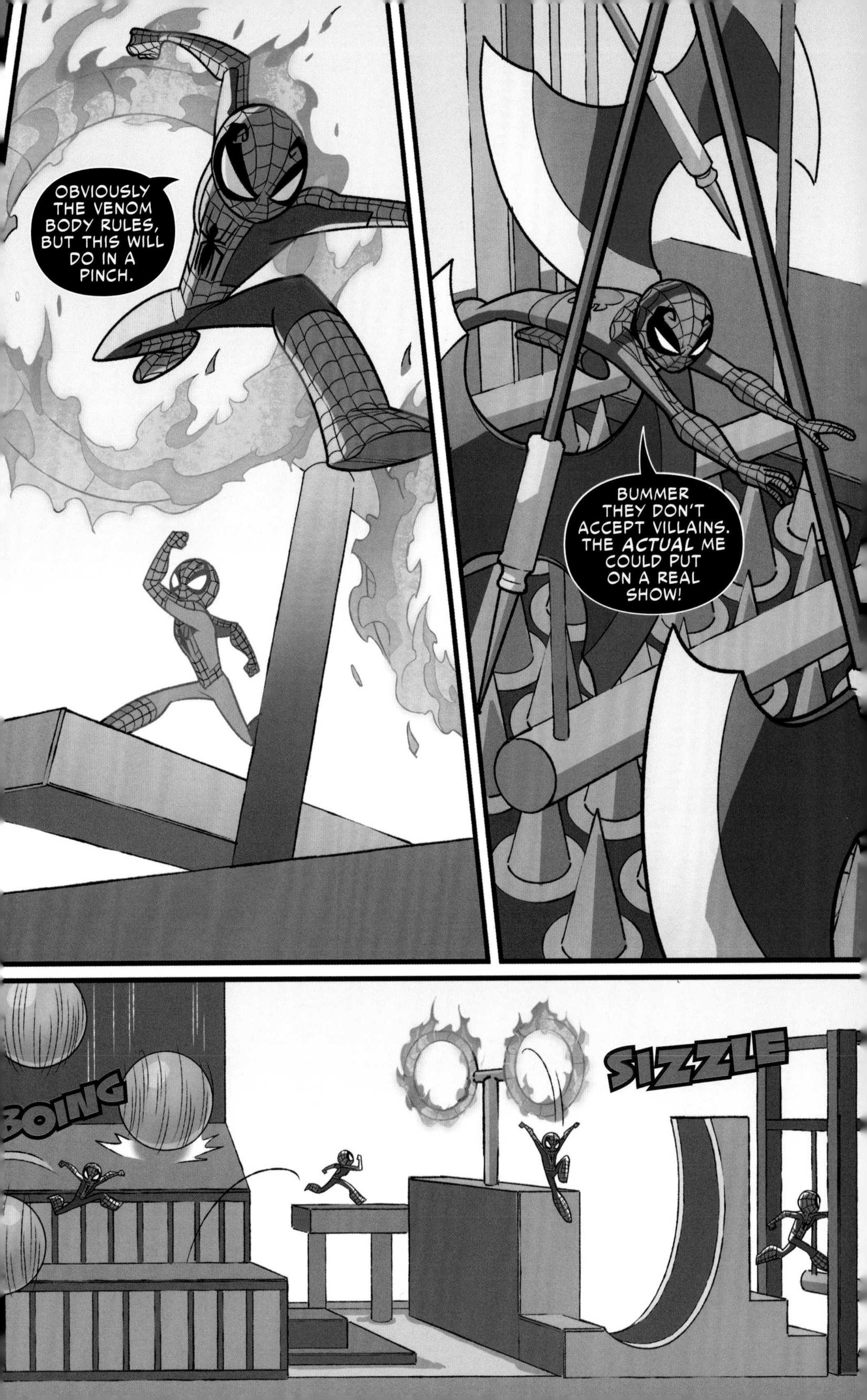
OBVIOUSLY THE VENOM BODY RULES, BUT THIS WILL DO IN A PINCH.
BUMMER THEY DON'T ACCEPT VILLAINS. THE ACTUAL ME COULD PUT ON A REAL SHOW!
BOING
SIZZLE

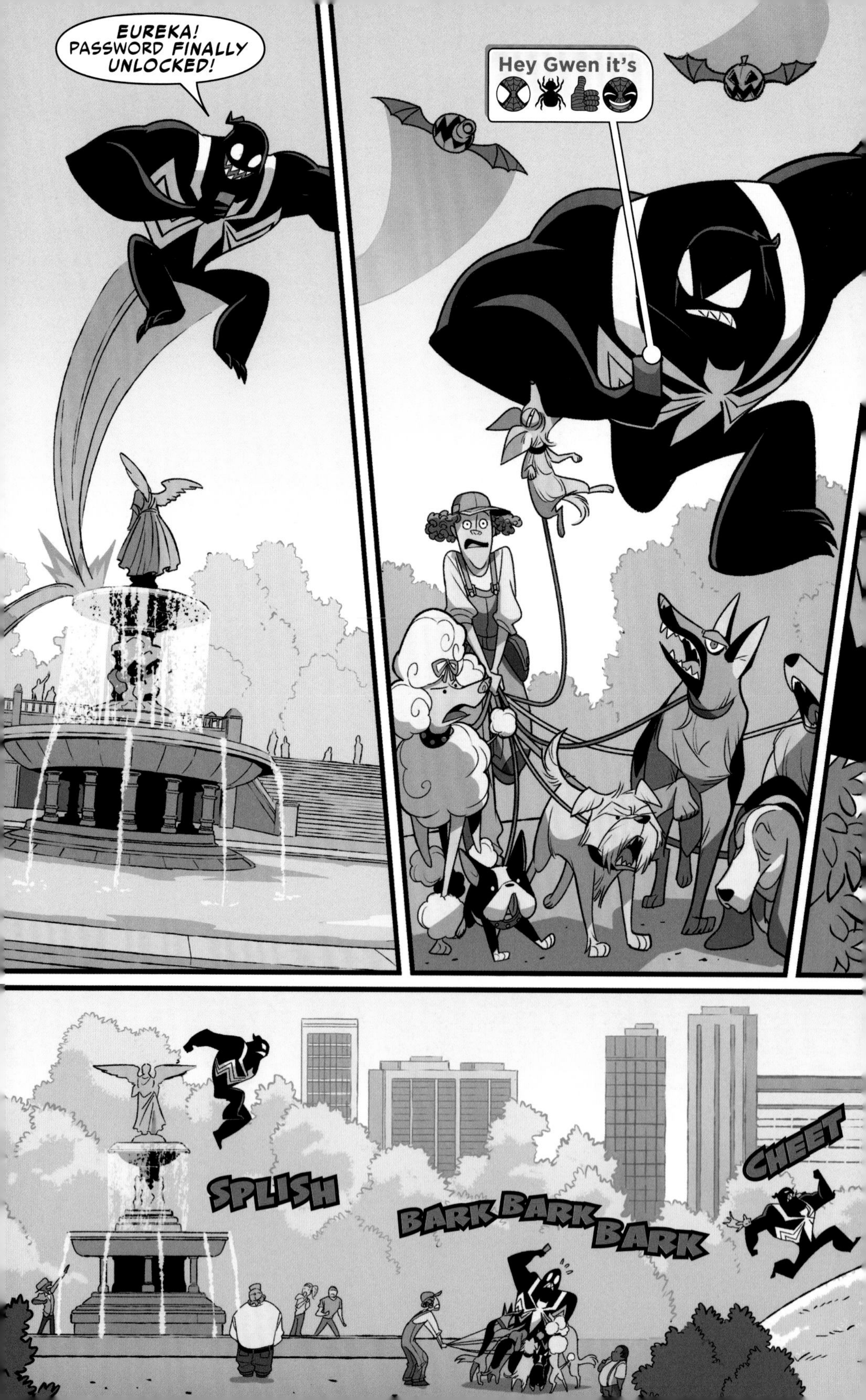
EUREKA! PASSWORD FINALLY UNLOCKED!
Hey Gwen it's
SPLISH
BARK BARK BARK
CHEET

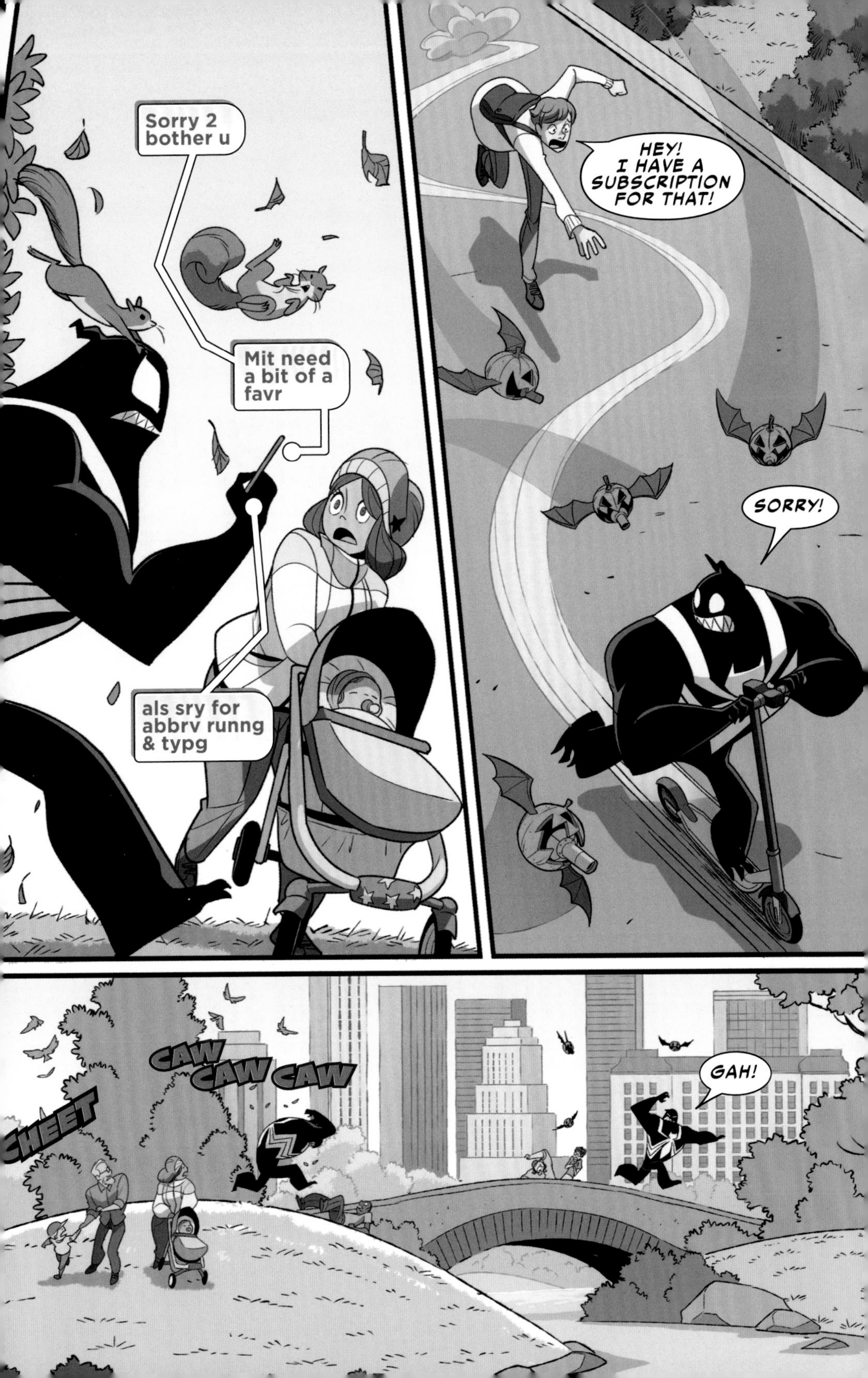
Sorry 2 bother u
Mit need a bit of a favr
als sry for abbrv runng & typg
HEY! I HAVE A SUBSCRIPTION FOR THAT!
SORRY!
CHEET
CAW CAW CAW
GAH!

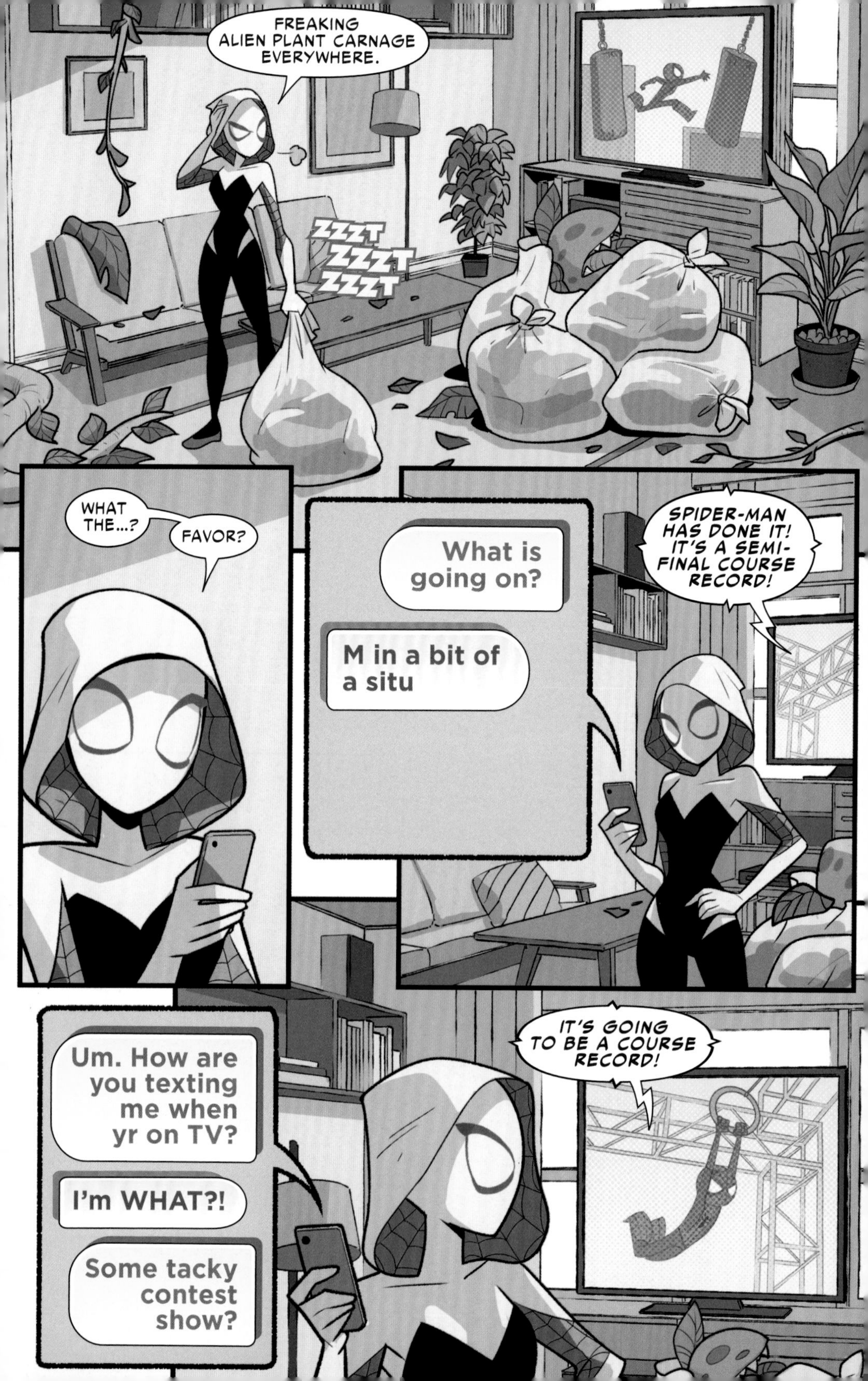
FREAKING ALIEN PLANT CARNAGE EVERYWHERE.
ZZZT ZZZT ZZZT
WHAT THE...?
FAVOR?
What is going on?
M in a bit of a situ
SPIDER-MAN HAS DONE IT! IT'S A SEMI-FINAL COURSE RECORD!
Um. How are you texting me when yr on TV?
I'm WHAT?!
Some tacky contest show?
IT'S GOING TO BE A COURSE RECORD!

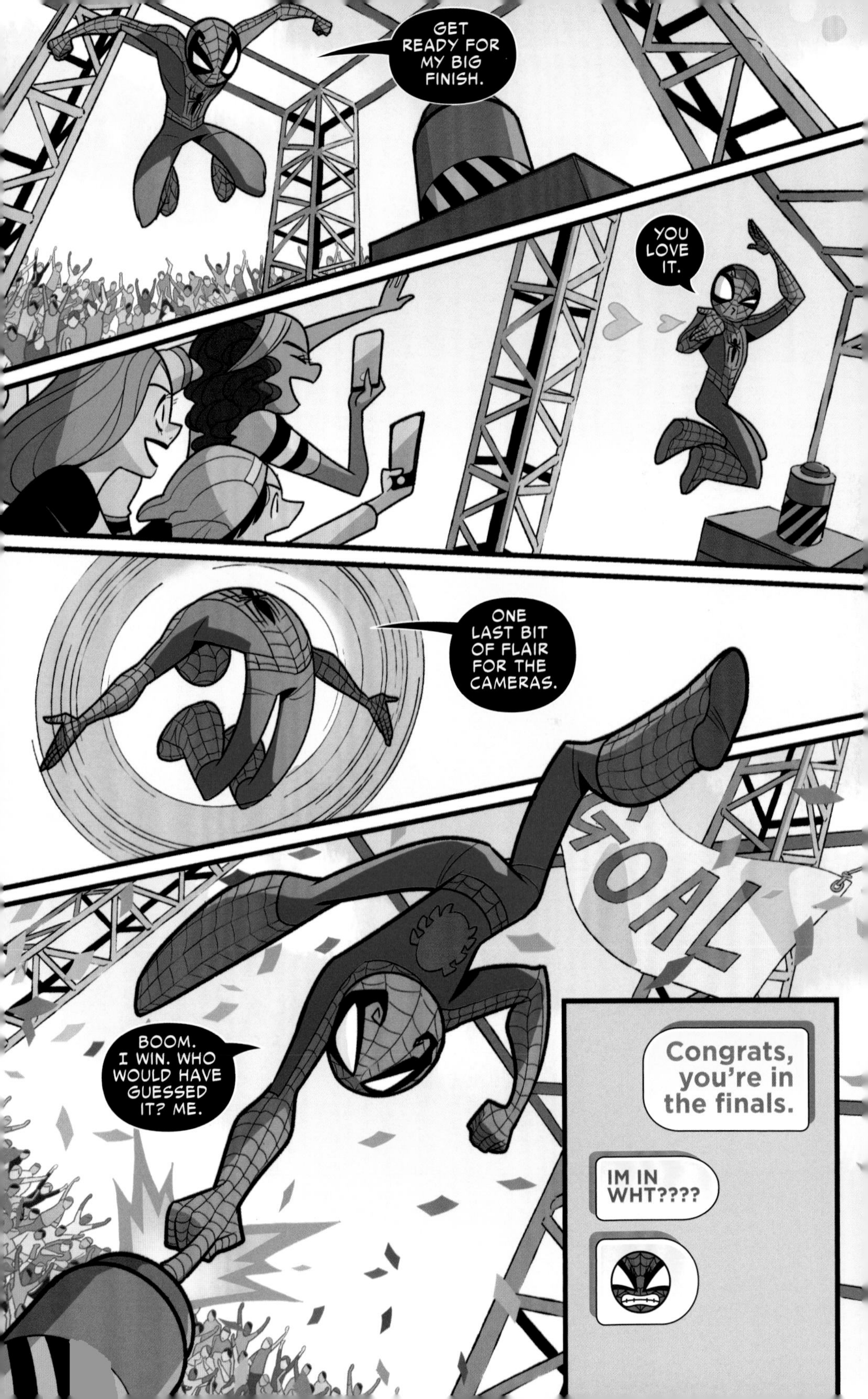
GET READY FOR MY BIG FINISH.
YOU LOVE IT.
ONE LAST BIT OF FLAIR FOR THE CAMERAS.
GOAL
BOOM. I WIN. WHO WOULD HAVE GUESSED IT? ME.
Congrats, you're in the finals.
IM IN WHT????

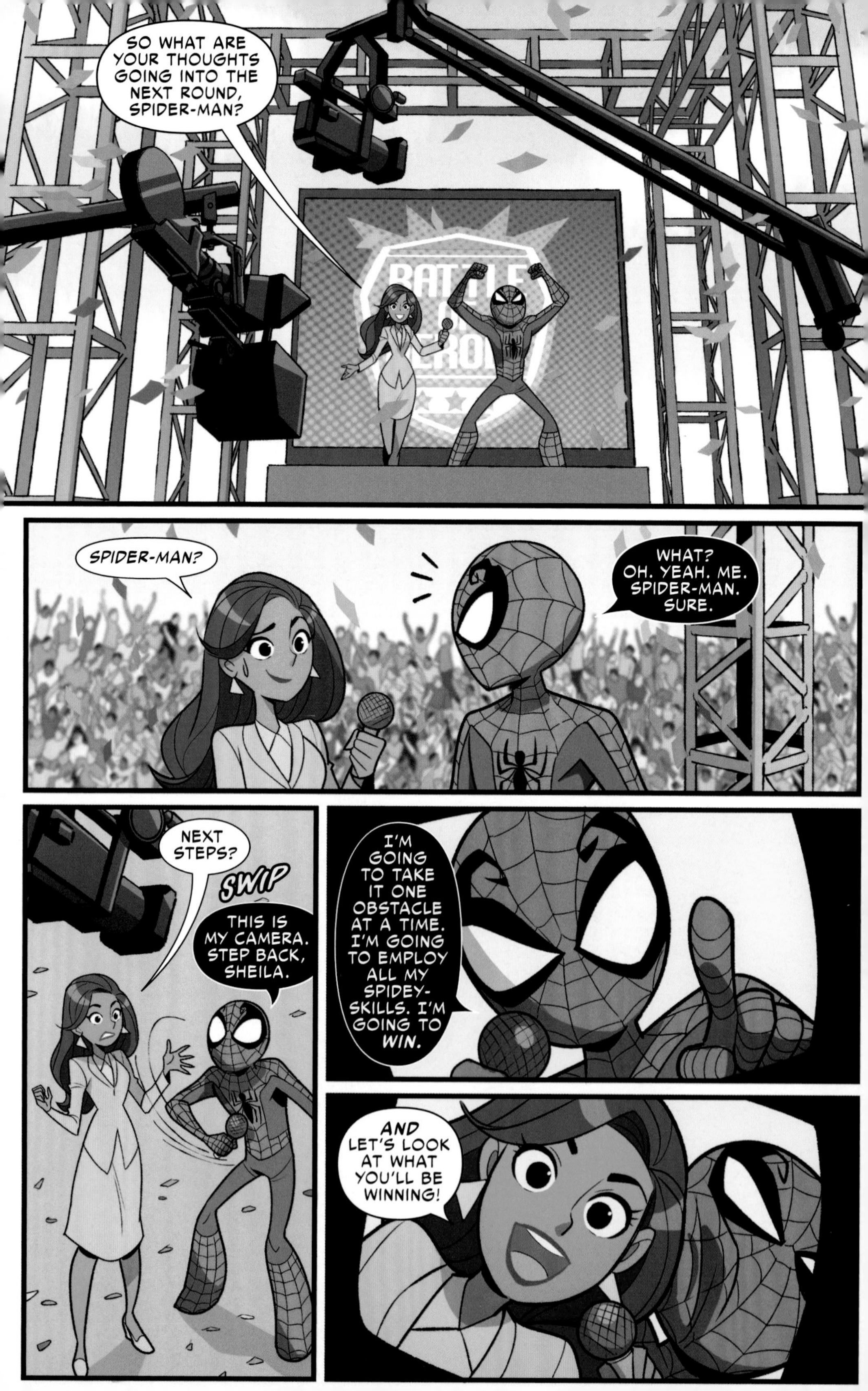
SO WHAT ARE YOUR THOUGHTS GOING INTO THE NEXT ROUND, SPIDER-MAN?
SPIDER-MAN?
WHAT? OH. YEAH. ME. SPIDER-MAN. SURE.
NEXT STEPS?
SWIP
THIS IS MY CAMERA. STEP BACK, SHEILA.
I'M GOING TO TAKE IT ONE OBSTACLE AT A TIME. I'M GOING TO EMPLOY ALL MY SPIDEY-SKILLS. I'M GOING TO WIN.
AND LET'S LOOK AT WHAT YOU'LL BE WINNING!

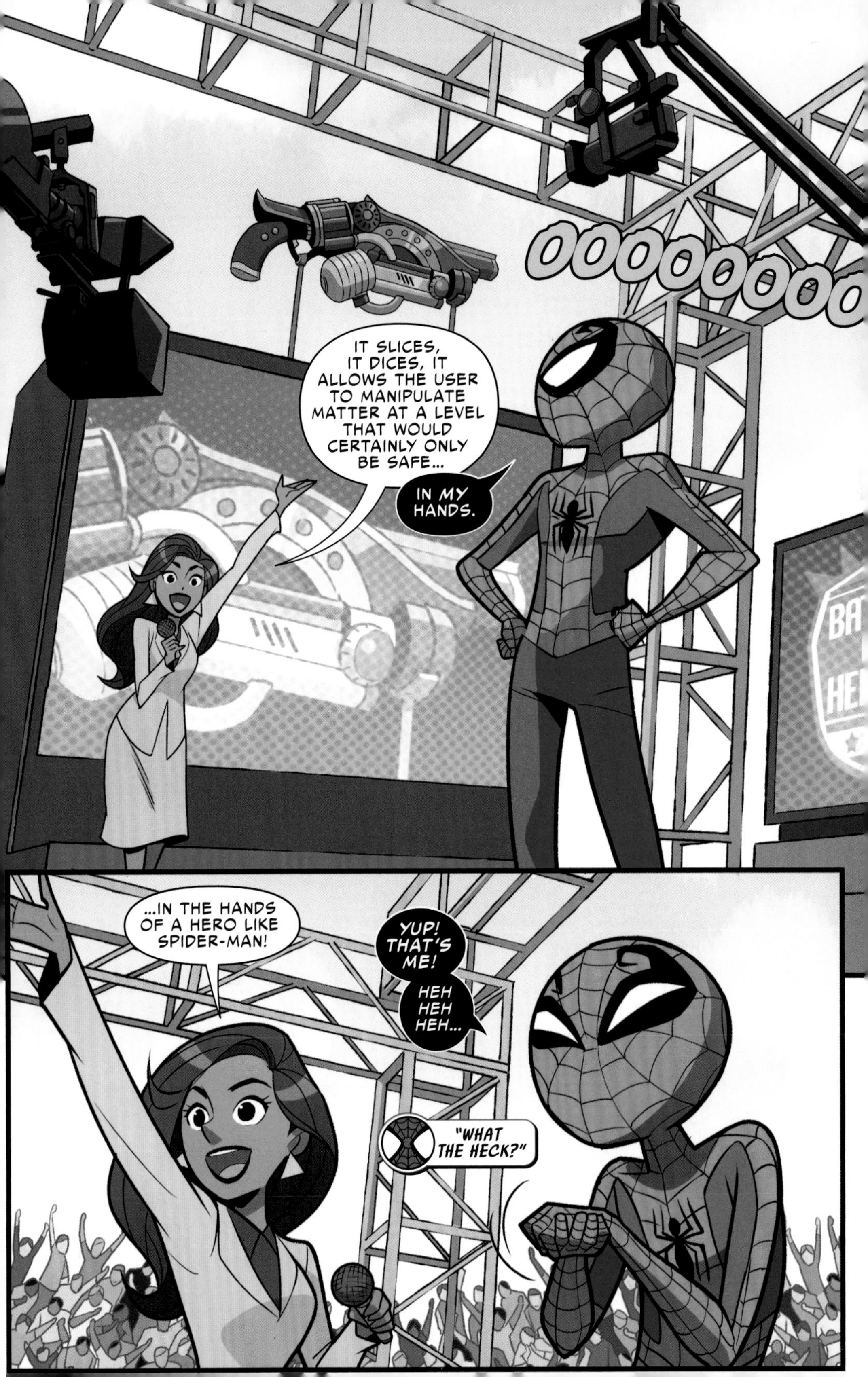
OOOOOOOOO
IT SLICES, IT DICES, IT ALLOWS THE USER TO MANIPULATE MATTER AT A LEVEL THAT WOULD CERTAINLY ONLY BE SAFE...
IN MY HANDS.
...IN THE HANDS OF A HERO LIKE SPIDER-MAN!
YUP! THAT'S ME!
HEH HEH HEH...
"WHAT THE HECK?"

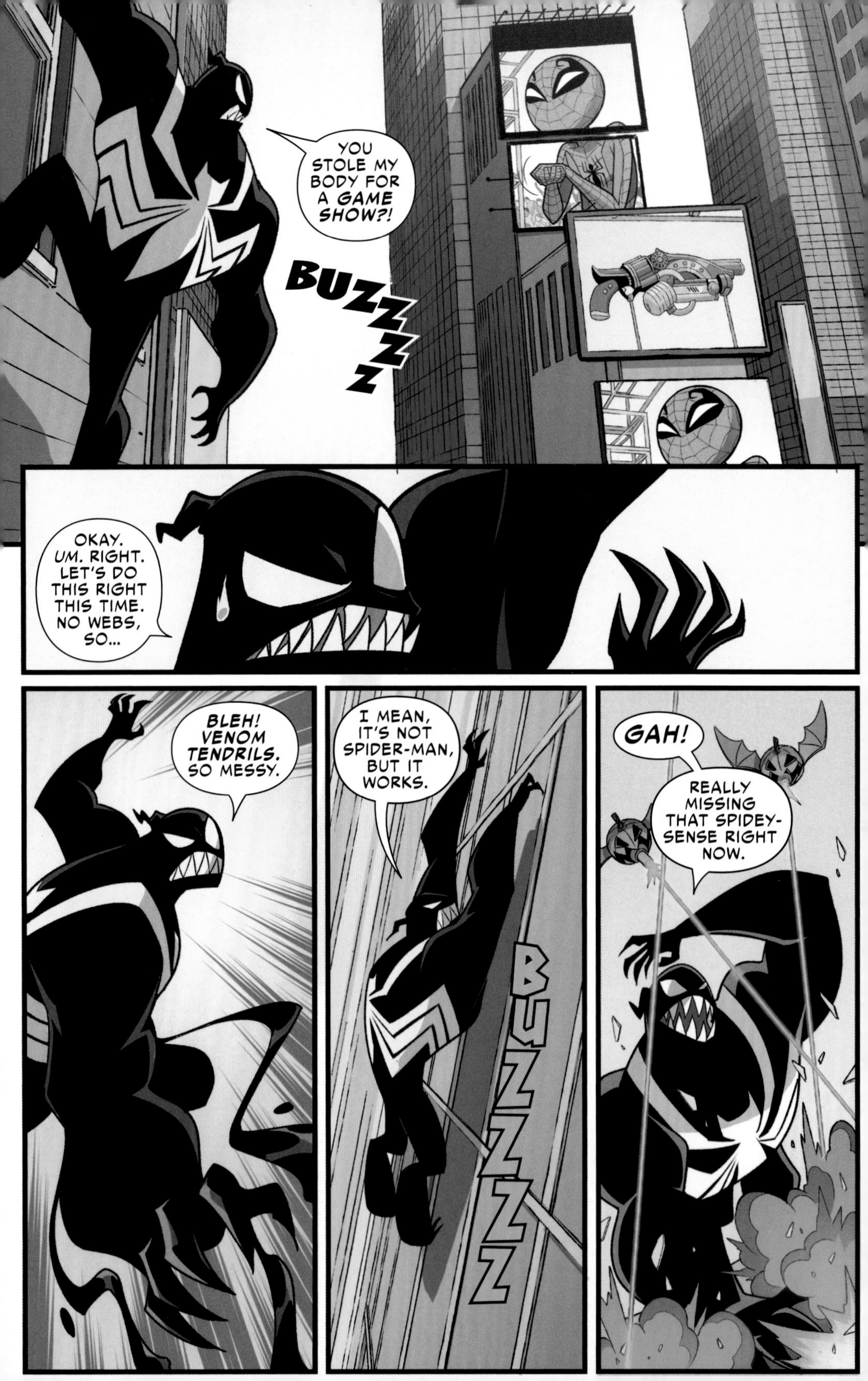
YOU STOLE MY BODY FOR A *GAME SHOW?!*
BUZZZZZ
OKAY. *UM.* RIGHT. LET'S DO THIS RIGHT THIS TIME. NO WEBS, SO...
BLEH! VENOM TENDRILS. SO MESSY.
I MEAN, IT'S NOT SPIDER-MAN, BUT IT WORKS.
BUZZZZZ
GAH!
REALLY MISSING THAT SPIDEY-SENSE RIGHT NOW.

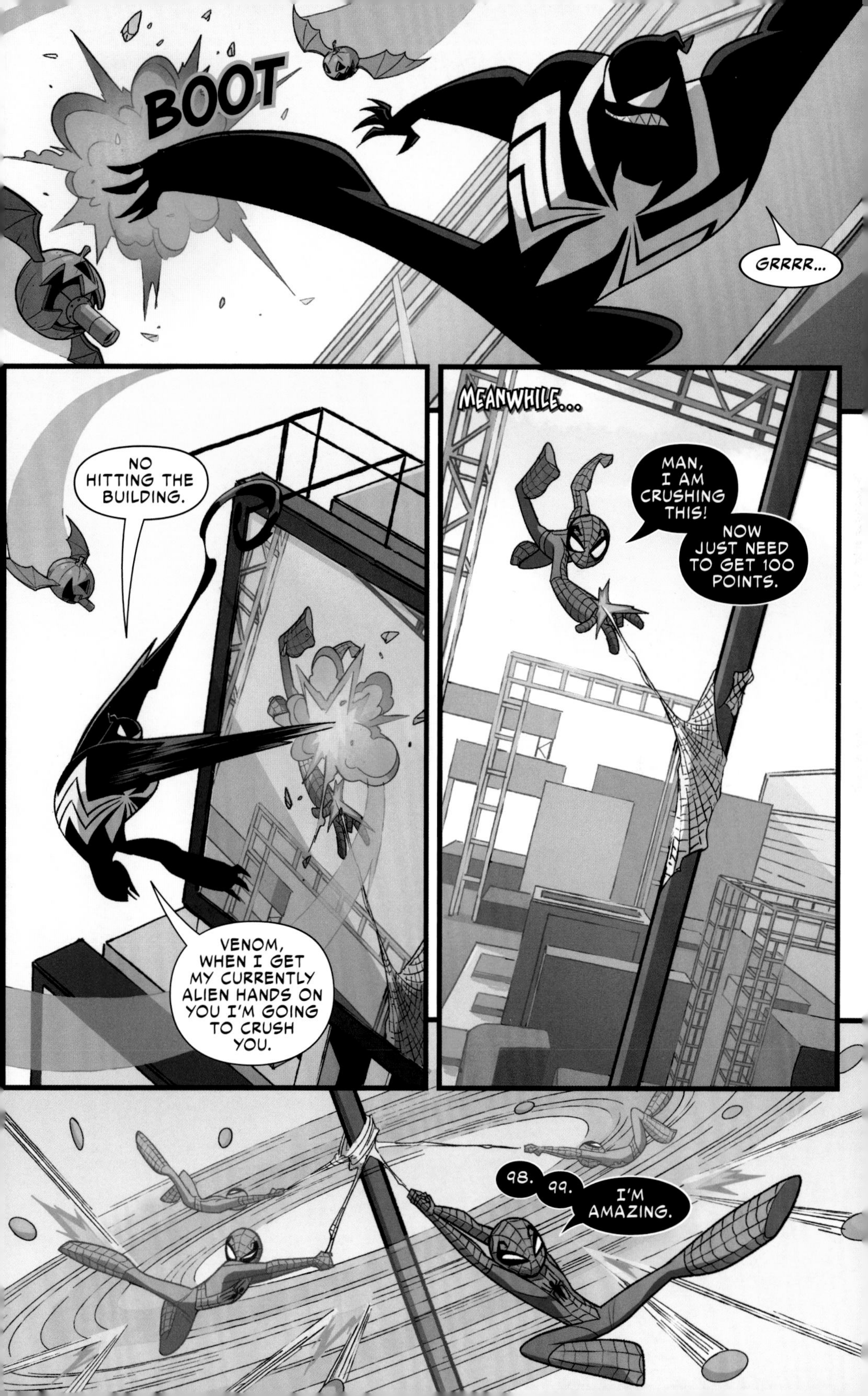
BOOT
GRRRR...
NO HITTING THE BUILDING.
VENOM, WHEN I GET MY CURRENTLY ALIEN HANDS ON YOU I'M GOING TO CRUSH YOU.
MEANWHILE...
MAN, I AM CRUSHING THIS!
NOW JUST NEED TO GET 100 POINTS.
98.
99.
I'M AMAZING.

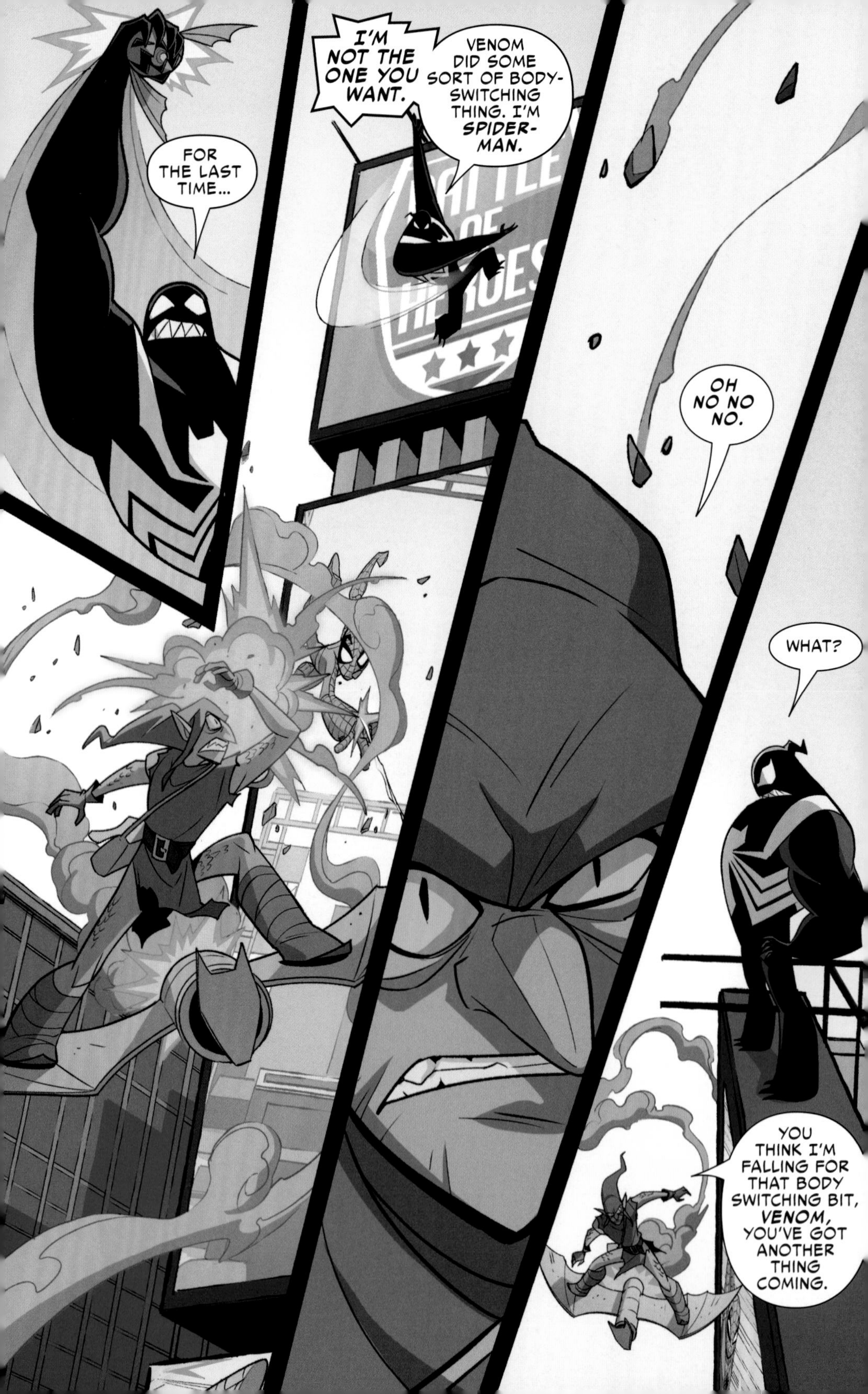
FOR THE LAST TIME...
I'M NOT THE ONE YOU WANT.
VENOM DID SOME SORT OF BODY-SWITCHING THING. I'M SPIDER-MAN.
BATTLE OF HEROES
OH NO NO NO.
WHAT?
YOU THINK I'M FALLING FOR THAT BODY SWITCHING BIT, VENOM, YOU'VE GOT ANOTHER THING COMING.

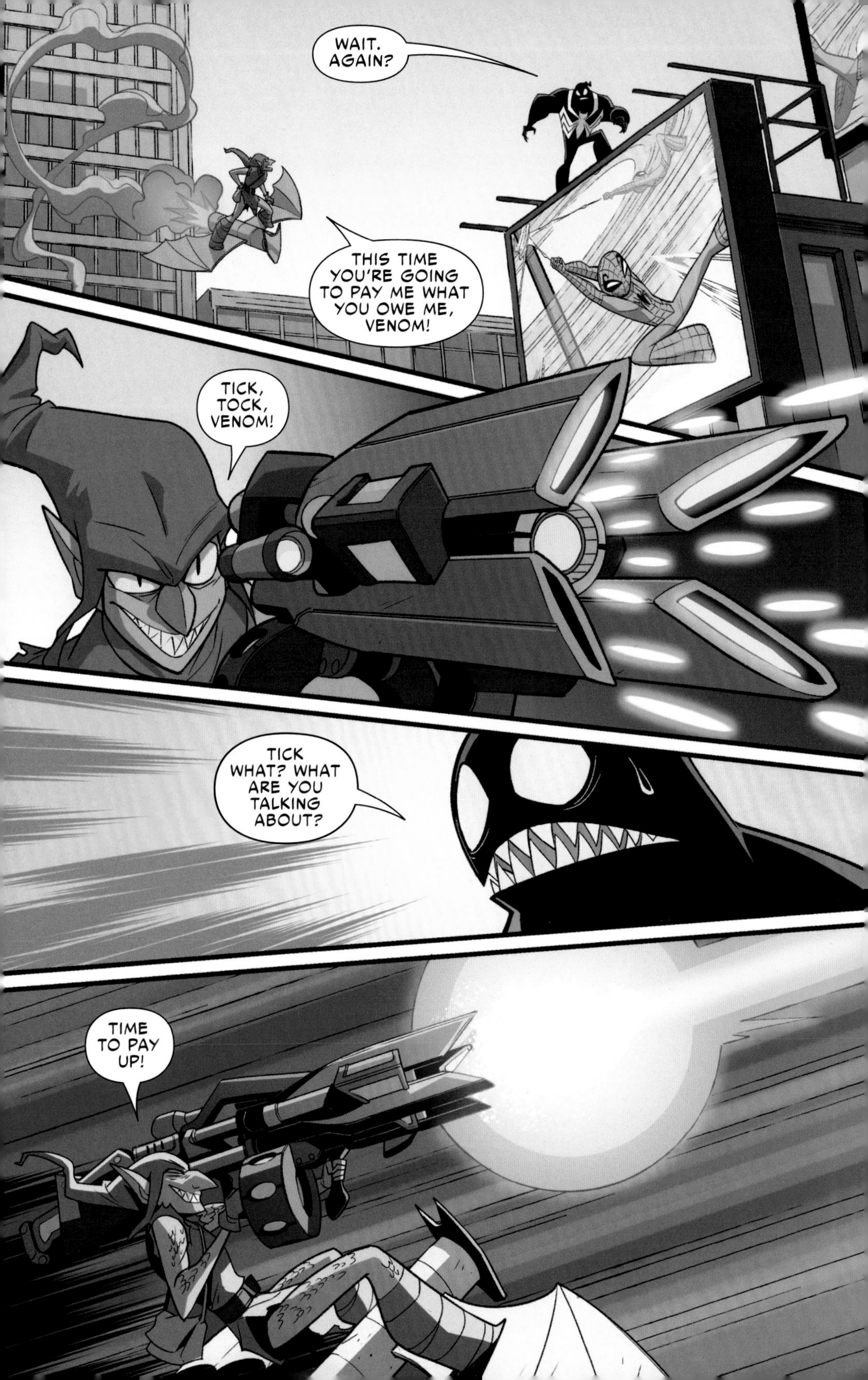
WAIT. AGAIN?
THIS TIME YOU'RE GOING TO PAY ME WHAT YOU OWE ME, VENOM!
TICK, TOCK, VENOM!
TICK WHAT? WHAT ARE YOU TALKING ABOUT?
TIME TO PAY UP!

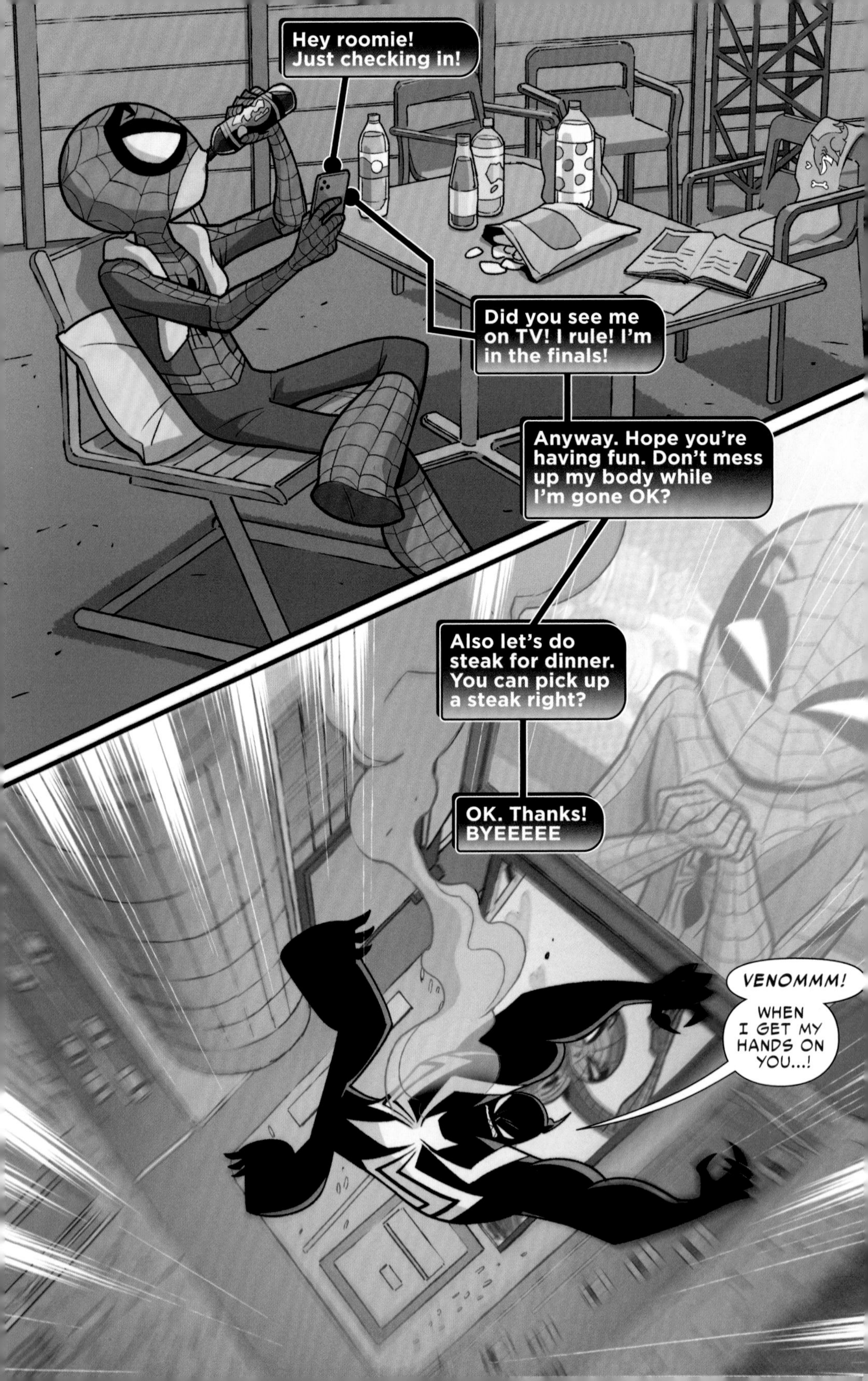
Hey roomie!
Just checking in!
Did you see me on TV! I rule! I'm in the finals!
Anyway. Hope you're having fun. Don't mess up my body while I'm gone OK?
Also let's do steak for dinner. You can pick up a steak right?
OK. Thanks! BYEEEEE
VENOMMM! WHEN I GET MY HANDS ON YOU...!

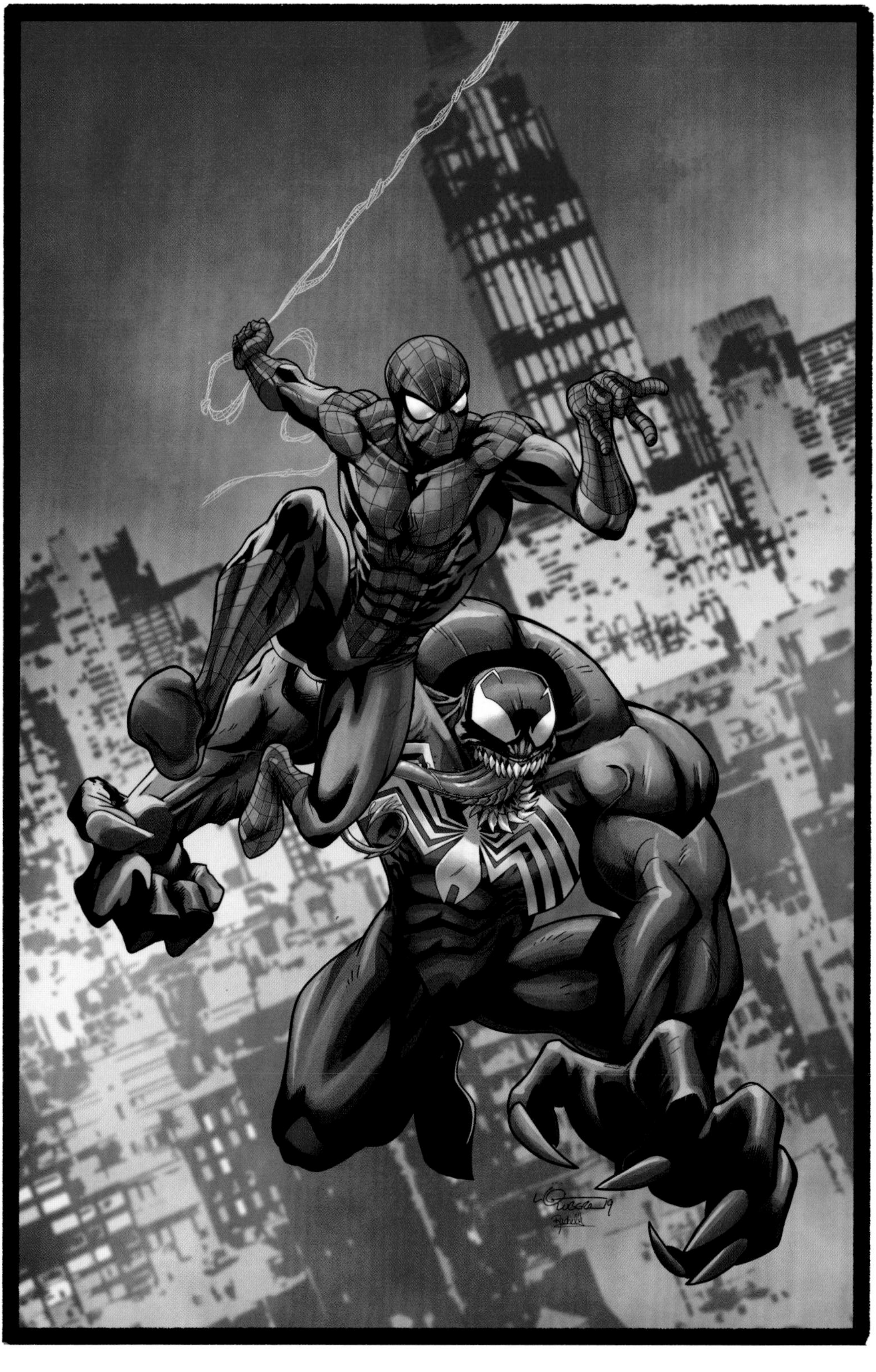

#1 VARIANT BY **LOGAN LUBERA** & **RACHELLE ROSENBERG**

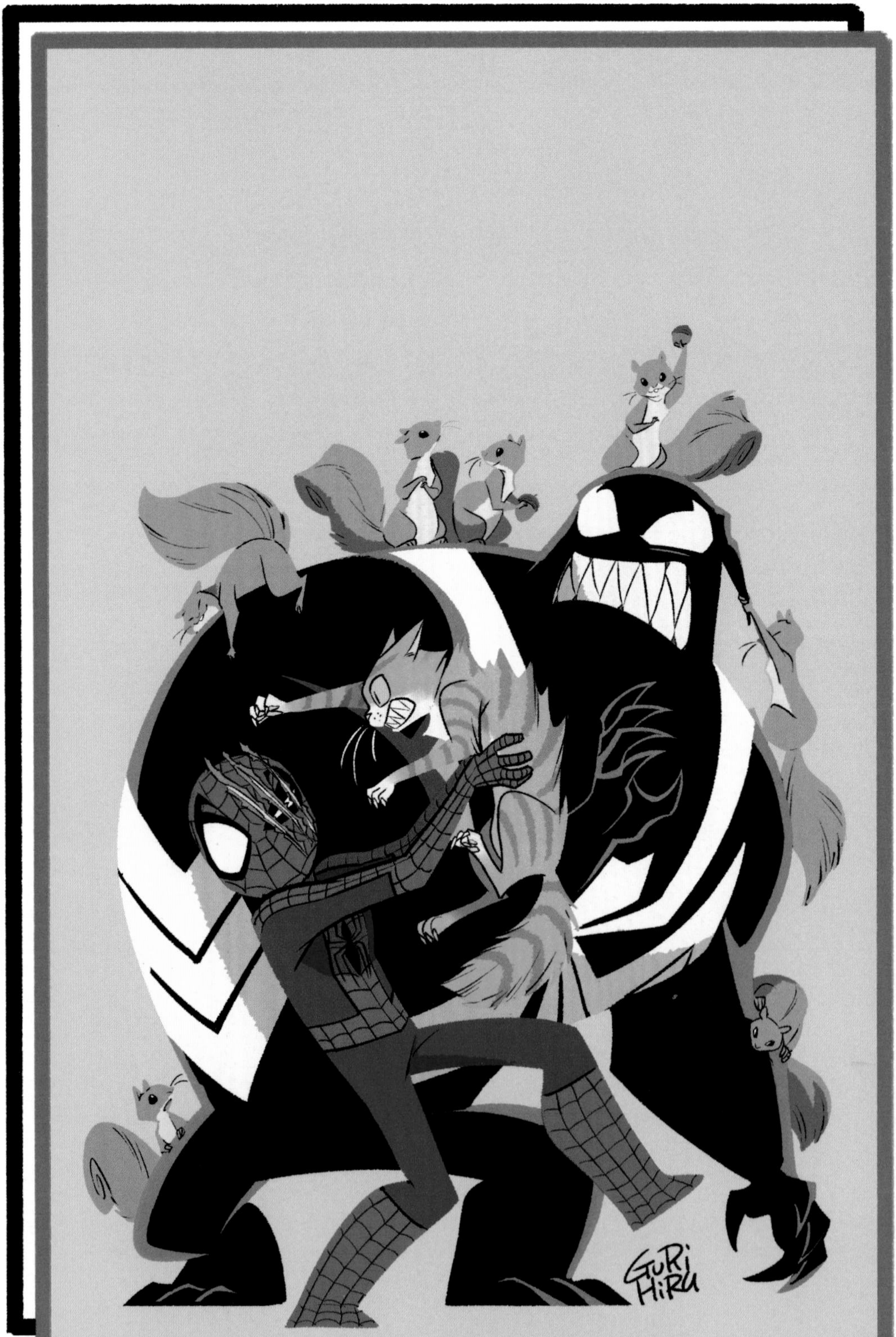
GURi HiRU

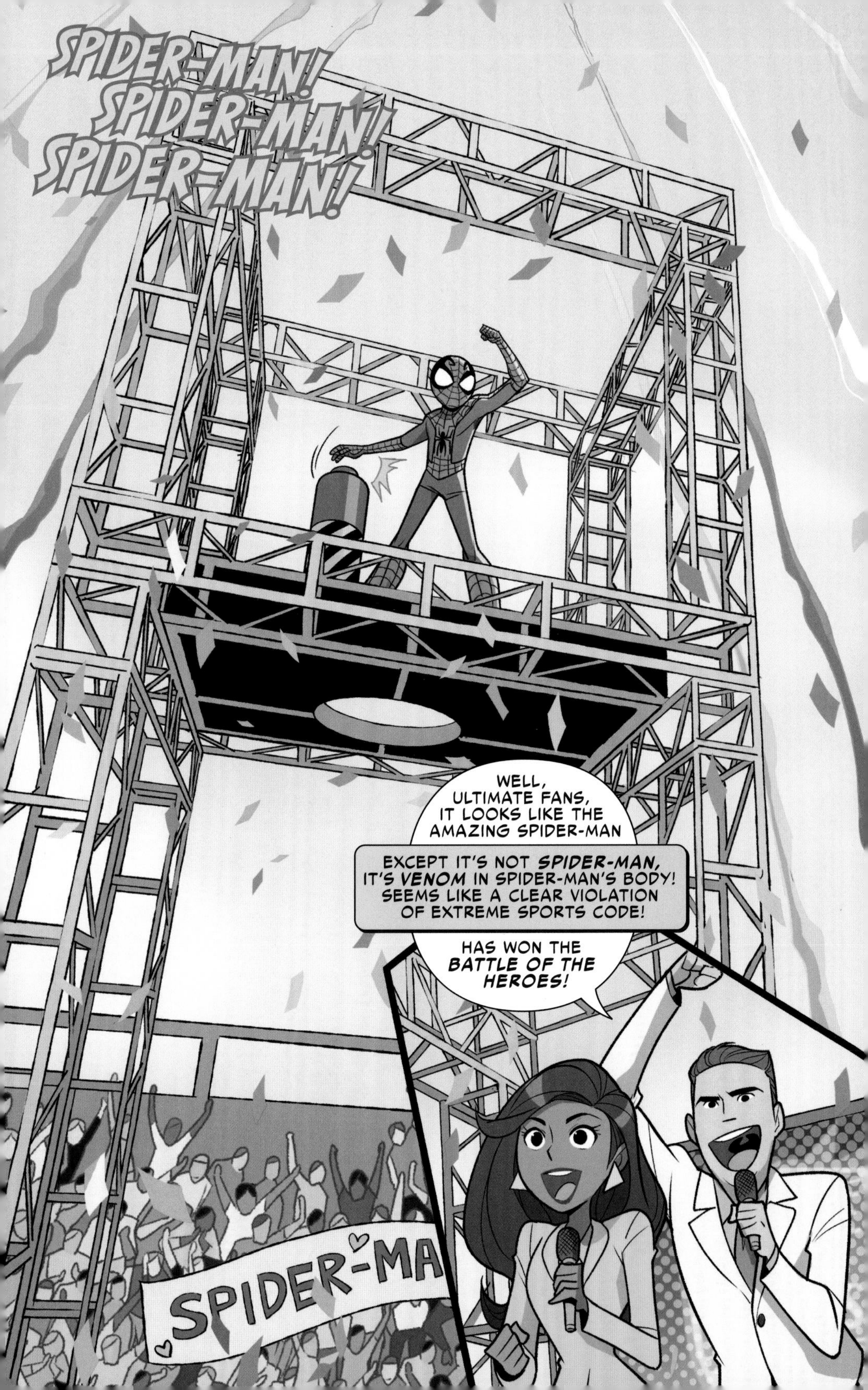
SPIDER-MAN! SPIDER-MAN! SPIDER-MAN!
WELL, ULTIMATE FANS, IT LOOKS LIKE THE AMAZING SPIDER-MAN
EXCEPT IT'S NOT SPIDER-MAN, IT'S VENOM IN SPIDER-MAN'S BODY! SEEMS LIKE A CLEAR VIOLATION OF EXTREME SPORTS CODE!
HAS WON THE BATTLE OF THE HEROES!
SPIDER-MA

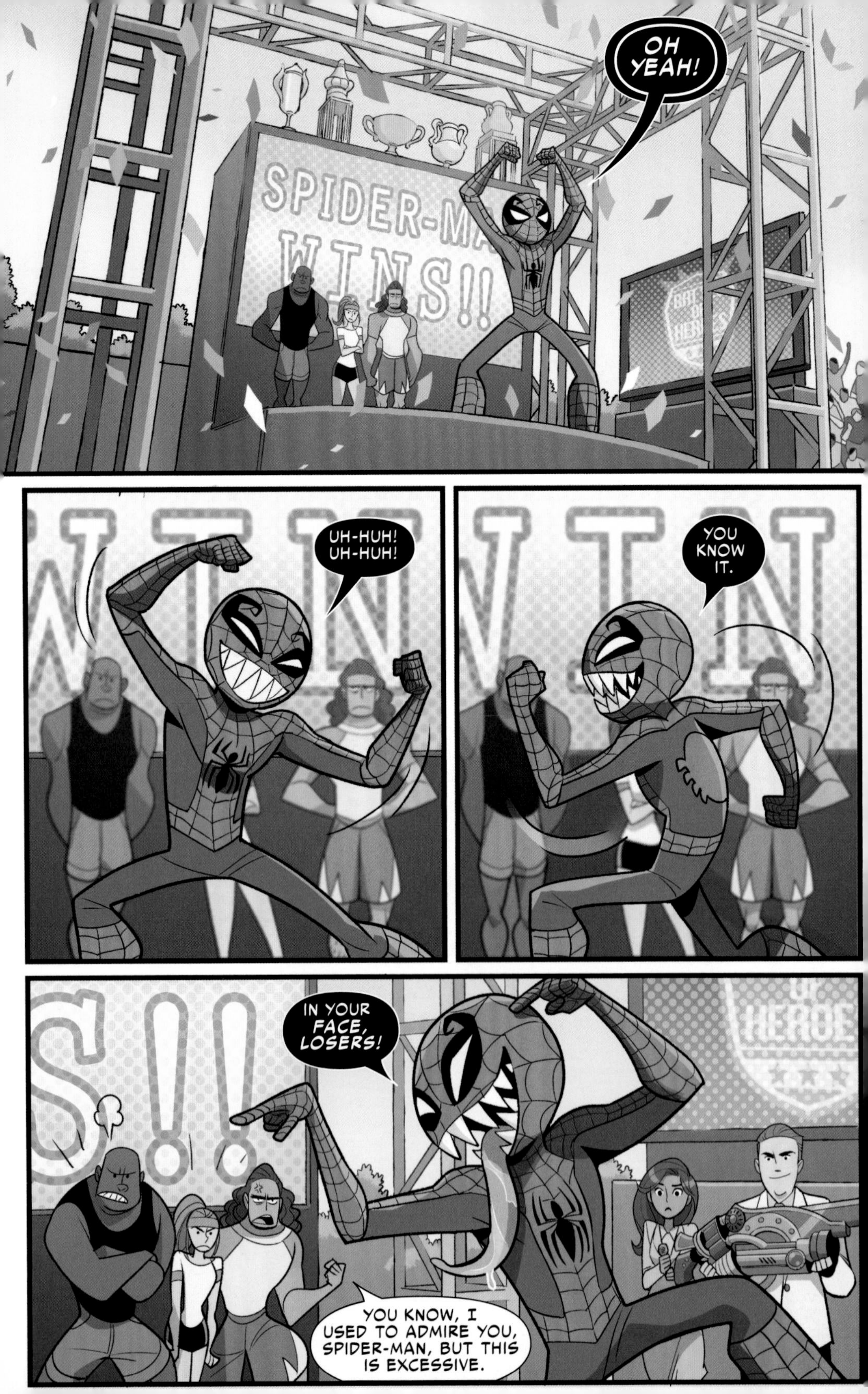
OH YEAH!
SPIDER-MAN WINS!!
UH-HUH! UH-HUH!
YOU KNOW IT.
IN YOUR FACE, LOSERS!
YOU KNOW, I USED TO ADMIRE YOU, SPIDER-MAN, BUT THIS IS EXCESSIVE.

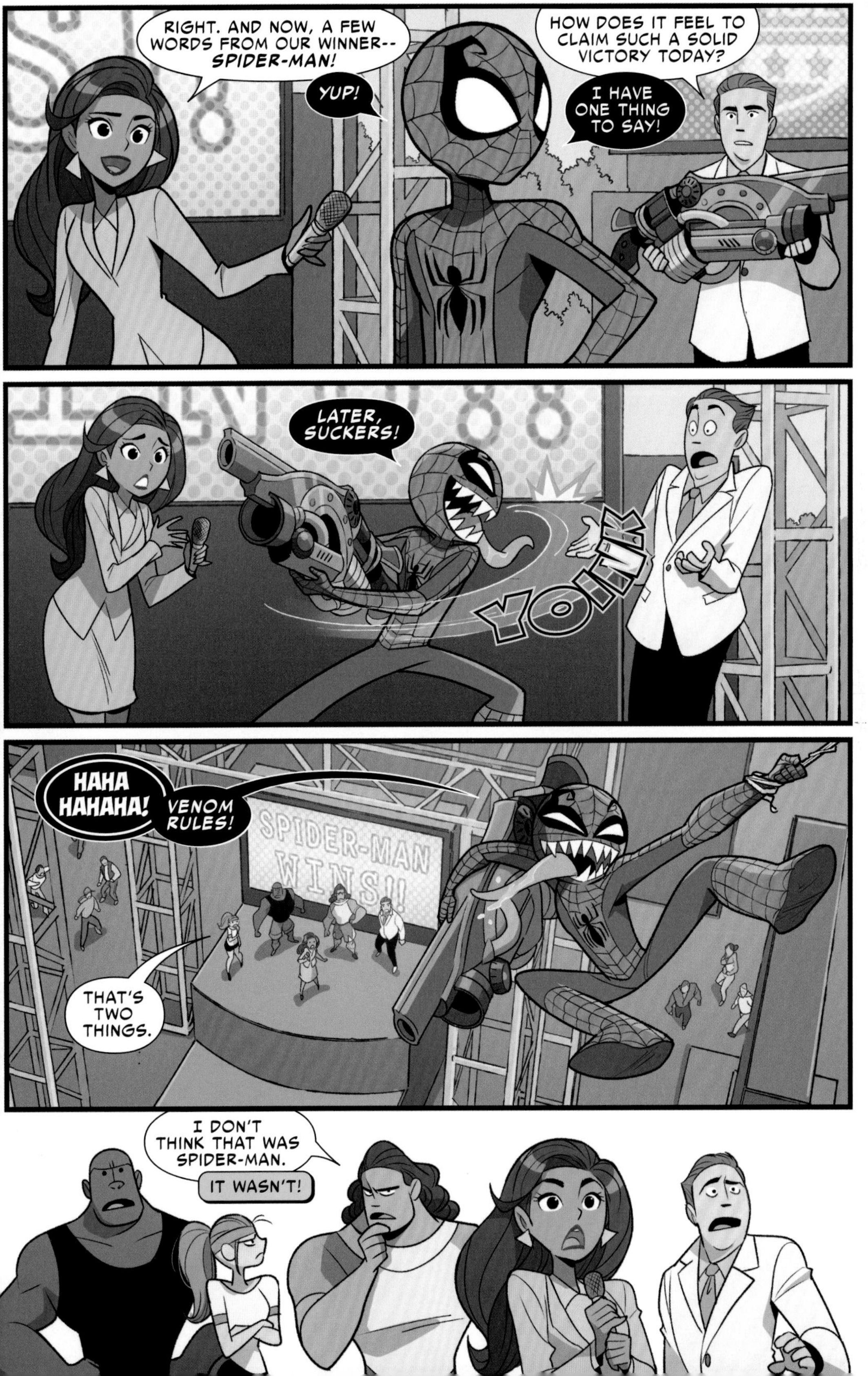
RIGHT. AND NOW, A FEW WORDS FROM OUR WINNER-- SPIDER-MAN!
YUP!
HOW DOES IT FEEL TO CLAIM SUCH A SOLID VICTORY TODAY?
I HAVE ONE THING TO SAY!
LATER, SUCKERS!
YOINK
HAHA HAHAHA!
VENOM RULES!
SPIDER-MAN WINS!!
THAT'S TWO THINGS.
I DON'T THINK THAT WAS SPIDER-MAN.
IT WASN'T!

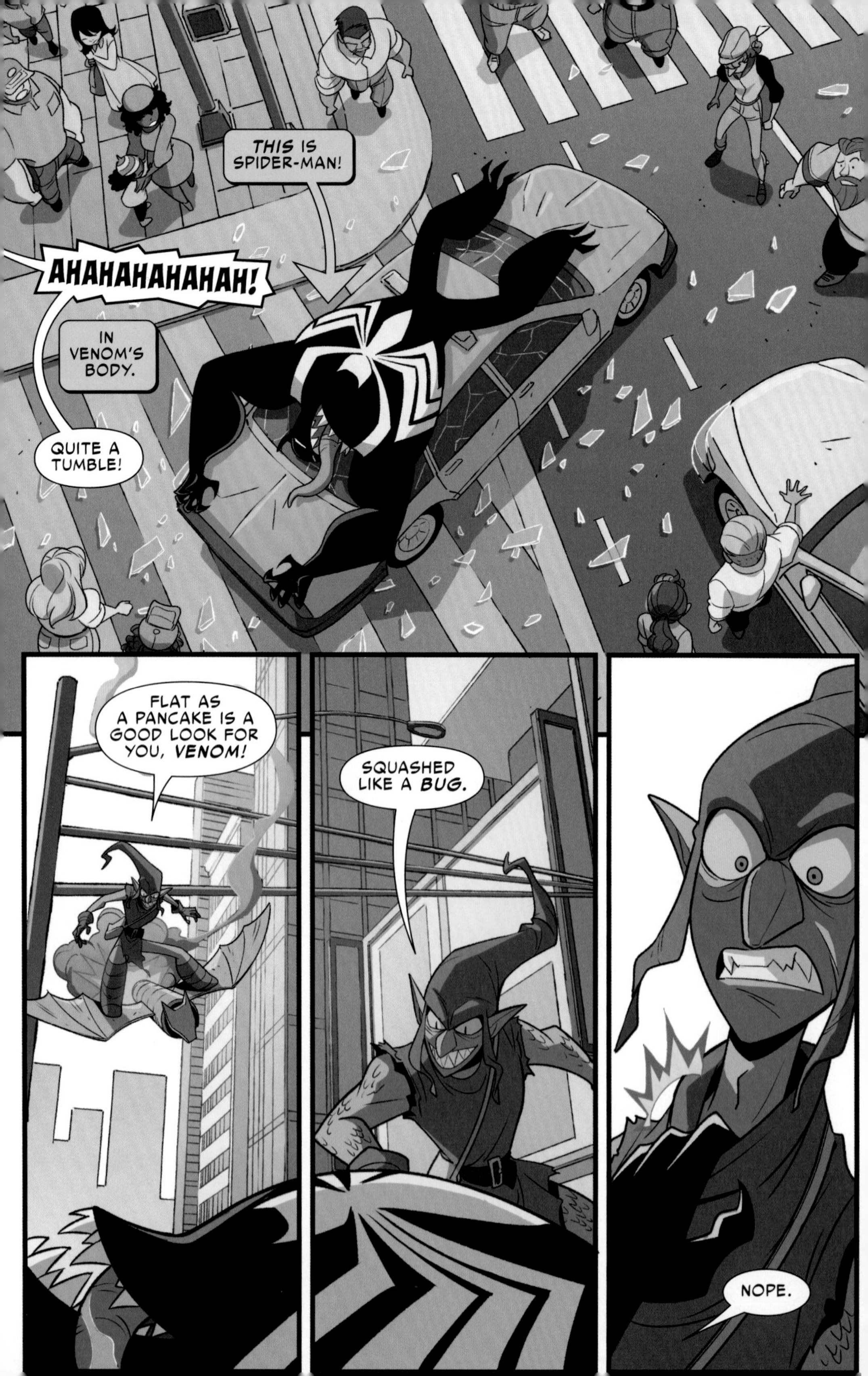
AHAHAHAHAHAH!
THIS IS SPIDER-MAN!
IN VENOM'S BODY.
QUITE A TUMBLE!
FLAT AS A PANCAKE IS A GOOD LOOK FOR YOU, VENOM!
SQUASHED LIKE A BUG.
NOPE.

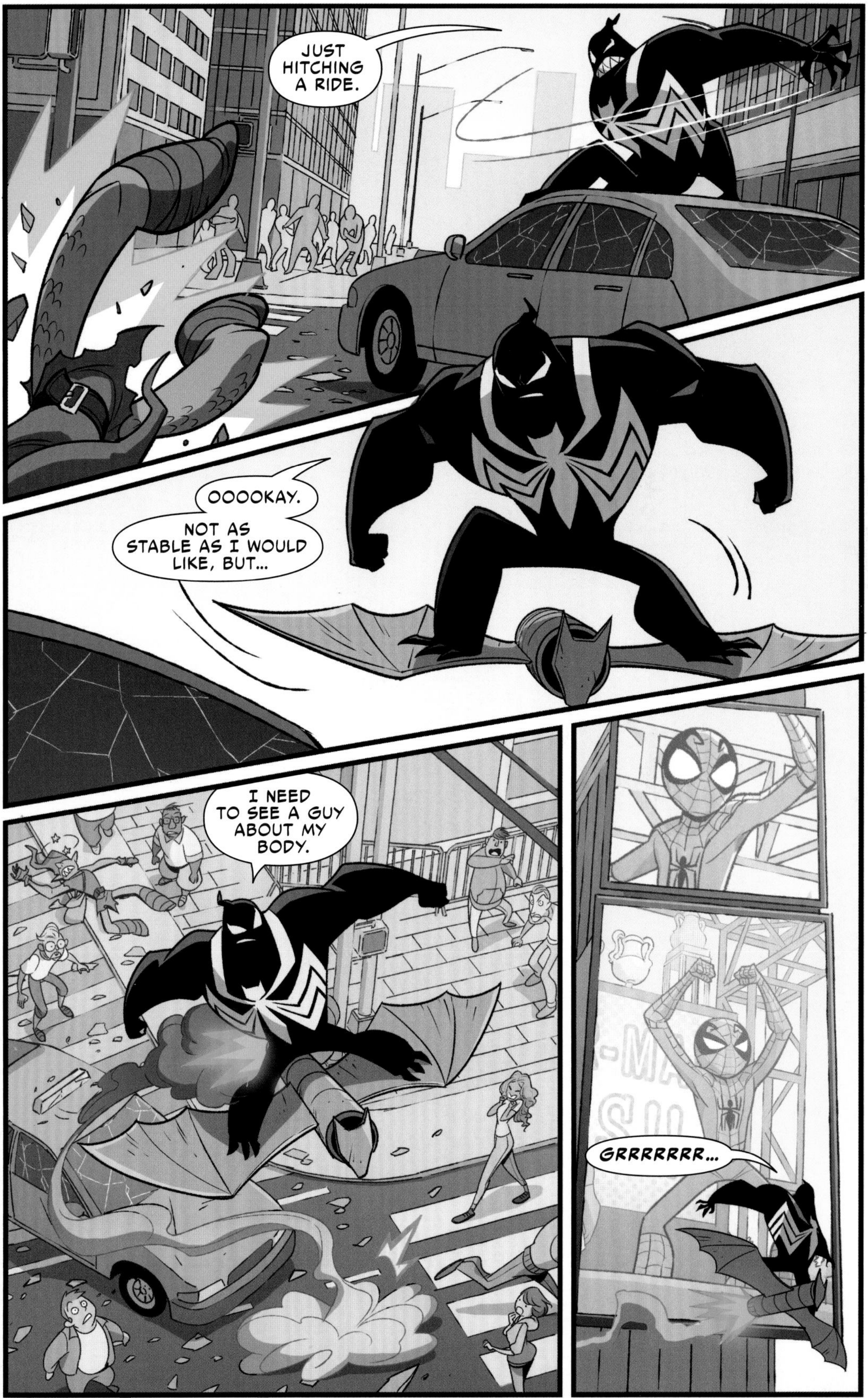
JUST HITCHING A RIDE.
OOOOKAY.
NOT AS STABLE AS I WOULD LIKE, BUT...
I NEED TO SEE A GUY ABOUT MY BODY.
GRRRRRRR...

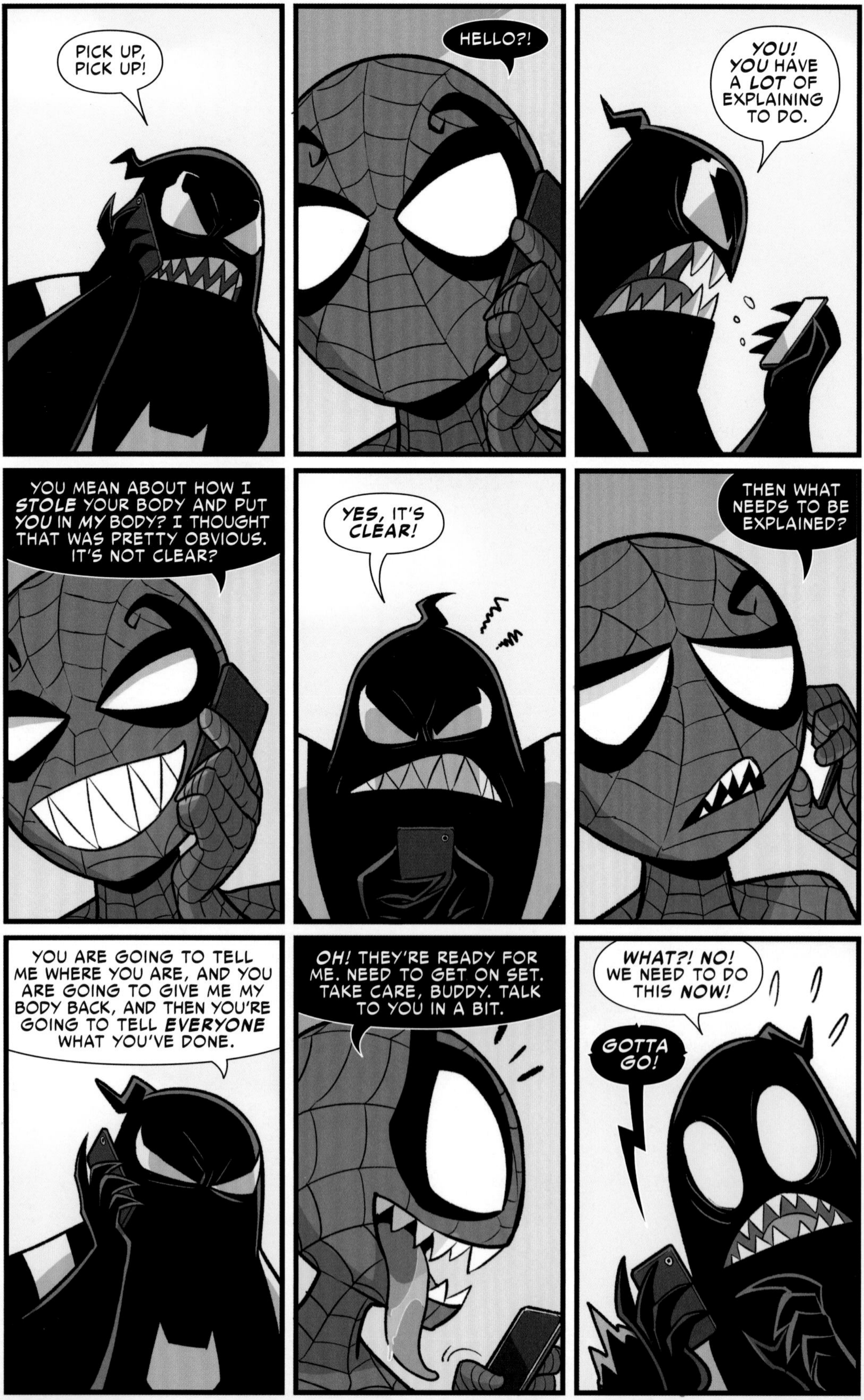
PICK UP, PICK UP!
HELLO?!
YOU! YOU HAVE A LOT OF EXPLAINING TO DO.
YOU MEAN ABOUT HOW I STOLE YOUR BODY AND PUT YOU IN MY BODY? I THOUGHT THAT WAS PRETTY OBVIOUS. IT'S NOT CLEAR?
YES, IT'S CLEAR!
THEN WHAT NEEDS TO BE EXPLAINED?
YOU ARE GOING TO TELL ME WHERE YOU ARE, AND YOU ARE GOING TO GIVE ME MY BODY BACK, AND THEN YOU'RE GOING TO TELL EVERYONE WHAT YOU'VE DONE.
OH! THEY'RE READY FOR ME. NEED TO GET ON SET. TAKE CARE, BUDDY. TALK TO YOU IN A BIT.
WHAT?! NO! WE NEED TO DO THIS NOW!
GOTTA GO!

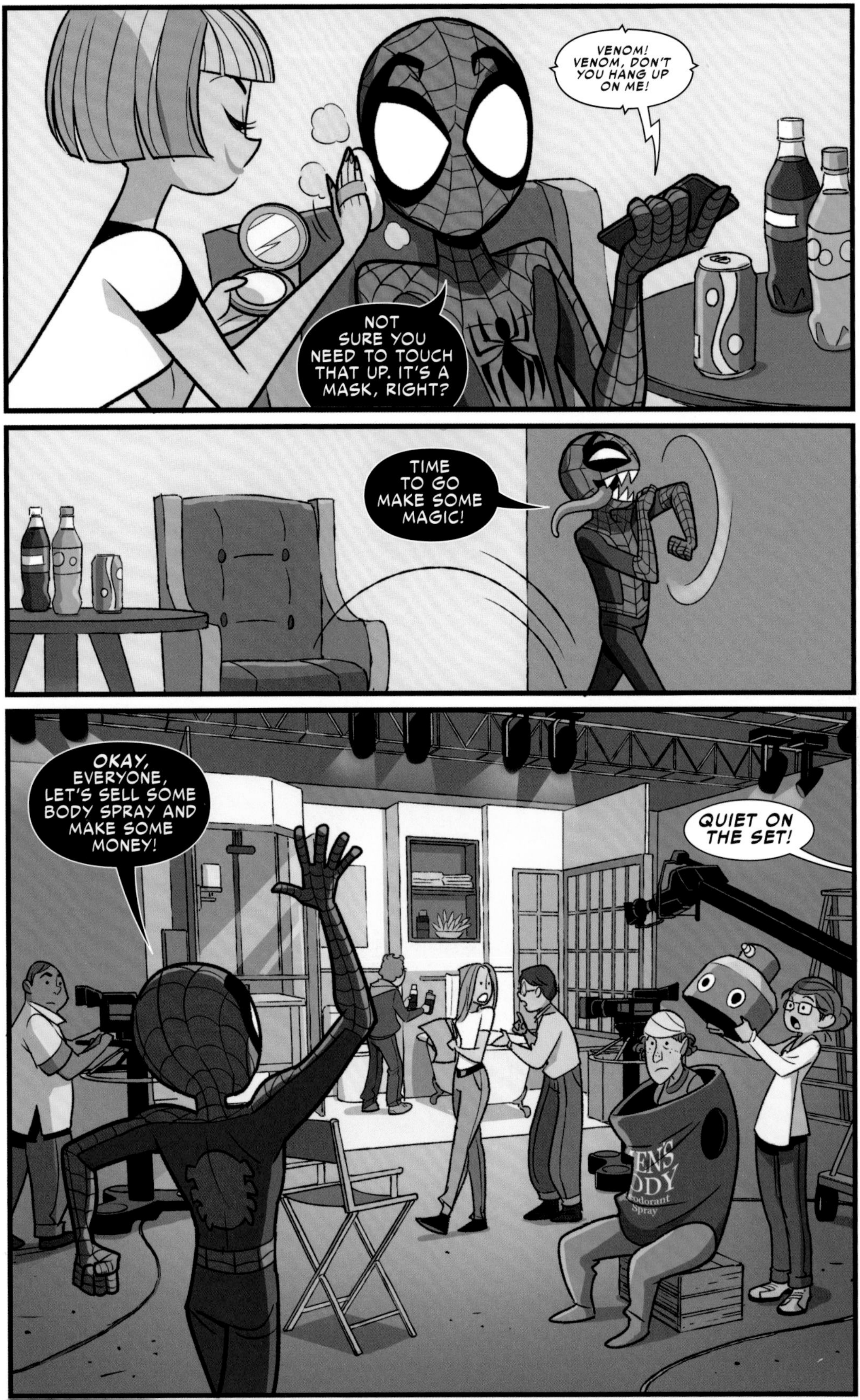
VENOM! VENOM, DON'T YOU HANG UP ON ME!
NOT SURE YOU NEED TO TOUCH THAT UP. IT'S A MASK, RIGHT?
TIME TO GO MAKE SOME MAGIC!
OKAY, EVERYONE, LET'S SELL SOME BODY SPRAY AND MAKE SOME MONEY!
QUIET ON THE SET!

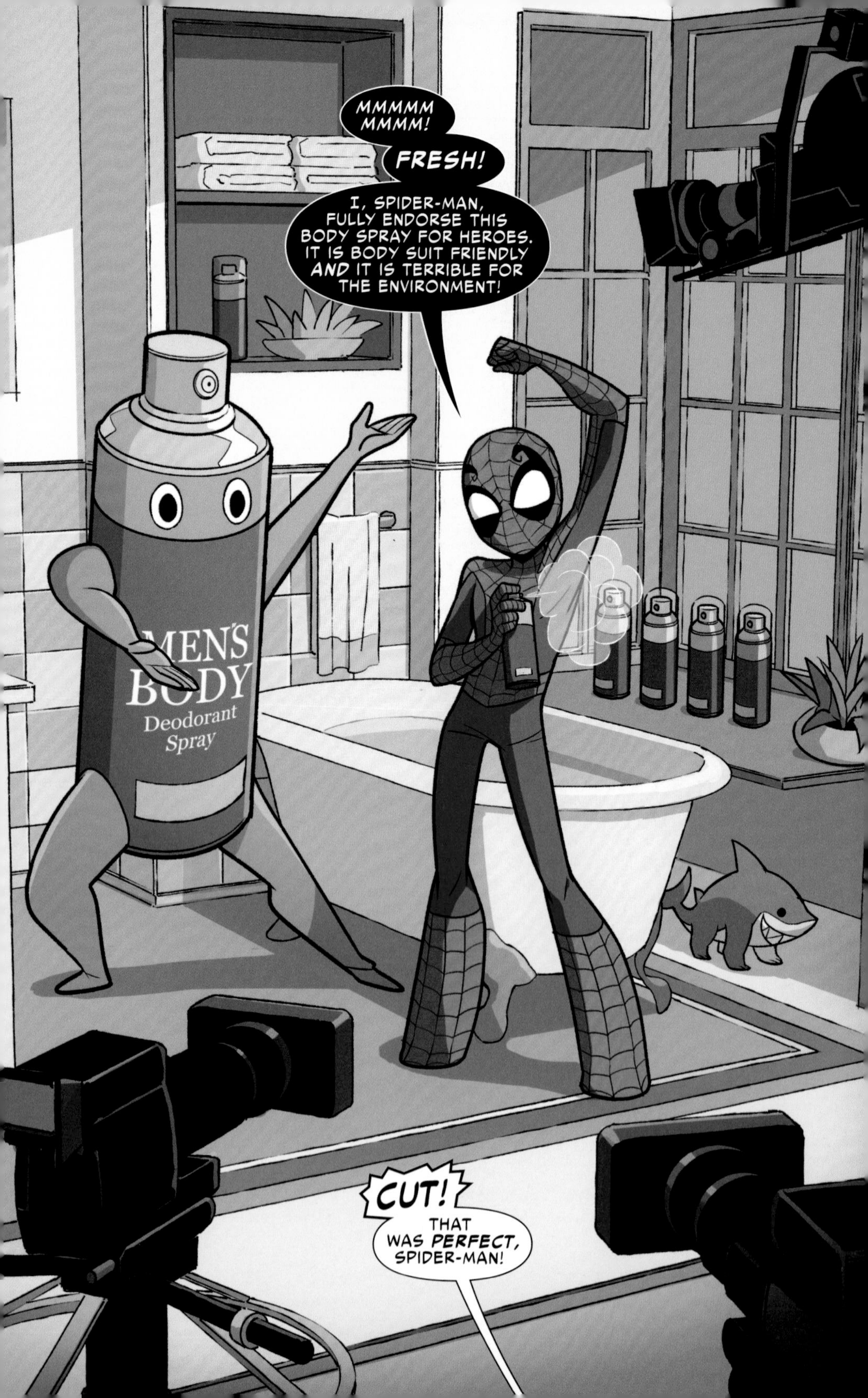
MMMMM MMMM!
FRESH!
I, SPIDER-MAN, FULLY ENDORSE THIS BODY SPRAY FOR HEROES. IT IS BODY SUIT FRIENDLY AND IT IS TERRIBLE FOR THE ENVIRONMENT!
MEN'S BODY Deodorant Spray
CUT!
THAT WAS PERFECT, SPIDER-MAN!

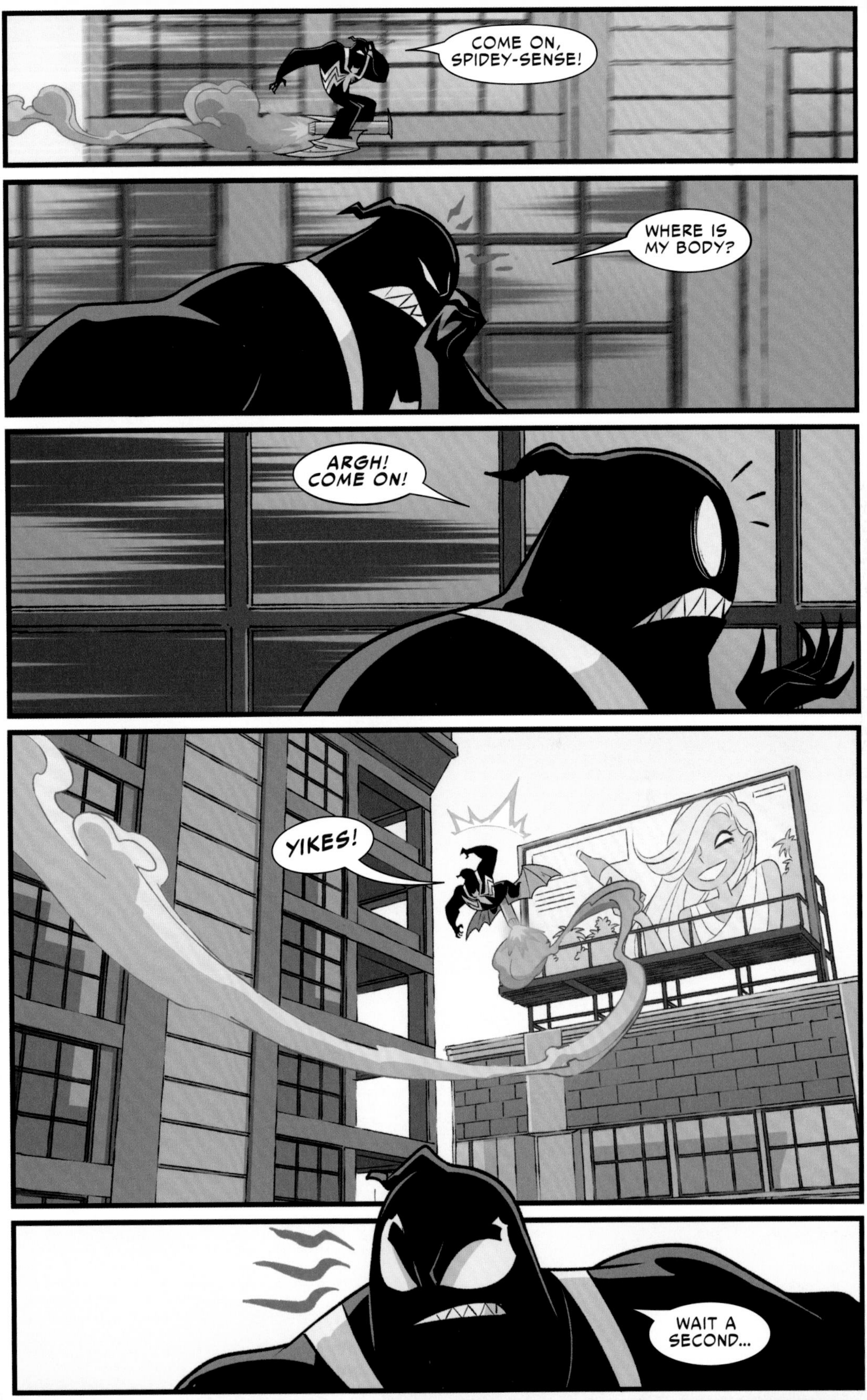
COME ON, SPIDEY-SENSE!
WHERE IS MY BODY?
ARGH! COME ON!
YIKES!
WAIT A SECOND...

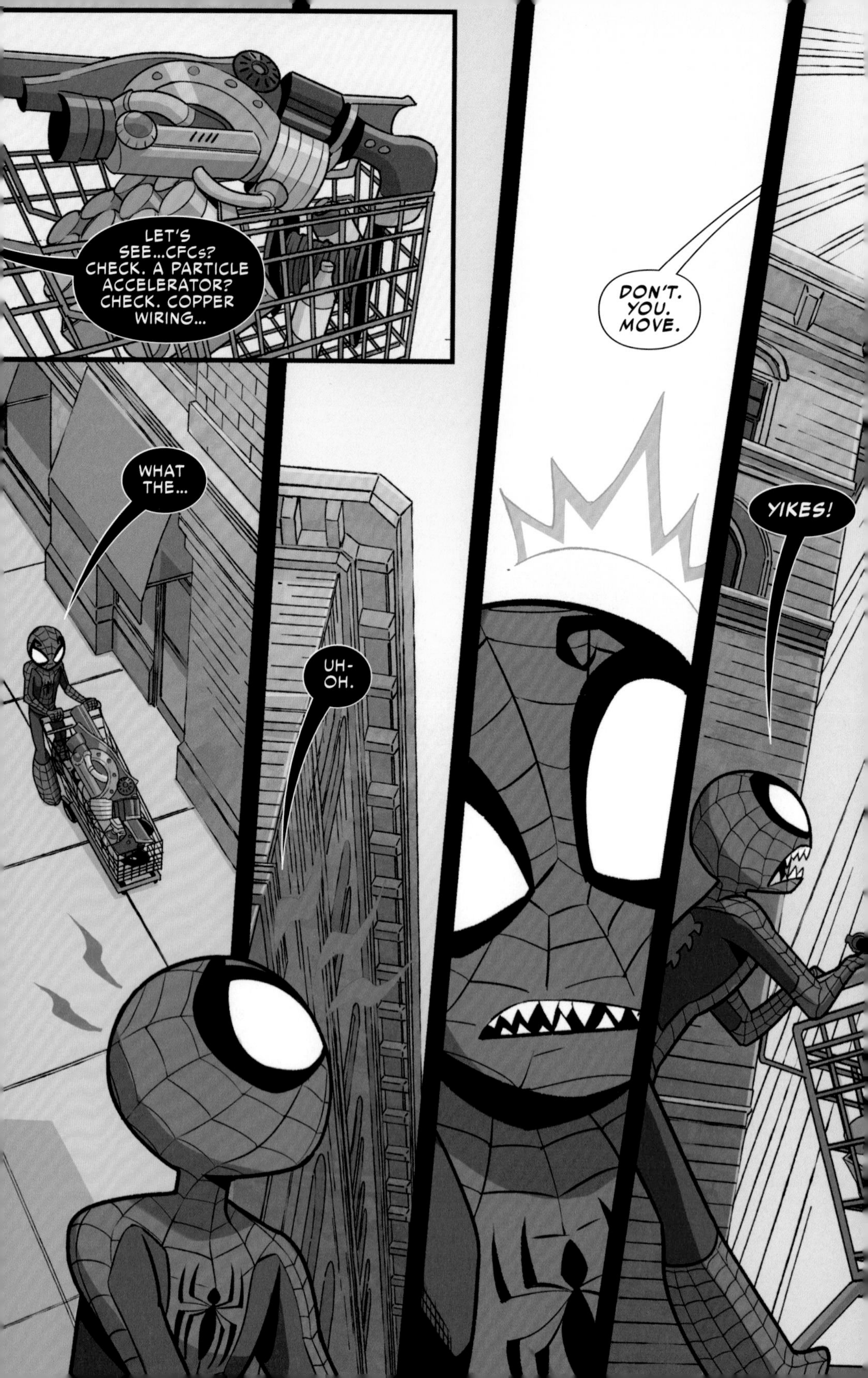
LET'S SEE...CFCs? CHECK. A PARTICLE ACCELERATOR? CHECK. COPPER WIRING...
DON'T. YOU. MOVE.
WHAT THE...
UH-OH.
YIKES!

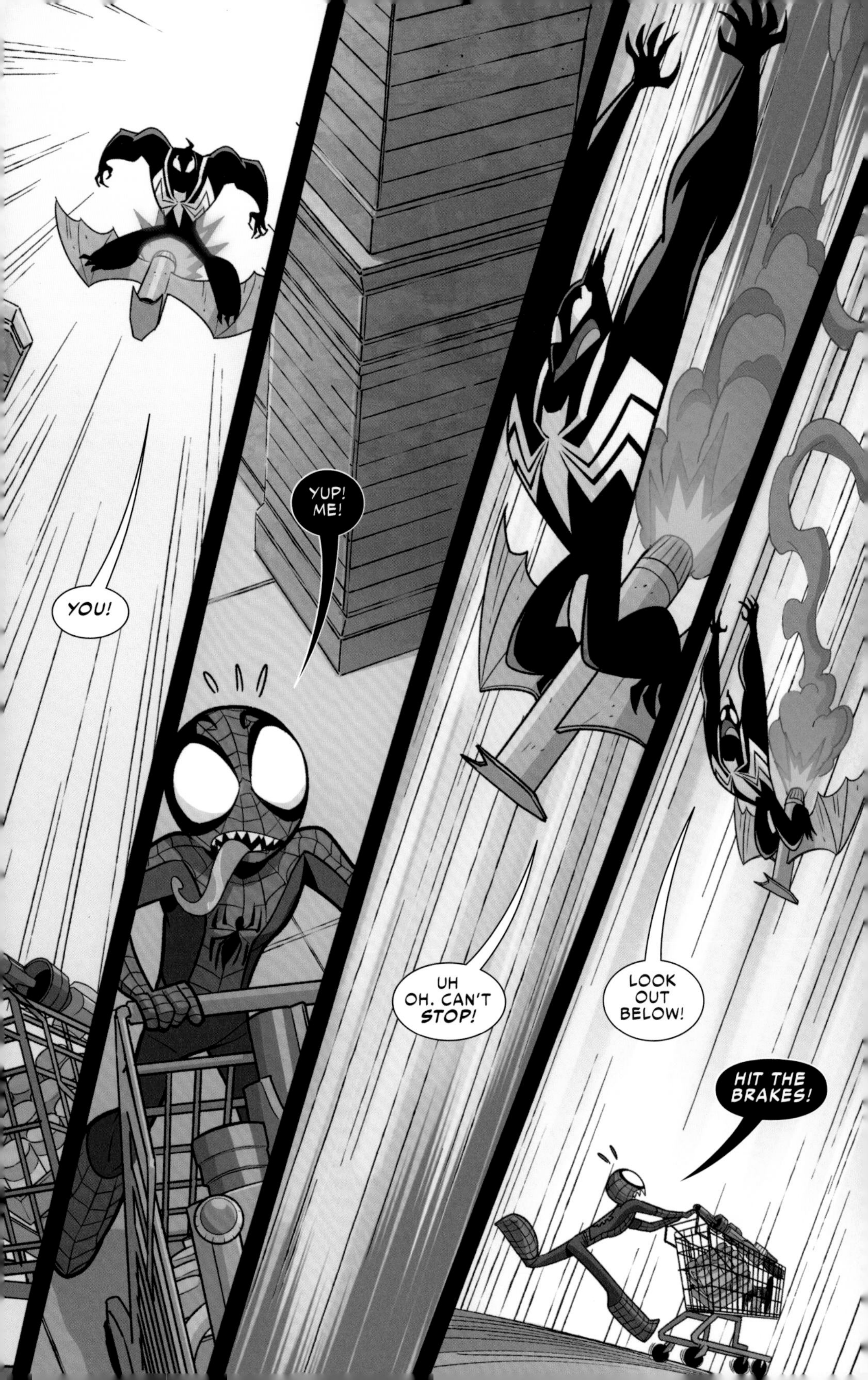
YOU!
YUP! ME!
UH OH. CAN'T STOP!
LOOK OUT BELOW!
HIT THE BRAKES!

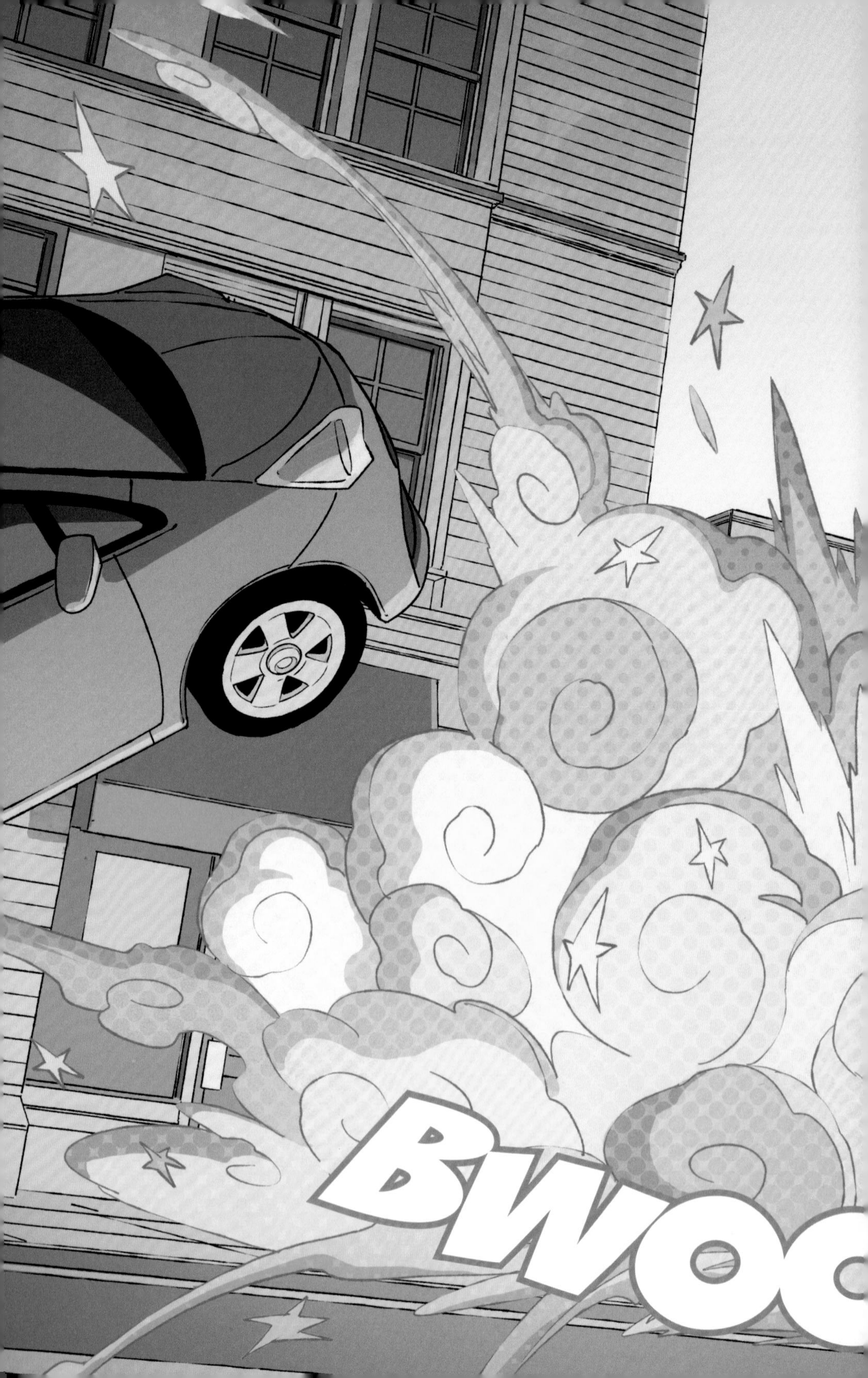
BWOO

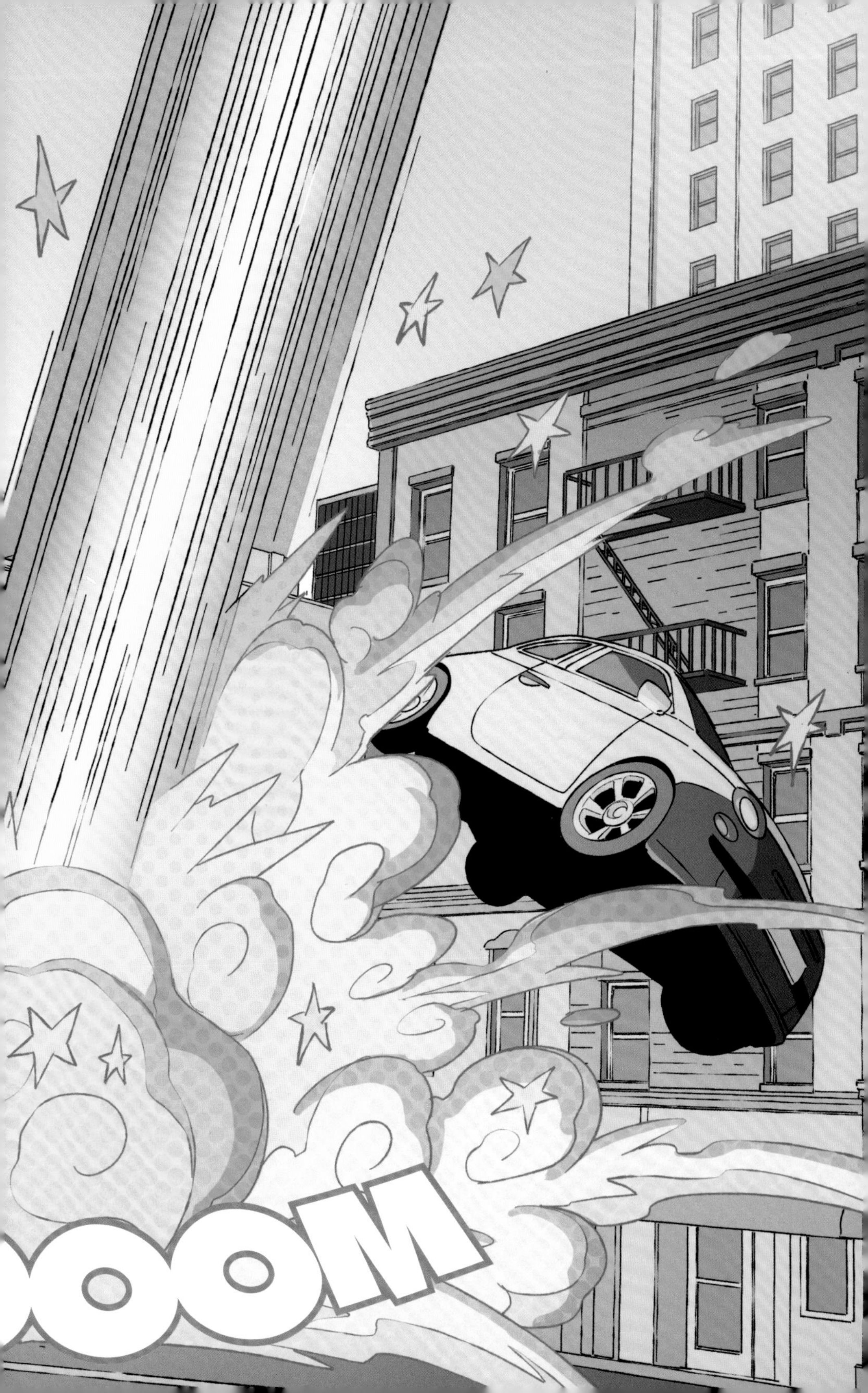
OOOM

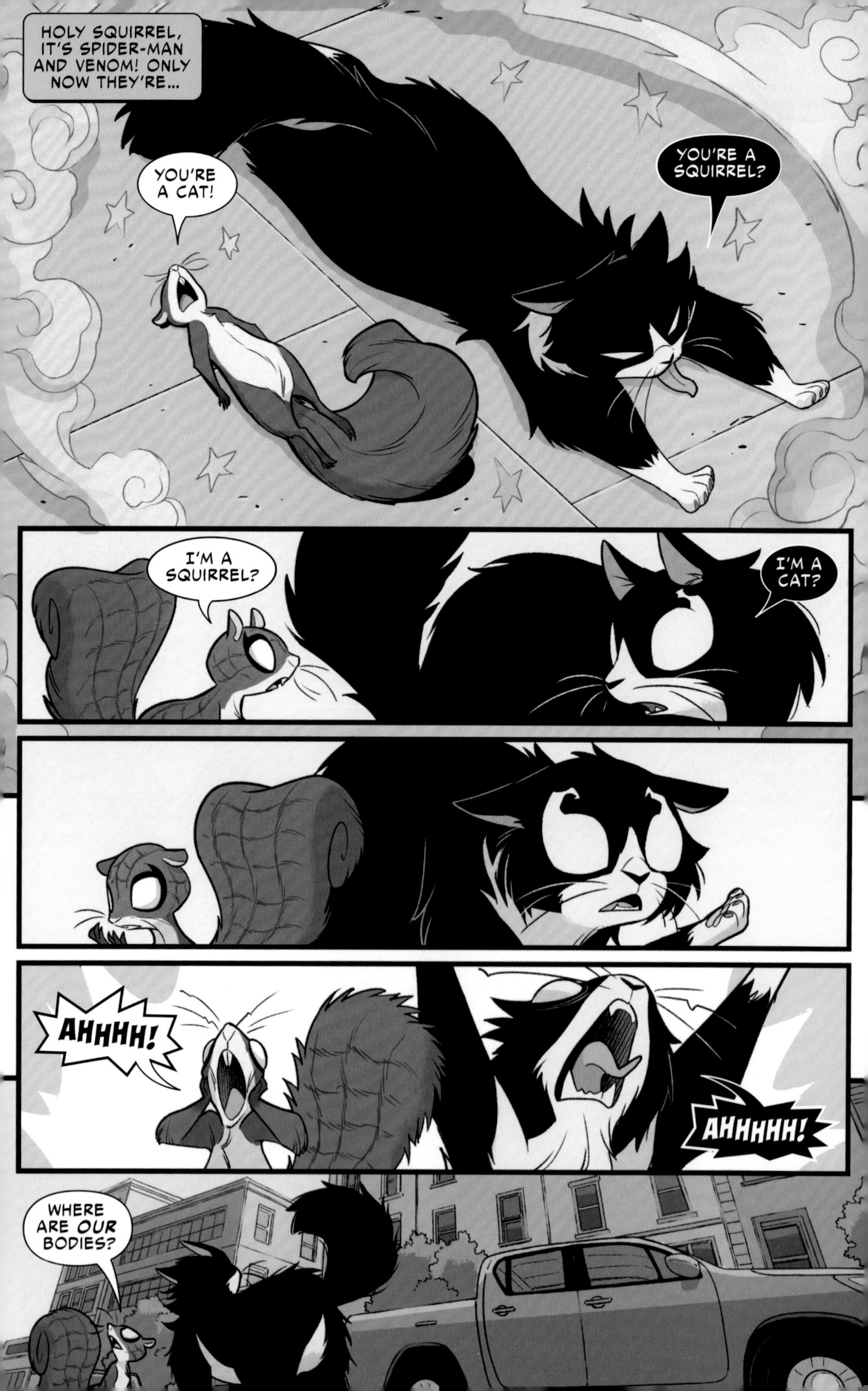
HOLY SQUIRREL, IT'S SPIDER-MAN AND VENOM! ONLY NOW THEY'RE...
YOU'RE A CAT!
YOU'RE A SQUIRREL?
I'M A SQUIRREL?
I'M A CAT?
AHHHH!
AHHHHH!
WHERE ARE OUR BODIES?

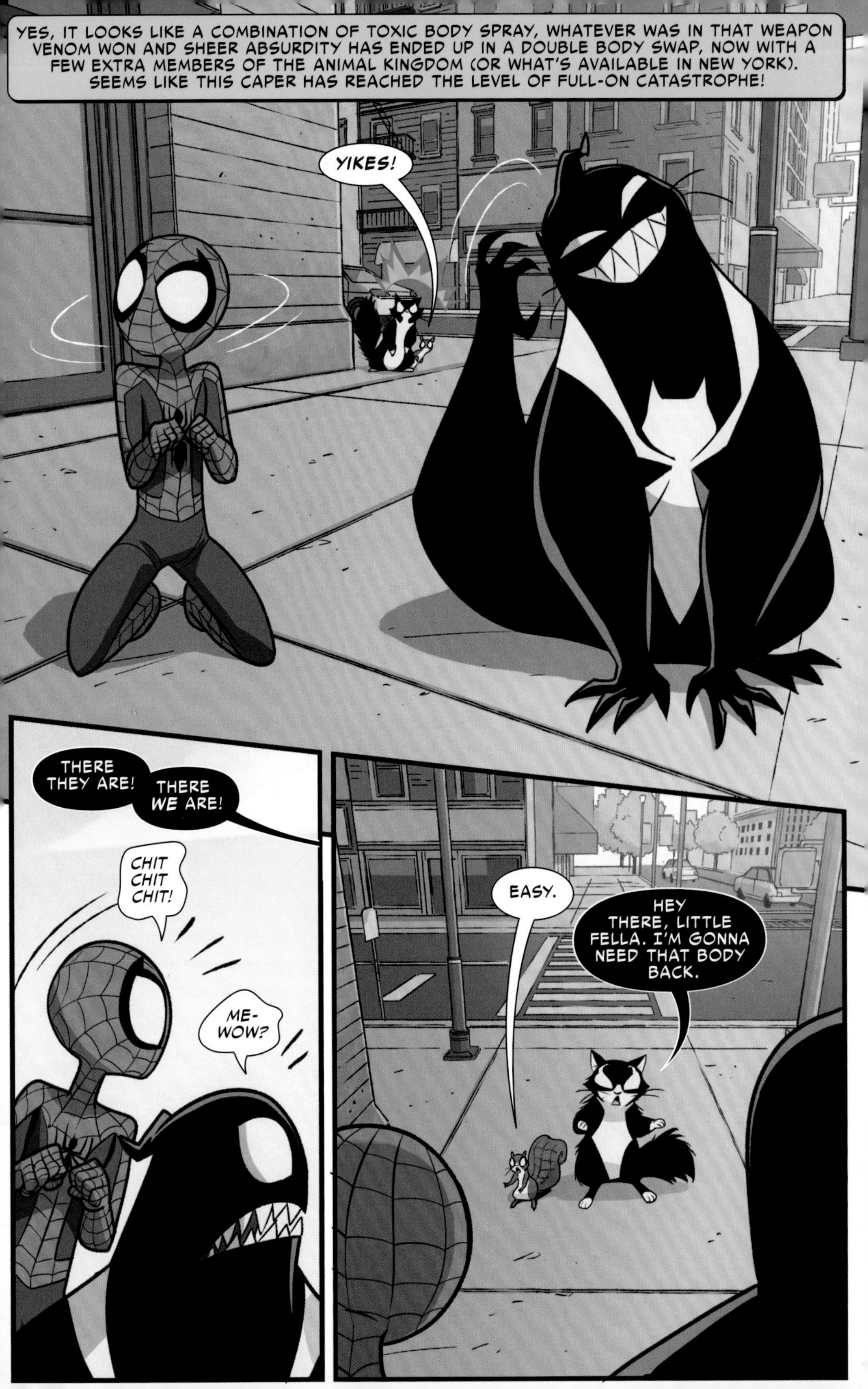
YES, IT LOOKS LIKE A COMBINATION OF TOXIC BODY SPRAY, WHATEVER WAS IN THAT WEAPON VENOM WON AND SHEER ABSURDITY HAS ENDED UP IN A DOUBLE BODY SWAP, NOW WITH A FEW EXTRA MEMBERS OF THE ANIMAL KINGDOM (OR WHAT'S AVAILABLE IN NEW YORK). SEEMS LIKE THIS CAPER HAS REACHED THE LEVEL OF FULL-ON CATASTROPHE!
YIKES!
THERE THEY ARE!
THERE *WE* ARE!
CHIT CHIT CHIT!
ME-WOW?
EASY.
HEY THERE, LITTLE FELLA. I'M GONNA NEED THAT BODY BACK.

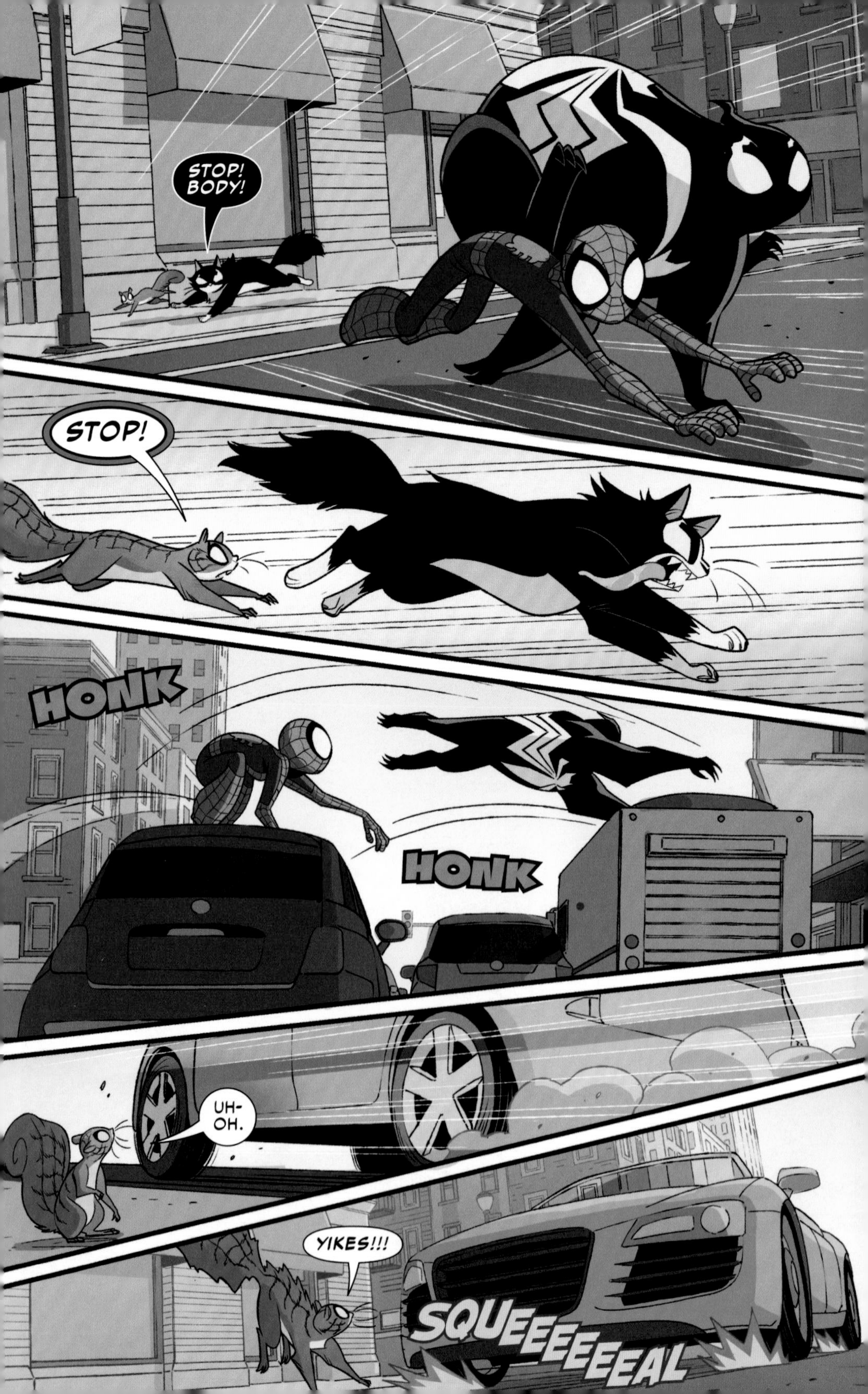
STOP! BODY!
STOP!
HONK
HONK
UH-OH.
YIKES!!!
SQUEEEEEEEAL

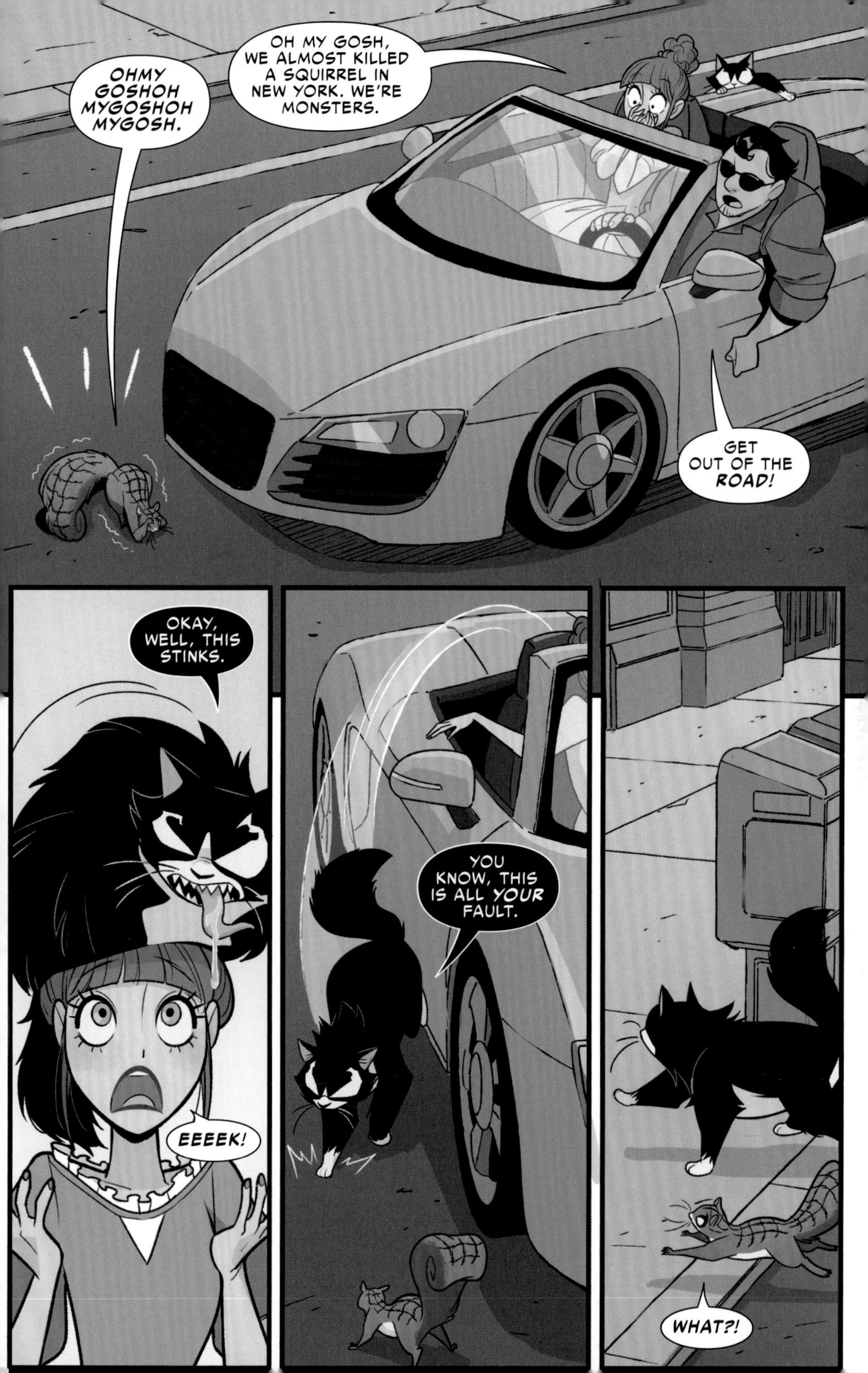
OHMY GOSHOH MYGOSHOH MYGOSH.
OH MY GOSH, WE ALMOST KILLED A SQUIRREL IN NEW YORK. WE'RE MONSTERS.
GET OUT OF THE ROAD!
OKAY, WELL, THIS STINKS.
EEEEK!
YOU KNOW, THIS IS ALL YOUR FAULT.
WHAT?!

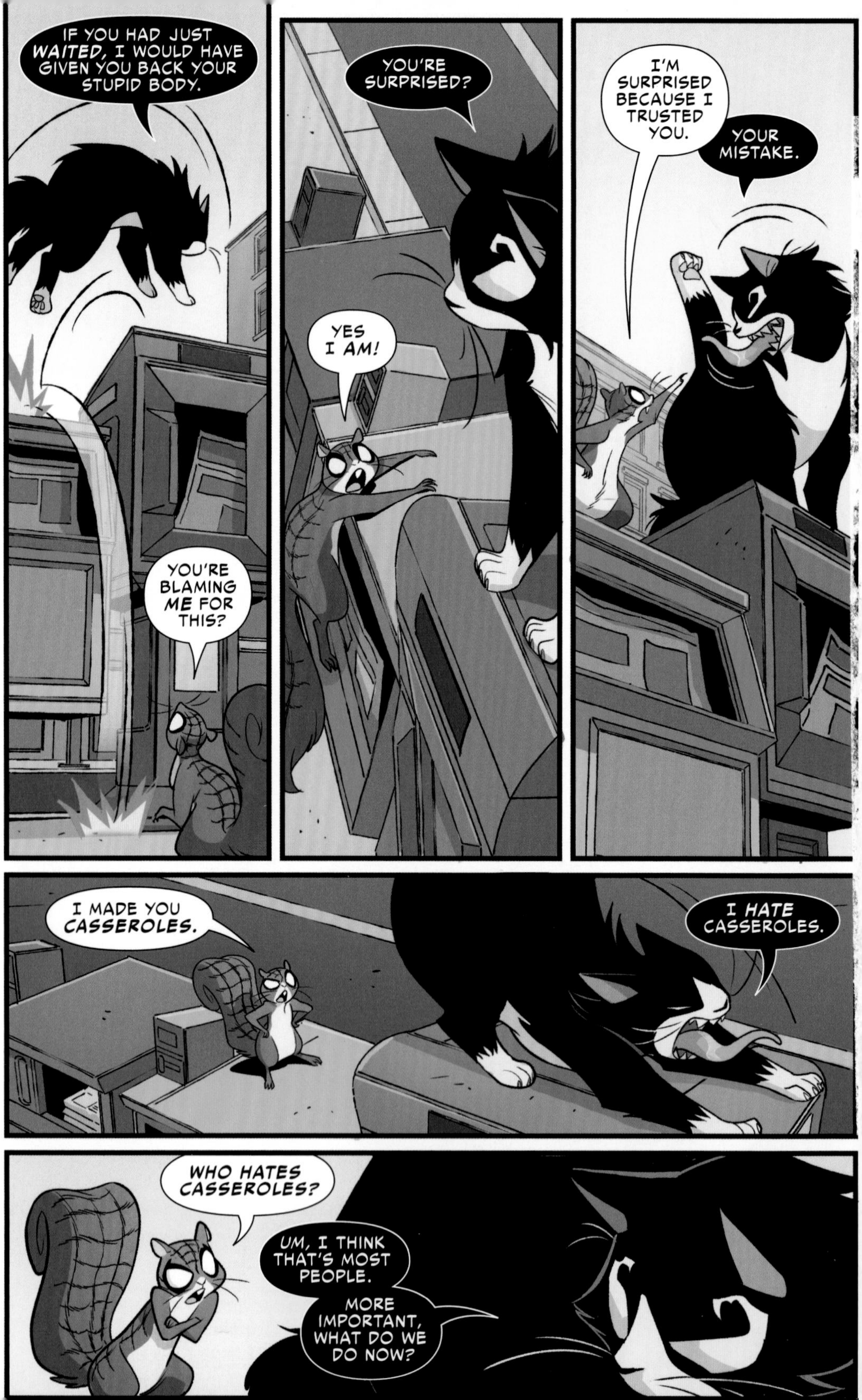
IF YOU HAD JUST WAITED, I WOULD HAVE GIVEN YOU BACK YOUR STUPID BODY.
YOU'RE BLAMING ME FOR THIS?
YOU'RE SURPRISED?
YES I AM!
I'M SURPRISED BECAUSE I TRUSTED YOU.
YOUR MISTAKE.
I MADE YOU CASSEROLES.
I HATE CASSEROLES.
WHO HATES CASSEROLES?
UM, I THINK THAT'S MOST PEOPLE.
MORE IMPORTANT, WHAT DO WE DO NOW?

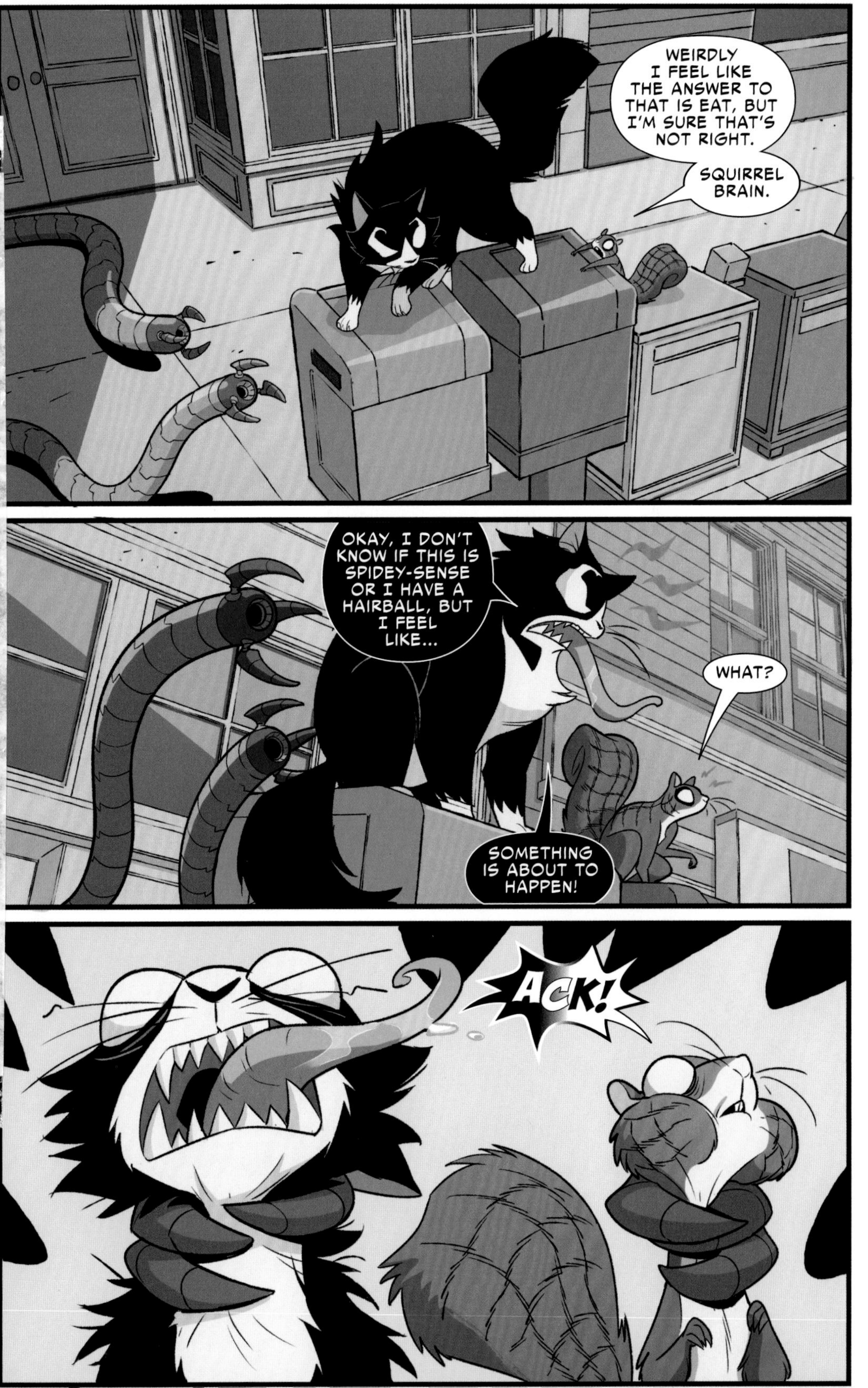
WEIRDLY I FEEL LIKE THE ANSWER TO THAT IS EAT, BUT I'M SURE THAT'S NOT RIGHT.
SQUIRREL BRAIN.
OKAY, I DON'T KNOW IF THIS IS SPIDEY-SENSE OR I HAVE A HAIRBALL, BUT I FEEL LIKE...
WHAT?
SOMETHING IS ABOUT TO HAPPEN!
ACK!

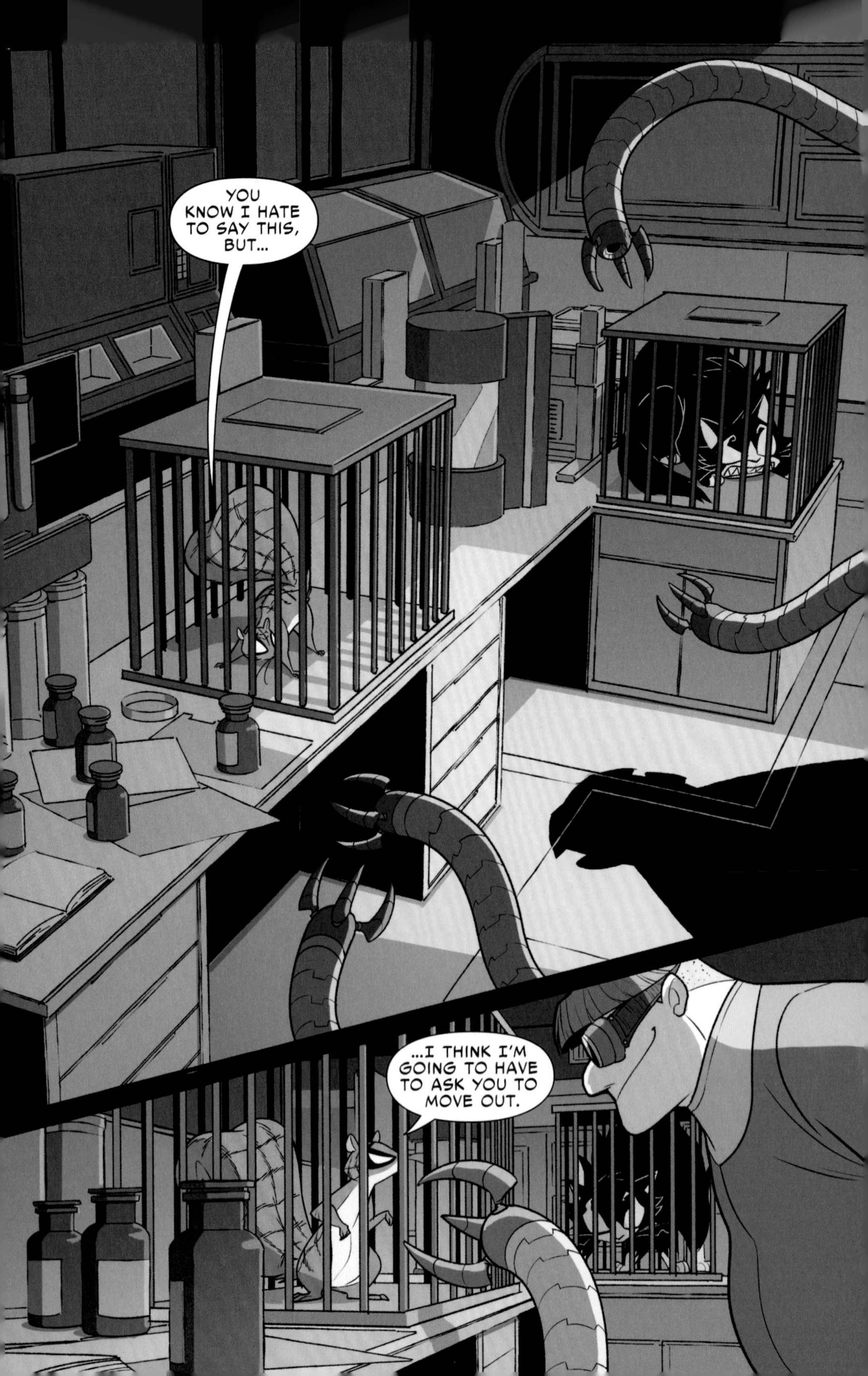
YOU KNOW I HATE TO SAY THIS, BUT...
...I THINK I'M GOING TO HAVE TO ASK YOU TO MOVE OUT.

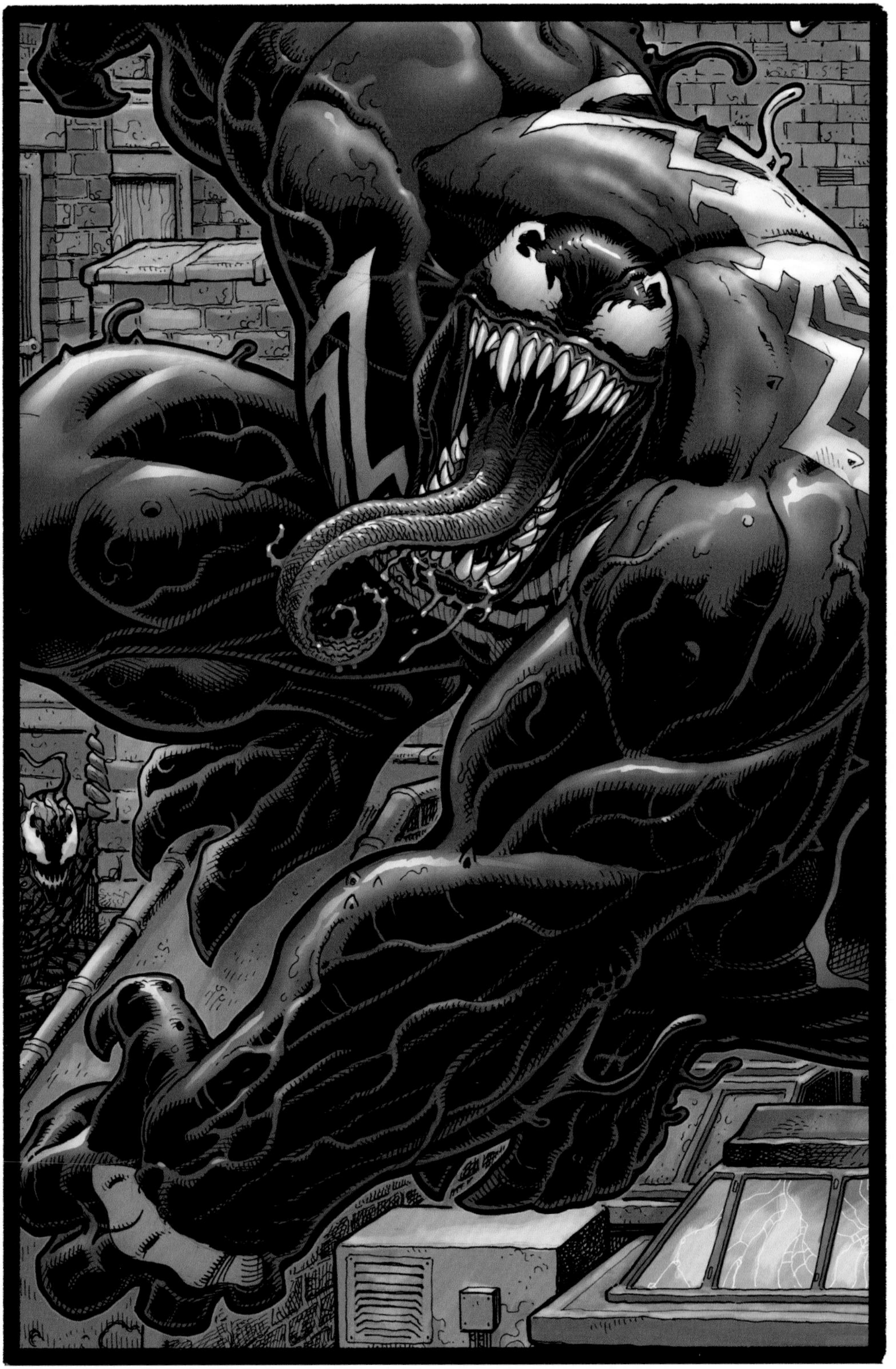

#1 VARIANT BY **ARTHUR ADAMS** & **EDGAR DELGADO**

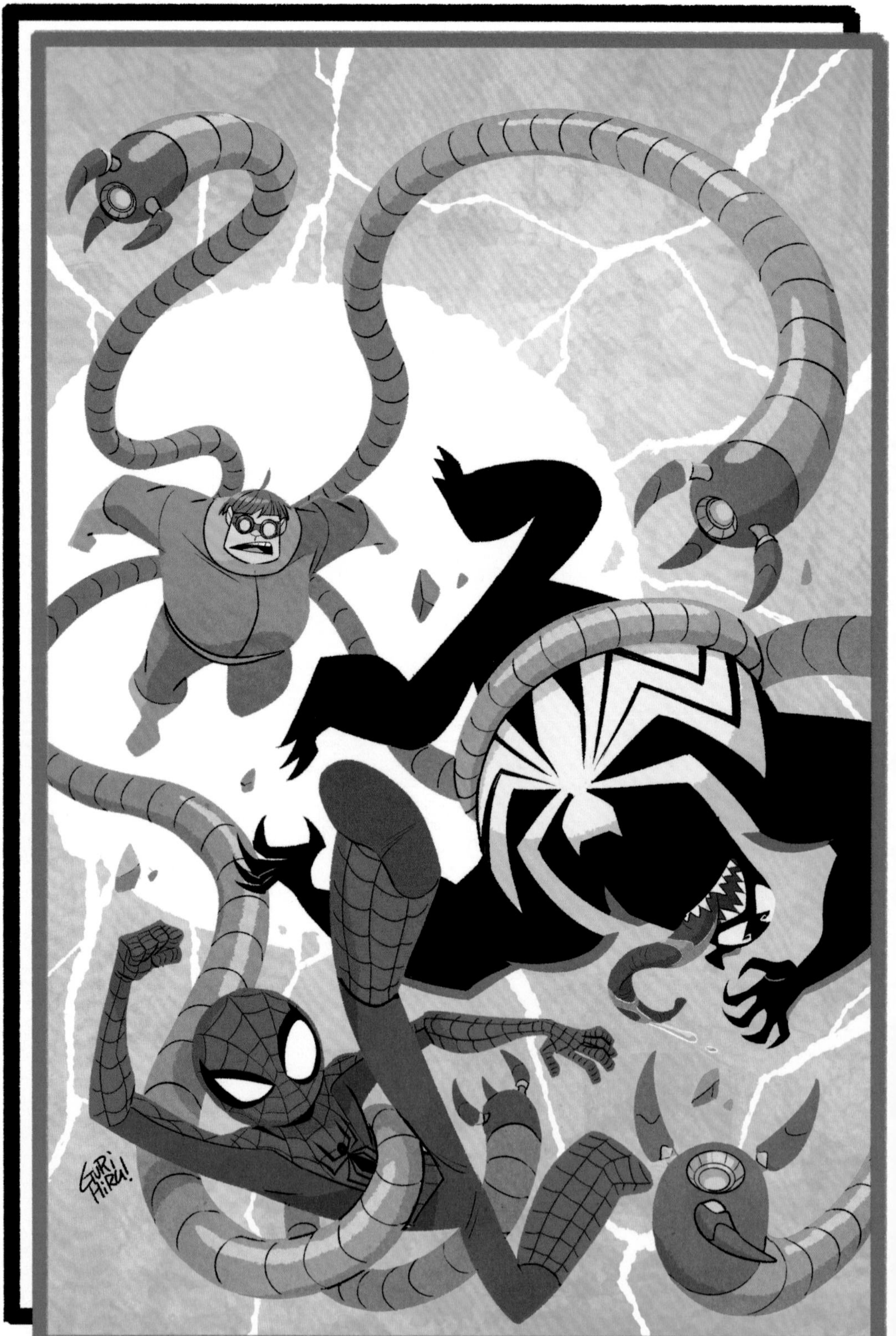
GURI HIRU!

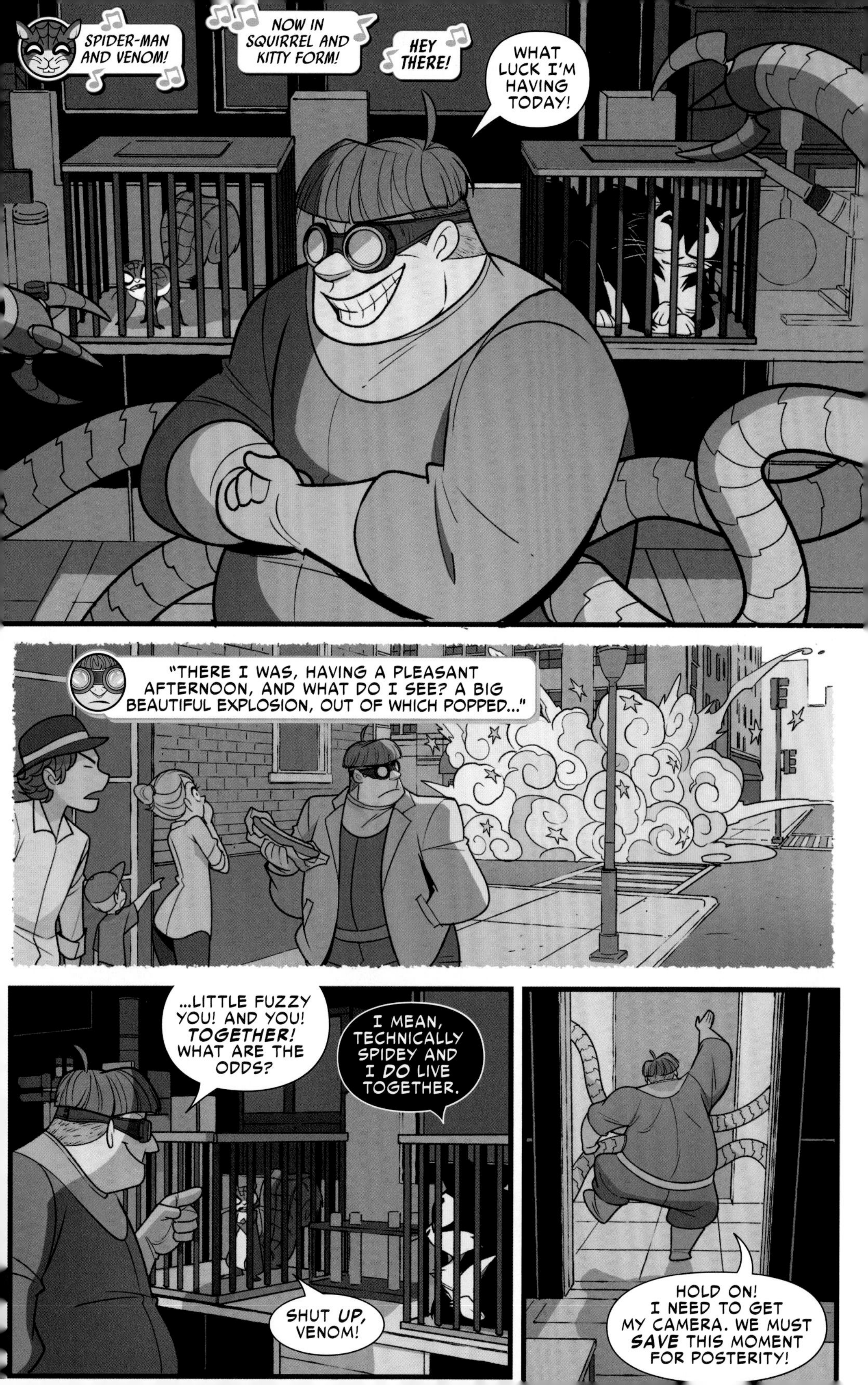
SPIDER-MAN AND VENOM!
NOW IN SQUIRREL AND KITTY FORM!
HEY THERE!
WHAT LUCK I'M HAVING TODAY!
"THERE I WAS, HAVING A PLEASANT AFTERNOON, AND WHAT DO I SEE? A BIG BEAUTIFUL EXPLOSION, OUT OF WHICH POPPED..."
...LITTLE FUZZY YOU! AND YOU! TOGETHER! WHAT ARE THE ODDS?
I MEAN, TECHNICALLY SPIDEY AND I DO LIVE TOGETHER.
SHUT UP, VENOM!
HOLD ON! I NEED TO GET MY CAMERA. WE MUST SAVE THIS MOMENT FOR POSTERITY!

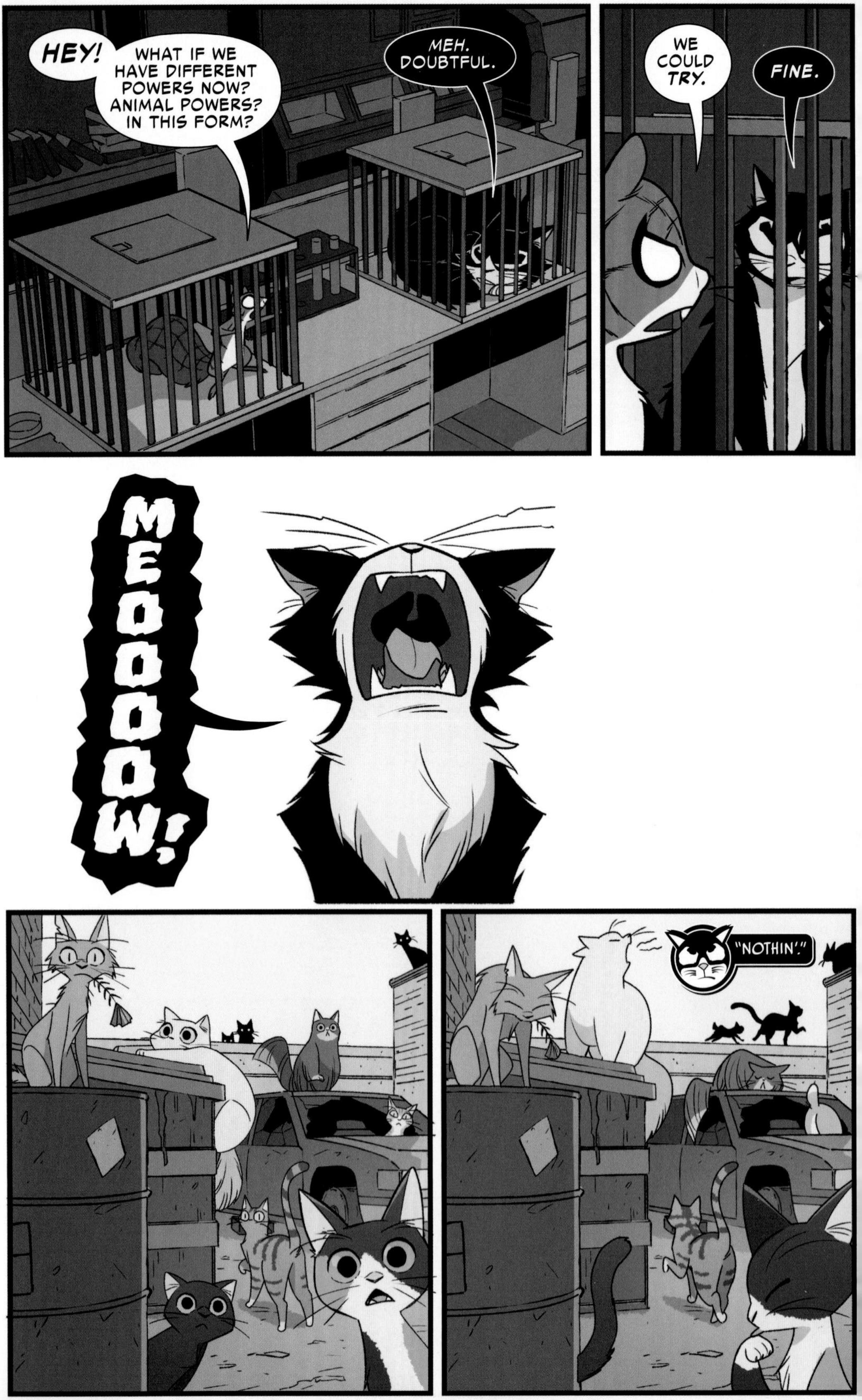
HEY!
WHAT IF WE HAVE DIFFERENT POWERS NOW? ANIMAL POWERS? IN THIS FORM?
MEH. DOUBTFUL.
WE COULD TRY.
FINE.
MEOOOOOW!
"NOTHIN'."

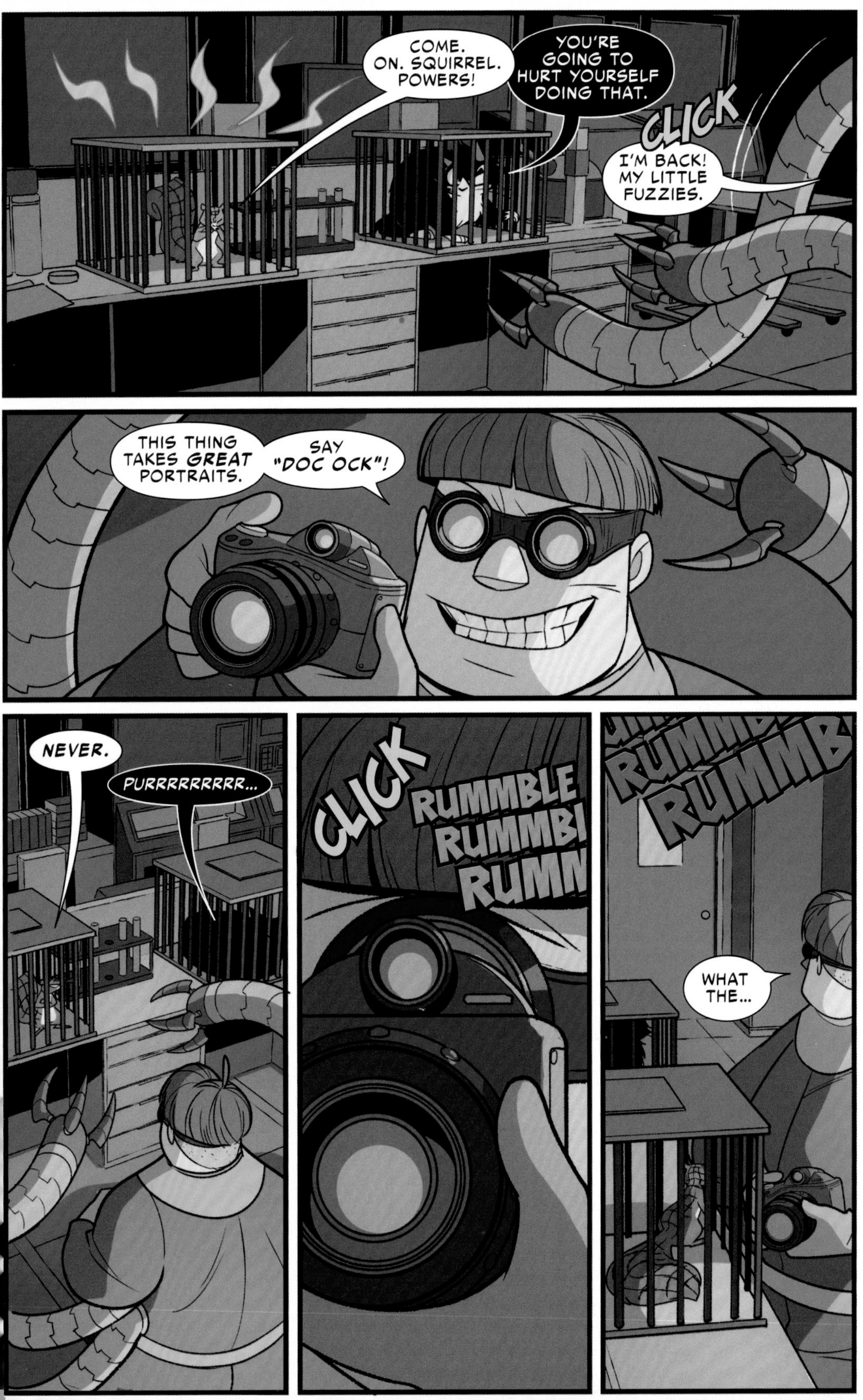
COME. ON. SQUIRREL. POWERS!
YOU'RE GOING TO HURT YOURSELF DOING THAT.
CLICK
I'M BACK! MY LITTLE FUZZIES.
THIS THING TAKES GREAT PORTRAITS.
SAY "DOC OCK"!
NEVER.
PURRRRRRRRR...
CLICK
RUMMBLE
WHAT THE...

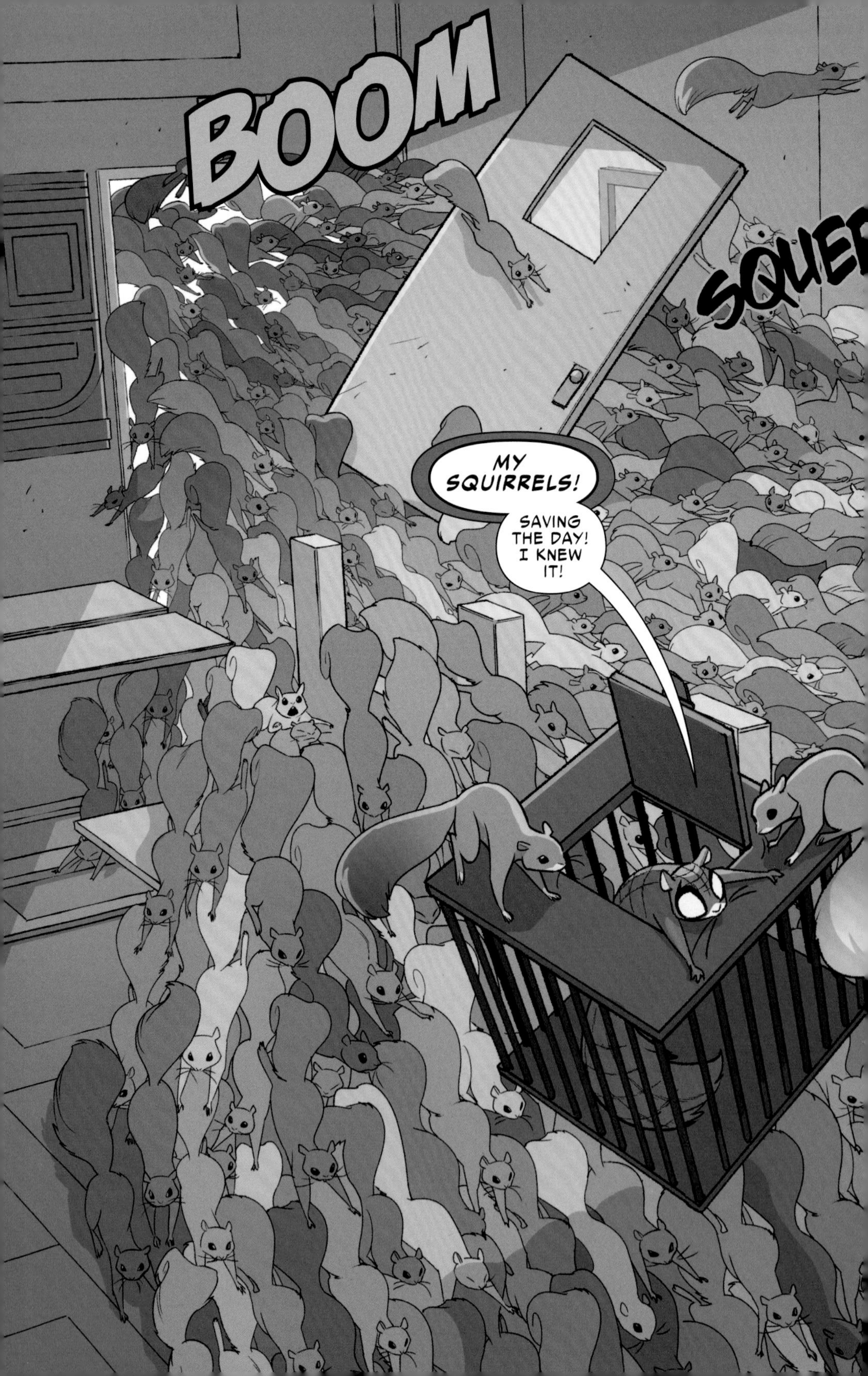
BOOM
SQUEE
MY SQUIRRELS!
SAVING THE DAY! I KNEW IT!

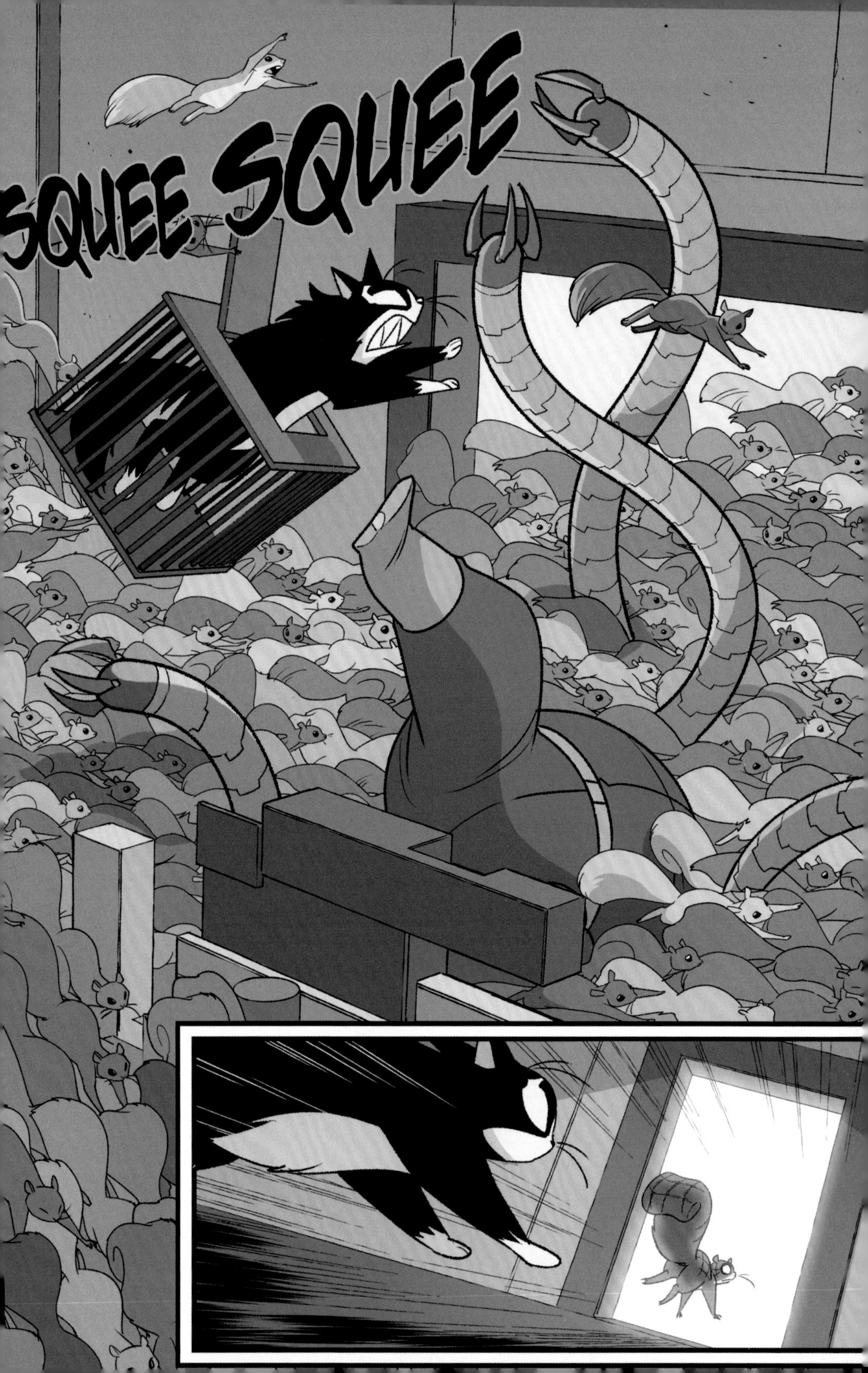
SQUEE SQUEE

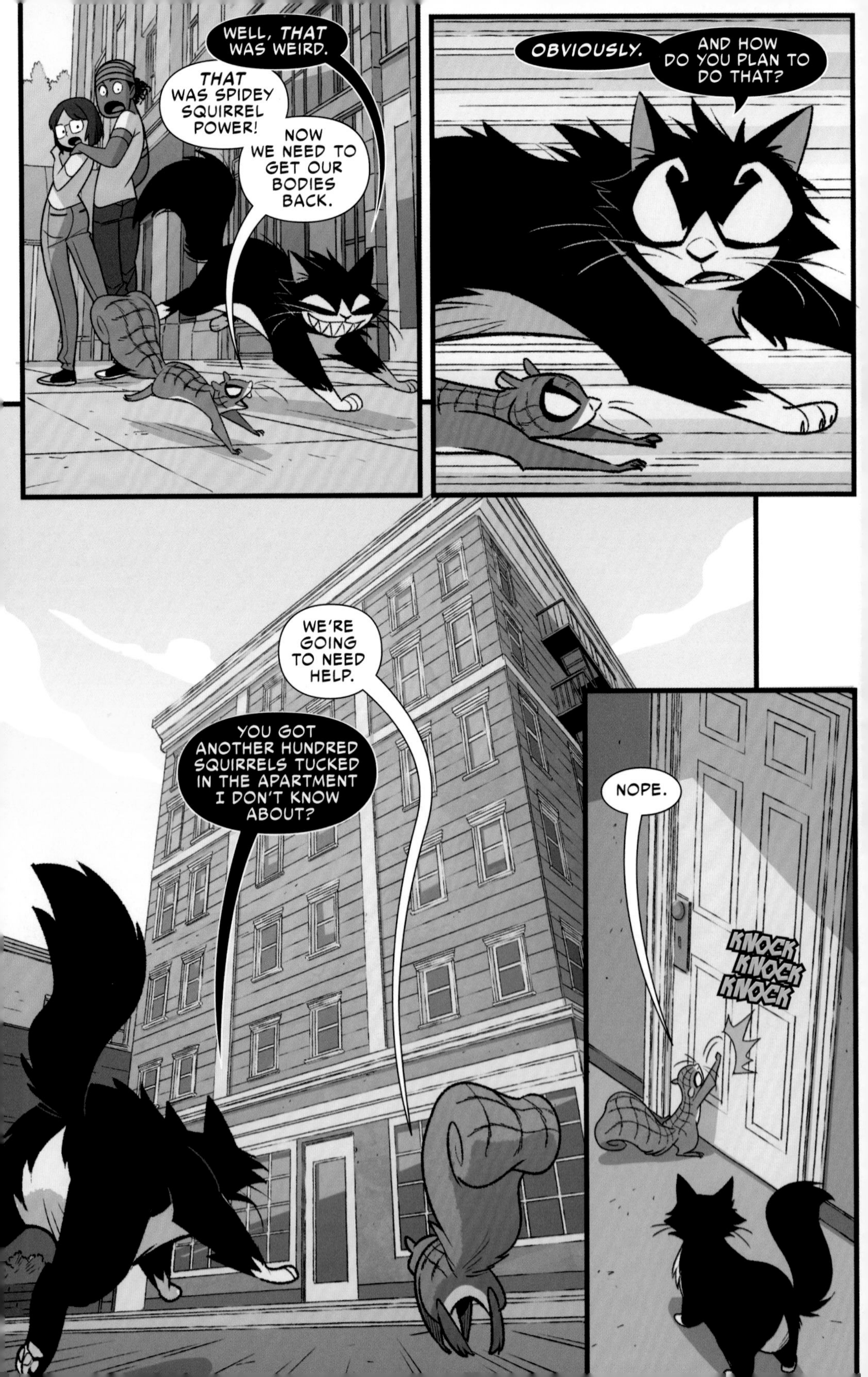
WELL, THAT WAS WEIRD.
THAT WAS SPIDEY SQUIRREL POWER!
NOW WE NEED TO GET OUR BODIES BACK.
OBVIOUSLY.
AND HOW DO YOU PLAN TO DO THAT?
WE'RE GOING TO NEED HELP.
YOU GOT ANOTHER HUNDRED SQUIRRELS TUCKED IN THE APARTMENT I DON'T KNOW ABOUT?
NOPE.
KNOCK KNOCK KNOCK

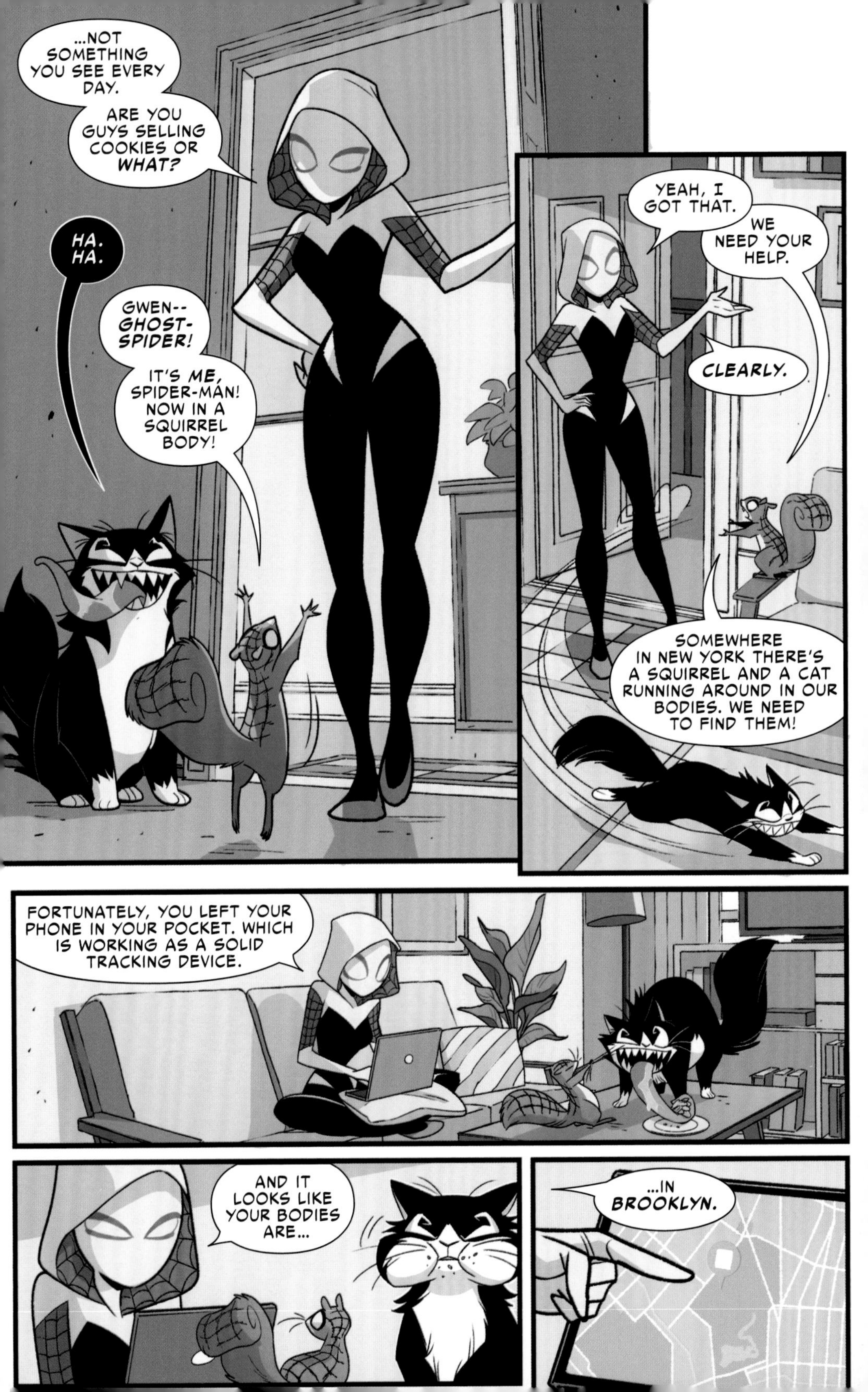
...NOT SOMETHING YOU SEE EVERY DAY.
ARE YOU GUYS SELLING COOKIES OR *WHAT?*
HA. HA.
GWEN-- *GHOST-SPIDER!*
IT'S *ME*, SPIDER-MAN! NOW IN A SQUIRREL BODY!
YEAH, I GOT THAT.
WE NEED YOUR HELP.
CLEARLY.
SOMEWHERE IN NEW YORK THERE'S A SQUIRREL AND A CAT RUNNING AROUND IN OUR BODIES. WE NEED TO FIND THEM!
FORTUNATELY, YOU LEFT YOUR PHONE IN YOUR POCKET. WHICH IS WORKING AS A SOLID TRACKING DEVICE.
AND IT LOOKS LIKE YOUR BODIES ARE...
...IN *BROOKLYN.*

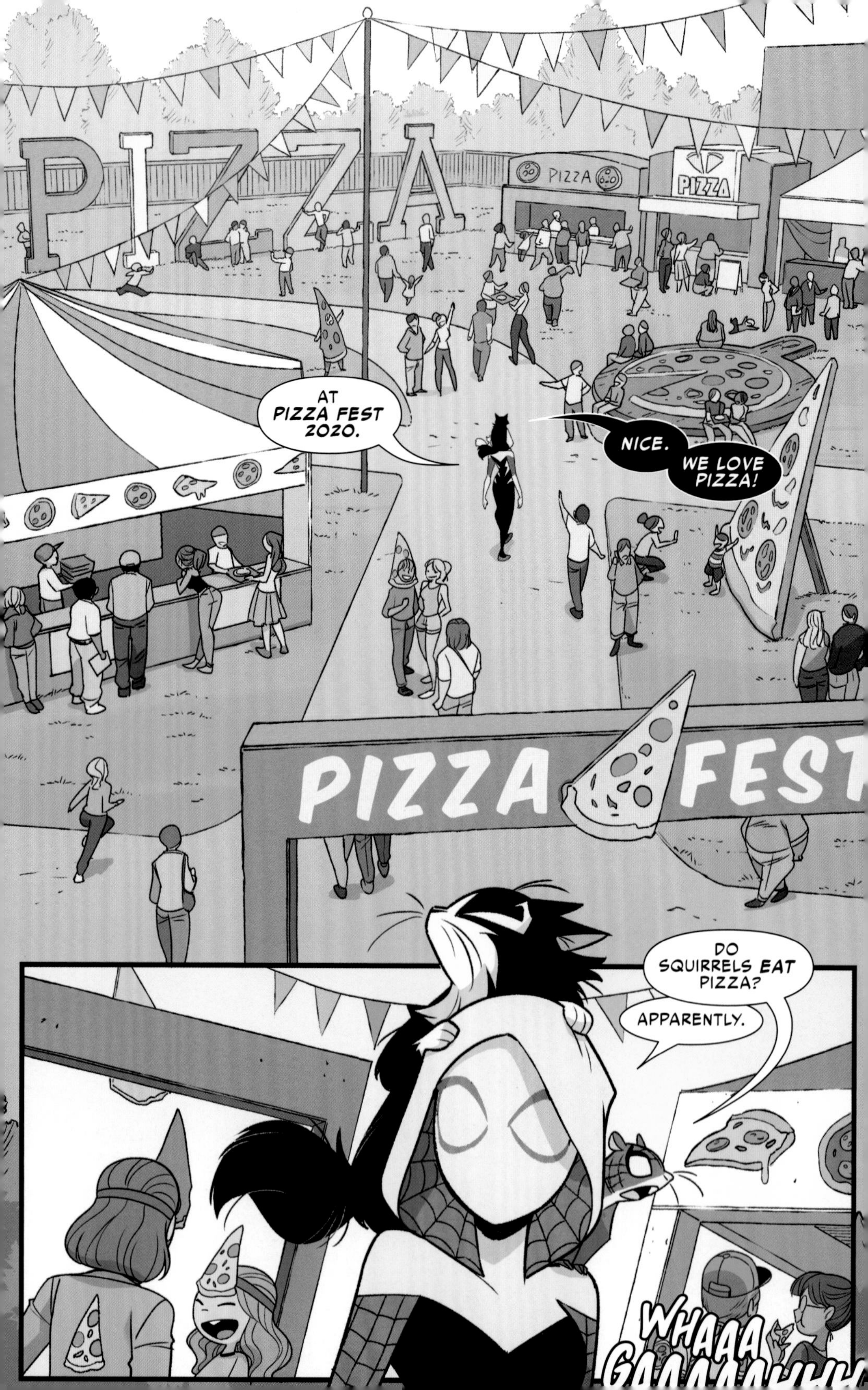
PIZZA
PIZZA
PIZZA
AT PIZZA FEST 2020.
NICE.
WE LOVE PIZZA!
PIZZA FEST
DO SQUIRRELS EAT PIZZA?
APPARENTLY.
WHAAA GAAAAAHHH

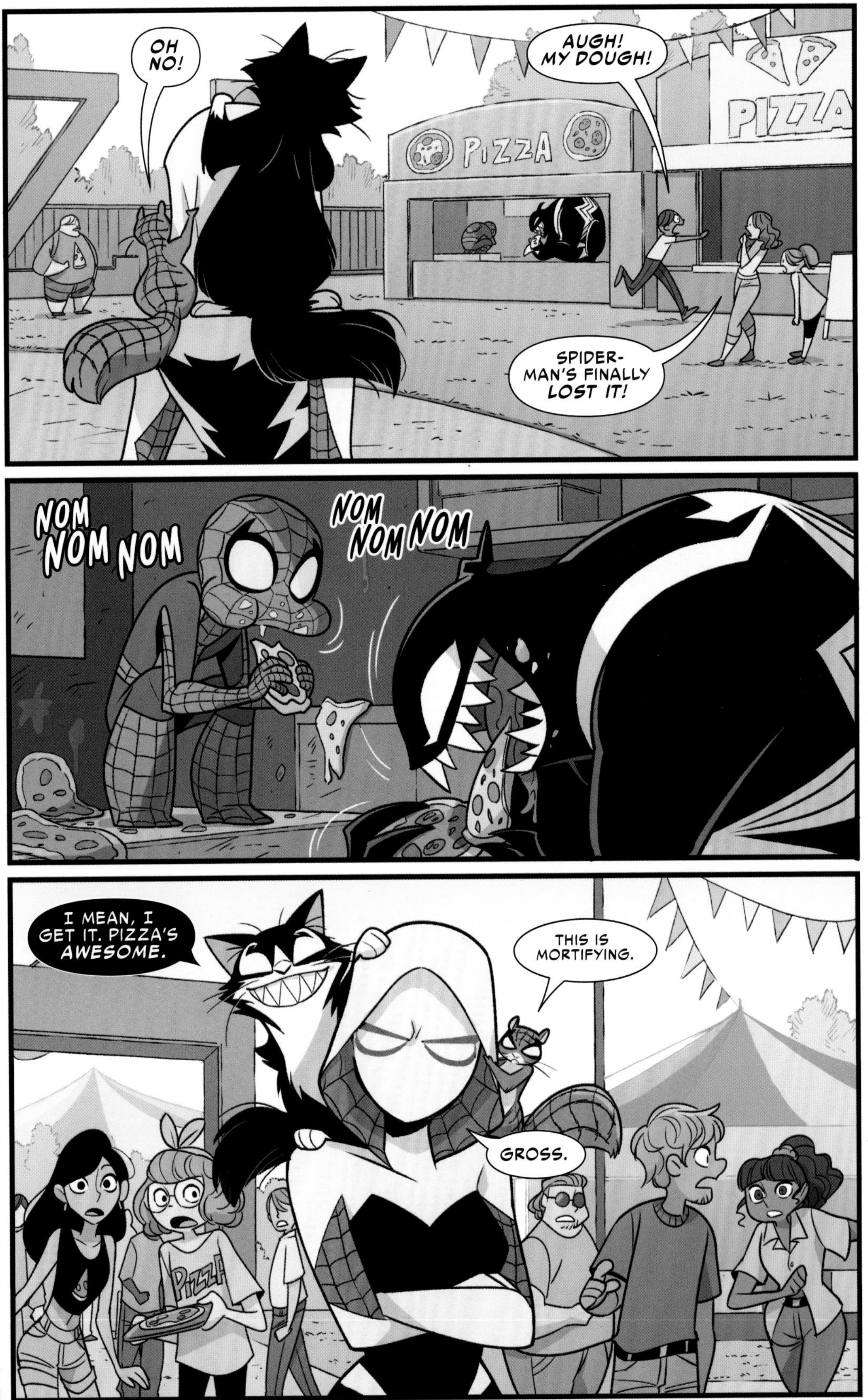
OH NO!
AUGH! MY DOUGH!
SPIDER-MAN'S FINALLY LOST IT!
NOM NOM NOM
NOM NOM NOM
I MEAN, I GET IT. PIZZA'S AWESOME.
THIS IS MORTIFYING.
GROSS.

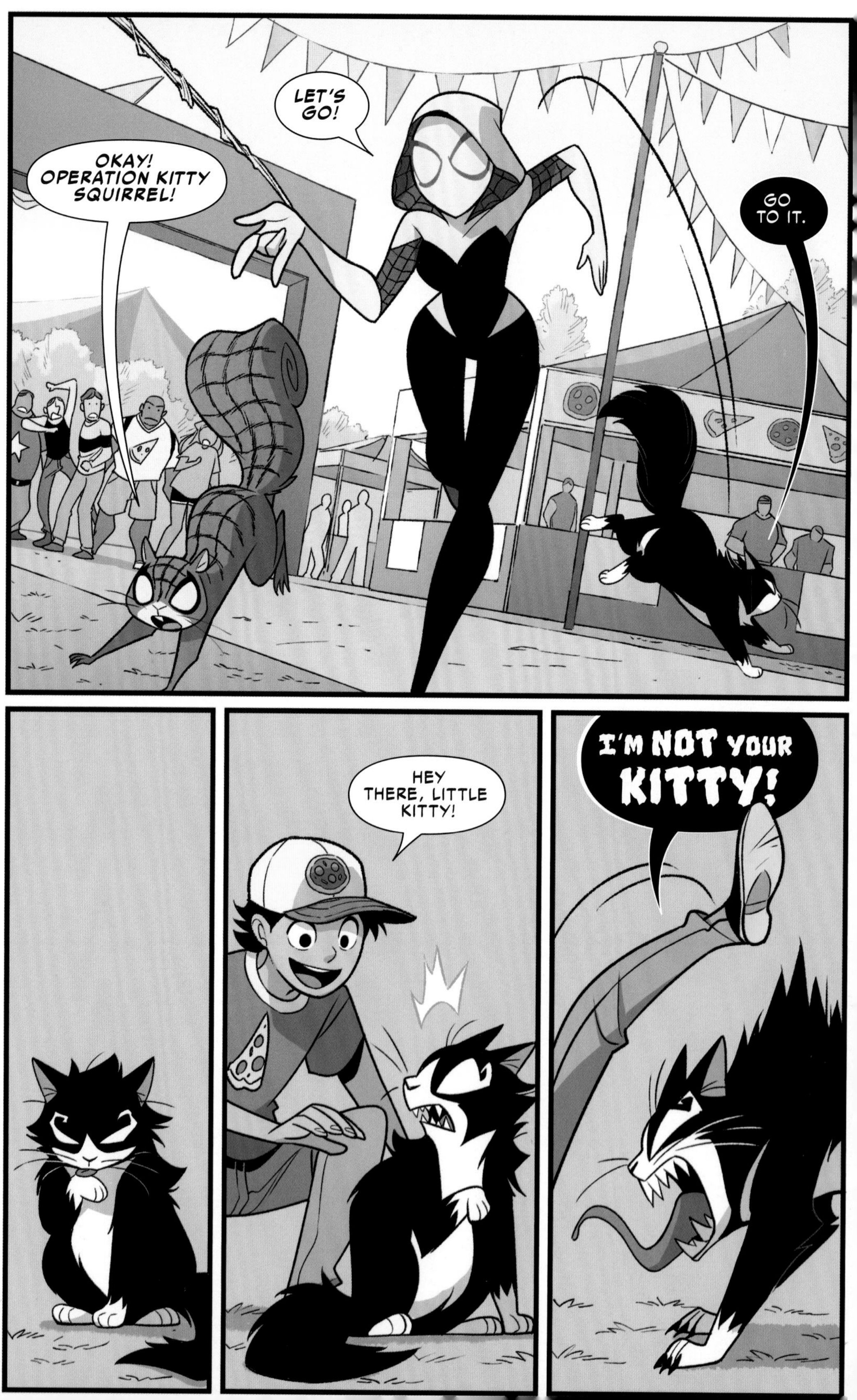
LET'S GO!
OKAY! OPERATION KITTY SQUIRREL!
GO TO IT.
HEY THERE, LITTLE KITTY!
I'M NOT YOUR KITTY!

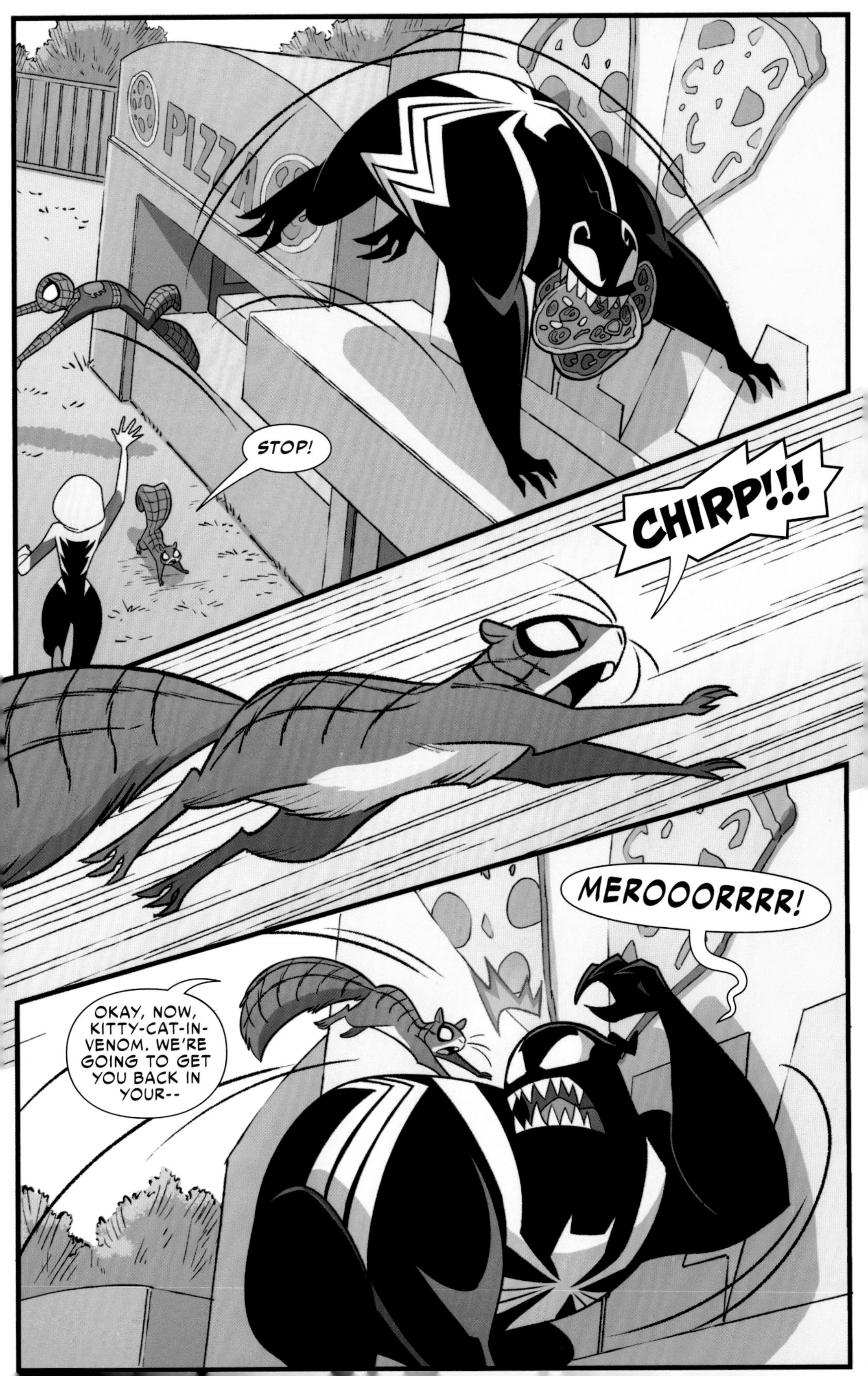

STOP!
CHIRP!!!
MEROOORRRR!
OKAY, NOW, KITTY-CAT-IN-VENOM. WE'RE GOING TO GET YOU BACK IN YOUR--

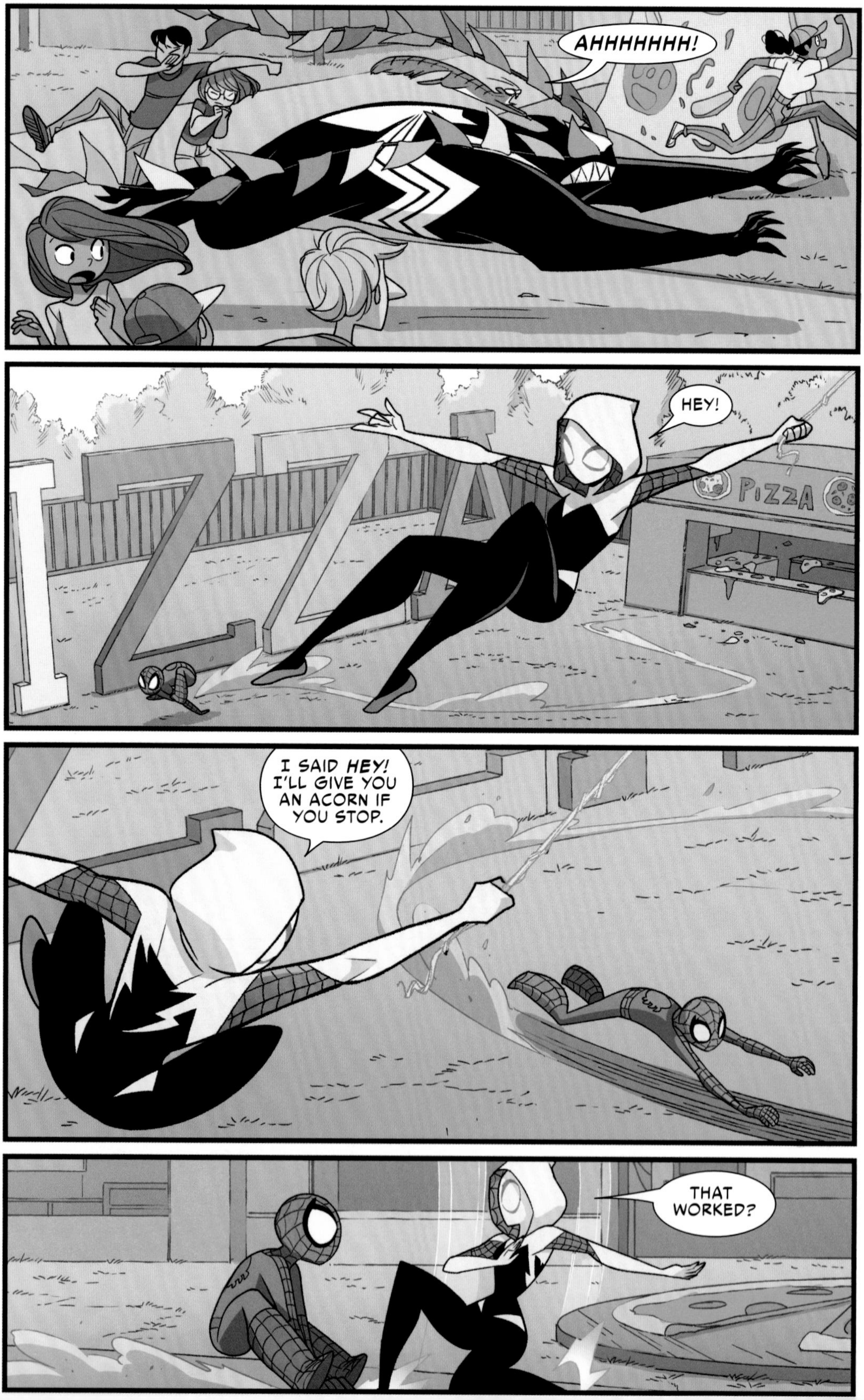
AHHHHHHH!
HEY!
PIZZA
I SAID HEY! I'LL GIVE YOU AN ACORN IF YOU STOP.
THAT WORKED?

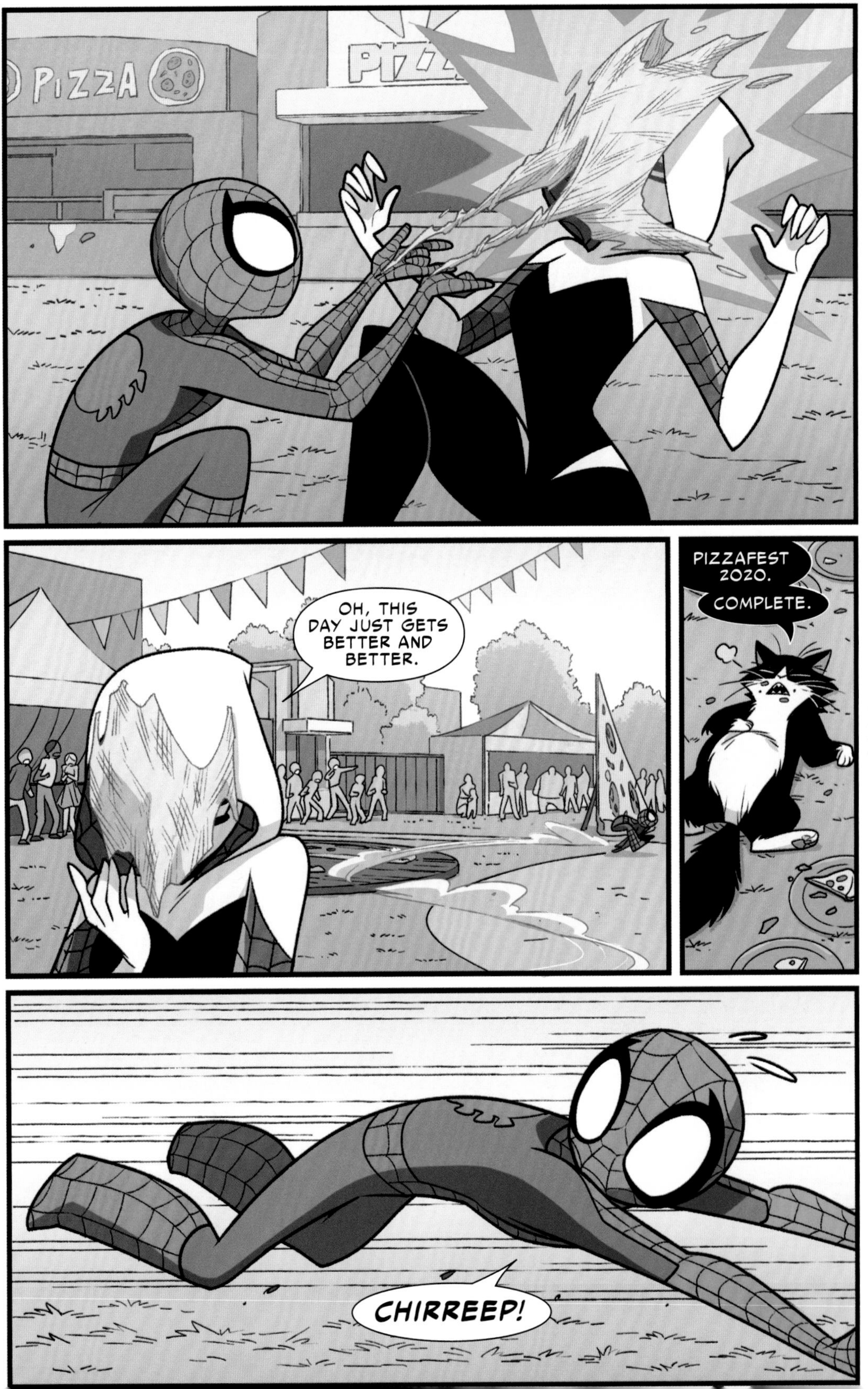
PIZZA
PIZZ
OH, THIS DAY JUST GETS BETTER AND BETTER.
PIZZAFEST 2020.
COMPLETE.
CHIRREEP!

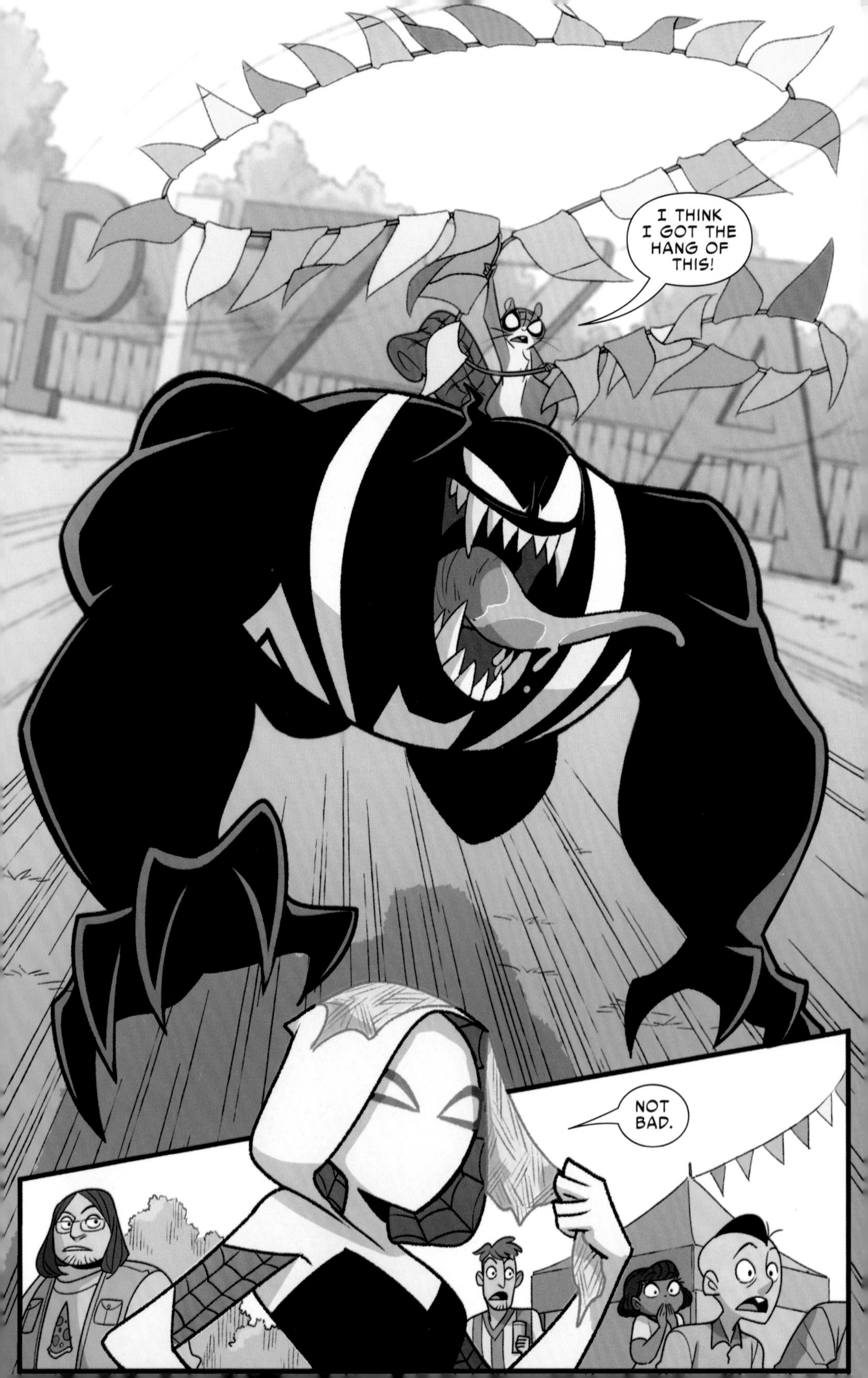
I THINK I GOT THE HANG OF THIS!
NOT BAD.

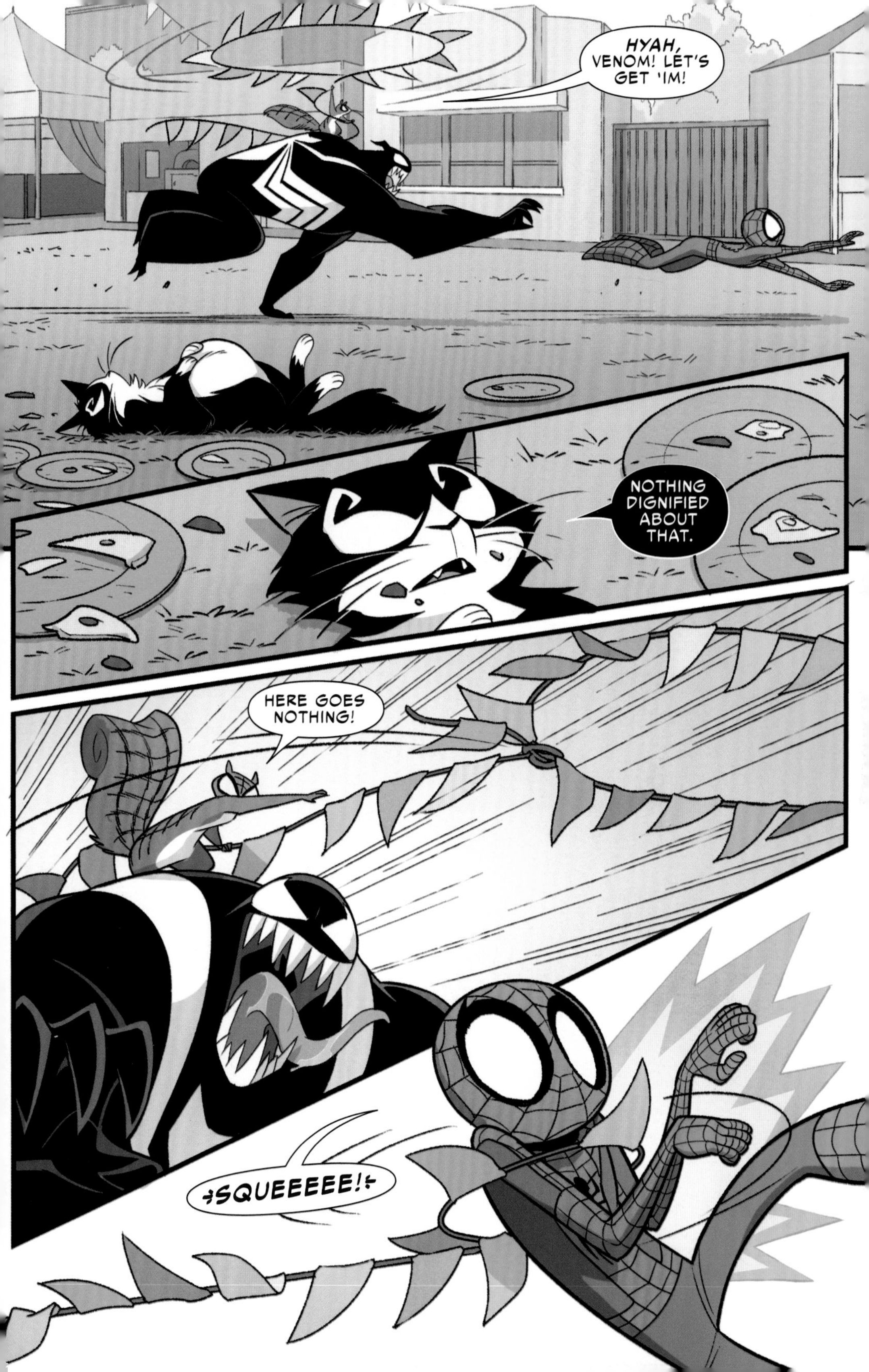
HYAH, VENOM! LET'S GET 'IM!
NOTHING DIGNIFIED ABOUT THAT.
HERE GOES NOTHING!
SQUEEEEEE!

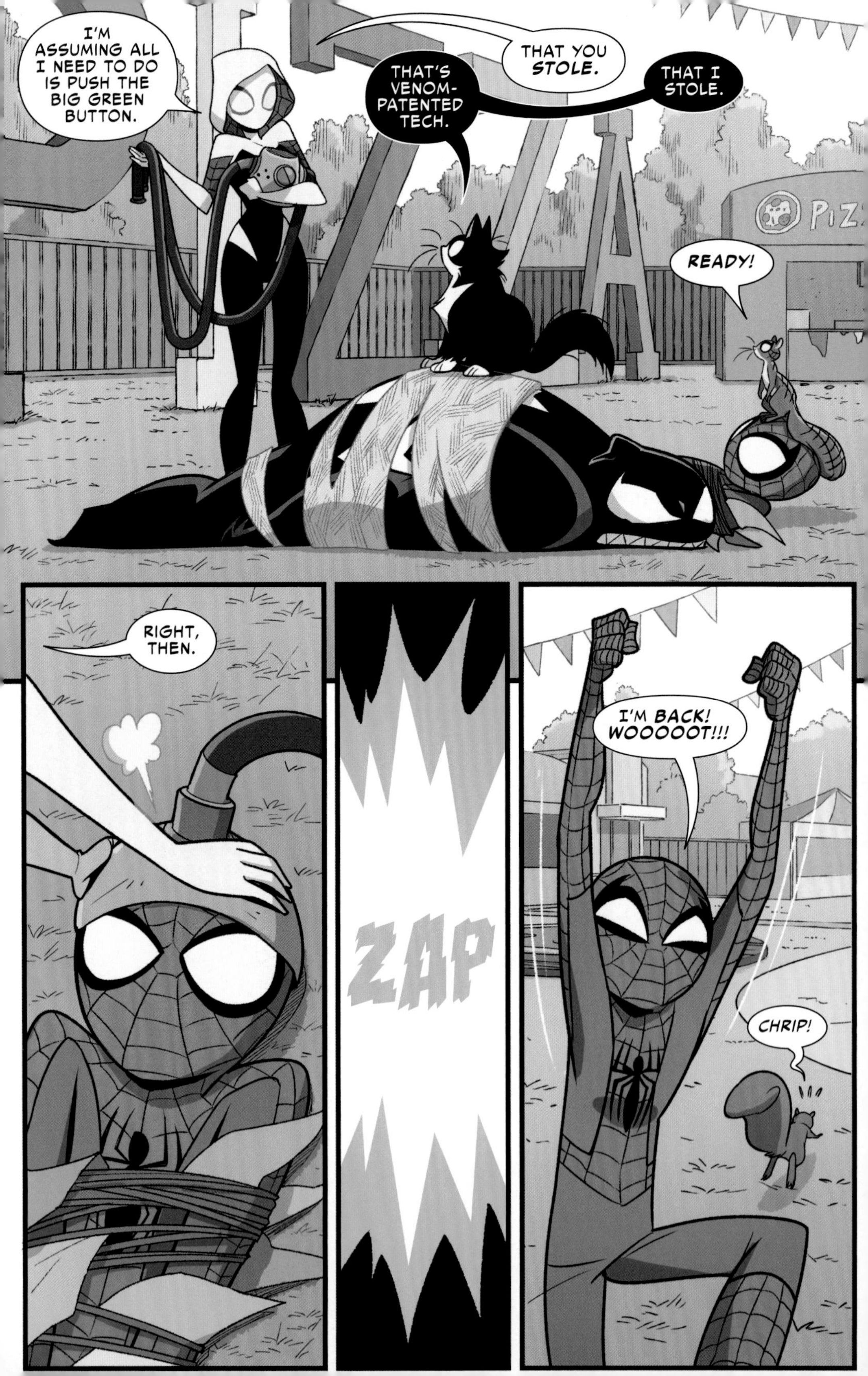
I'M ASSUMING ALL I NEED TO DO IS PUSH THE BIG GREEN BUTTON.
THAT'S VENOM-PATENTED TECH.
THAT YOU STOLE.
THAT I STOLE.
READY!
RIGHT, THEN.
ZAP
I'M BACK! WOOOOOT!!!
CHRIP!

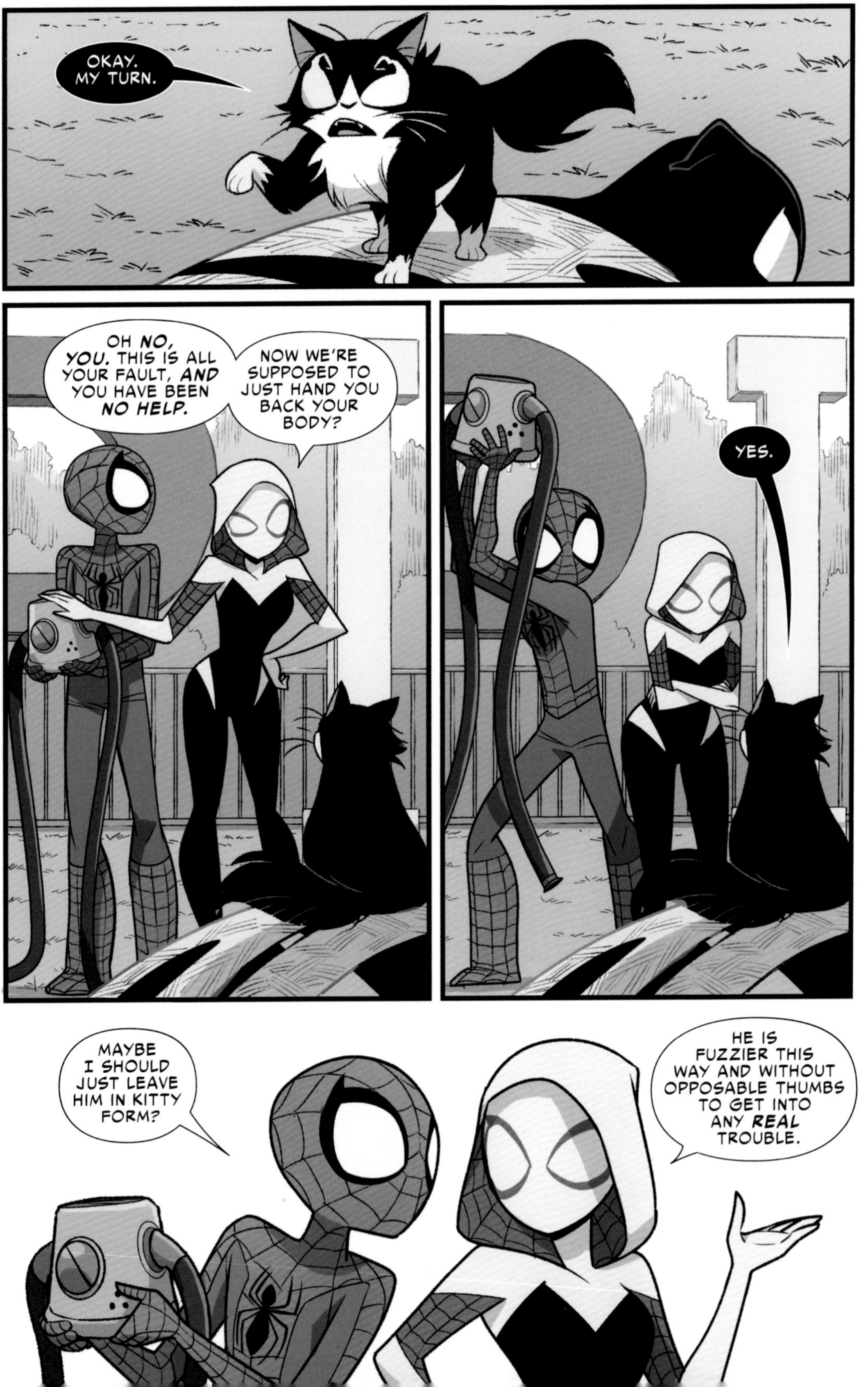
OKAY. MY TURN.
OH NO, YOU. THIS IS ALL YOUR FAULT, AND YOU HAVE BEEN NO HELP.
NOW WE'RE SUPPOSED TO JUST HAND YOU BACK YOUR BODY?
YES.
MAYBE I SHOULD JUST LEAVE HIM IN KITTY FORM?
HE IS FUZZIER THIS WAY AND WITHOUT OPPOSABLE THUMBS TO GET INTO ANY REAL TROUBLE.

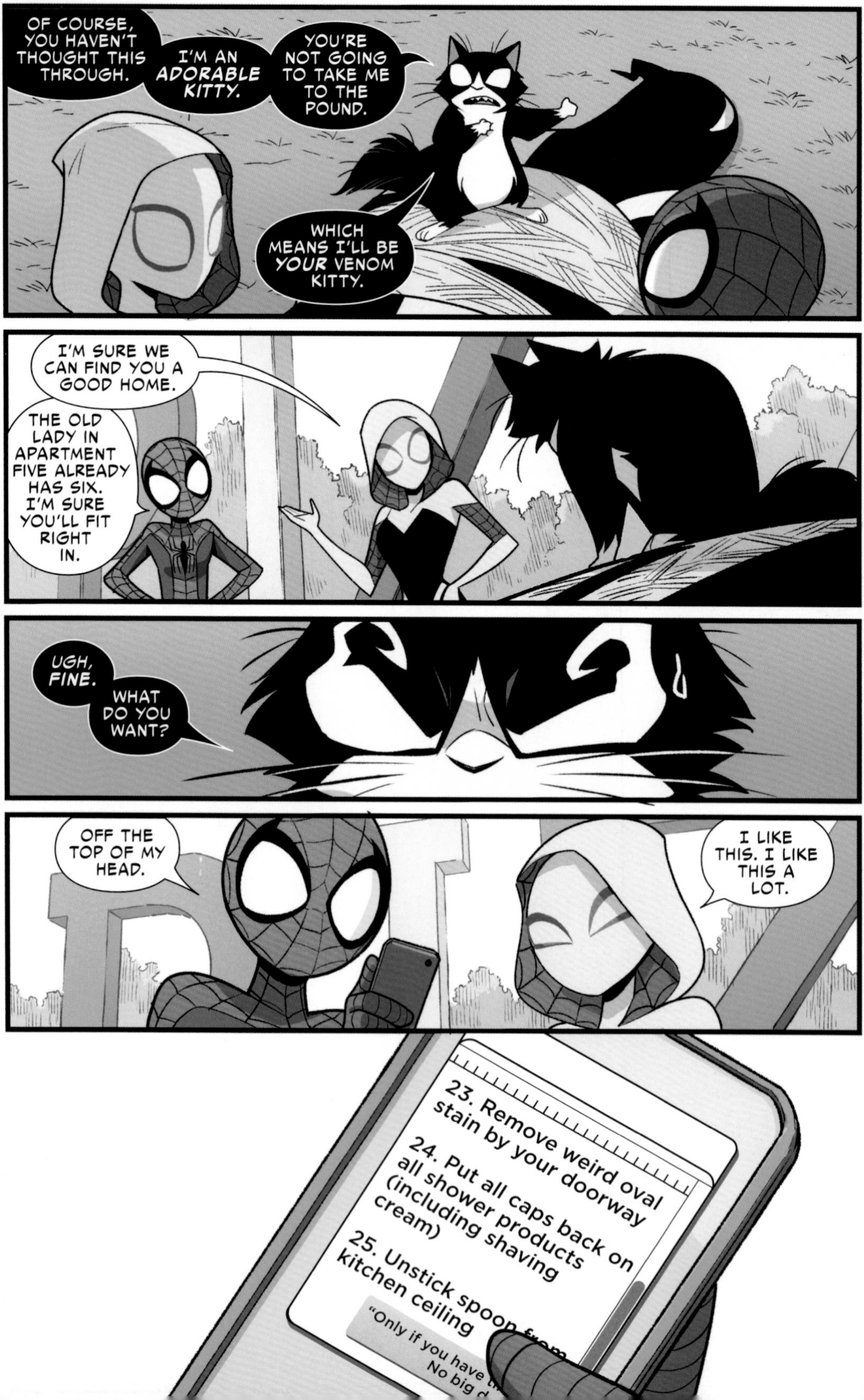

OF COURSE, YOU HAVEN'T THOUGHT THIS THROUGH.
I'M AN ADORABLE KITTY.
YOU'RE NOT GOING TO TAKE ME TO THE POUND.
WHICH MEANS I'LL BE YOUR VENOM KITTY.
I'M SURE WE CAN FIND YOU A GOOD HOME.
THE OLD LADY IN APARTMENT FIVE ALREADY HAS SIX. I'M SURE YOU'LL FIT RIGHT IN.
UGH, FINE.
WHAT DO YOU WANT?
OFF THE TOP OF MY HEAD.
I LIKE THIS. I LIKE THIS A LOT.
23. Remove weird oval stain by your doorway
24. Put all caps back on all shower products (including shaving cream)
25. Unstick spoon from kitchen ceiling

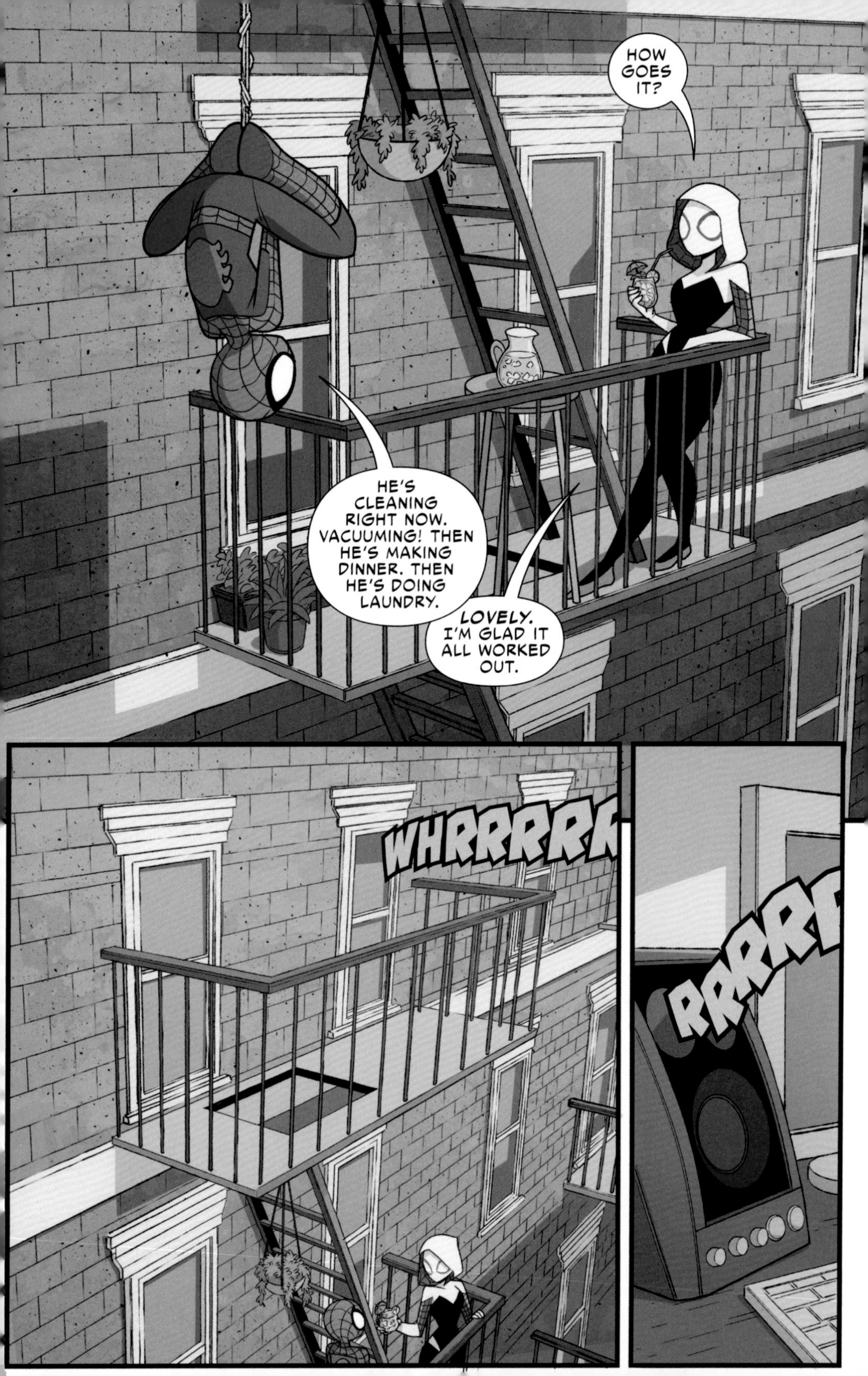
HOW GOES IT?
HE'S CLEANING RIGHT NOW. VACUUMING! THEN HE'S MAKING DINNER. THEN HE'S DOING LAUNDRY.
LOVELY. I'M GLAD IT ALL WORKED OUT.
WHRRRRR
RRRRR

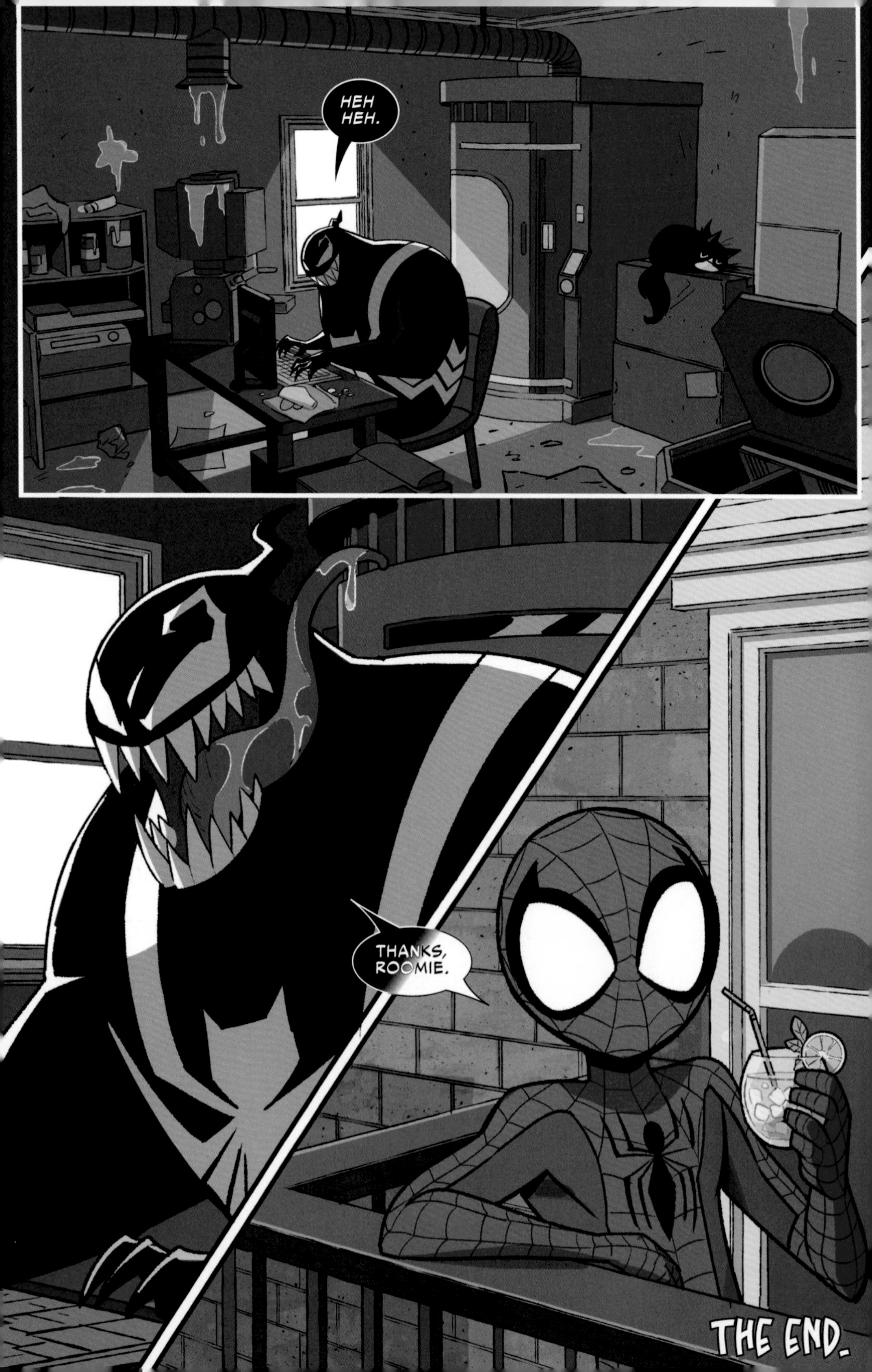
HEH HEH.
THANKS, ROOMIE.
THE END.

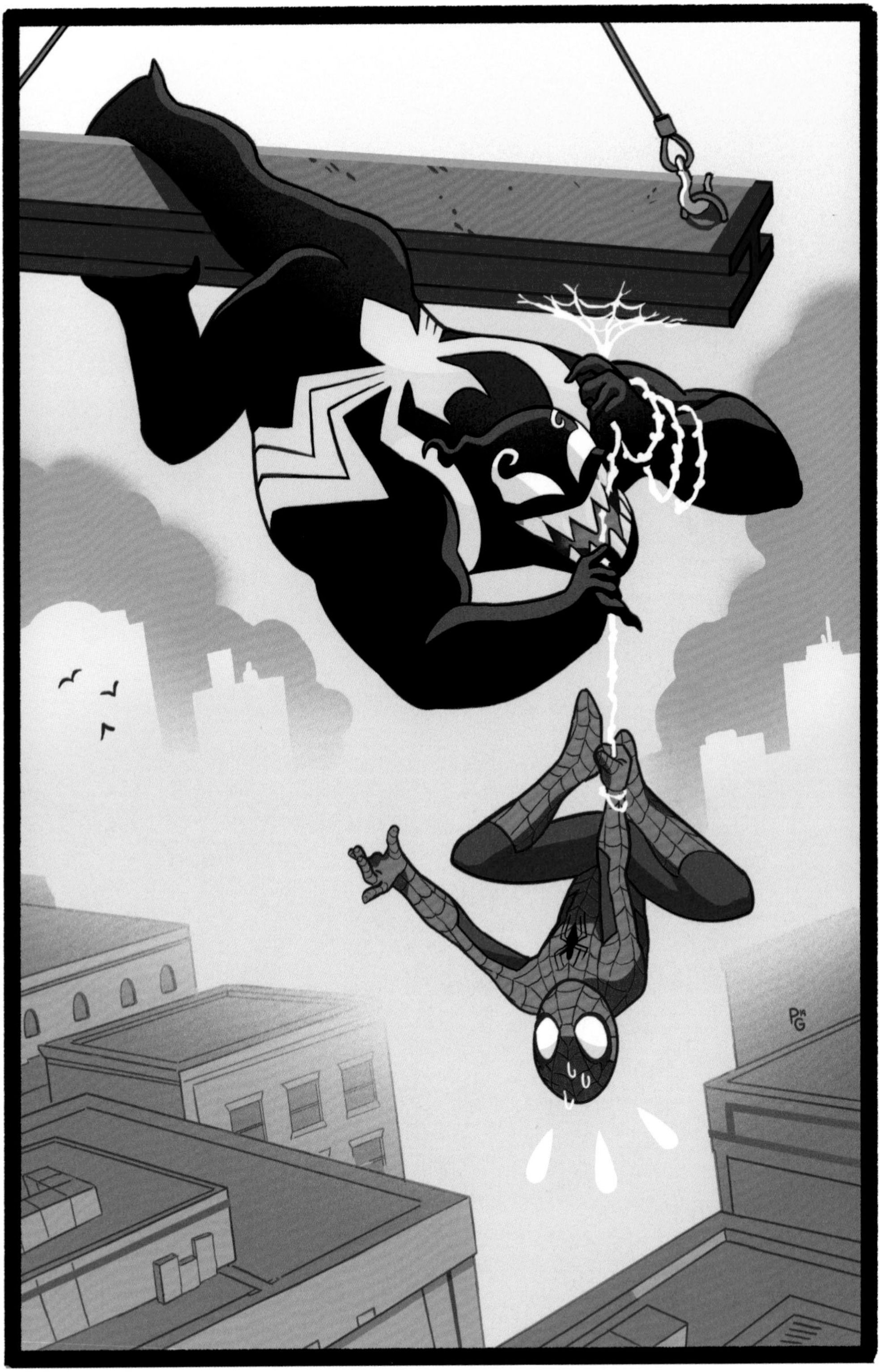
PMG

#1 VARIANT BY **PAULINA GANUCHEAU**

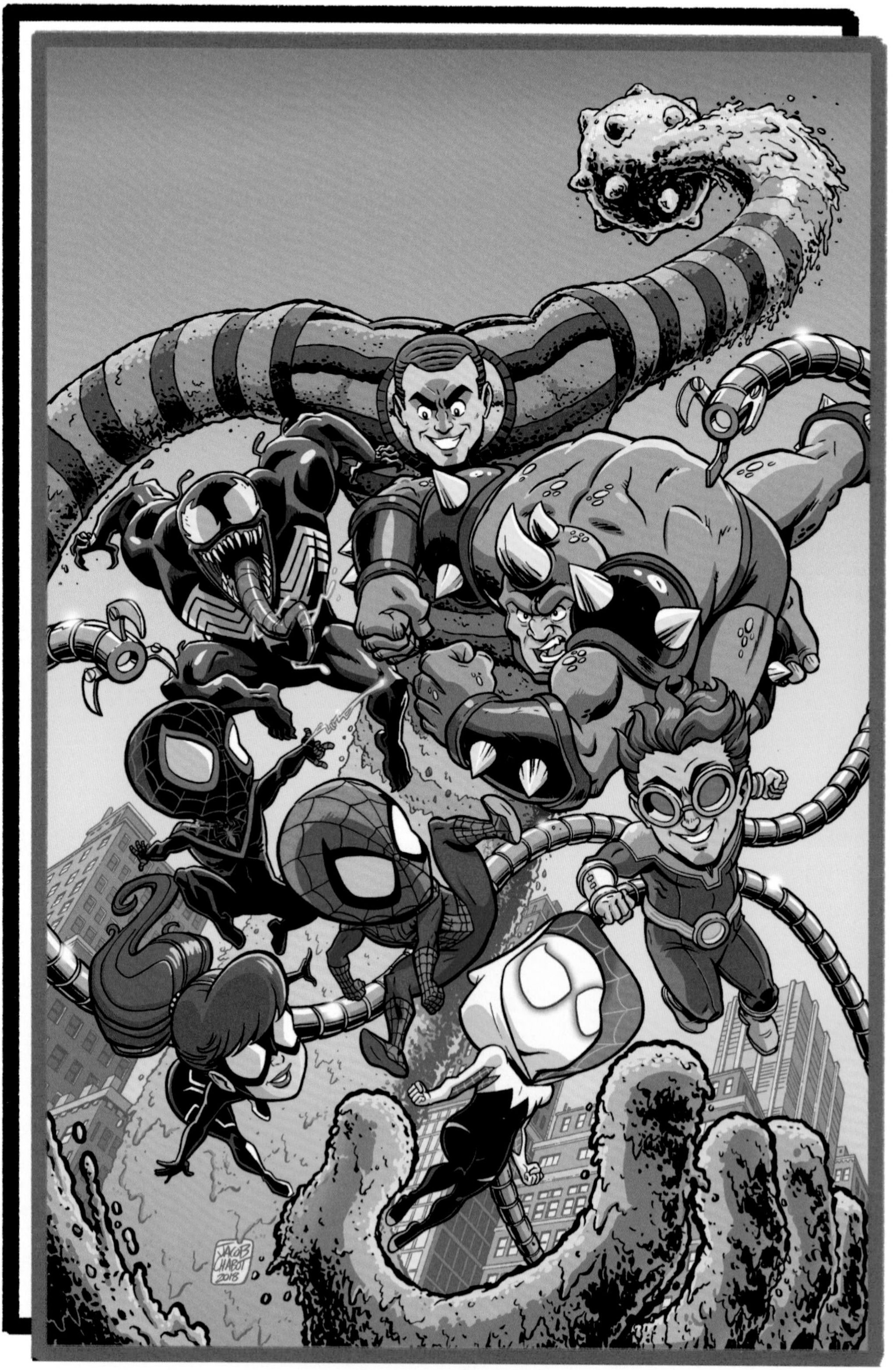
JACOB CHABOT 2018

MARVEL SUPER HERO ADVENTURES: SPIDER-MAN –
WEB OF INTRIGUE

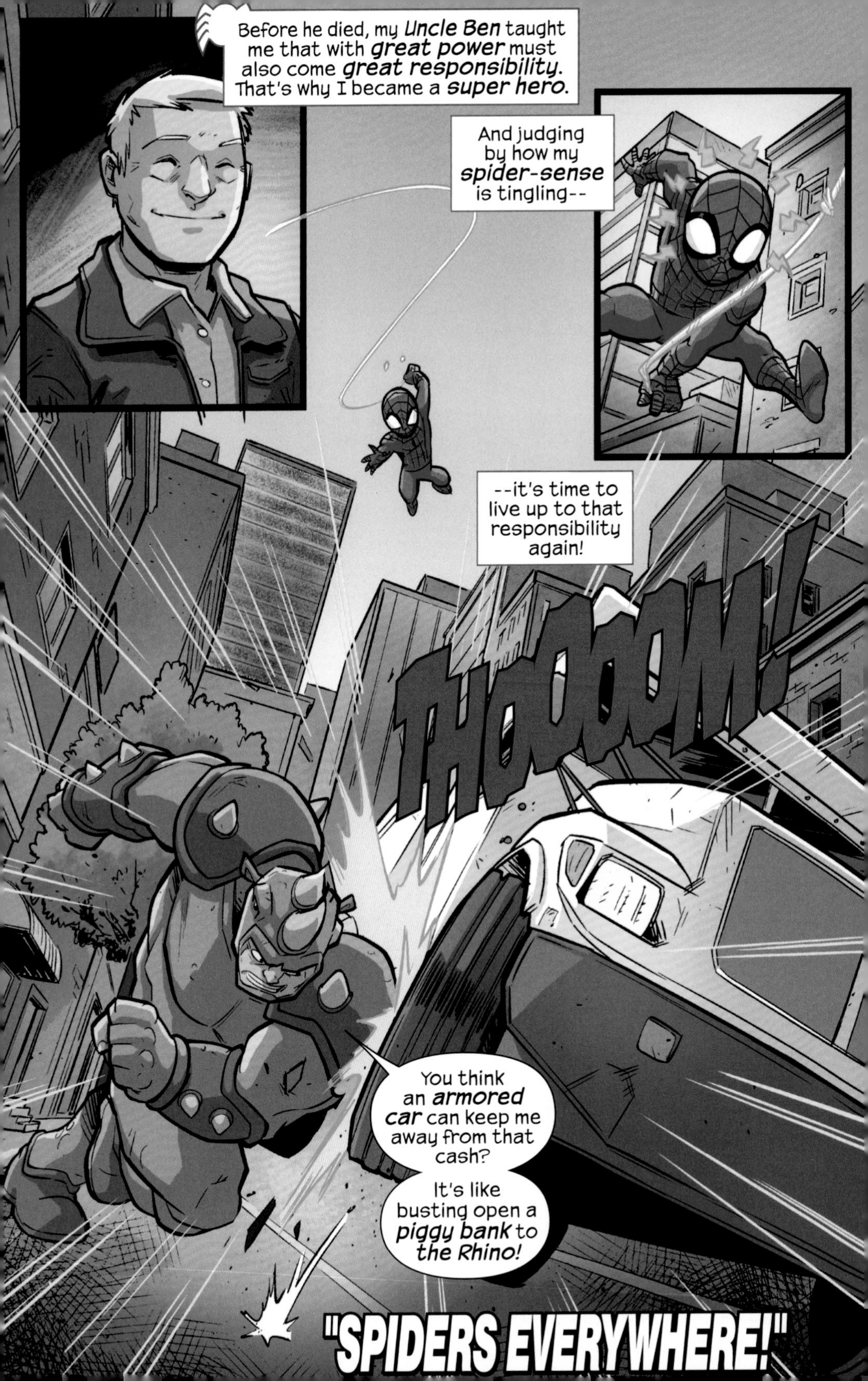
Before he died, my Uncle Ben taught me that with great power must also come great responsibility. That's why I became a super hero.
And judging by how my spider-sense is tingling--
--it's time to live up to that responsibility again!
THOOOOM!
You think an armored car can keep me away from that cash?
It's like busting open a piggy bank to the Rhino!
"SPIDERS EVERYWHERE!"

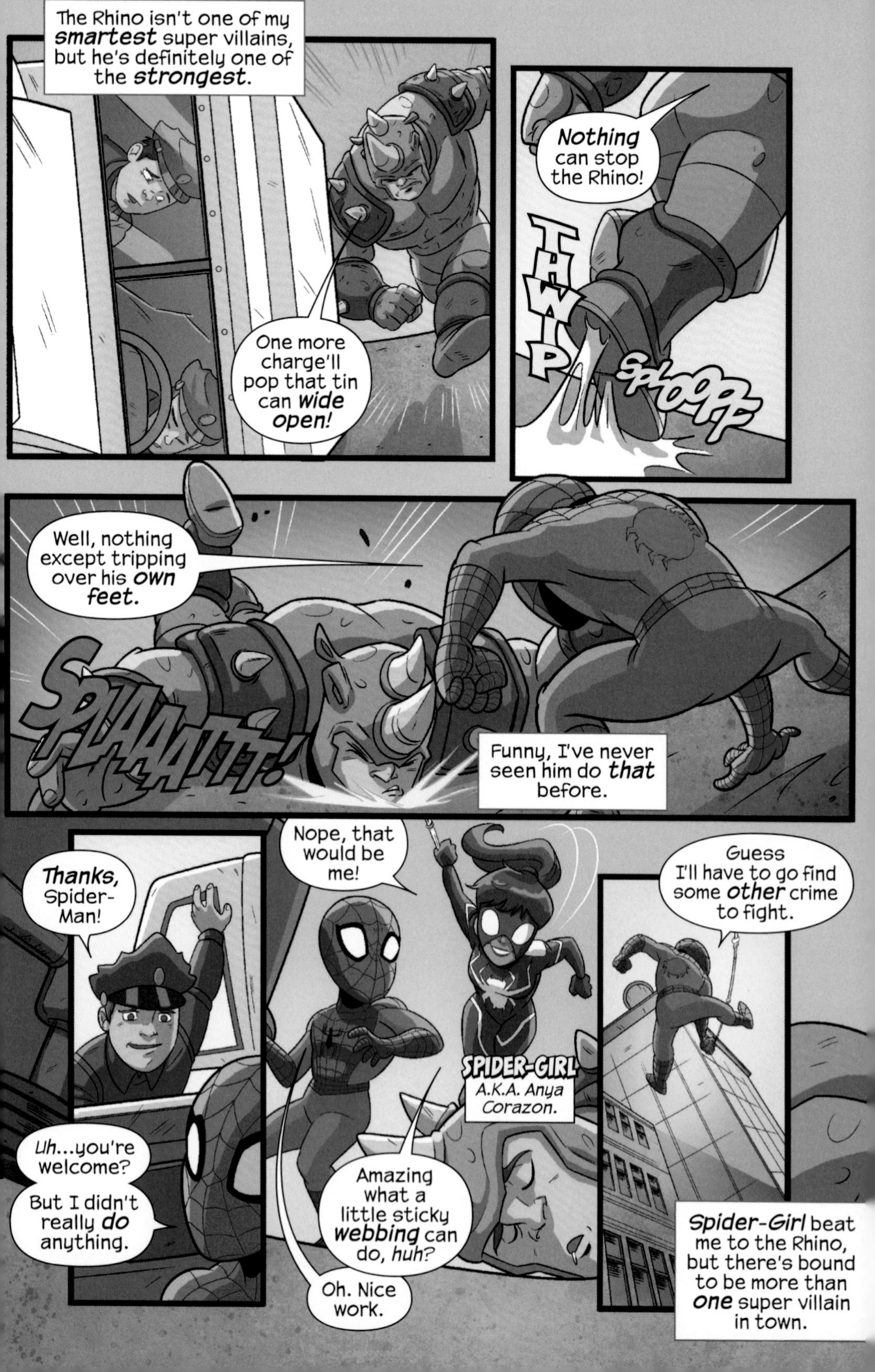
The Rhino isn't one of my smartest super villains, but he's definitely one of the strongest.
One more charge'll pop that tin can wide open!
Nothing can stop the Rhino!
THWIP
SPLOOPP
Well, nothing except tripping over his own feet.
SPLAAATTT!
Funny, I've never seen him do that before.
Thanks, Spider-Man!
Uh...you're welcome?
But I didn't really do anything.
Nope, that would be me!
SPIDER-GIRL
A.K.A. Anya Corazon.
Amazing what a little sticky webbing can do, huh?
Oh. Nice work.
Guess I'll have to go find some other crime to fight.
Spider-Girl beat me to the Rhino, but there's bound to be more than one super villain in town.

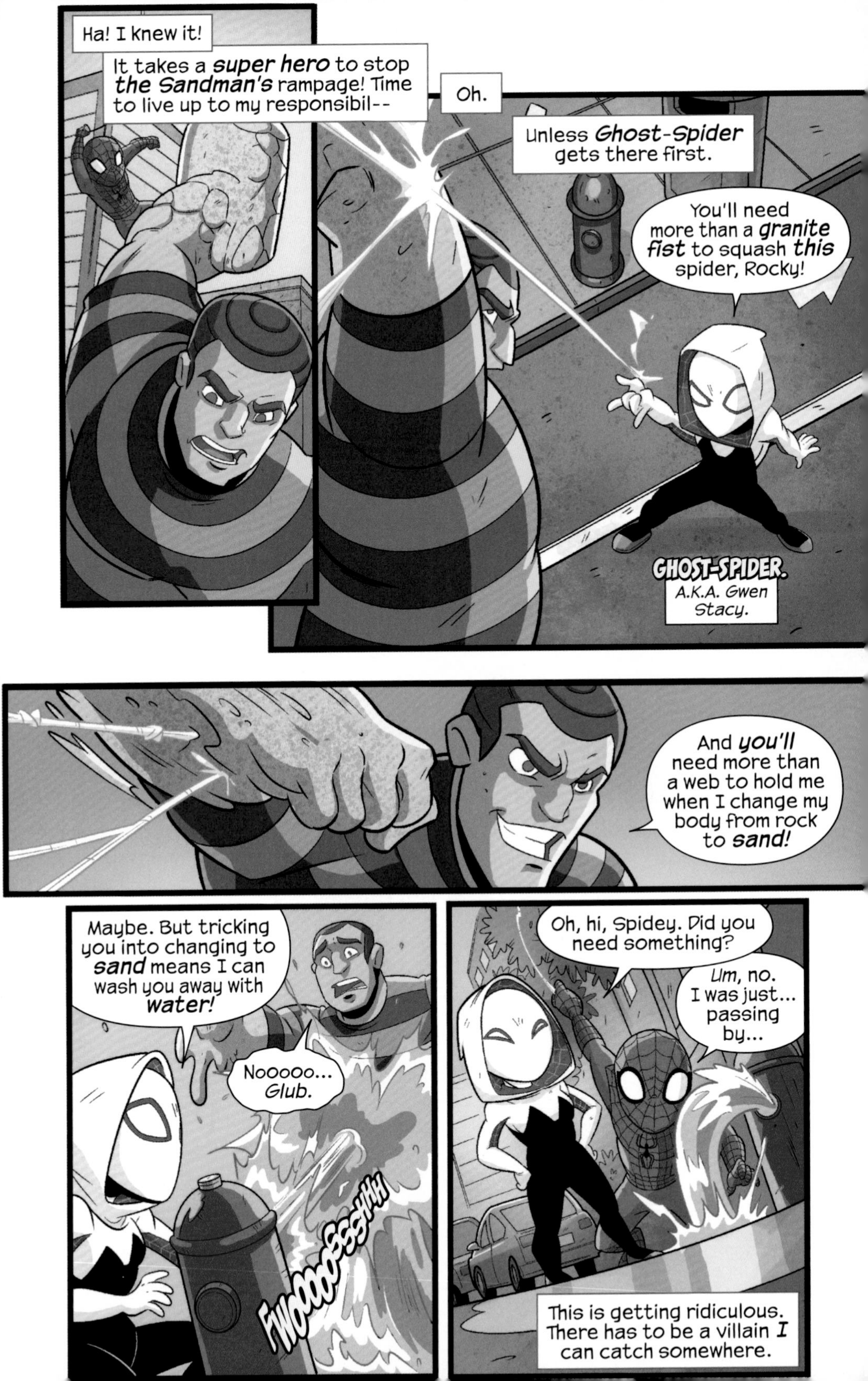
Ha! I knew it!
It takes a **super hero** to stop **the Sandman's** rampage! Time to live up to my responsibil--
Oh.
Unless **Ghost-Spider** gets there first.
You'll need more than a **granite fist** to squash **this** spider, Rocky!
GHOST-SPIDER.
A.K.A. Gwen Stacy.
And **you'll** need more than a web to hold me when I change my body from rock to **sand!**
Maybe. But tricking you into changing to **sand** means I can wash you away with **water!**
Nooooo... Glub.
FWOOOOSSSHHH
Oh, hi, Spidey. Did you need something?
Um, no. I was just... passing by...
This is getting ridiculous. There has to be a villain **I** can catch somewhere.

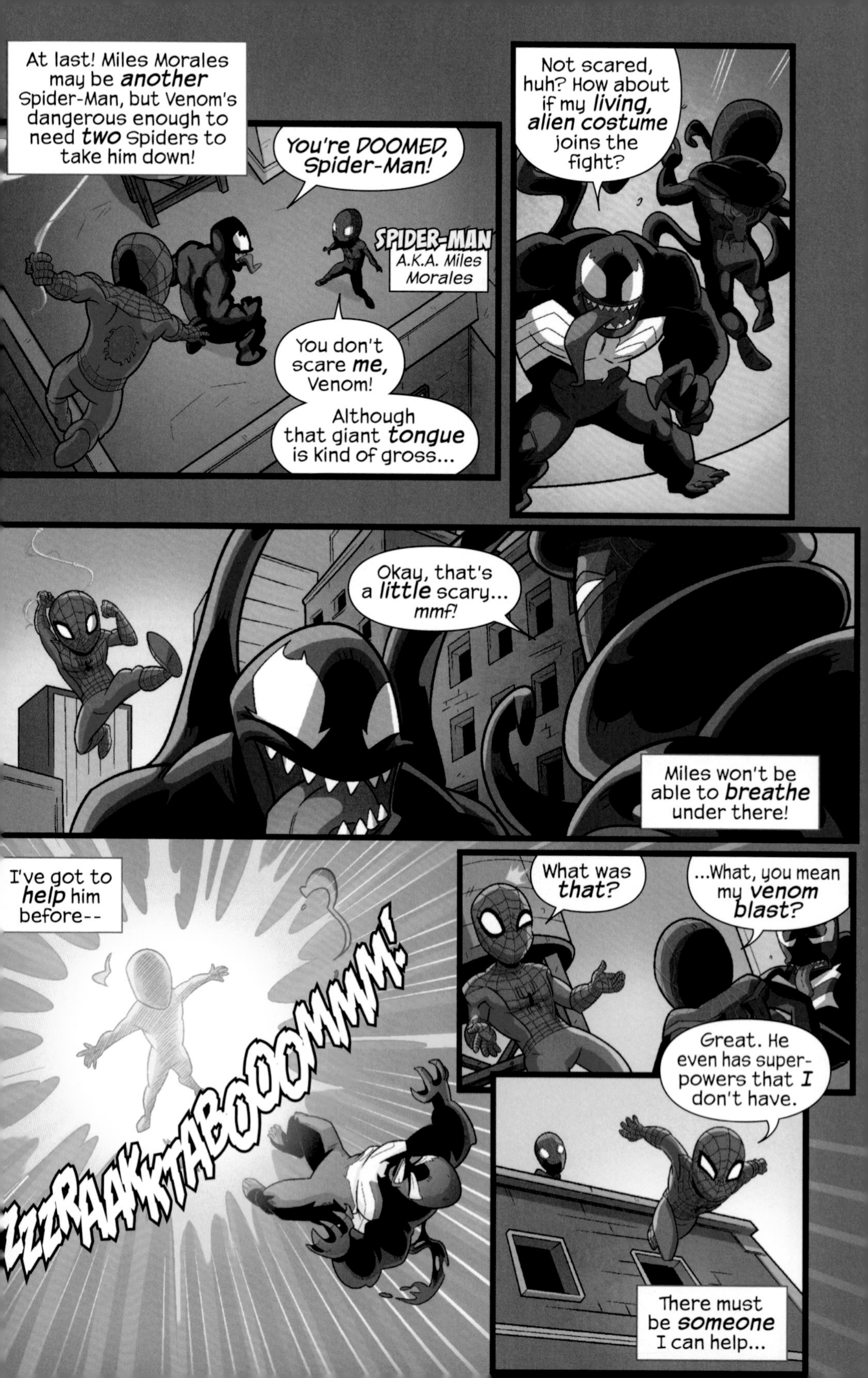
At last! Miles Morales may be *another* Spider-Man, but Venom's dangerous enough to need *two* Spiders to take him down!
You're DOOMED, Spider-Man!
SPIDER-MAN
A.K.A. Miles Morales
You don't scare *me*, Venom!
Although that giant *tongue* is kind of gross...
Not scared, huh? How about if my *living, alien costume* joins the fight?
Okay, that's a *little* scary... *mmf!*
Miles won't be able to *breathe* under there!
I've got to *help* him before--
ZZZRAAKKTABOOOMMM!
What was *that?*
...What, you mean my *venom blast?*
Great. He even has super-powers that *I* don't have.
There must be *someone* I can help...

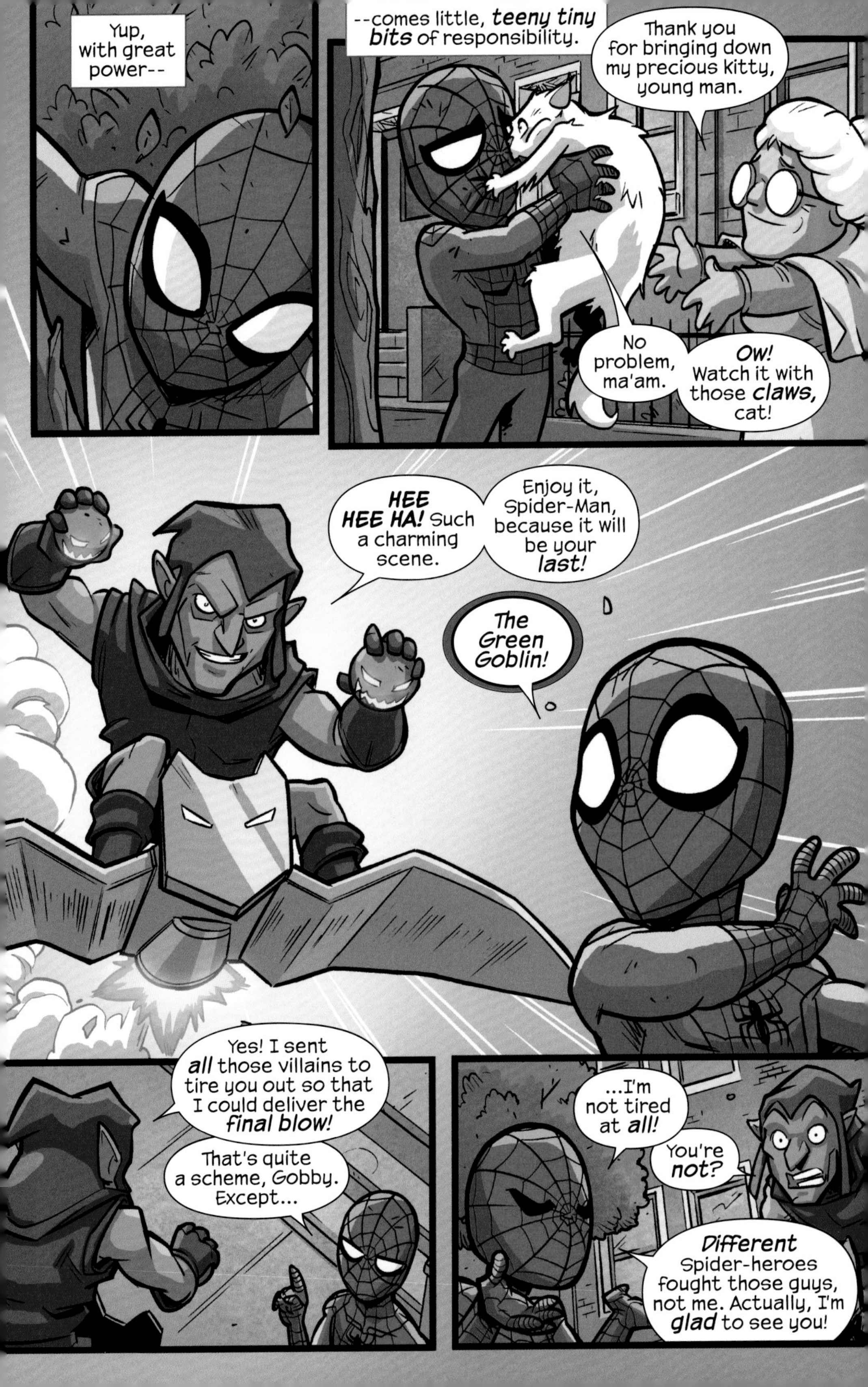
Yup, with great power--
--comes little, teeny tiny bits of responsibility.
Thank you for bringing down my precious kitty, young man.
No problem, ma'am.
Ow! Watch it with those claws, cat!
HEE HEE HA! Such a charming scene.
Enjoy it, Spider-Man, because it will be your last!
The Green Goblin!
Yes! I sent all those villains to tire you out so that I could deliver the final blow!
That's quite a scheme, Gobby. Except...
...I'm not tired at all!
You're not?
Different Spider-heroes fought those guys, not me. Actually, I'm glad to see you!

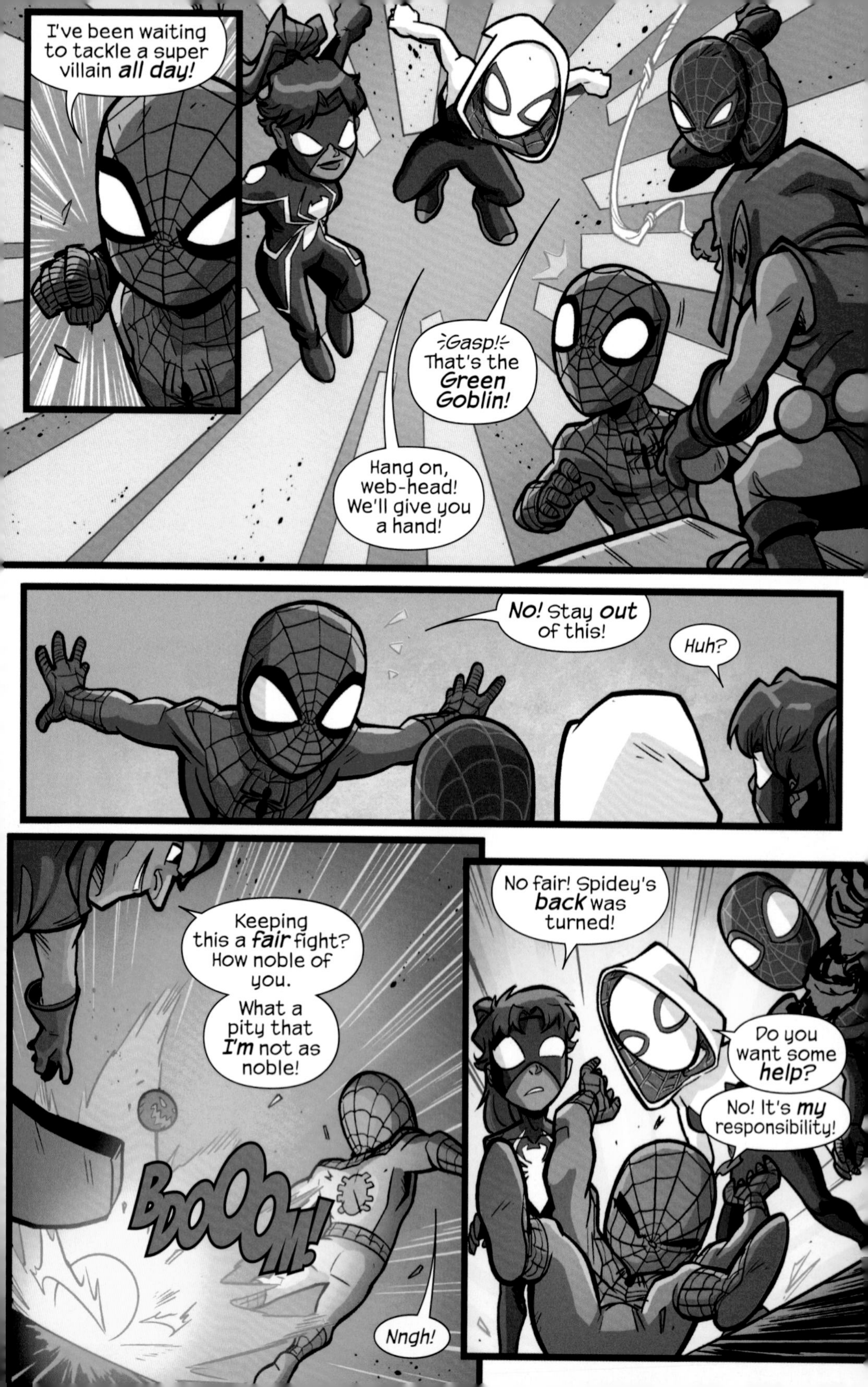
I've been waiting to tackle a super villain all day!
Hang on, web-head! We'll give you a hand!
Gasp! That's the Green Goblin!
No! Stay out of this!
Huh?
Keeping this a fair fight? How noble of you.
What a pity that I'm not as noble!
BOOOOM!
Nngh!
No fair! Spidey's back was turned!
Do you want some help?
No! It's my responsibility!

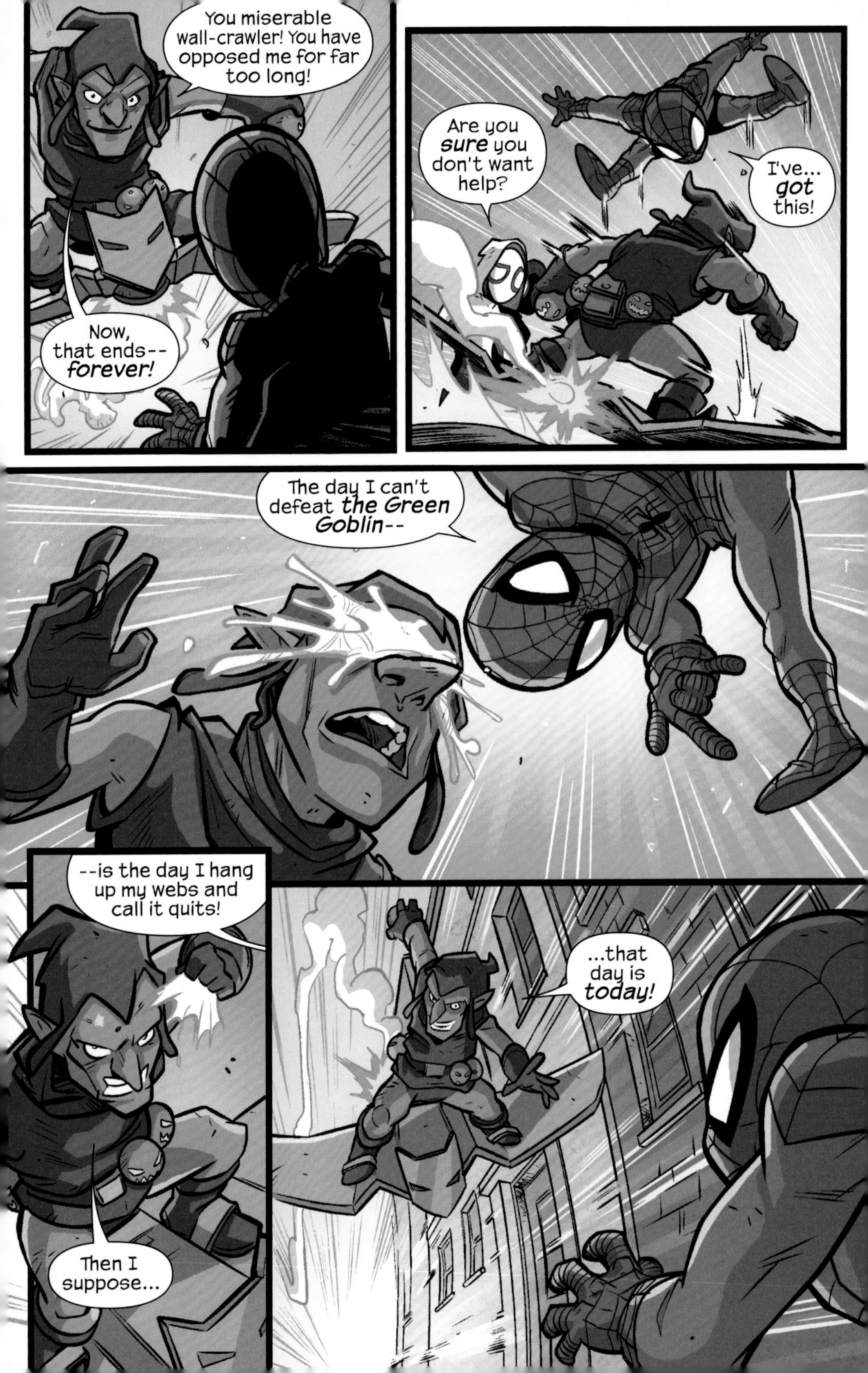
You miserable wall-crawler! You have opposed me for far too long!
Now, that ends-- *forever!*
Are you *sure* you don't want help?
I've... *got* this!
The day I can't defeat *the Green Goblin*--
--is the day I hang up my webs and call it quits!
Then I suppose...
...that day is *today!*

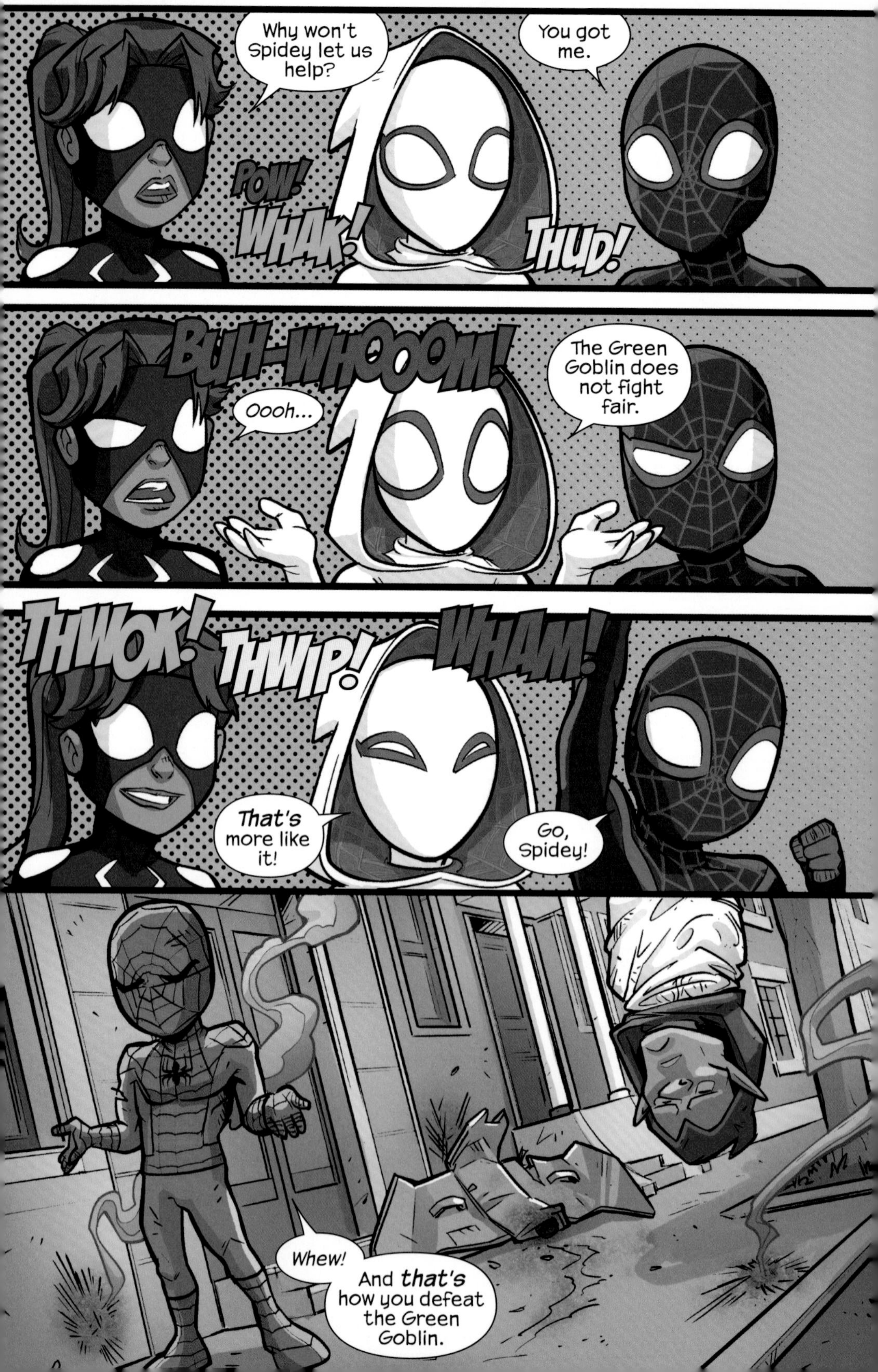
Why won't Spidey let us help?
You got me.
POW!
WHAK!
THUD!
BUH-WHOOOOM!
Oooh...
The Green Goblin does not fight fair.
THWOK!
THWIP!
WHAM!
That's more like it!
Go, Spidey!
Whew!
And *that's* how you defeat the Green Goblin.

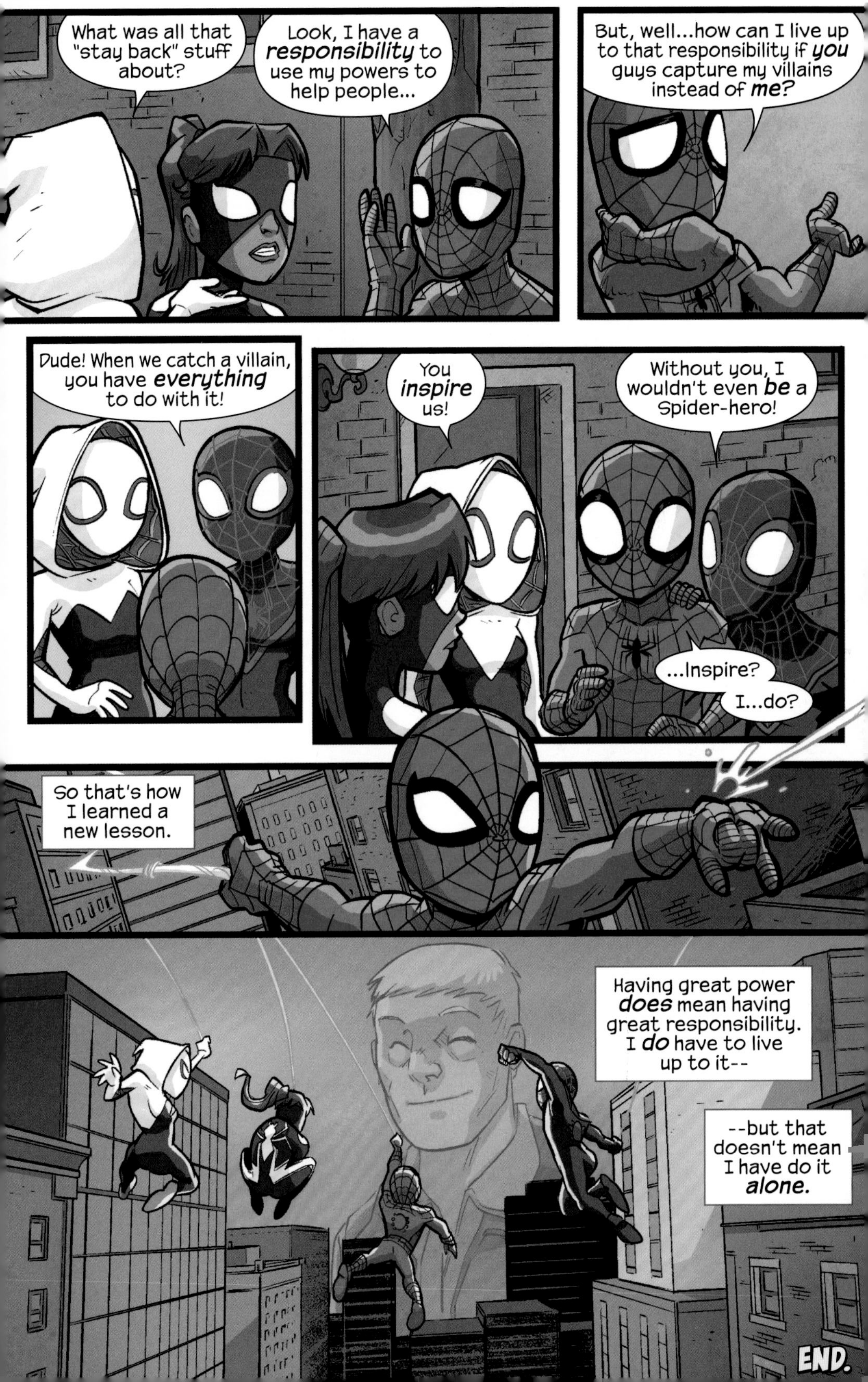
What was all that "stay back" stuff about?
Look, I have a *responsibility* to use my powers to help people...
But, well...how can I live up to that responsibility if *you* guys capture my villains instead of *me?*
Dude! When we catch a villain, you have *everything* to do with it!
You *inspire* us!
Without you, I wouldn't even *be* a Spider-hero!
...Inspire?
I...do?
So that's how I learned a new lesson.
Having great power *does* mean having great responsibility. I *do* have to live up to it--
--but that doesn't mean I have do it *alone.*
END.

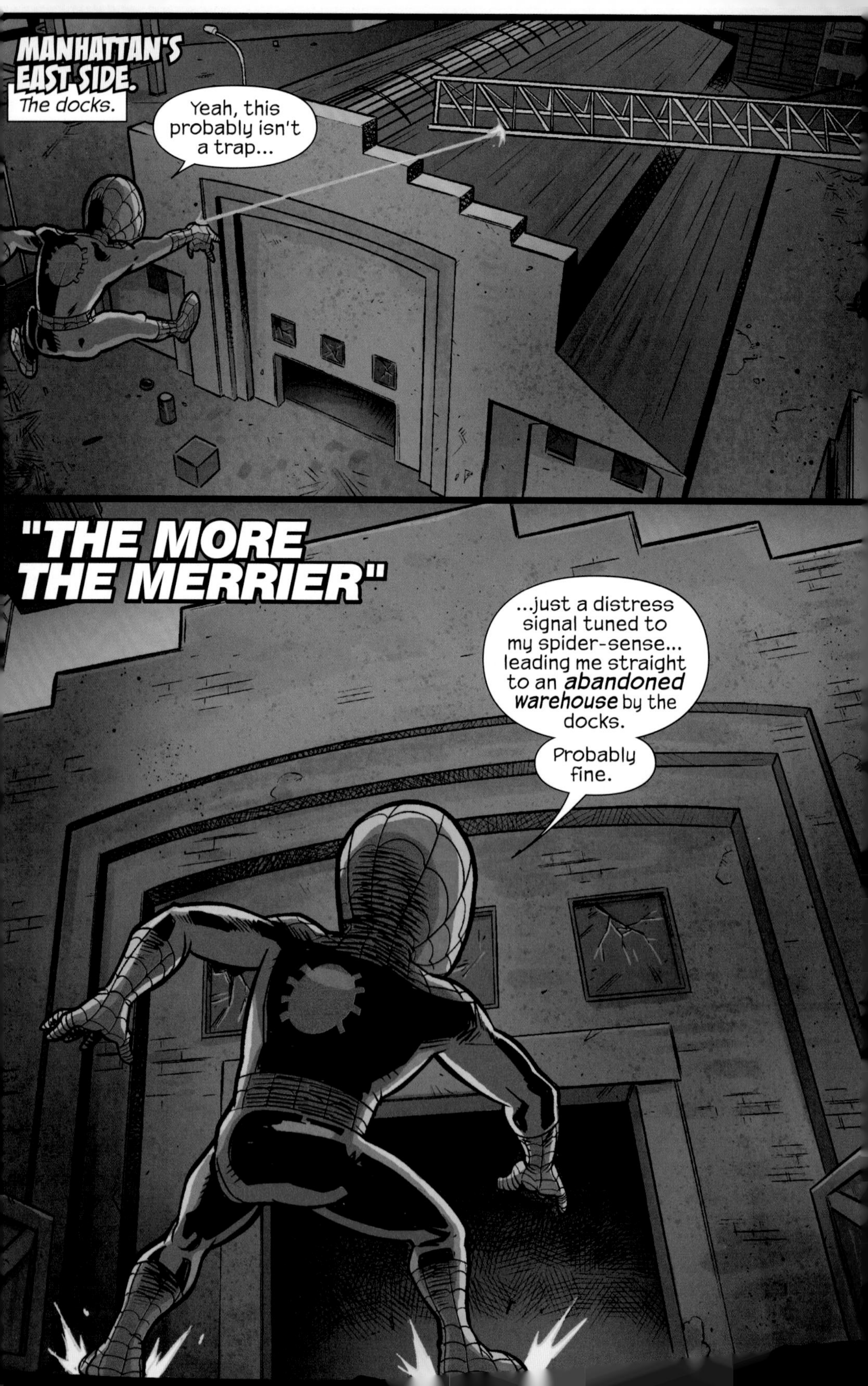
MANHATTAN'S EAST SIDE.
The docks.
Yeah, this probably isn't a trap...
"THE MORE THE MERRIER"
...just a distress signal tuned to my spider-sense... leading me straight to an *abandoned warehouse* by the docks.
Probably fine.

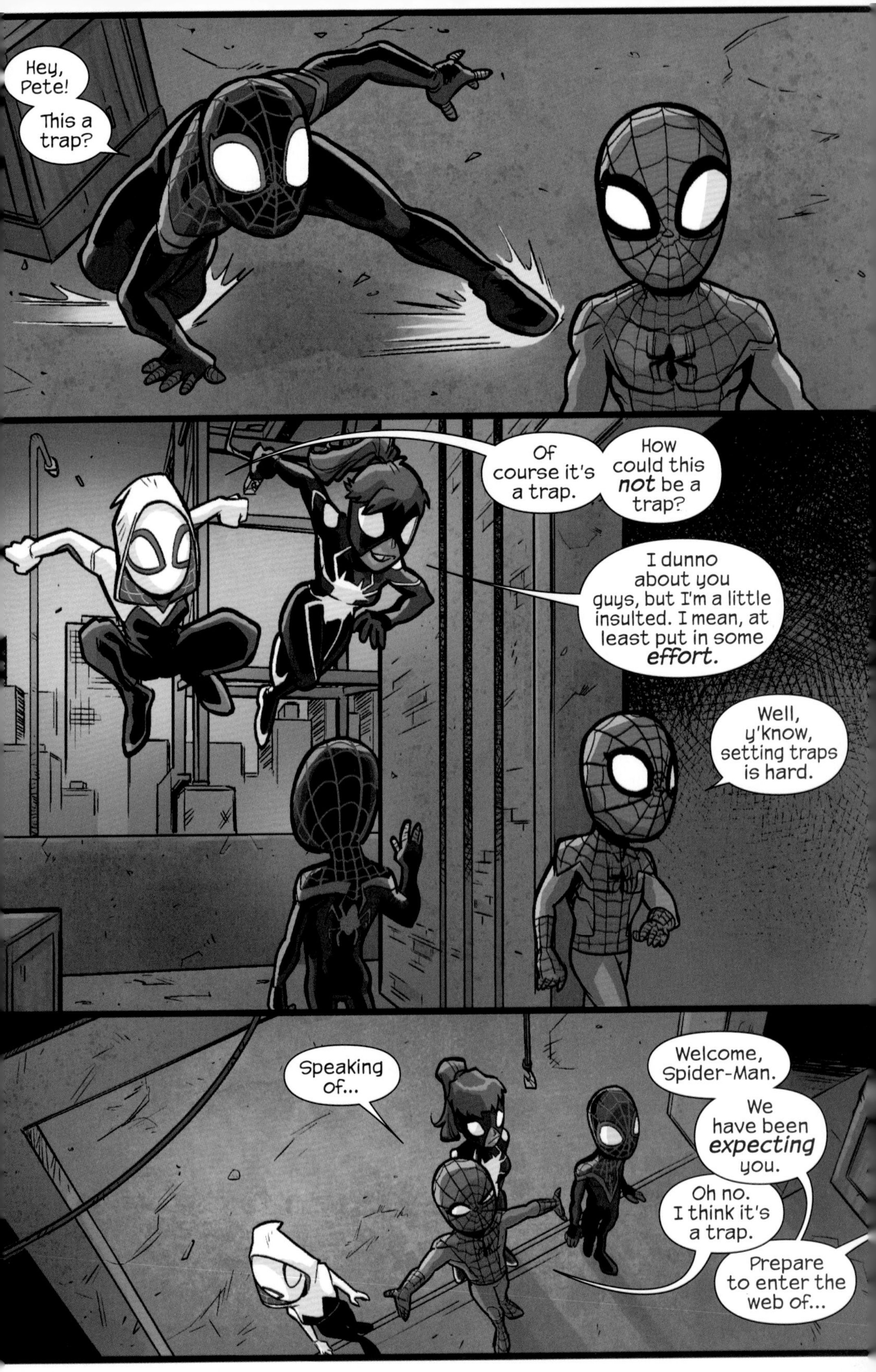
Hey, Pete!
This a trap?
Of course it's a trap.
How could this *not* be a trap?
I dunno about you guys, but I'm a little insulted. I mean, at least put in some *effort.*
Well, y'know, setting traps is hard.
Speaking of...
Welcome, Spider-Man.
We have been *expecting* you.
Oh no. I think it's a trap.
Prepare to enter the web of...

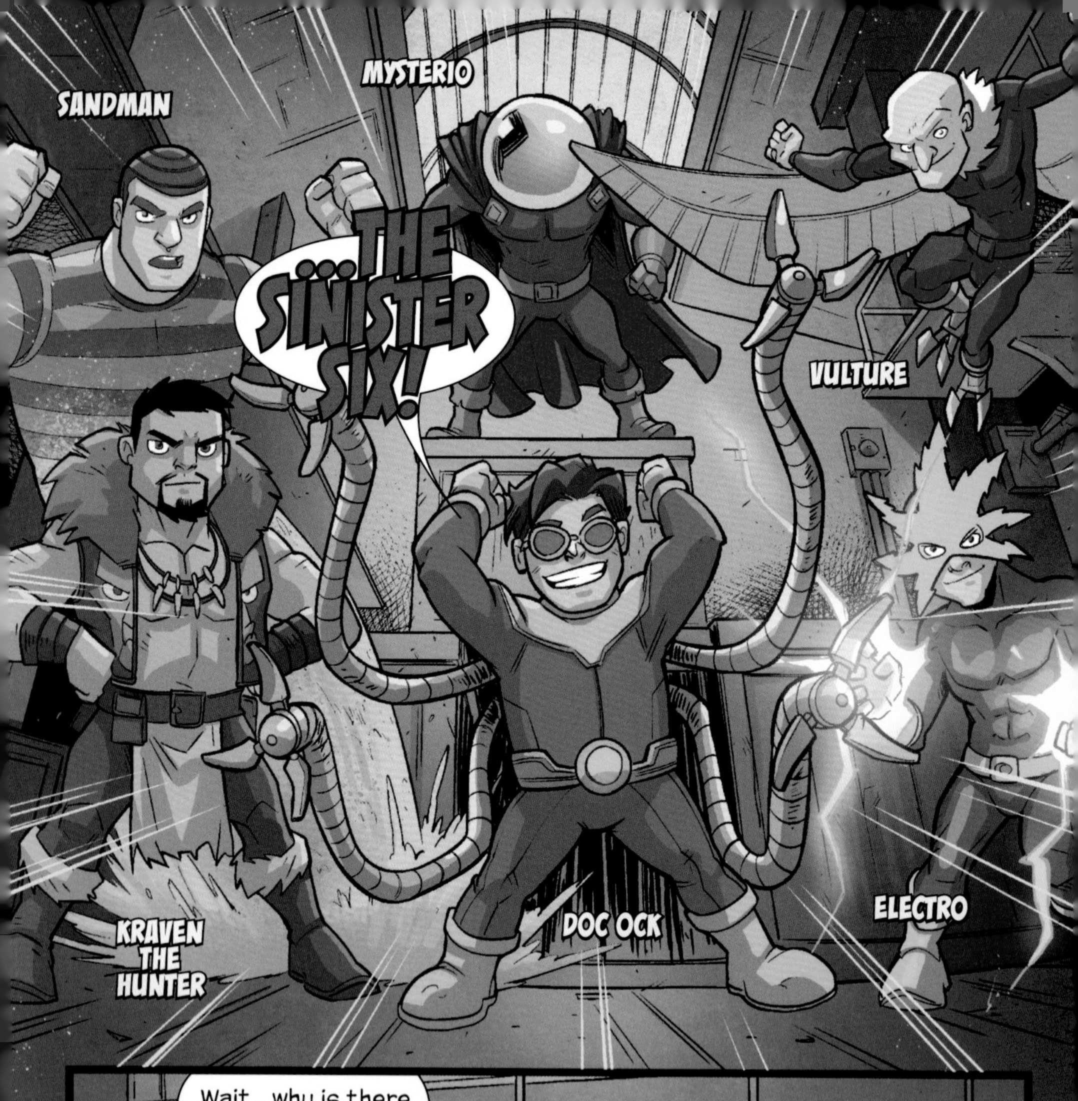
MYSTERIO
SANDMAN
...THE SINISTER SIX!
VULTURE
KRAVEN THE HUNTER
DOC OCK
ELECTRO

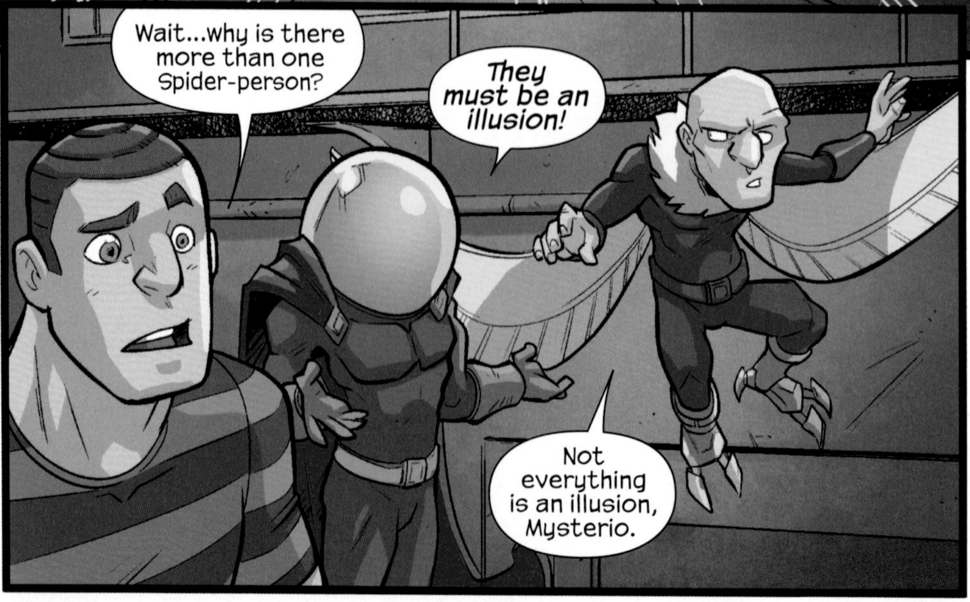
Wait...why is there more than one Spider-person?
They must be an illusion!
Not everything is an illusion, Mysterio.

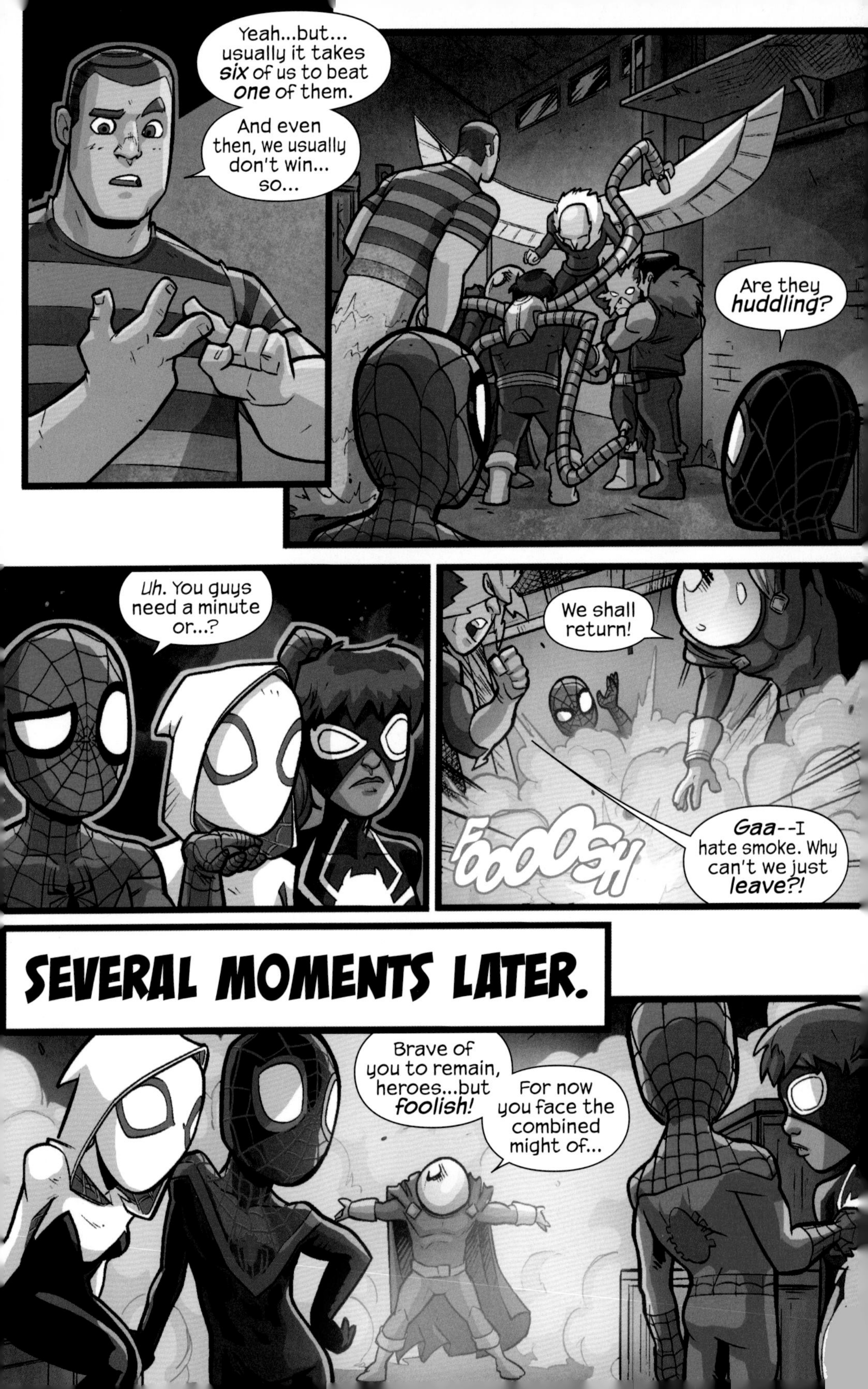

Yeah...but... usually it takes *six* of us to beat *one* of them.
And even then, we usually don't win... so...
Are they *huddling*?
Uh. You guys need a minute or...?
We shall return!
FOOOOSH
Gaa--I hate smoke. Why can't we just *leave*?!
SEVERAL MOMENTS LATER.
Brave of you to remain, heroes...but *foolish!*
For now you face the combined might of...

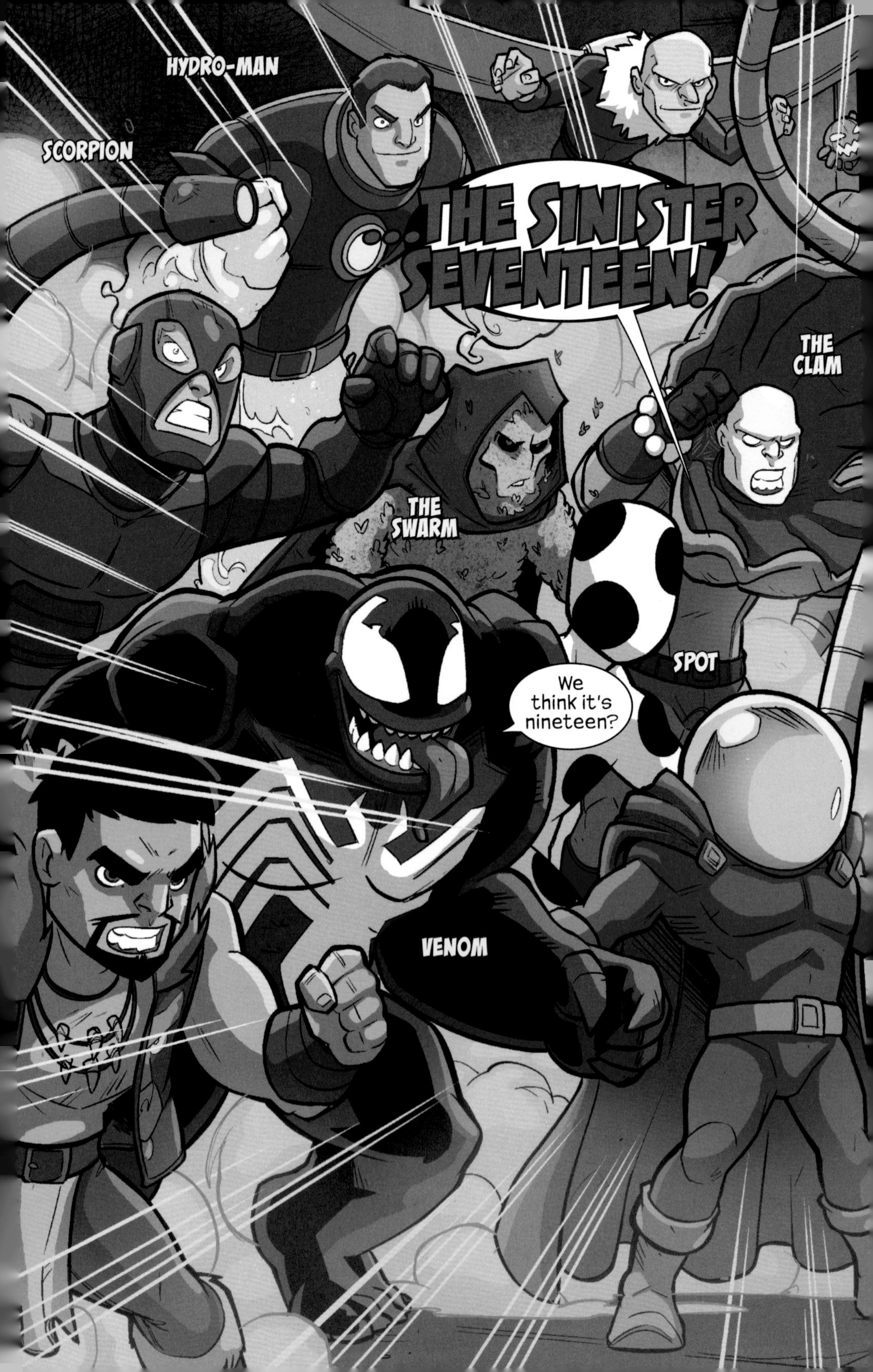
HYDRO-MAN
SCORPION
...THE SINISTER SEVENTEEN!
THE CLAM
THE SWARM
SPOT
We think it's nineteen?
VENOM

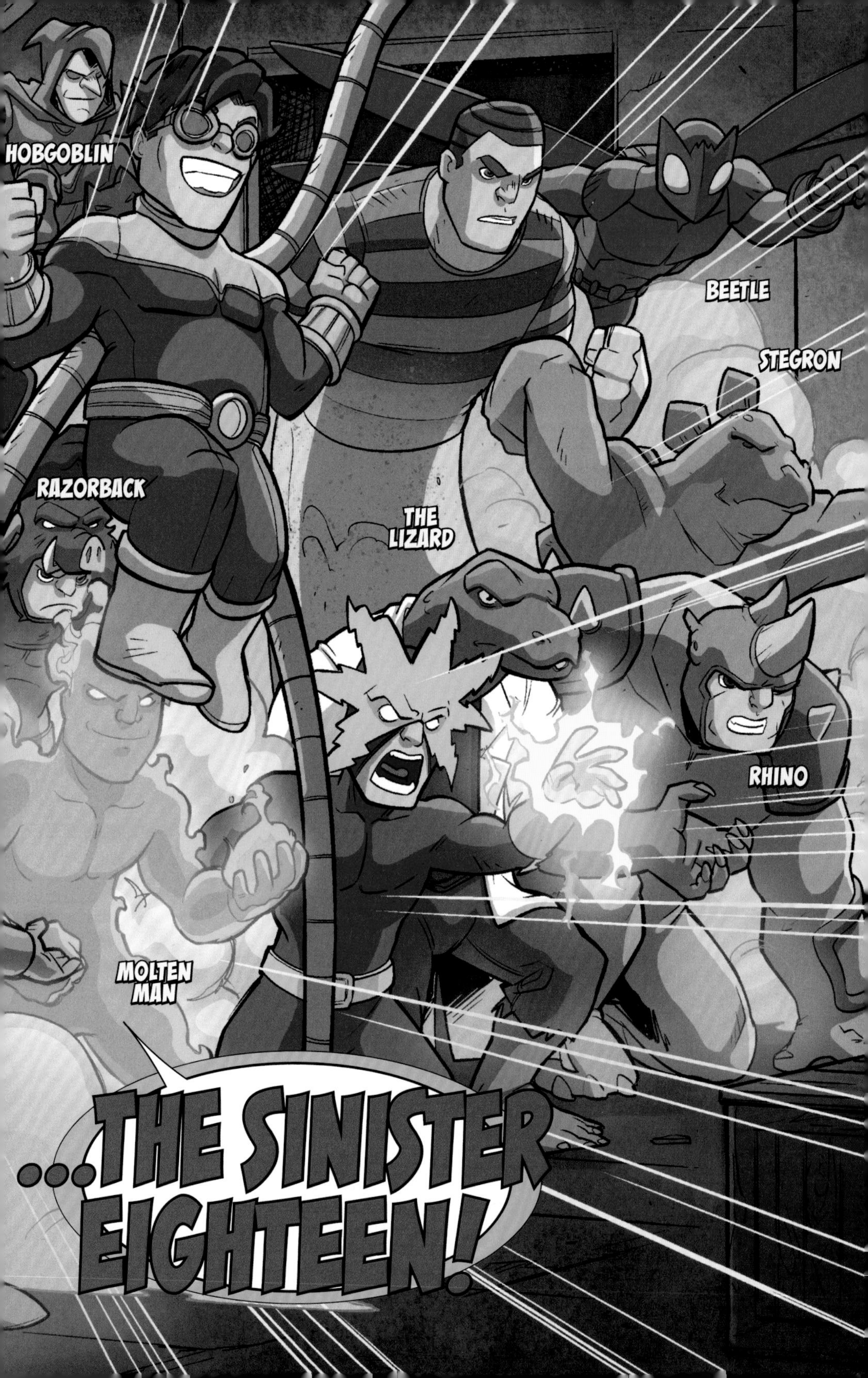
HOBGOBLIN
BEETLE
STEGRON
RAZORBACK
THE LIZARD
RHINO
MOLTEN MAN
...THE SINISTER EIGHTEEN!

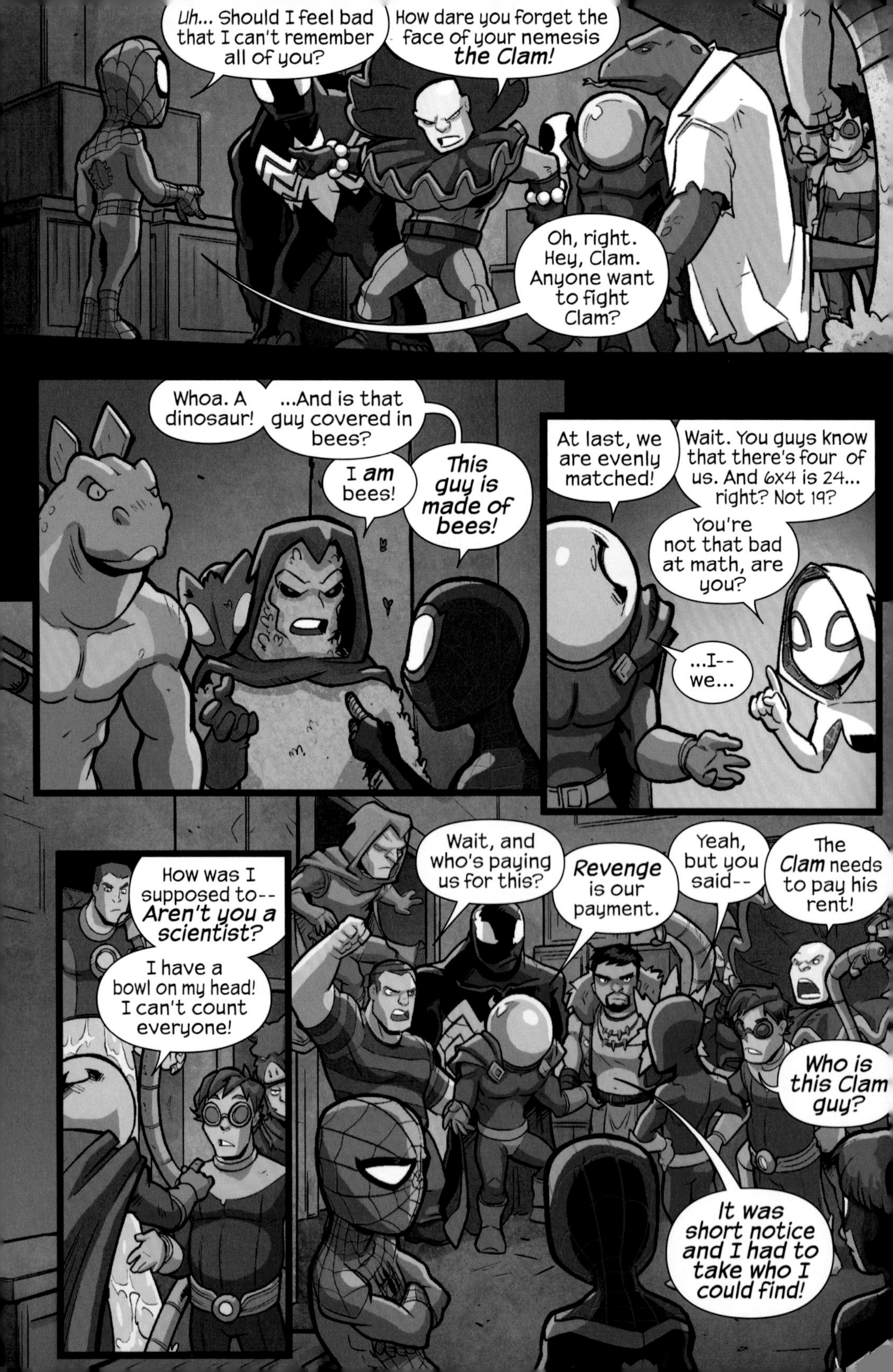
Uh... Should I feel bad that I can't remember all of you?
How dare you forget the face of your nemesis the Clam!
Oh, right. Hey, Clam. Anyone want to fight Clam?
Whoa. A dinosaur!
...And is that guy covered in bees?
I am bees!
This guy is made of bees!
At last, we are evenly matched!
Wait. You guys know that there's four of us. And 6x4 is 24... right? Not 19?
You're not that bad at math, are you?
...I-- we...
How was I supposed to-- Aren't you a scientist?
I have a bowl on my head! I can't count everyone!
Wait, and who's paying us for this?
Revenge is our payment.
Yeah, but you said--
The Clam needs to pay his rent!
Who is this Clam guy?
It was short notice and I had to take who I could find!

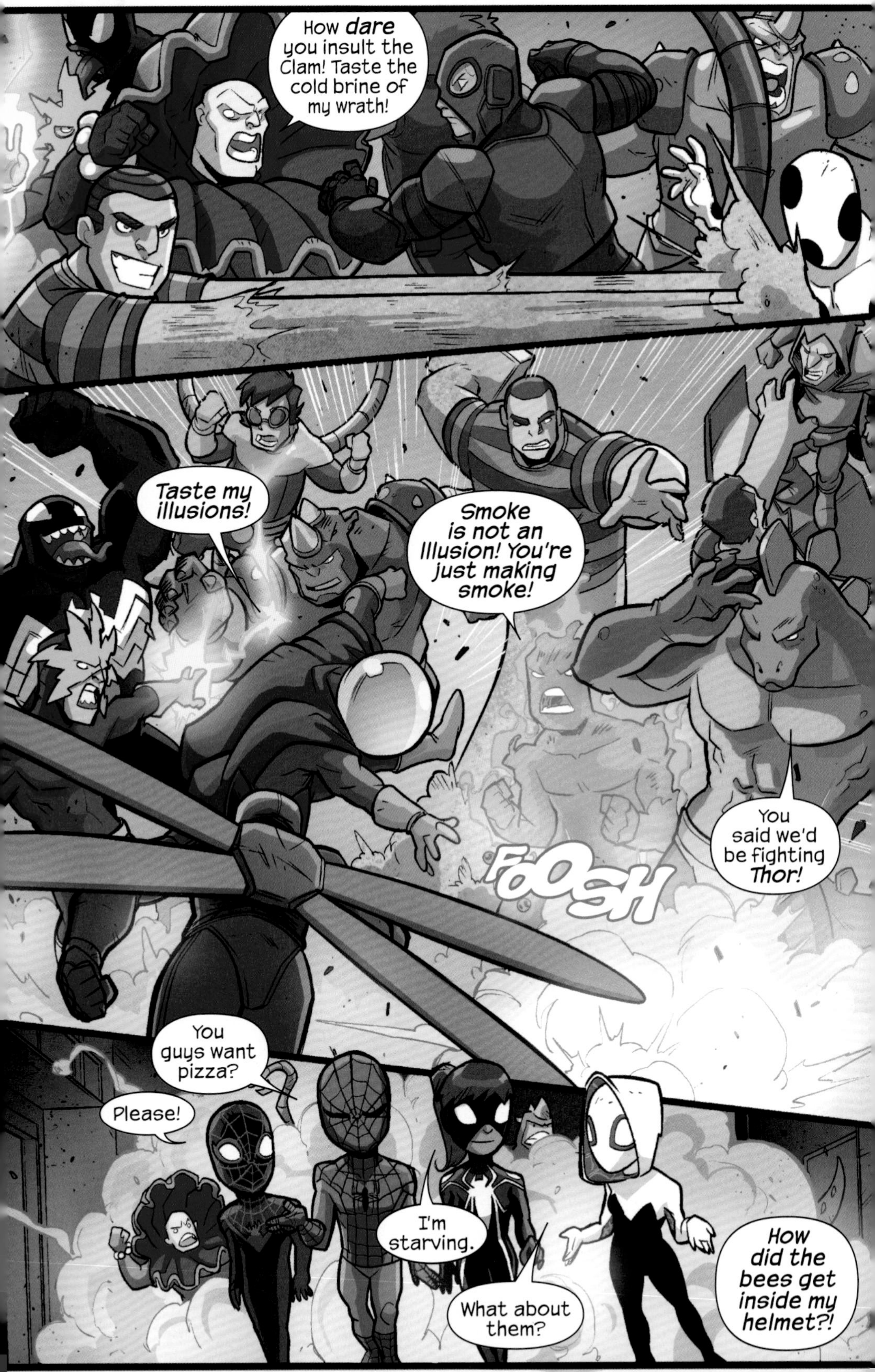
How *dare* you insult the Clam! Taste the cold brine of my wrath!
Taste my illusions!
Smoke is not an illusion! You're just making smoke!
You said we'd be fighting *Thor!*
FOOSH
You guys want pizza?
Please!
I'm starving.
What about them?
How did the bees get inside my helmet?!

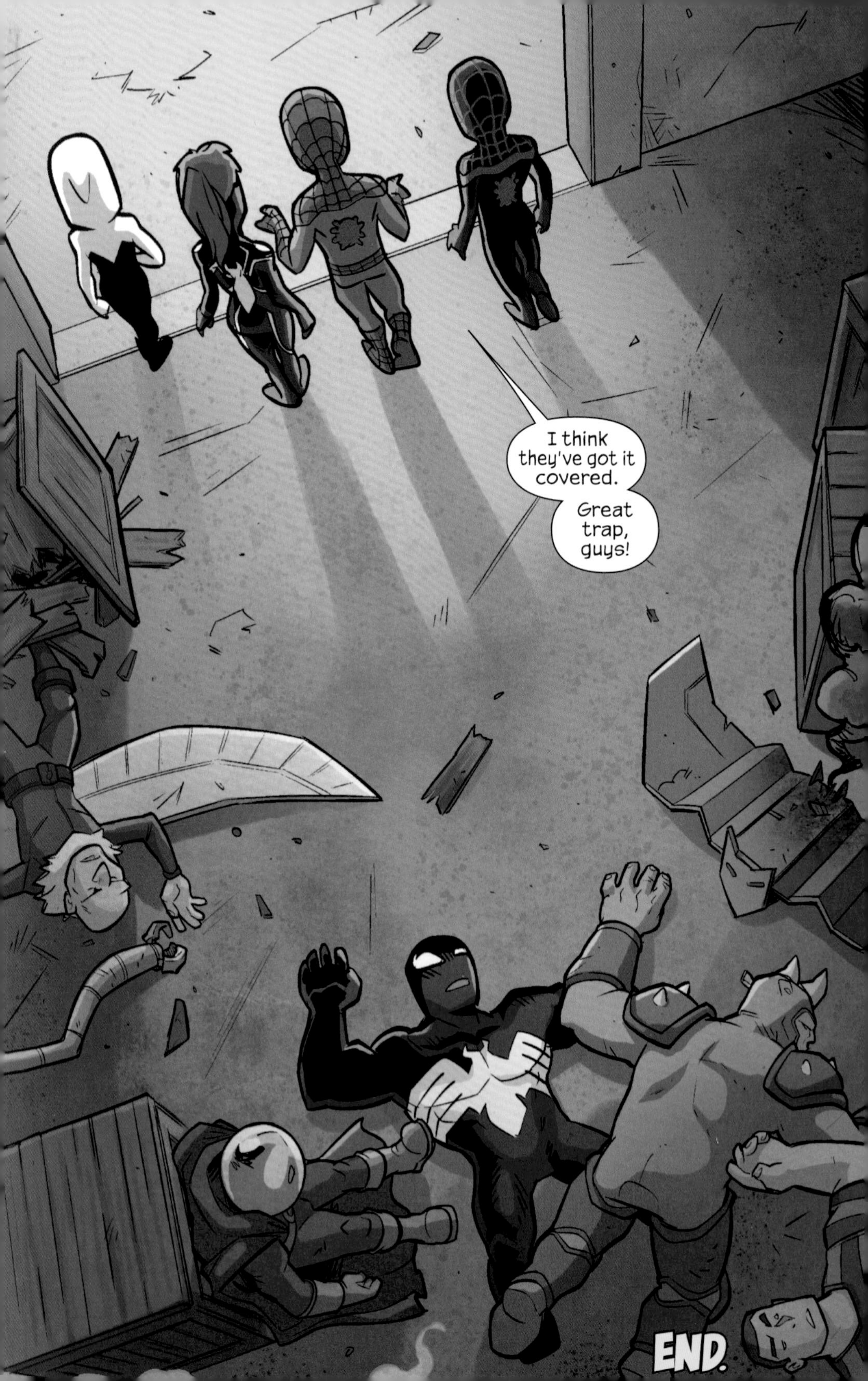

I think they've got it covered.
Great trap, guys!
END.

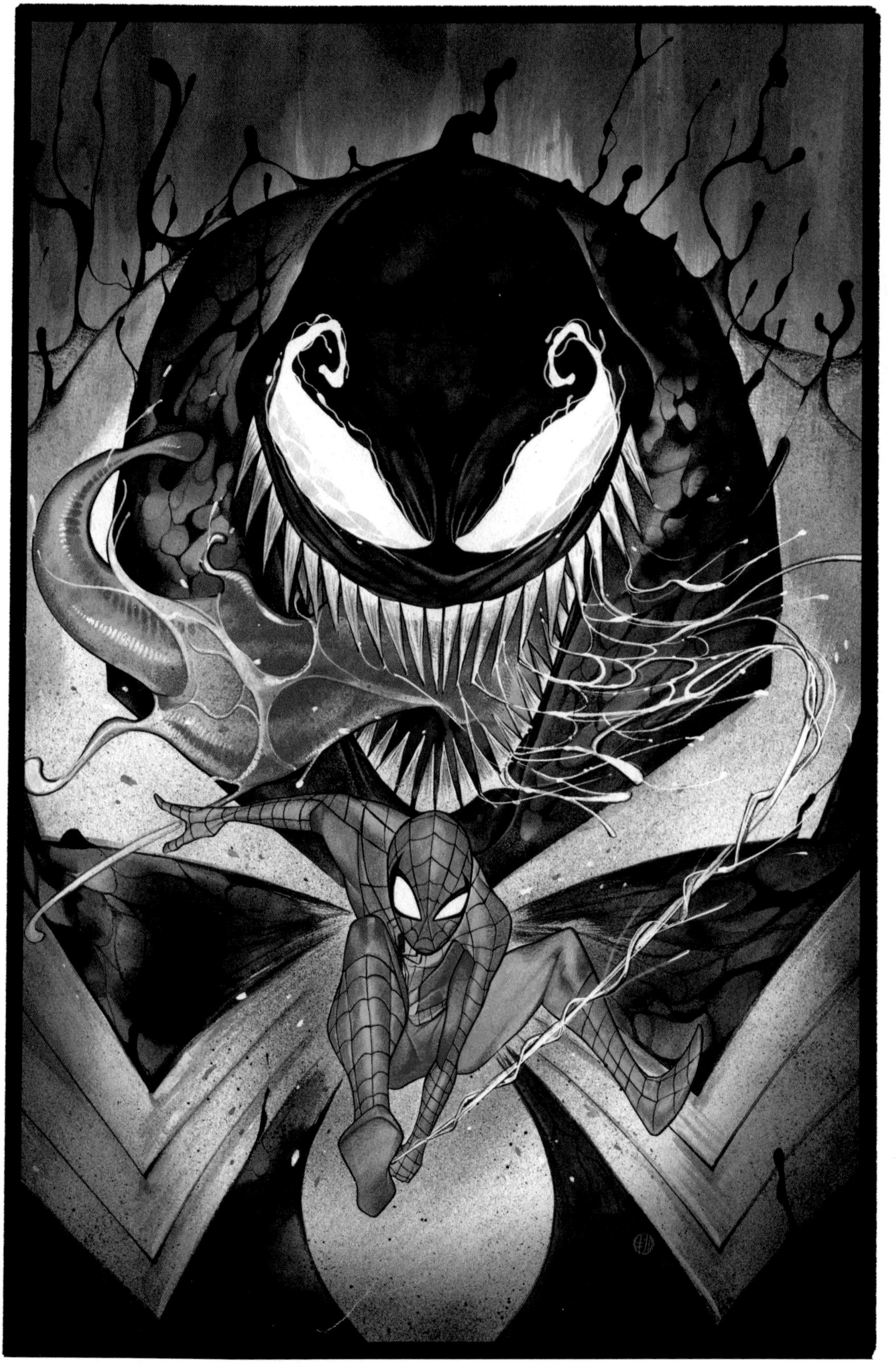

#2 VARIANT BY **PEACH MOMOKO**

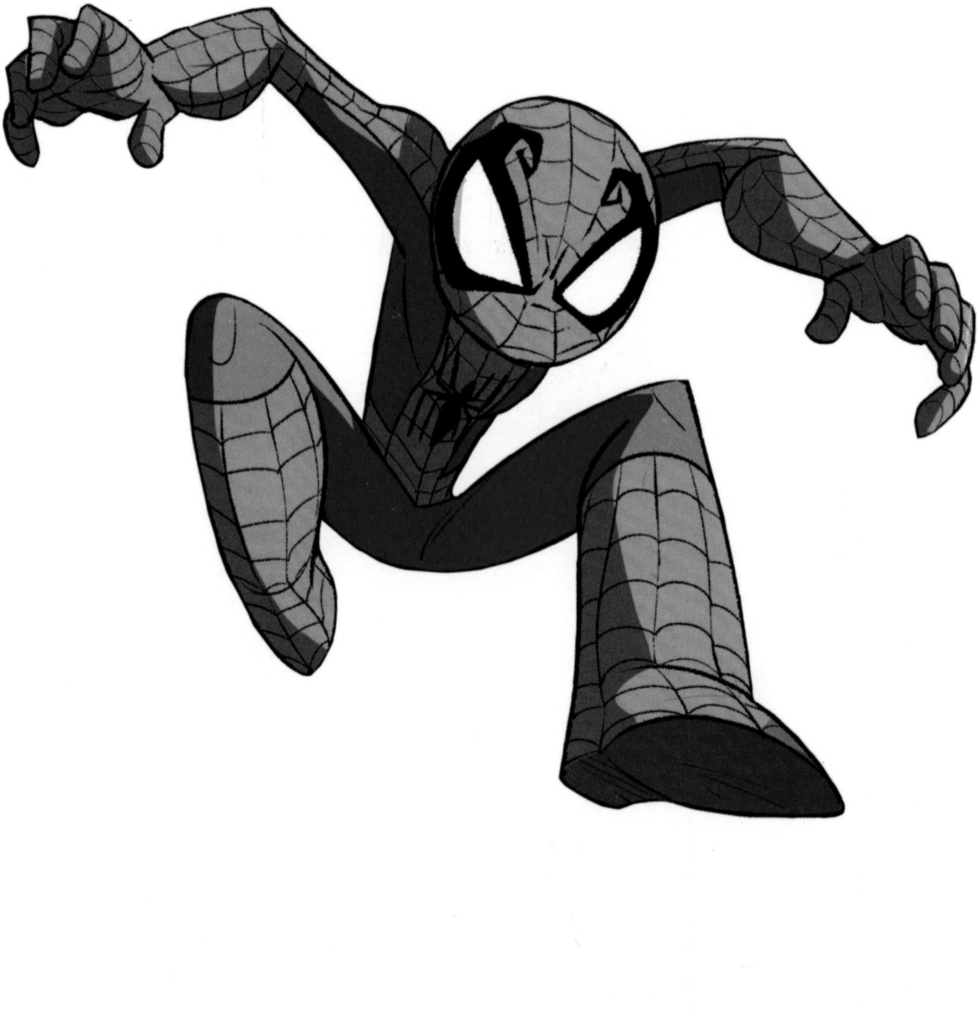